THE DARKNESS WITHIN
BOOK ONE

Skyla Raines

THE BEAUTIFUL DEAD

THE BEAUTIFUL DEAD
Copyright © Skyla Raines, 2025

Without limiting the rights under copyright reserved above, no part of this publication may be reproduced, stored in or introduced into a retrieval system, or transmitted in any form or by any means (electronic, mechanical, photocopying, recording, or otherwise) without the prior written permission of the copyright owner. This is a work of fiction. Names, characters, places, and incidents are either the product of the author's imagination or are used fictitiously, and any resemblance to actual persons, living or dead, business establishments, events, or locales is entirely coincidental.

Cover Design: Design by Kage
Model: Charlie Edwards
Photographer: Jack Edwards
Formatting: Michaella Dieter
Editor: Campfire Edits

BEFORE YOU READ

Please note this book has dark elements and contains themes which some may find difficult read. Your mental health is important, so if you need a more detailed content list, please check page 541.

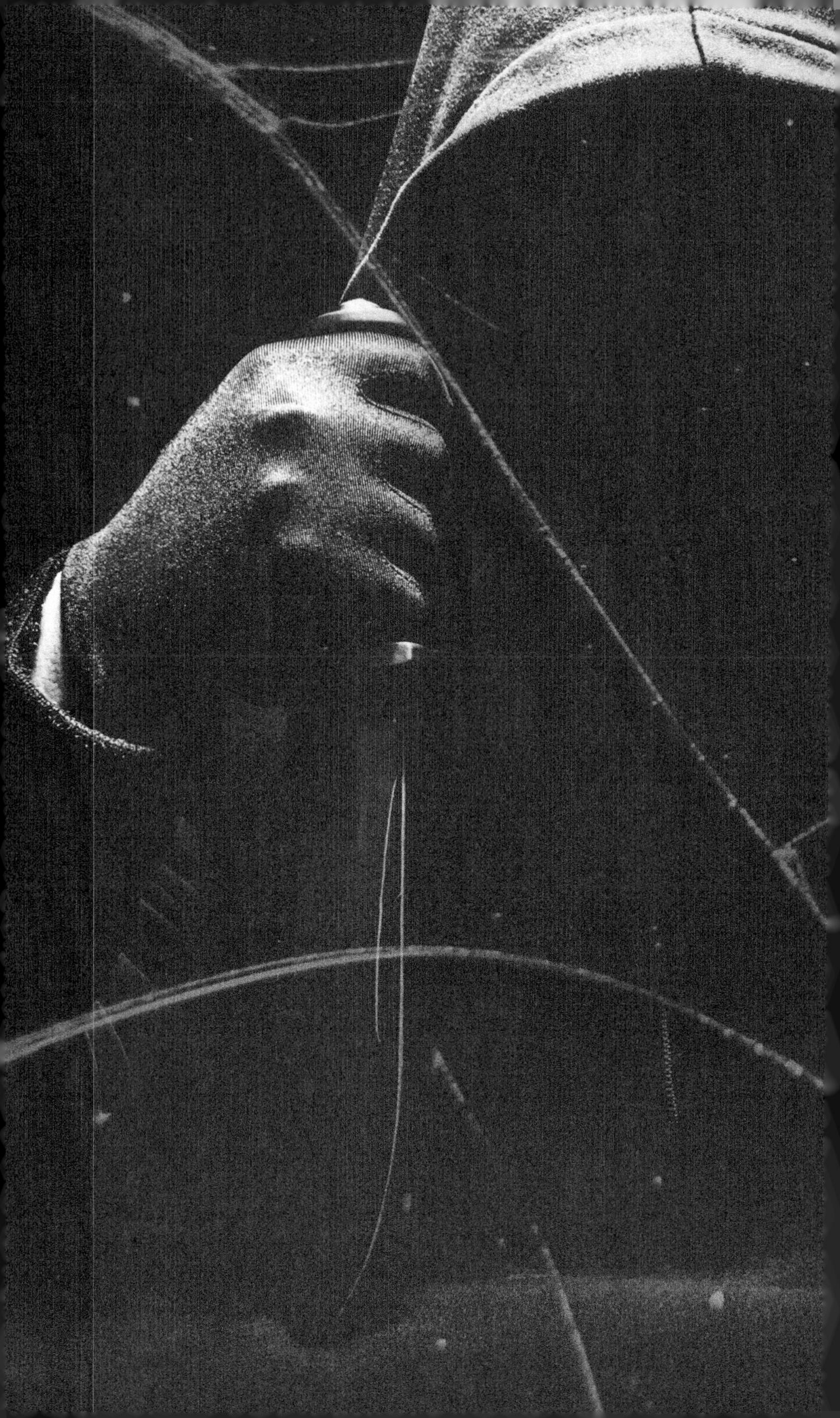

To those who walk the line between fear and fascination, who are obsessed with what hides in the shadows. May your dreams be as twisted and exhilarating as the stories you dare to live.

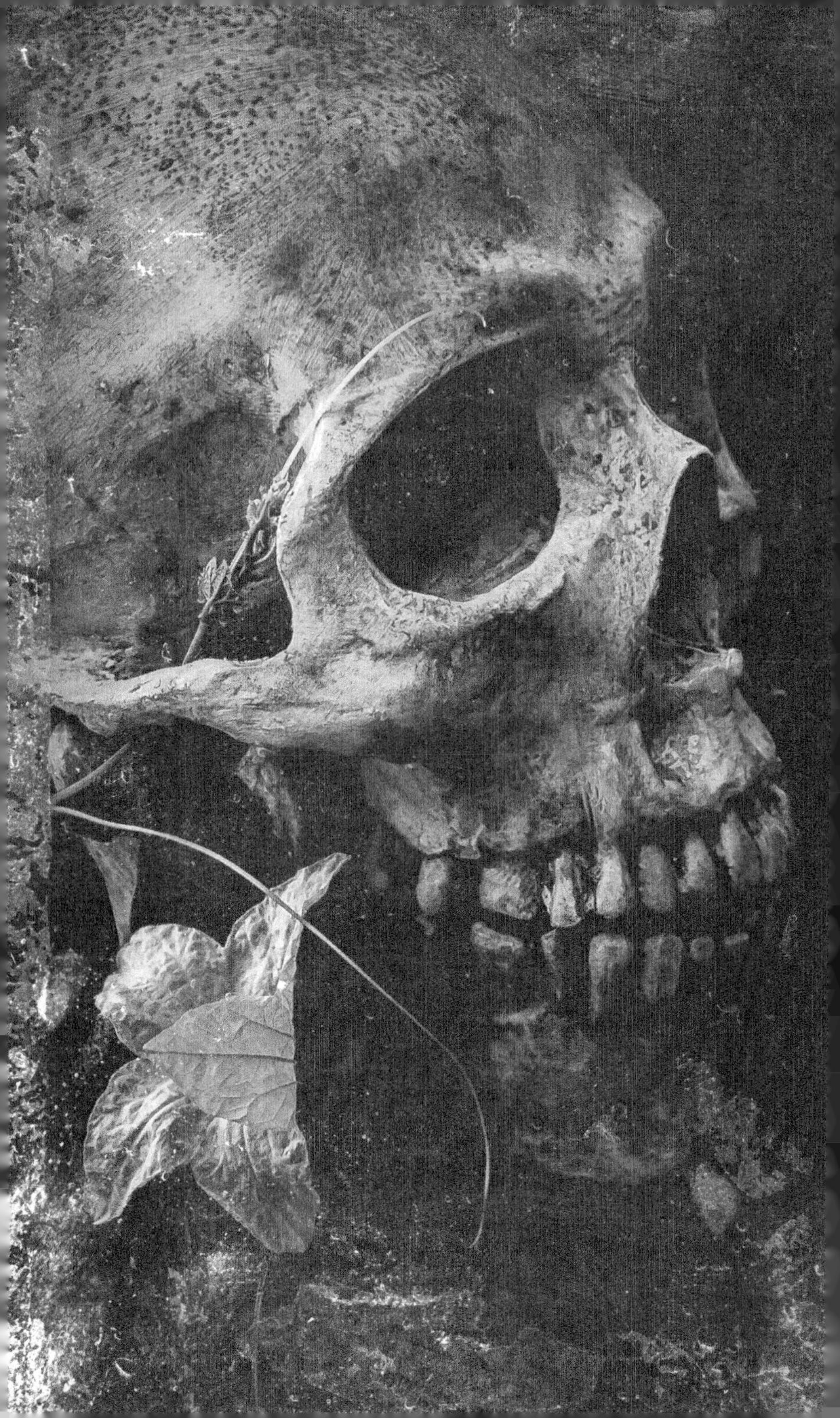

1. DOMINO

"No! No more, please... no more."
    The sharp point of my switchblade sliced through the skin of his fingertips—not too deep, but enough to make it feel like liquid fire was licking at his nerves. His hand twitched and jerked with every kiss of the blade, tiny beads of blood blooming against his skin. I watched, fascinated, as they slid down his fingers in rivulets of red, weaving between the fine hairs and pooling around the chains that bound his wrists.

    Muffled whimpers bled into hollow screams, the echoes ricocheting off the damp concrete walls. The stench of bodily fluids and copper thickened the air—an odor that would send a weak man running in terror. But to me, this was home.

    My playground.

A place where my monster could breathe. A world of my own design, where the rules of society held no power. Here, I stood above the law that the sheep so blindly followed. Here, I was judge, jury, and executioner.

No one was safe from the wrath of the DeMarcos.

No one was safe from me.

David—Davey—Rutter was the current object of my sadistic fixation. He hung limply, trapped in a never-ending cycle of disorientation and pain. His shoulders slowly separated under his hefty weight, tendons straining, ready to snap. Head thrown back, he howled, spittle flying from his lips as one of my—our—soldiers tightened the crank, raising him higher off the floor. It gave me easy access to his toes, where I gave them the same focused attention as his fingers.

My blade sliced through the layers of toughened skin like butter. His blood rushed to the surface quickly, aided by gravity and the fact that he'd been hanging for hours already.

No matter how much I wanted every crimson drop of his blood to spill across the tiled floor, to revel in the power of watching him take his final breath as the light faded from his eyes, I couldn't... not yet. Rutter had information I needed—information my father had instructed me to extract by any means necessary. But I had to leave him alive. People would notice if the Chief of Police suddenly turned up as a mutilated bag of bones or disappeared altogether.

Breathing but irrevocably broken—that, I could do.

Sparing Rutter's life would come at a price, one he had no choice but to pay: a life of servitude to the devil —Federico DeMarco. I had manipulated Rutter with bribes and blackmail until now, but it was time to show him why my name was feared above all, even my father's.

Smoke curled lazily from the cigarette between my lips as I lit it and wiped the bloodied blade against my thigh. With a single nod, I motioned for one of the nameless soldiers to lower the crank, dipping his sliced toes into acidic lemon juice. Bracing my foot against the brittle wall behind me, I watched, motionless, enraptured by his suffering.

Rutter writhed in his restraints, the thick chains biting into his blood-slicked wrists. His tanned skin prickled with goosebumps in the frigid air. A blindfold covered his eyes, and noise-canceling headphones blared Tchaikovsky's *Nutcracker Suite* interspersed with torturous moments of utter silence as I sliced into him in the semi-darkness.

"Make it stop. Make it stop...please," he whimpered weakly, his chains rattling like some obscure puppet on a string.

A cruel smile flickered at the corners of my lips. He had no idea of the level of pain he was about to endure. All because he couldn't do what he was told to do. Actions had consequences after all; it wasn't like he hadn't been warned what would happen if he stepped out of line.

The tip of his big toe brushed the liquid first. He flinched, gasping for breath, muscles rigid as the pain worked its way through his body to his brain. I tipped my head to the side and marvelled at the look of torture that broke across his face as he continued to descend.

"Legs!" I ordered.

Two of my men rushed toward Rutter, lifting the chained cuffs off the floor and securing them just above his ankles before tying them off. Now, he had no choice but to keep his feet immersed in the liquid.

Violent shudders wracked his body as both feet were forced down. Rutter gritted his teeth, blood seeping around them where they pressed into his cracked lips. A feeble attempt to hold back another scream—useless. It tore free, raw and jagged, punching out of his chest. Pain seared into each tiny cut on the soles of his feet. It probably felt like he was burning alive from the inside out. A hopeless whimper left his parched lips.

Fuck, he was a weak excuse for a man.

"He's pathetic," one of the soldiers chuckled, nudging the guy beside him, who nodded in agreement.

I shifted my gaze to them, arching a brow. Not that I disagreed, but he'd spoken out of turn.

"You think this is funny?"

The color drained from his face. His tanned complexion turned ghostly pale, and he shook his head with a wince. Smart. His silence was the only thing keeping him alive right now. I didn't have time for men who acted like idiots. Working beside me was an honor few earned—fewer still survived. That wasn't my fault.

I was my father's son. Cold. Ruthless.

"Why don't I tie you to a chair and do the same to your ass? *Maledetto idiota!*"

"N-no, sir." He shrank back, shoulders hunched, and slipped into the shadowed corner where the others waited for my command.

This was why I preferred working alone. My patience was a lit fuse, and people…people made simple things complicated. They wasted time, drained energy, and pulled me away from what I was meant to be doing. From spilling blood. From watching bodies go still, drained of life.

Smoke curled from my lips as I glared at them. The cigarette had burned down to the end, but instead of crushing it under my boot, I had a better idea.

I stepped forward, circling Rutter, sneering as urine trickled down his leg from his pathetic, flaccid cock. His broken whimpers grated on my last nerve. I slapped him hard, snapping his head to the side and forcing his focus back on me. He tried to anticipate my next move, but being unable to see me, his fear would override any logic left in his mind. I was everywhere and nowhere.

Power. Control.

The cigarette cherry sizzled against his exposed flesh, drawing another hoarse scream from his bloodied lips. The skin blistered, smoking as I pressed the ember deeper into his flabby gut. His body spasmed, but there was nowhere for him to go while he was trapped in my web.

Not until I decided.

Only when the embers finally died did I let the cigarette drop from my fingers. I relished every flinch, each futile thrash, every broken cry.

Pathetic.

"I can't... I can't take it anymore..."

I pulled a silver tin from my pocket, flipped it open, pulled out another cigarette, and lit it with a flick of my Zippo. The blue-yellow flame danced in the dim light, licking at the air between us. Rutter whimpered, his breath hitching as the heat singed the hair that covered his body.

This was the man entrusted to protect this city?

He wouldn't last a single day in my world.

Exhaling smoke through my nose, I reached out, plucking the headphones from his ears. I pressed a button in my pocket, flooding the soundproofed room with the music he'd been tormented by for hours.

I cut the blindfold from his face. His eyes—wild and bloodshot—locked onto mine, insipid brown irises swallowed by terror.

The tip of my blade traced down his nose, over his lips, gliding lower until it hovered just below his neck. A single bead of red welled around the steel as I increased the pressure.

"You're wasting your breath," I said coldly. "No one's coming."

His panicked gasps filled the room. He rattled his chains harder, the clang of metal against metal blending with his desperate moans.

A chuckle rumbled in my throat, low and dark, curling my lips into something that barely passed for a smile. A fresh wave of goosebumps rippled across his skin—a visceral display of fear, so pure, so delicious.

If only his men could see him now.

So fucking pathetic.

My hand latched onto his jaw, blunt nails digging into clammy flesh. I leaned in, inhaling the sharp scent of his terror.

There was beauty in this—the fragile balance between life and death, hanging by a thread only I controlled.

His survival.

His agony.

Every ounce of his existence now belonged to me. And I liked holding that power. Releasing him, I stepped back, wiping his sweat and snot on my jeans.

"Do you know why you're here?" I asked, tilting my head like I was speaking to a child.

He shook his head violently, sweat plastering graying hair to his temples.

"N-no."

My gaze hardened. Rutter flailed helplessly, grasping for answers he wouldn't get from me. Then—*finally*—recognition flickered in his hollow eyes. His brain was catching up.

"B-business... j-just business," he croaked. "It's nothing personal... DeMarco, please—"

I laughed, the sound completely void of warmth. "That's where you're wrong."

I leaned in, my breath ghosting against his sweat-damp skin. His shudder made a smirk strain my lips.

"Everything is personal."

His face crumpled as the truth sank in.

I knew everything. Nothing he could say would change that. Watching him process it was like witnessing a car crash in slow motion—inevitable, brutal.

I pulled my switchblade from my jacket, the wolfs head handle gleaming under the dim light. The blade caught the glow, sharp and unforgiving. He whimpered, his entire body going rigid.

Good.

"Your officers arrested six of my men," I said, my tone devoid of emotion, as if discussing the weather. "Six of my soldiers are rotting behind bars because you decided to play hero."

I scraped the tip of the blade down his neck, tracing the delicate line of his carotid artery.

"You think you can interfere in my business and just walk away?" I murmured. "You seem to have forgotten who you work for, who truly holds the power in Marlow Heights, *Chief*."

His lips trembled. "I-I can fix it. I'll drop the charges. Please... I—"

"Shhh." I pressed the blade against his skin. A thin bloom of crimson welled beneath the pressure. "That's not how this works. You don't get to play savior and erase the consequences."

Control.

It thrummed through me, sharpening my senses. Every flinch, every ragged breath, fed something dark and primal inside me. He deserved this. They all did. A lifetime of lies and corruption finally balanced by the edge of my knife as I delivered my retribution.

I gripped his chin, tipping his head back, carving the blade through skin—slow, deliberate, shallow enough to sting but not maim. Blood welled up, glistening as his body spasmed against the restraints.

The music swelled, drowning out his hoarse screams as I dipped a finger into the lemon juice and traced the fresh wound.

"You have children, don't you?" I asked conversationally.

His chin bobbed in a frantic nod, tears spilling down his face.

"Good." I smiled. "Then you understand what it's like to lose something you care about."

His sobs grew desperate. "Please... I-I'll do anything…"

"Then tell me—" I tightened my grip. "—why did you break our agreement?"

Rutter squeezed his eyes shut and shook his head as much as he could in my grasp.

"Who paid you to raid my shipment?"

He froze. Every muscle in his body went taut. His

head twitched in tiny, involuntary shakes, like a puppet with its strings tangled.

Ah. There it was.

The truth—rotting inside him like a corpse, waiting to be unearthed.

"Give me a name."

"T-there is... n-no—"

My hand cracked across his face, the wet slap echoing through the room. I wrenched his head back, fingers tangled in his damp hair, bending his neck at an unnatural angle.

"Do you think I'm *stupid*?" I bellowed, spit flying.

"N-no..." he rasped. "I-I would... n-never..."

I leaned in, my lips brushing the shell of his ear.

"Remember this moment," I murmured. "The moment you realized you were powerless. The moment your life stopped belonging to you. The moment you watched your child break before your eyes."

His sobs turned frantic. "How... how can I stop this?"

"By following my rules." The words settled between us like poison already swallowed. "And by giving me that name. It's simple, really."

The bloodied edge of my switchblade gleamed as I twirled it between my fingers. Rutter whimpered but stayed silent.

Disappointing. But not surprising.

They always thought they had a choice. They never understood the weight of their decisions—until I burned the consequences into their flesh.

At my signal, the last notes of *Tchaikovsky's Nutcracker Suite* faded into obscurity. Overhead, the grimy ceiling lights flared to life, making Rutter recoil.

Too bad. There was nowhere left to hide.

"Five..."

"Four..."

"Three... How is Ashley? He enjoying college?"

His spine snapped straight. "Y-you leave him out of this."

"Why?" I smirked. "Are you going to save him? Protect him?"

I waited.

Waited for a father to value his son's life over his own greed. Waited for him to *fight* for something other than himself.

But... nothing.

"Two... Last chance. Give me a name."

If I had a heart, it might have broken for the boy. But empathy? Emotion? They were foreign languages to me. Instead, I exhaled a soft, measured breath.

"One." The number rang out like a death knell. "Bring him in."

The guards nodded and left the door open. I wanted Rutter to *hear* it, and the moment his son's screams echoed down the damp corridor, something inside him shattered.

"NOOOOO! You leave him alone!"

His cries meant nothing. He'd been given a choice and spit in its face.

And now, he had to *live* with that.

Ashley's scream tore through the room, and for the first time, Rutter went silent. His head jerked toward the open doorway, his body straining against the cuffs. "G-get off me!"

A smile spread across my lips, my cock thickening.

I loved it when they fought back, watching their eyes widen as they realized it wasn't an act, that the hunger in me was real.

I could have a willing body anytime—at twenty-five, I'd had more than enough of *easy*.

The sound of my belt buckle unfastening jolted Rutter back to life. His shattered brown eyes locked onto my hand as I toyed with my zipper.

Then, his gaze met mine—widening in horror—giving me exactly what I craved.

"N-no. Anything but that."

A hollow chuckle left my lips. I shook my head.

"Too late for that now."

He broke completely then, blubbering nonsense about second chances and forgiveness.

Begging.

Pleading.

But I wasn't listening anymore.

His *fear* sang louder than any plea ever could.

Straightening, I pocketed the blade just as Ashley was dragged into the room. The boy hit the ground hard, shoved to his knees at my feet.

"No," Rutter sobbed, eyes bulging. "Don't you dare fucking touch him."

He thrashed violently, blood pooling around his wrists where the cuffs bit into flesh.

"You shouldn't have tried to be a hero, *Chief*."

Tears streamed down his cheeks, and his body shook so hard he could barely breathe.

The acrid scent of urine burned my nose. I inhaled deeply, letting the rush settle into my bones.

My blood *sang* as he suffered.

Rutter's pupils were blown black, the whites nearly red from burst capillaries. His terror filled the room, thick as smoke.

I let it feed me. Let it *consume* me.

And fuck, it was intoxicating.

Ashley trembled at my feet, his bound hands curled into fists against the cold concrete. Blood bloomed across his split lip in perfect contrast to his pale, unblemished skin.

I crouched beside him, letting my fingers ghost over his curls before gripping a fistful of his hair and wrenching his head back.

His breath hitched.

"Look at him, Chief." My voice was velvet-wrapped steel. "Look at your son. Your blood. Your legacy."

Rutter's entire body convulsed against the restraints. "Please—"

I tugged harder, forcing Ashley's neck to arch, exposing the frantic pulse beating just beneath the surface.

"You're going to give me that name now."

A strangled sob wrenched from Rutter's throat. "I— I can't—"

I sighed, almost disappointed.

Then, with deliberate slowness, I ran my thumb across Ashley's trembling lower lip, smearing the blood that had pooled there. His whole body jerked.

"You know," I mused, tracing the curve of Ashley's jaw with the flat of my blade, making him flinch at the touch of cold steel. "I never cared much for mercy. I find it... wasteful. You know what I do like, though?" I continued, my lips brushing his ear. "Breaking beautiful things."

"You know what I do like, though?" I continued, my lips brushing his ear. "Breaking beautiful things."

Ashley whimpered before Rutter screamed, "NO! STOP! PLEASE, FOR GOD'S SAKE!"

The raw agony in his voice was exquisite. I trailed the knife lower, pressing the tip against Ashley's collarbone, just hard enough to dimple the skin. The boy shook violently, his gasps ragged, erratic.

"One name," I whispered.

Rutter choked on a sob. "I-I swear, I d-don't—"

I rolled my eyes, the blade sinking just deep enough to draw a single ruby bead of blood. Ashley yelped, his body twisting against the guards' hold. I swiped it up with my finger, dragged it across his lips, and pushed up to my feet. My eyes fixed on the trembling boy at my feet as I pulled my throbbing cock out of my jeans and slowly stroked it.

Ashley recoiled, but his eyes tracked every move of my hand. I watched Rutter come apart as I traced the tip of my cock along his son's lips.

"STOP! STOP I-I'LL TELL YOU!"

I stilled.

Rutter sagged against the cuffs, his body wracked with uncontrollable tremors. "Please," he whispered, "Just... just let him go."

I smirked, sinking my fingers further into the boy's curls and tightening my grip. "Open," I ordered quietly. The room fell silent as the grave as he followed my command without question. Soft pink lips parted for me, and I rested the tip on his tongue.

"If you bite me, I will kill you."

The boy's eyes widened in fear and resignation, but the slight movement of his head let me know he understood. Tightening my hold, I thrust all the way to the back of his throat with a snap of my hips and lost myself in the wet heat of his untouched mouth. Rutter screamed, turning rabid as I fucked Ashley's throat raw, starved him of oxygen while tears streamed down his face.

"Fuck!" I grit out, euphoria dancing through my blood.

"GET THE FUCK OFF HIM. I'LL KILL YOU."

My head fell back on my shoulders as I laughed.

"You will do exactly as I say." I yanked the boy's head until his nose was buried against my groin and held him there while Rutter seethed.

"You won't get away with this."

"I will," I said simply. "Because if you step a foot out of line again, I will come for your wife. Mary." Rutter blanched. "The twins, Jane and Jessica."

"No," he whispered brokenly.

"Then I'll leave Ashley's body in your trunk for you to find."

Rutter whimpered, the fight drained from him completely. "Y-you, win."

"Name."

A pause.

Then, barely above a breath— "Calloway."

The name slithered through the air, curling around my senses like a serpent.

I chuckled, low and dark.

"Now that wasn't so hard, was it?" I pulled my cock from Ashley's mouth and grunted as thick ropes of cum lashed over his face.

Rutter gasped, his head dropping forward, his entire body defeated.

I hummed, basking in the afterglow before pushing the boy away like a discarded plaything. The guards caught him before he hit the ground, but the boy had already gone limp—spent, ruined, utterly broken.

I flicked my knife clean, watching Rutter's tears fall freely, his face a portrait of utter devastation.

I drank it in, savoring it.

The agony.

The submission.

The end of a man who once thought himself untouchable.

I smirked as I tucked myself away and dialed my father's number.

"Is it done?"

"Yes."

"Name?"

"Calloway. A Gallo enforcer."

"Fuck! Get it done."

The line went dead, and I knew my night wasn't over yet. No one would be left standing in our way. I'd pick the Gallos off one by one if I had to because Marlow Heights was ours.

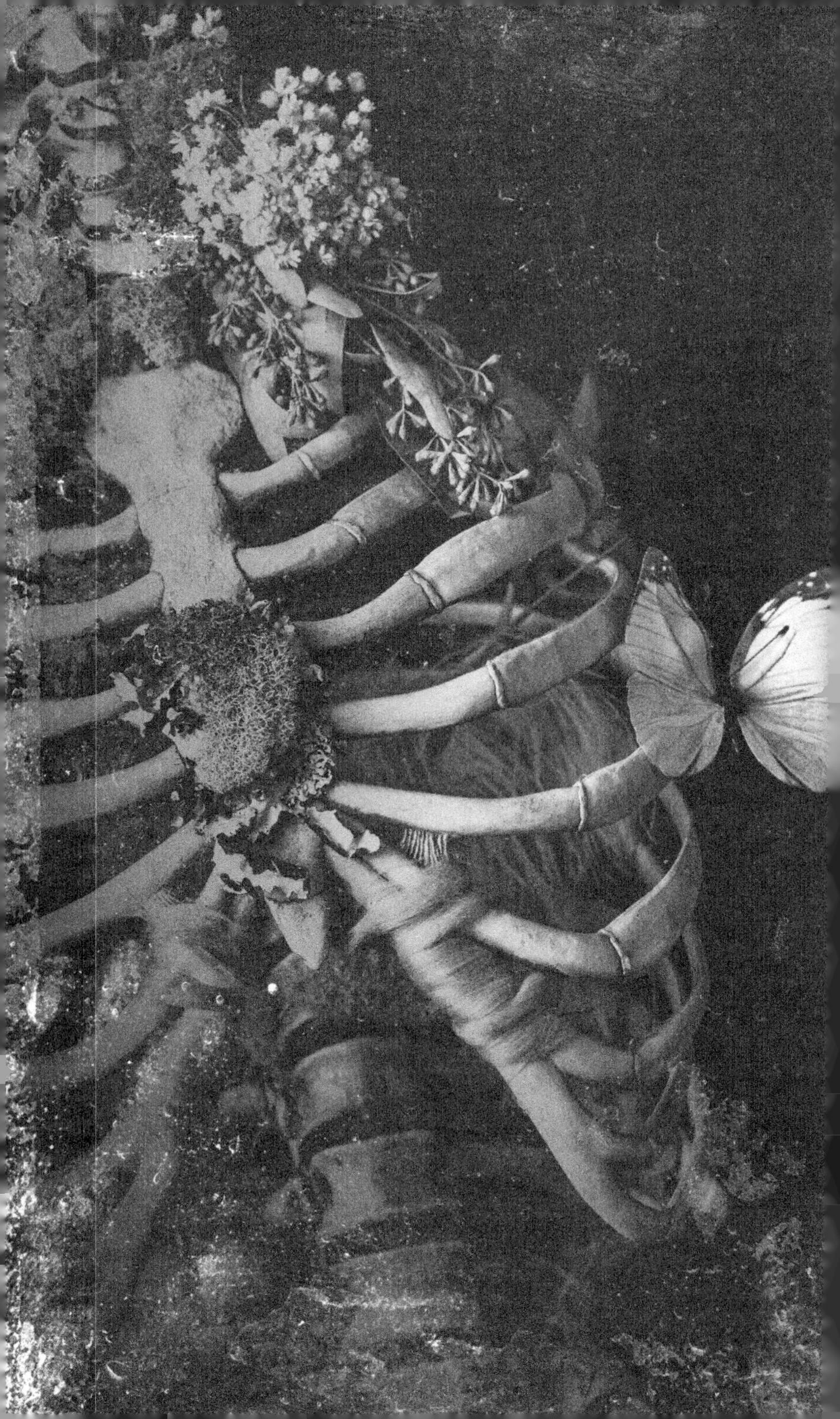

2 REMI

"Are you ready to go, kid?"

I grunted in acknowledgment and stuffed the last of my clothes into my backpack.

It felt strange—leaving the only place I'd ever known. A fourth-floor walk-up wasn't much, but it had been home. Now, it was nothing more than an empty shell, stripped of the life we'd carved into its walls.

"Get moving then," Arti grumbled, already heading for the door. "I can't wait for ya any longer. The drive's gonna take a few hours, if not longer. Your mother needs to get to the home so her condition stays stable."

Like I didn't know that.

I hated the way people spoke to me—like I was slow and needed things spelled out. Just because I wasn't wide-eyed and wagging my tail at the world didn't mean I was stupid. People never got that. They saw a kid who didn't fit into their neat little boxes and decided he was broken. That was fine. Let them think what they want.

I bit the inside of my cheek, doing a final sweep of the apartment to make sure I hadn't left anything important. It wasn't like I could afford to replace things. I knew that better than most.

The last year had been hell—balancing school, finances, and working nights at The Hollow bussing tables just to keep food on the table. Every penny from Mom's insurance—along with anything else I could scrape together—had been funneled into her medical bills, as if keeping her breathing mattered more than keeping the lights on.

And now, after all that, we were leaving.

Leaving Cedarbrook. Leaving behind the life I'd tried so damn hard to hold together with my own two hands.

All for a woman who didn't even know she was alive.

I should have been relieved when she woke up from the coma. That's what a *good* son would have felt. Instead, all I could think about was how unfair it was that she came back *like this*—half a person, her brain wrecked beyond repair. She needed oxygen just to get through the day. Couldn't move without help. Couldn't *speak*.

Existing like that wasn't life.

It was suffering.

She should have died. I knew it, and maybe, somewhere in that broken brain of hers, she knew it too. It would have been a mercy.

Instead, she clung on, breathing, blinking, *waiting*. And now we were moving across state lines so she could waste away in some nursing home under the care of an aunt I'd never met. That was her future. That was mine.

Nothing here for me anymore.

Not that there ever was.

It wasn't like I had friends. People were too much work, and I'd never had the patience for their bullshit. Because I wasn't a brown-nosing little kiss-ass who hung on every word the jocks spewed, or played any sports, I'd been marked an outcast.

That suited me just fine because the living were exhausting.

The dead were easier.

I'd always preferred the cemetery anyway—the quiet, the stillness, the reminder that none of us got out of this alive. Life was a fleeting illusion, a single bright spark that was swallowed by the darkness of eternity when our hearts gave out. It was the only certainty in the world, and most people feared it but me…?

I was fascinated by something so permanent.

The idiots at school didn't get that. They ran around like they were untouchable, like they'd never have to face the same decay and rot as the corpses buried six feet under.

But they would. Every single day they woke up was just one day closer to the end. And I was the only one who seemed to *see it*.

The door to the private ambulance slammed shut, harder than necessary, but I didn't care if it pissed off Arti or his team. It wasn't like Mom would notice. It wasn't like she'd give a shit.

So why should I?

"Jesus, kid." Arti shot me a glare from the driver's seat. "You're a fucking mess."

I rolled my eyes, shoving my bag between my feet as I tried to get comfortable on the rock-hard bench seat. The only things I needed were my sketchbook, camera, and pencils. I'd have to pick up a new set of charcoals once Mom was settled, but for now, I had bigger problems—like tuning out Arti's relentless chatter.

The engine rumbled to life, and the ambulance lurched forward, leaving Cedarbrook behind. Good riddance.

Five minutes in, and my ears were already bleeding from Arti's voice. If I had to endure the entire drive with him running his mouth like this, I'd throw myself out of the moving vehicle. I could just visualize the way my skin would paint the blacktop as we drove down the interstate. Beautiful.

The last few years had drained me, physically and mentally. I wasn't just tired—I was bone-deep exhausted. The kind of fatigue that sleep wouldn't fix. The kind that lived in my muscles, weighed down my limbs, made every step feel like I was trudging through knee-deep mud and battling against a riptide.

I needed silence. Darkness. Solitude.

I shifted, curling up on the seat with my hoodie bunched beneath my head against the cool window. The steady vibration of the road hummed through me, lulling my body into something close to rest. So close but perpetually out of reach, I popped in my AirPods, turned on my favorite serial killer podcast, and finally—*finally*—unconsciousness claimed me.

A PRICKLE OF UNEASE CREPT UP MY SPINE, YANKING ME from sleep. Adrenaline shot through my system as my eyes snapped open. The world outside was pitch-black.

Not the hazy, congested blue of Cedarbrook, but a deep, endless void.

"Welcome back, kid." Arti's chuckle grated on my nerves.

I shot him a glare and sat up, stretching as my joints cracked in protest. My eyes caught the clock on the dashboard, the green segments showed six p.m. Five hours. I'd been out for nearly five hours. What the fuck? No wonder I felt like utter shit, and my head was pounding like a motherfucker.

"Five hours?" My voice was rough with sleep.

Arti shrugged. "Storm slowed us down. Visibility was shit, everyone was crawling."

"Huh." I scrubbed a hand down my face.

"Almost there. 'Bout twenty minutes out."

There wasn't much to see in the darkness as I trained my gaze on the window. We weren't in a city, no bright lights and streets lined with clubs and bars. Just an empty, winding road that looked straight out of a horror movie. Tall, skeletal trees lined the narrow path, their branches draped in something that could've been moss—or something worse. The weak arc of the ambulance's headlights barely cut through the gloom, leaving too many shadows for my imagination to fill in the blanks.

Brielle had mentioned they lived outside the city, near Hollow Pines National Park. Her care home—aptly named *Hollow Pines Care Home*—backed right up against it.

We veered off the road, the ambulance's headlights sweeping over a weathered sign. The lettering was barely legible, but according to the GPS, we were in the right place.

"You have reached your destination." The distorted female voice announced, flat and emotionless.

I stared at the driveway ahead, which resembled a dirt track. Potholes—some deep enough to swallow a wheel—scarred the road leading up to the home. Neglected. Forgotten. If Brielle took care of her patients the way she did this place, Mom was not in safe hands.

Hollow Pines Care Home emerged through the misty drizzle. The massive, white building loomed in the darkness, its long, barred windows staring blankly ahead. The place reminded me of an old asylum, the kind of institution people whispered about but never acknowledged. We passed the front, heading for the back entrance as per Brielle's instructions. The ornate main doors weren't equipped for patients arriving in hospital beds like Mom, but what she called the servants' entrance was.

Arti turned and reversed us toward the back entrance, shut the engine off, and rolled his neck before running his fingers through his hair. The double doors behind us swung open, revealing two figures silhouetted against the harsh light that spilled out from the home.

Brielle and Brock, I assumed. Having never met them, I had no clue what or who I was looking for. No childhood photos. No family visits. Nothing. With a sigh, I slung my bag over my shoulder and climbed out just as Arti did.

"Get the doors for me, kid."

His dismissive tone grated my nerves, but I moved to unlock the ambulance doors and shoved back one heavy lever at a time. The two nurses who'd accompanied us stiffened at the gust of cold air, scurrying to tuck extra blankets around Mom's fragile frame.

The rain slicked my hoodie, soaking through the

material in seconds as I yanked out the running boards from beneath the ambulance. The metal groaned under my grip, the chill biting at my fingers as I lowered them to the ground, the gravel crunching beneath my feet as I worked.

The pitchy, feminine laugh that cut through the night had me glancing over my shoulder to see what was going on. Brielle stood too close to Arti, a manicured hand resting lightly on his arm as they lost themselves in conversation.

But it wasn't her that held my attention. It was him, the broad, silent figure standing just off to the side—Brock. His stance was rigid, hands clenched at his sides, his stare locked onto me with the kind of hostility that burned cold against my skin.

I didn't know the guy from Adam, but judging by the way he was looking at me, he sure as hell had already made up his mind about me. Most people would've been unsettled. Maybe even intimidated.

I just didn't give a shit and let it roll off my back.

It was already clear—this wasn't going to be anything like the picture Brielle had painted over the phone. That the family who hadn't known I'd existed were excited to get to know me and welcome my mom back into the fold. It had sounded too good to be true when the words had left her lips, but now? Reality proved they were just a pretty picture she'd wanted to paint to get me here.

The question was why?

Growing up, Mom never talked much about her family. She never fit in, she'd said. And I was better off not knowing them. But she'd also mentioned—vaguely—that if we ever needed help, there was a seventy percent chance they'd be there for us.

"It'ss w-worth a...ssshot."

Her words echoed in my head, slightly slurred from her first, smaller stroke. Seventy percent weren't great odds, but it was better than nothing. And now I was all out of options, with no savings left and her insurance drained. It wasn't like I had anyone else I could ask for help.

It had been just me and mom growing up. Dad died on active duty when I was two, but beyond that, he was a ghost. There were no photos, medals, or even letters from him for me to read to get to know him.

No proof he'd ever really existed.

Not that it mattered. Even my own mother struggled to understand me. So why would a bunch of strangers parading as my family be any different?

I was better off alone. I'd always known that.

The nurses maneuvered Mom's bed down the ramps, their hurried footsteps echoing across the bricked driveway as they wheeled her inside. The open doors spilled warm light onto the rain-slicked ground, a stark contrast to the cold seeping into my bones. Water dripped from my hair, rolling down my face as I shoved the ramps back into place and slammed the ambulance doors shut.

My hoodie clung to me, heavy with rain, as I trudged toward the entrance. One of the double doors had already swung closed, but before I could step inside, Brielle blocked my path.

Her expression was unreadable at first, but her pale blue eyes were frigid—empty of the warmth I'd expected.

"What are you doing?" Her tone matched the ice in her gaze.

I hesitated. Why did it suddenly feel like I was trespassing?

"I just..." I cleared my dry throat. "I wanted to make sure Mom was settled in, and—"

"Angelica is fine," she cut in with a clipped voice. "Arti and the nurses will take care of that."

"Okay, but can I—"

"No." The word was a slap.

She braced her arm against the doorway, leaning in just enough to make her point clear.

"You need to find somewhere to stay."

Wait. I blinked at her, rainwater stinging my eyes. "But I thought—"

She laughed. Sharp. Mocking. "There's no room for you here."

My stomach dropped. "But you said—" I fisted my soaked hair, frustration clawing at my skin like fire ants. "You said I could stay here with Mom."

"That was then. This is now."

Her gaze raked over me, slow and deliberate, disgust curling her lip.

"Angelica is here, and she'll be looked after," she said, like it was some great favor. Like I was the outsider. "You, however, don't belong here."

I could barely breathe. This couldn't be happening. "But...where am I supposed to go?"

She shrugged. "The mountains? The city? I don't give a shit. Just get gone. If I see your face around here again, I'll call the cops."

I opened my mouth to argue—to fight, to demand answers—but then, I felt it. The presence behind her. A shadow. Brock. I wasn't short at 5'11, but he towered over me. Broad and thickly muscled. The kind of muscle that looked less like hard work and dedication and more like a side effect of a roid addiction. And his glare? It was a warning. A threat.

But it was lost on me.

I smoothed every trace of emotion from my face, watching Brock like he was nothing more than a mildly interesting experiment. His control started to crack.

The twitch of an eye. The clench of his teeth. Veins pulsing beneath stretched skin as his grip tightened on the doorframe behind Brielle.

"She told you to leave," he said, voice low and seething like a ticking time bomb. "Or do I need to remove you from the property?"

I rolled my eyes. Tilting my head, I studied them like they were animals in a zoo. "I don't care about staying where I'm not wanted," I said evenly. "But I want to see my mom. The doctors said she doesn't have long."

For the briefest moment, something flickered in their eyes, but it was gone before I could name it. Then, the door slammed shut in my face.

I exhaled slowly, staring at the weathered wood. Well, I guess I have my answer.

A stray stone sat near my boot, and I kicked it hard, watching it ricochet off the brick driveway before vanishing into the dark. My heart thudded, an uncomfortable, restless beat against my ribs.

Turning on my heel, I headed back toward the ambulance to grab my duffel—the only real proof I existed. Because if I stood there any longer, I'd do something stupid.

Like breaking in or making a point no one gave a shit about. I was good at picking locks, but my kit was buried at the bottom of my bag, the one I didn't have.

Arti was leaning against the front of the ambulance,

cigarette dangling between his fingers. The smoke curled into the damp air, the scent sharp and familiar.

"I'm sorry, kid," he said, voice rough.

I didn't answer. What was there to say?

"Want one?" He held the pack out toward me, flicking the bottom so a cigarette popped forward.

I hesitated but fuck it. Taking one between my lips, I let him light it. The first inhale hit my lungs like fire, and I coughed hard, doubling over for a solid minute.

Arti chuckled. "Been a while?"

I glared at him through watering eyes, but he only smirked, taking another drag. The cherry flared bright red in the darkness. "I'd offer to take you into the city, but…" He trailed off, chewing his cheek like he wasn't sure how to say what came next.

I spared him the effort. Shrugging my duffel over my shoulder, I unzipped it just enough to pull out my puffer jacket and tug it on over my backpack. The rain was picking up. I couldn't afford to let my sketchbook get wet. Or my camera. They were irreplaceable. Pieces of me, scrawled in ink and graphite.

"If you head that way—" Arti gestured toward the treeline. "—it's about a forty-minute walk into town. Once you hit the main strip, go three blocks down. You'll find Denny's Diner. If anyone knows where you can crash, it's Denny and Doll."

I nodded. "Thanks."

It felt strange—this random act of kindness from someone who owed me nothing. But I'd take it.

"Hey, kid?"

Halfway across the driveway, I glanced over my shoulder. "Yeah?"

"What's your number?"

Unease curled in my stomach. My shoulders tensed, hunching against the rain. "Why?"

Arti let out a flat laugh. "So I can let you know when they're gone. You can come see your mom."

Oh. My throat tightened. I hadn't expected that. "I, uh…" I shifted on my feet, forcing my expression to stay neutral. "I don't have one."

His brow furrowed.

"Had to sell it to keep the lights on," I admitted. "Got sick. Couldn't work."

Arti studied me for a long moment, then nodded like it made perfect sense. "When you get one, tell Doll to let me know."

I gave him a two-fingered wave and kept walking.

His voice chased after me. "I'll check in with her until then, yeah? Just… check in with Doll every day."

I didn't answer, slipping into the shadows beyond the treeline. The night swallowed me whole. The path ahead was well worn, but the trees loomed overhead like silent sentinels. Moonlight trickled through the canopy in broken shards, painting the forest floor in silver and shadow. I wasn't sure how much it would help.

But I wasn't in a position to complain. All I could do was follow my feet; what will be, will be. I slid my AirPods in, and Every Me Every You by Placebo drowned out the howling of the wind ripping through the trees.

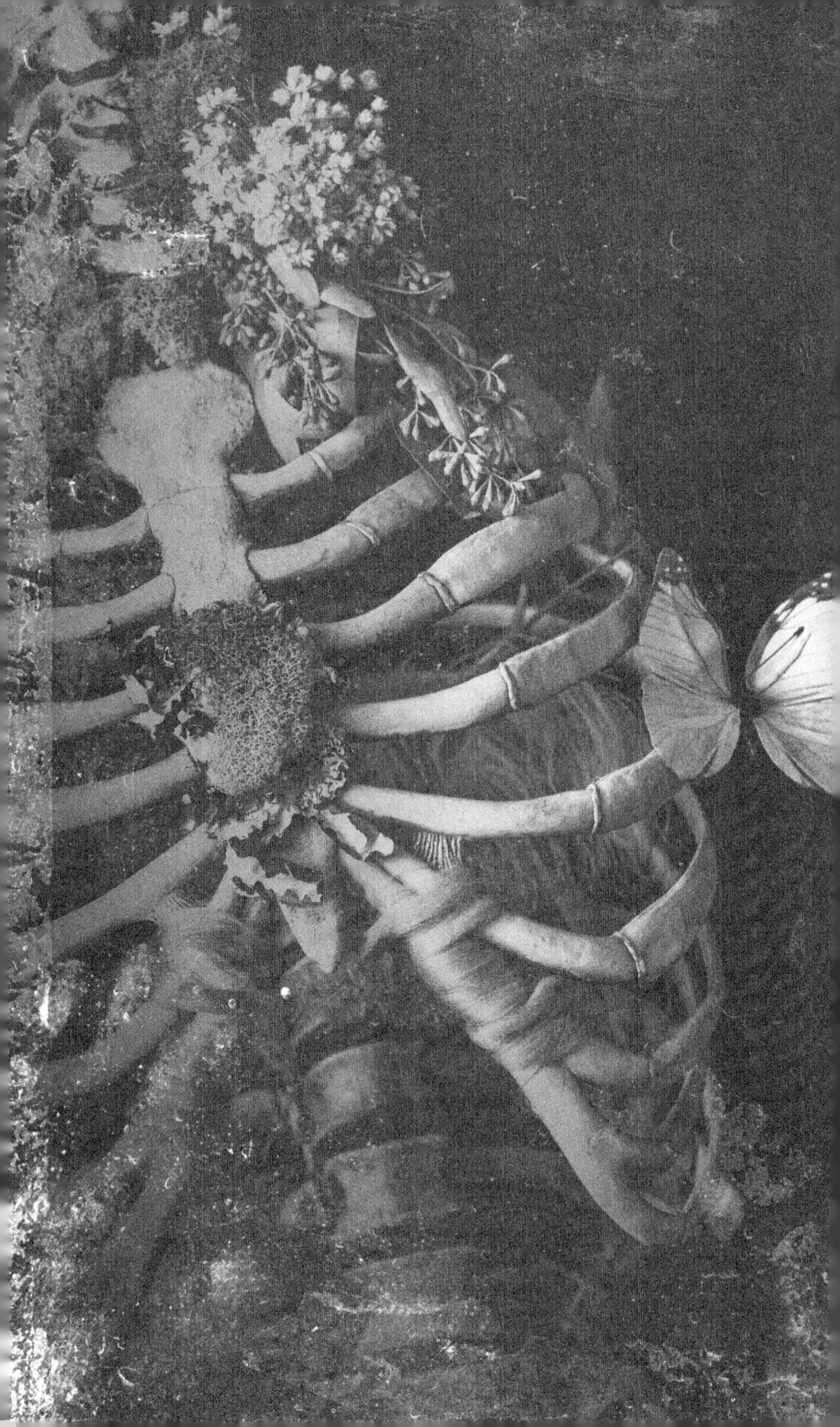

3 REMI

Denny's Diner looked like it had seen better decades. Paint peeled from the weathered wooden exterior, curling like dead leaves. Above the entrance, a neon purple sign flickered erratically, missing an N, so it read *De_ny's* instead.

The bell above the door jangled as I stepped inside. Rain running in rivulets down my face, soaking into my hoodie. Small puddles pooled around my boots on the faded black-and-white checkered floor.

The place smelled like stale coffee and grease—comforting in a way I didn't expect.

It wasn't empty, but it was close. A couple of men sat at the counter, hands curled around steaming mugs. Thick beards. Dirty jeans. Flannel jackets. Either passing through or lying low, trying to disappear into the cracks of the world.

In the far booth, a group of college kids picked at baskets of fries, their laughter too loud for the quiet space. The hum of life vibrated through this place, low and steady.

"Take a seat, darlin'. I'll be over in a minute."

The woman behind the counter didn't even glance my way. Gray hair twisted into a messy bun and her grease-stained apron that looked like it used to be white had the Denny's logo across her chest. She fit the diner like she'd always been here.

I shrugged, heading for the booth in the far corner—the one where an overhead light had burned out, leaving it cloaked in shadow. It felt safer there, out of sight.

The red leather was cracked and split at the seams, but it was dry. I slid into the seat, my weight deflating the cushion beneath me. Shrugging off my soaked jacket, I draped it over the opposite bench and then pulled my sketchbook from my bag.

The plastic menu was laminated to the tabletop, edges curling with age. The selection wasn't bad, typical greasy diner food.

The thought of food made my stomach roll. I hadn't eaten since last night, not the slightest bit hungry, but I knew I needed to eat. I just… I had to at least try.

"What can I get ya, darlin'?"

I looked up.

The waitress smiled, eyes crinkling at the corners. "You're new."

I nodded. "Yeah."

"You here for Deveraux? Heard it's good."

"Yeah." That had been the plan. Before everything fell apart. Before I realized that I had nowhere to stay. The scholarship covered tuition but not food. Not a roof over my head. The fifty bucks in my pocket wouldn't last long. I'd need a job—fast.

"Do you need a minute?"

I blinked, confused. "What?"

Her lips twitched. "To order, honey."

"Oh." My face warmed. "Uh… coffee and cheesy fries."

"Great choice, hun."

She held out her hand. "I'm Doll."

I hesitated. I wasn't a fan of physical contact. People were too hot and their skin too soft. Touch repelled me. Still, I forced my hand into hers for the briefest shake before retreating.

"I'll bring it over in a sec," she said, either not noticing or not commenting on my discomfort. "If you need anything, let me know."

"Sure."

The shadows felt heavier as she walked away. They felt like home.

I flipped open my sketchbook to a blank page—crisp white, like fresh bone stripped of flesh. My pencil hovered for a moment before my gaze wandered across the diner, taking in the shifting crowd.

The energy had changed. The group on the other side of the diner had grown.

The latest additions were not college kids. They sat like kings in their own space, backs to the walls, eyes tracking movement like hunters. Men in their mid to late twenties, but the weight they carried aged them beyond their years. Something clung to them—a darkness, an aura of violence and control that made the others give them a wide berth.

They weren't just passing through. That's when I noticed the discarded newspaper on the table across from me. I snatched it up, flipping it open in search of rental listings or shelters—anything that could tell me where I'd be sleeping tonight. But it was the bold headline that caught my attention:

WHISPERS OF WAR: DEMARCO VS. GALLO— WHO WILL FALL FIRST?

What the hell was that supposed to mean? Everyone knew cities thrived on corruption, built on a web of lies so thick it was impossible to untangle. But this?

A feud between influential families?

Something darker?

Was the underworld on the verge of war?

Would the streets run red until only one side remained standing? Or was it a case of mutually assured destruction? Images flicked through my mind like a twisted fantasy of darkness. Hiding in the shadows, watching death and destruction first hand. Guns or blades?

A clatter of porcelain snapped me from my thoughts. "I wouldn't pay too much attention to that," Doll said, setting my coffee and fries down beside the paper.

I glanced up. "Do you know anything about it?"

She hesitated for half a second too long. "There's not much to say," she murmured. "Just don't get lost in the shadows."

"Huh?"

She shook her head, brushing it aside. Subject closed. "I got a text from Arti," she said instead. "Told me you were coming by. Said you're looking for a room?"

"Something like that."

Doll's lips pressed into a thin line. "Brielle is a selfish bitch." She placed a hand over her chest. "You didn't hear that from me, but it's better to stay away from her and her family."

I scoffed. "Kinda hard when she's my aunt."

Her eyes darkened. "Family isn't defined by blood, kid."

I tipped my head slightly, watching her. This was the longest conversation I'd had with anyone in months.

"Or at least, it doesn't have to be," she continued. "Find your people. Your person. Then you'll know what family truly is."

She glanced toward the group of men at the far end of the diner, something unreadable flickering across her face.

"But take my word for it," she muttered. "These streets aren't safe anymore."

I exhaled slowly. "Thanks, but I have nowhere to go."

"There's a shelter down on Clayburn Avenue. If they have space, they're open until midnight."

She grabbed a napkin and scribbled out a rough map. "Words can be forgotten," she said. "Ask for Tilly."

Before I could say anything else, she hurried back toward the kitchen—Where the cook was losing his shit in the kitchen over a table of high schoolers inhaling their weight in fries.

By the time I looked up, the diner had transformed. What had been nearly deserted was now buzzing with life—the heartbeat of the city thrumming between these walls. The diversity was staggering.

College kids. Strangers on the run. Workers just trying to make it through another night to rinse and repeat the following day. The noise rose like a wave, crashing over me, pressing against my ribs.

I wasn't leaving anytime soon—not with the rain lashing down in thick sheets against the sidewalk. The streets beyond the glass were swallowed by darkness, and I wondered...

What secrets did they hold? Did the wind whisper the city's nightmares to those who knew how to listen?

My pencil spun between my fingers, a quiet rhythm against the chaos in my mind. Blood. Bone. The fragility of life.

People mistook life for power, but power wasn't in living—it was in taking. A bullet. A blade. A whisper of poison in the bloodstream. Life could be snuffed out in a breath, stolen before a scream could form. That was real power. To wield it. To control it. To decide.

I wondered what that kind of power felt like.

Would it be a slow burn, seeping into your veins, intoxicating? Or would it be instant, a spark of adrenaline, a rush so consuming it became impossible to stop?

The world faded as my pencil scratched across the page. Lines and shadows formed vertebrae, each delicate curve stretching into an exposed spine. Bone by bone, the skeleton took shape. Ribs jutted out, arching across the thick white paper, brittle yet unyielding as they formed from nothing.

Vines sprouted from the broken ground. They twisted between the bones, curling like hungry fingers, pulling the skeleton downward—back into the earth, back into the abyss. Like hands from hell, clawing to reclaim what had been lost.

There was beauty in death. A purity that life smothered and twisted, distorting it into something it was never meant to be.

The bones told a story, a struggle that reality lied to you about. The sharp lines carved into them, the fusion of the bone plates, were like little bread crumbs that bore the brutal truth. You could learn so much from them if only you took the time to look closely and piece them all together.

"That's not something you see every day."

My pencil halted mid-stroke. A slow, creeping sensation of awareness trickled down my spine. His voice was a rasp of gravel, sliding over me like a blade against my skin. I looked up, locking onto dark green eyes that held too many secrets. Even lost in shadow, they seemed to see me in a way no one ever had.

My heart skipped—not in fear, not exactly. Intrigue, maybe?

"Or maybe it is…?"

There was something in the way he said it, an unspoken weight behind the words. A test. A challenge. A flicker of amusement ghosted across his features, but his stare remained steady, searching. The diner had quieted, all waiting to see what would happen next.

Without breaking eye contact, he reached out. A single tattooed finger dragged my sketchbook across the table, slow and deliberate. He turned it toward himself, releasing me from the intensity of his gaze—but not from its effect.

"You like art?"

"You don't?" I shot back, my voice steadier than I expected.

His mouth curved, something unreadable in his expression as he settled into the opposite side of the booth. When he finally looked up again, the dim light caught in his eyes—green laced with flecks of metallic gold. Hypnotic. Dangerous.

"Certain types."

A cryptic answer. A warning? An invitation?

His attention dropped back to my sketch. I watched as his fingers traced the lines—not touching, just hovering—a breath away from the penciled ribs and twisting vines. The way he studied it was almost reverent, like he understood the darkness woven between the lines.

Like he recognized it.

Now that he was distracted, I took my chance to observe him in return. Jet-black hair, a close fade shaved at the sides, the outline of a tattoo barely visible beneath. The longer strands on top were wild, like he'd spent hours running his fingers through them in frustration. Stubble framed a sharp jaw, lips that looked too soft for someone so unnerving. A silver ring pierced his nose, a delicate chain hanging from one ear with an inverted cross.

The contrast of sharp, masculine lines and something almost… sinisterly beautiful.

Tattoos crawled up his hands and disappeared beneath the sleeve of his black leather jacket, the fabric pulled back just enough to hint at more ink covering his arms. His left wrist was adorned with a silver chain, and the fingers of his right hand had thick rings on them. Adornment or armor?

"The force required to carve bone like that… mmm."

I stiffened. Had I heard him right? He hadn't meant to say it aloud, had he? It was more of a thought, slipping past his lips unbidden. His fingers flexed against the table, but he didn't correct himself.

Instead, he asked, "Do you only draw?"

I hesitated. "What do you mean?"

He made a slow, deliberate gesture with his hand, the thick silver chain around his wrist catching the light. "Do you work with other... mediums? That's the word, isn't it?"

Something about the way he said it sent a shiver through me. "I take photographs, too."

"Nothing... real?"

I shook my head, uneasy now. Instinct told me to take my sketchbook back, but when I reached for it, he held it in place with just a finger.

"I'm no sculptor."

"That's a shame," he murmured, leaning back in his seat. "Nothing like the real thing."

The real thing? He couldn't mean actual bone, could he?

The thought burrowed under my skin, sinking its teeth into the deepest, darkest part of me—the part that had always wondered. How much pressure would it take to carve into bone without shattering it? How would it feel beneath my fingers? Would the blade vibrate up my arm as it sliced?

"Art takes many forms."

His voice was velvet, but the edge beneath it was steel. He finally released my sketchbook, and I wasted no time closing it, tucking it safely into my bag. He didn't stop me. Just watched.

"You're new."

"So I'm told."

"You staying with family?"

I exhaled sharply, scrubbing a hand down my face. What was this—an interrogation? "No. My plans have changed."

"So where then?"

"That's a work in progress."

A slow nod. He flexed his fingers again, drawing my attention to his rings. Thick. Heavy. Not just for decoration.

Doll appeared beside us, placing a to-go cup in front of him with a wary glance in my direction. She didn't say a word. Just turned on her heel and left without looking back.

His chuckle was quiet. Hollow.

"I'm here to finish my degree at Devereux University," I found myself saying, as if filling the silence would make it easier to breathe. "Forensic anthropology. Got a scholarship."

Something flickered in his expression at that but was gone before I could name it.

He leaned back, settling into the seat like he owned it. Like he owned the room. And maybe he did, because the second he walked in, the diner had shifted. The space around us was different now.

"You know... this is my table. No one sits here."

His Adam's apple bobbed as he swallowed his drink, and my eyes followed the movement without thinking. My body reacted before my mind could catch up. Heat coiled low in my stomach, warming the blood in my veins.

Confusion rippled through me at my body's reaction. I didn't react like this to people. I could appreciate beauty across any gender—always had—but I'd never felt it like a spark against dry kindling before. Never like this.

He placed his cup on the table with a soft thud, his smirk curling slow and cruel. "You're different."

A statement. A realization? A warning or maybe a threat.

He didn't wait for a response as he slipped out of his

seat fluidly. Muscles coiling and bunching under the straining material of his jacket. A ripple passed through the diner, conversations fading in his wake as he sauntered to the door.

At the front, the table of men stood as he approached. Their movements were sharp, practiced. Not just deference but discipline. They flanked him, moving in sync as he stepped outside, and the night swallowed them whole as they melted into the shadows.

With them gone, the silent moment shattered. Air rushed back into the room, but the weight of their absence lingered. Then—I felt it. A subtle but undeniable shift. Every gaze turned in my direction as they studied me like an exhibition. Recognition or fear flickered across their faces. Faces that had smiled at me before now judged me.

I was no longer just the boy in the dark corner. No longer invisible. Something had changed. They might not have understood why, but instinctively, unconsciously—they recoiled.

Marked me as an outsider, someone whom they should keep their distance from. As one, they built their walls up and turned back to their private conversations.

"Top-up?" Doll's voice cut through the tension, her coffee pot poised.

I nodded. "Sure."

As she poured, her voice dropped to a whisper, like she was sharing a secret rather than a warning. "Be careful."

I raised a brow.

"He's not like everyone else."

I tilted my head. "Neither am I." The words left my mouth before I had time to process them.

Doll's expression flickered—understanding? Concern? She reached out, her fingers barely grazing the air near my shoulder. I flinched.

She hesitated, then pulled back. But her voice hardened. "Maybe not. But you're not like him." Something in her tone tickled the back of my mind; it was more than caution. Conviction maybe? A warning.

Before I could press her for more, I exhaled, mentally exhausted. "Mind if I stay and draw?"

She paused, and all I could hear was the sound of my heart beating in my ears. Her features smoothed, the practiced ease returning along with the smile on her lips. "'Course, darlin'."

I reached into my pocket and pulled out my wallet for the cash to pay—I didn't have much— but she waved me off.

"On the house. Something tells me you need it more than I do."

I opened my mouth to argue, but she silenced me before I could.

"You don't mind loading the dumpsters for me at the end of the night, that is?"

A trade. That was fair. "Of course not."

Satisfied, she moved through the diner, slipping back into routine—orders taken, drinks refilled. The world around me settled, falling back into rhythm.

I was quickly forgotten by the other patrons as I disappeared back into my own world. I pulled my sketchbook free and let the pencil glide over paper, coaxing the image to life—fractured bone, splintered under pressure. Swirling shadows, curling into the vines, stretching from the page as if they could reach out and pull you in.

I pressed harder, the graphite deepening, darkening. Everything else faded as I added flecks of blood glistening in the unseen light. There was only art and a feeling that, somehow, the shadows were watching.

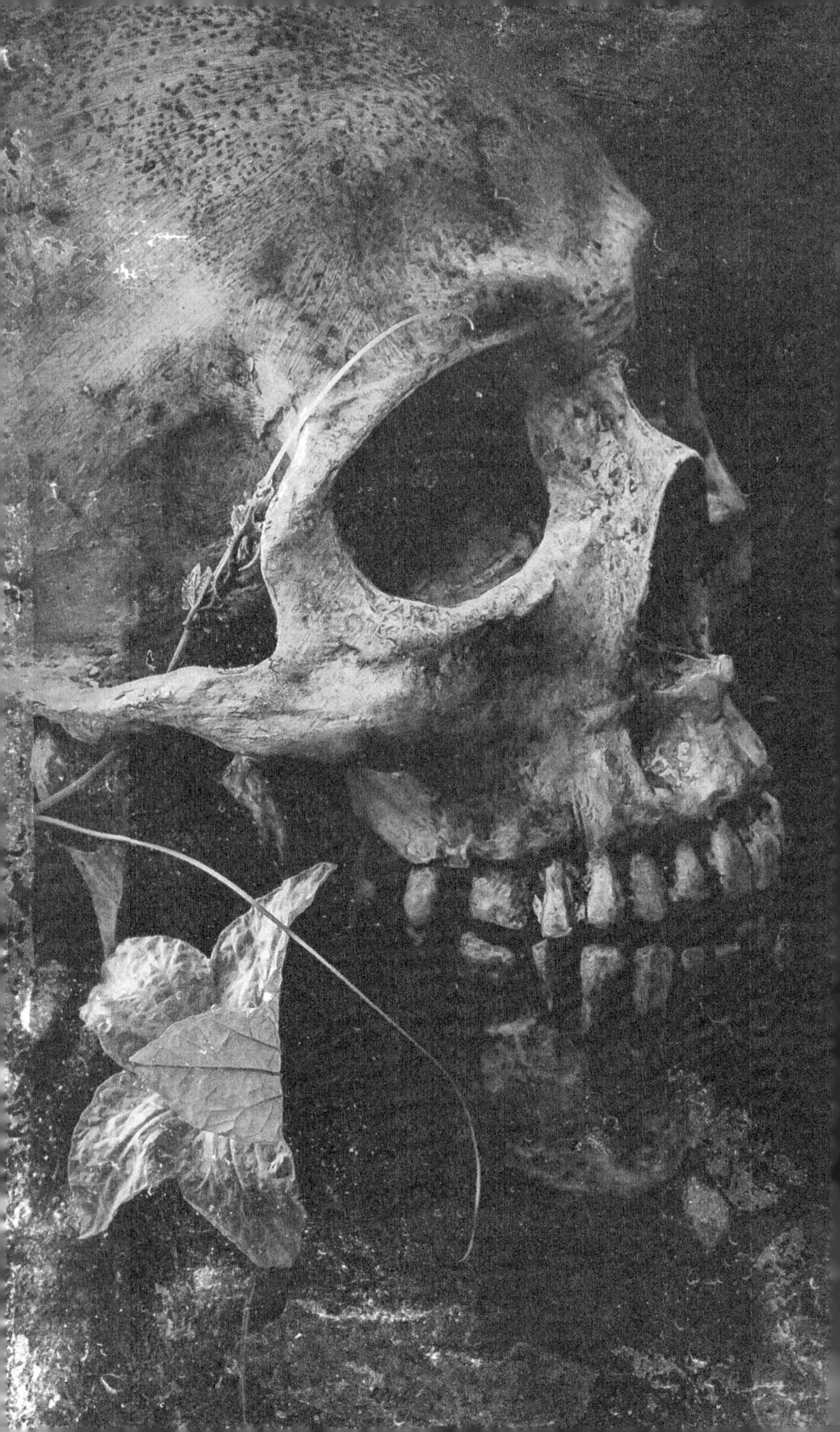

4 DOMINO

Darkness and rain cloaked me, offering the cover I needed to move unseen through the shadowed streets. The cold wind whipped around me, chafing against my skin, and the blood in my veins sang. After leaving Denny's, I sent my men to Blackwater Docks to receive and transport the incoming drug shipment. Our deliveries were being targeted on multiple fronts, but with Chief Rutter taken care of, there was only one loose end to tie up.

But the streets had been silent the last few days, giving me no answers. My patience was hanging on by a thread. It wouldn't be long before the streets ran red as I hunted down the rats that were hiding in the gutters.

Once they'd received their instructions and were strapped up and in position, I slipped back into the city alone. That's when I felt it. Eyes on me. A slow prickle of unease ran down my spine, the hairs on the back of my neck stood on end. My hands clenched into fists at my sides before I shoved them into my pockets.

I moved through the rain-slick streets, my steps almost silent against the wet asphalt. But beneath the faint noise of my movement, there it was—a second set of footsteps. Faint. Careful. He tried to blend into the night, but the delayed echo of his steps was impossible to miss if you were paying attention. And I was; I never let my guard down. In my world, you always had to be prepared for the one you trusted most to sink a knife into your back.

Amateur.

He might as well have had a spotlight on him—careless, overconfident. Tonight's hunt would be entertaining. I couldn't wait to show him the error of his ways.

The shift had already happened, even if he didn't know it yet. No longer the hunter—he was the hunted, dangling from strings only I could cut.

A Gallo. It was always them. Like cockroaches crawling out of the woodwork, infesting every crack and crevice.

They had been trying to sink their claws into Marlow Heights for as long as I'd been alive. My father had kept them at bay for twenty years. Now, that duty was mine. One day, I would inherit his title. Don. And this city would be my kingdom.

To say my father relied on me would be an understatement. The gunshot wound to his leg had never healed right, leaving him dependent on a cane for anything more than a short distance. If he wasn't personally handling an interrogation in the compound's basement, he sent me.

I had been the face of the DeMarco empire for five years now, and my reign of terror was undefeated.

The only way the Gallo family would ever take Marlow Heights was if my cold, dead body burned in the pits of hell. And that wasn't happening.

I would fight to my last breath, meeting them blow for blow, my grin bloodstained and feral.

Because I lived for this.

The brutality. The violence. The power.

The art of it.

Leaving macabre scenes for the pigs to stumble upon, watching them fumble for answers, knowing I was untouchable—it was a pastime I indulged in. My control was absolute. A mockery of everything they stood for. And I loved every second of it.

Especially when the body they found belonged to one of their own.

The shipment had come in at the docks, the lawless side of the city. A place where men like me ran the streets, peddling products to the underprivileged masses—people Marlow Heights' officials kept down by any means necessary.

Religion parading as politics.

Taxes.

Unemployment.

A system designed so the rich grew richer, and the poor got crushed beneath their feet.

If I were the kind of man who cared, maybe it would have mattered. But I wasn't.

We used districts across the river to run our operations. No one looked too closely at the abandoned warehouses, the crumbling factories left behind by the industrial revolution. The exteriors remained untouched, forgotten relics of a city that had long since moved on. But inside?

Inside, they were whatever I needed them to be. Drug processing centers. Interrogation rooms. Training facilities. Execution hubs. And then, of course—my playground.

A place only I knew how to reach. A secret buried so deep that even my most trusted men had no idea where it was. And it would stay that way.

Using my knowledge of the backstreets, I led the Gallo soldier straight into my web. He thought he was the one hunting. He had no idea.

The alley stretched before me, dark and silent. Walls slick with rain. The hum of the city barely reached this place—a dead zone. Forgotten.

Perfect.

Taking measured steps, hands loose at my sides, I moved deeper into the shadows. Every movement deliberate and controlled. Baiting my prey until he was exactly where I wanted him.

I wasn't in a rush. I enjoyed this. Almost as much as I enjoyed watching the light leave their eyes. The trick was letting him believe he had the upper hand.

I felt him before I heard him. The shift in the air as he lurked behind me, the tremor in his breath as he fought to control it. People never realized how loud fear made them. The harder they tried to be quiet, the louder they became.

A two-story wall rose in front of me, halting my progress. I tilted my head back slightly, just enough. Hesitation. An act. The idiot took the bait.

Footsteps. Fast. Confident. Stupid. His voice, thick with arrogance. "You should be afraid."

A sigh slipped from my lips—more disappointment

than anything. Slowly, I turned to face him. Hands still loose at my sides, posture relaxed. But inside? A tightly coiled spring.

Watching.

Measuring.

Calculating.

Every breath he took. The weight shifts in his stance. The slight tremble in his fingers. He was telegraphing his next move before his brain had even made the decision. The Gallo soldier stood there, gun in hand, smirking like a man who thought he was in control.

He wasn't.

I took him in, my expression unreadable.

The twitch in his trigger finger. His stance—too stiff, too rigid. Muscles locked up with tension. He wasn't a killer. He was a thug playing pretend.

My hollow laugh echoed around us, empty and cold.

A flinch racked through his body, forcing him to shift unevenly on his feet.

"I wouldn't be afraid," I murmured, voice like a blade sliding free of its sheath. "Even if there were ten of you."

His smirk faltered. Tension crept in, curling at the corners of his eyes. His tongue darted out, wetting his lips. Fear. Just a flicker. Just enough. He fought to school his features, to keep his mask in place. But that's all it was. A mask.

A child, standing before a lone wolf. And he knew it. Not enough to make him back down. But enough to make him realize that something was very, very wrong.

I took a step forward, anticipation thrumming through my veins.

"Why are you here?" My voice was calm. Measured.

A hunter in its element. As I closed the distance between us, the last vestiges of his bravado cracked.

The real fear began to set in.

The soldier rolled his shoulders, masking his discomfort with bravado. "Maybe we got tired of your family thinking they own this ci—"

He never got to finish. My fist collided with his nose before the last word left his mouth. The satisfying crunch of cartilage beneath my knuckles sent a sharp thrill through me.

The idiot stumbled back, clutching his face, blood seeping between his fingers. His eyes widened in pain and shock. As if he hadn't expected me to strike first.

Rookie mistake.

Never underestimate your opponent.

He recovered quickly, anger twisting his features. "You son of a—"

His weight shifted. He favored his right side. Predictable. I dodged his punch with ease, stepping into his space and grabbing him by the head. My knee drove into his ribs with brutal precision.

Crunch.

A wheezing gasp tore from his throat as he staggered back, clutching his side. He collapsed against the wall, struggling for breath. But he wasn't done yet—there was still fight left in him.

I tilted my head, watching with cold detachment. Too much emotion. Too much hesitation. Weak.

"That all you got?" he spat, wiping blood from his mouth. "No wonder your family's losing ground."

I sighed, already bored. "You talk too much."

In one moment, I was across the alley, in his face. My forearm braced against his neck, pinning him in place. He barely had time to react before my right fist snapped forward—a vicious hook to the jaw.

His head whipped sideways. His body followed. The Gallo crumpled to the ground, dazed but still breathing. That was the problem with guys like this. They didn't know when to stay down.

With a sudden burst of energy, he pushed up and lashed out, boot aimed at my ribs. I caught the kick on my forearm, but the force knocked me back just enough for him to yank a gun from his waistband.

His confidence soared, bloodied lips curling into a grin.

Stupid. He had no idea who he was dealing with. Before he could pull the trigger, I moved. Steel whispered as I flicked open the switchblade from the sheath at the base of my spine.

A flash of silver in a blur of movement. The blade kissed his throat. Not deep enough to kill. But enough to make him feel it. Blood welled around the cold steel. His breath hitched, his pupils blown wide.

I drank in every second of his terror. "Too slow."

His entire body trembled, pulse hammering against the blade's edge. I could feel it—the exact moment he realized he was outmatched.

I savored it. Consumed it.

Predictably, like a trapped rat, he panicked. His elbow slammed into my ribs, throwing his weight into the strike. The slick handle of my blade slipped from my fingers, clattering across the alley.

I had exactly one second to react before he lunged. We hit the ground hard, fists flying. His knuckles cracked against my cheekbone. A solid hit.

I grinned.

His eyes widened.

Wrong move.

He swung again. This time, I caught his fist midair and wrenched it backward. His shoulder popped, the socket giving way with a sickening snap. He screamed, but that didn't stop him.

Through sheer adrenaline, he slammed his forehead into mine, rattling my skull. My grip loosened just enough for him to scramble free, shoving me off with a desperate kick to my ribs.

I barely felt it.

The second my back hit the concrete, I rolled, dodging the wild punch he aimed at my face. He overextended, momentum carrying him forward. I capitalized on the mistake, twisting his arm behind his back and slamming him face-first into the ground.

Hard.

Blood smeared against the wet concrete as he groaned. I didn't give him a second to recover. Gripping his collar, I hauled him up and drove my knee into his stomach—once, twice, a third time—until he coughed up blood.

Still, he struggled. Still, he fought. I admired that. For a moment.

Then I slammed him against the wall, pinning him by the throat. His hands clawed at my wrist, but his strength was failing. The gun was gone. His weakened body trembled from the beating.

All that remained was the inevitable.

His last act of defiance came in the form of a broken, bloody smile. "Fuck... you."

I answered with a punch to the ribs, my knuckles connecting with the already-shattered bone. He gasped, his body spasming from the pain.

It was clear to see now—the shift in his eyes. The

realization. The fear. I dragged him down to the ground, straddling him, knees pinning his legs. Blood slicked my hands as I wrapped them around his throat. The red was beautiful against his pale, clammy skin.

His nails raked at my arms, a frantic, useless effort of a man who knew he was about to die. I didn't feel it. I only felt his pulse. The desperate flutter beneath my fingers. He gasped. Kicked. Choked. The scent of death filled the air.

I leaned in, voice a whisper. "This is what dying feels like."

Panic burst across his face. Pure. Unfiltered. Tears spilled from bloodshot eyes, capillaries bursting from the pressure. His lips tinged blue as his legs jerked in one final, useless struggle.

"Who sent you?"

His pulse stuttered. Weak. Fading.

"Who?"

Lips parted. A wet, gurgled breath. I loosened my grip. Just enough. His tongue clung to the roof of his mouth as he fought to form words.

"Who sent you to follow me?"

"D-D…" Blood bubbled past his lips.

"Say it." My voice dropped to a lethal growl.

A shuddering breath. "D…Diego."

Diego. Interesting. I'd expected the order to come from Enzo.

His pulse gave one final, weak flutter. One more squeeze—and it stopped.

Lifeless eyes stared up at the blackened sky. My face was the last thing he ever saw.

For a moment, I held on, fingers still pressed to his throat. I wanted to feel it. The slow, inevitable ebb of life. The moment power shifted.

Electric. Absolute.

Then, with a breath, I released him. I pushed to my feet, rolling my shoulders, blood dripping from my fingers. Another nameless body at my feet. I adjusted my jacket, smoothing out the wrinkles. With slow, deliberate care, I wiped my hands clean on his hoodie, then stepped over the corpse.

I turned, scanning the alley for my blade and his discarded gun—and froze.

Halfway down the alley, he stood. Ice-blue eyes. The guy from Denny's. He watched me, gaze unreadable, his pupils blown wide. But there was no fear.

Not a trace.

His breathing was steady. Even. He had just witnessed everything, watched me kill someone with my bare hands—and he was still standing there.

Watching. Unmoved by the brutality of the killing, but his eyes seemed slightly glazed like he was hypnotized as they stared at the body.

He moved toward me, fluid as liquid, his steps measured, deliberate. His gaze swept the ground, and for a moment, I thought he was avoiding my eyes.

Then I realized what he was looking for.

He stopped just shy of three feet from me, reaching down to pluck my switchblade from beneath a split garbage bag. With an unsettling ease, he turned it over in his fingers, testing the weight, the balance—like he'd done it before.

Like he knew what he was doing.

Maybe he did.

He closed the distance without hesitation, without fear, and held the knife out to me. Dark, thickened blood slicked his fingers, yet he seemed…unbothered. Almost at peace.

I took the blade, watching him closely as I wiped it on my jeans in a well-practiced motion—one I could do blindfolded.

His eyes never left mine.

Still, he remained at ease. Unflinching. Unshaken.

His fingers curled, rolling absently through the blood smeared across his skin. Testing its viscosity.

I waited for the inevitable.

The fear. The horror. The psychotic break that always came when people glimpsed the true depths of my world.

But instead, he met my stare with a cool, detached curiosity.

No fear.

Only fascination.

The silver flecks in his ice-blue eyes glowed in the dim alley light. His lips quirked at the corners, and then, with the slow confidence of a man who knew exactly what he was doing, he raised his bloodied hand to his face and breathed in.

A deep inhale. His thick, black lashes fluttered closed as if savoring the scent.

Something dark slithered through me, coiling tight around my spine.

Possession.

Lust.

Recognition.

Before I could think, I moved. My hand shot out, wrapping around his throat, lifting him clear off the ground. He barely had time to gasp before I drove him back into the wall.

Hard.

The impact stole the breath from his lungs, but his eyes—those fucking eyes—stayed locked on mine.

Then, he did the unthinkable.

He licked his lips, the tip of his tongue toying with black snake bite piercings.

Taunting.

Tempting.

His pulse remained steady beneath my fingers. Not a single stutter of fear. My thumb stroked the column of his throat, feeling the slow, controlled bob of his Adam's apple beneath my palm.

Still steady. Still calm.

Still fucking with me.

Heat surged through my veins, white-hot and electric. My cock pulsed, straining against the zipper of my jeans. The high of the kill burned through me, setting every nerve ending ablaze, making me feel invincible, unstoppable, untouchable—And now, this.

This fucking man.

A groan rumbled from deep in my chest. I slid the blade to his throat, pressing just hard enough for him to feel the promise of pain.

He didn't flinch.

Didn't fucking blink.

Instead, he tilted his chin up in invitation.

Something primal inside me snapped. I pressed closer, inhaling the scent of blood and desire as I dragged my nose along the sharp edge of his jaw, up to his cheek, across his lips, until my breath ghosted hot over his ear.

"Are you afraid?" I murmured, letting my lips brush the sensitive lobe.

His breath hitched.

His fingers twitched against my wrist. But he didn't push me away. Didn't struggle.

Didn't lie. "No." His voice was hoarse, wrecked.

He remained still. Allowed it. Encouraged it.

"No?"

I smiled against his skin, slow and sharp, then flicked my tongue along the curve of his ear, circling the cartilage, savoring the way he sucked in a sharp breath.

My free hand slid over his shoulder, dragging down his arm in a slow, lazy path, like I had all the time in the world.

I felt the shift beneath his skin.

The tension.

The heat.

The ache.

It mirrored my own. My palm flattened over his chest, pressing firm over his heart. His pulse jumped.

Finally. *Not so steady now, are you?*

I smirked, tightening my grip on his throat just enough to watch his pupils blow wide.

He wasn't afraid. No, this was something else entirely. And fuck, it was intoxicating.

"You're not afraid of me?"

He tilted his head, an almost mocking smile curling at the corner of his lips. "Should I be?"

I chuckled darkly, amused by his defiance. Curious. I took a slow step forward, closing the distance between us, so close now our breaths mingled, his exhale becoming my inhale. My lips brushed against his, barely there, teasing the edges of his sanity.

"Most run. But not you. You stand there... like you're waiting for me to show you something more."

I saw the flicker in his eyes—something dark, something that wanted to know. To understand.

My hand slid down his chest, fingers grazing across the ridges of his abs. His breath hitched at the subtle touch, his body stiffened before his chest rose with a ragged inhale. I leaned closer, my lips dangerously near his throat. His pulse hammered beneath my blade, each beat echoing louder in my ears.

"I think death is beautiful," he breathed, his voice low, rough with desire, maybe even with madness.

His words stirred something deep within me, something wild and primal, I couldn't help myself. My hand moved lower, feeling his length pressing against the zipper of his pants. Thick. Solid. Pulsing.

I felt his breath catch in his throat, his entire body responding to my touch. I wanted to hold him there, to make him ache for more. But I couldn't get lost in the moment. Not yet.

My hand pulled away slowly, and I watched how he shuddered at the loss of contact. His gaze followed the movement of the steel, the gleam of danger reflecting in his eyes before it was gone.

"Let's see how long you survive the wolves, *piccolo agnello*."

I sheathed my blade with a quick, deliberate motion, then took a step back, the distance between us growing again, but the tension hanging thick in the air.

The chill of the night settled around us, but the heat from our exchange still burned, coiling in the pit of my stomach. I turned on my heel, my boots clicking on the ground as I walked away, but not without one last glance over my shoulder.

He didn't chase. He didn't scream.

He stayed.

And that... was the most dangerous thing about him.

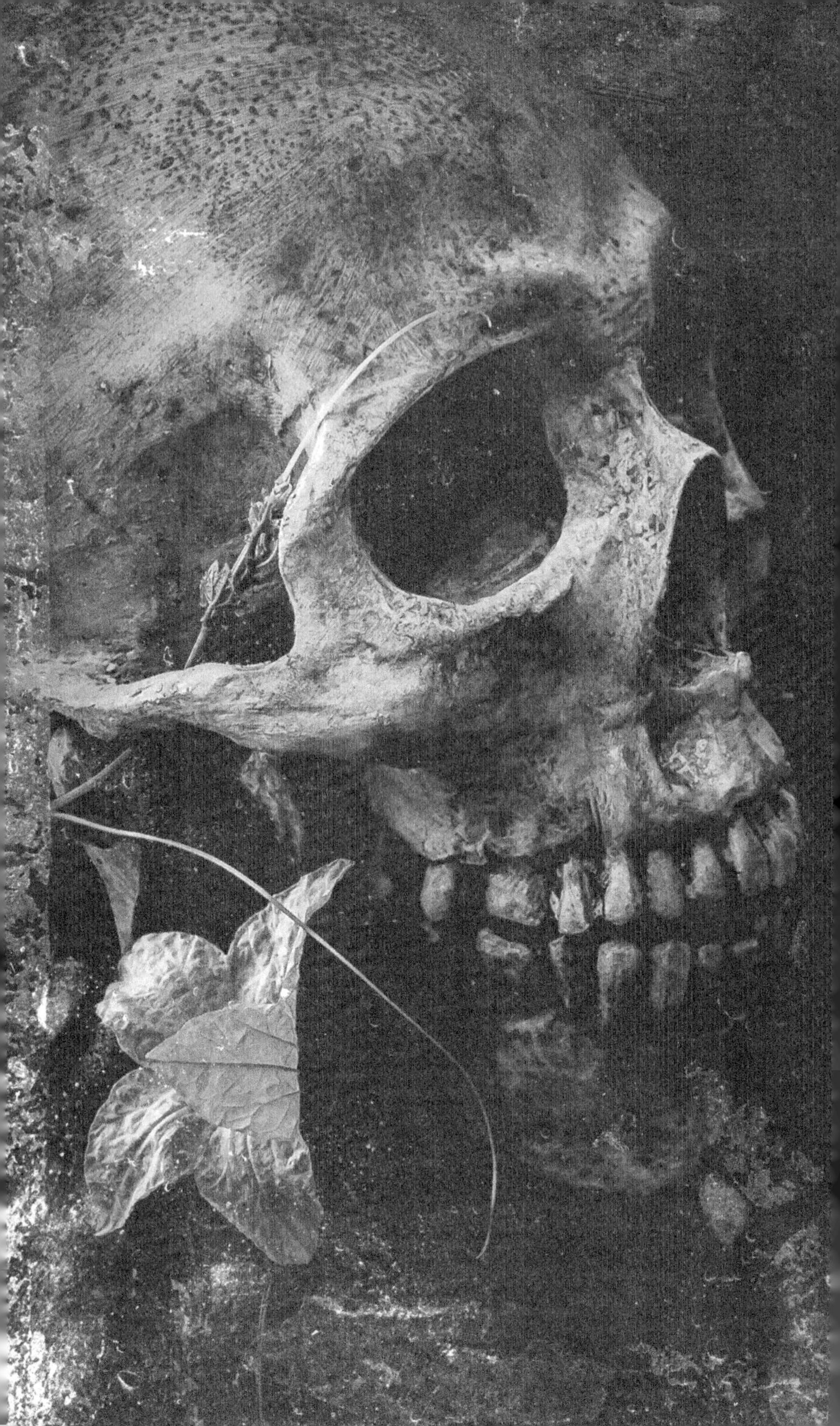

5 DOMINO

My Ninja H2R sliced through the rain-slicked streets, the roar of the engine reverberating off the towering buildings as I carved my way through the maze of Marlow Heights. The city blurred past me in streaks of neon and shadow, but my mind was locked onto one thing—him.

The guy from Denny's. Those piercing blue eyes and that wild black hair with the unusual white patch at the front were burned into my memory, lingering every time I closed mine.

I couldn't shake him. Couldn't silence the way he had looked at me, unflinching and steady, even after watching me rip the life from a man with my bare hands. He hadn't recoiled. Hadn't screamed. Hadn't even hesitated when he held my switchblade, dripping with fresh blood.

Instead, he had breathed it in. Enamored. Curious. Something more, darker, something I understood.

The streets were deserted at this hour, stripped of the mindless masses that usually filled them. I preferred it that way. People were either assets or annoyances, just playthings for leverage or power. I had no use for them.

But him?

He was different. He had sparked something inside me—unfamiliar and dangerous. It coiled in my chest, sharp and insatiable, a hunger I had only ever felt when I was watching the light fade from someone's eyes.

I needed to know more.

The underground parking garage swallowed me whole, the sound of my bike amplified by the unyielding concrete as I pulled into my designated space. The rain clung to me, dripping from my hair, sliding down my cold skin.

My pulse thrummed as a plan took shape, twisting in my mind. One person could get me what I wanted. I pulled my phone from my pocket as I strode toward the elevator. It rang once before a low moan echoed through the receiver.

"Ghost," I said, voice edged with impatience. "Meet me at my apartment in five. I don't care what you're doing—end it."

After a long pause, he said a single word. "Boss."

The line went dead. My hand clenched around my phone, the plastic creaking under the pressure as the steel doors slid open. I stepped inside, the mirrored walls reflecting my image, a darkness swirled in my eyes. Controlled. Dangerous.

My apartment spanned the entire top floor of Vesper Tower—a calculated move. The tallest building in the city, offering me unrestricted 360-degree views of

Marlow Heights. From here, I could see everything. Control everything. And no one could touch me. It was a far cry from my father's fortified compound on the outskirts of the city that he used as his base of operations. He hid behind his walls and armed guards, whereas I preferred to hide in plain sight.

The DeMarcos wore a legitimate face, a carefully constructed mask of wealth and enterprise. The casinos, the real estate empire, the exclusive clubs—money laundered clean while the real business thrived in the shadows.

Nothing happened in this city without my knowledge.

And yet, he had slipped through.

I stepped off the elevator, muscles wound tight, my blood still humming with that strange, restless edge. The city stretched out beyond the rain-streaked glass, a sea of flickering lights and endless night. But I wasn't looking at the view. I was thinking about him.

His steady breath. His unwavering stare. The way his pulse had thrummed beneath my fingertips—not with fear, but something else entirely. I tore off my jacket and threw it onto the couch, an act very unlike me, rolling my shoulders to shake the tension. It didn't help.

What was it about him? I didn't get curious about people. They were tools. Obstacles. Corpses. He was none of those. And yet, he had twisted his way into my thoughts, insidious and lingering like smoke. I had walked away. I should have forgotten him the second I turned my back.

But I hadn't.

The elevator doors slid open again. Ghost strode in like he owned the place, rolling his neck, irritation flickering in his eyes. I had interrupted something. I didn't care; his life was mine, and he knew it.

"Find out who he is," I ordered. Ghost didn't blink. He never asked who—just waited, expectant. "The guy from Denny's."

The words tasted like an admission. Like something I didn't want to acknowledge.

Ghost's brow twitched, unreadable. A smirk slid across his lips, a slow nod. He was already pulling out his phone. "You got a name?"

"No."

"A picture?"

My jaw tightened. That I didn't have either irritated me. I'd been too captivated by his presence. I should have forced his name from his lips. Should have taken a photo. Should have done something other than walk away after nearly kissing him, just because I wanted a taste.

Ghost smirked like he knew exactly what was unraveling inside my head. He let out a low whistle, rubbing the back of his neck. "Didn't take you for the type to get caught up over a pretty face."

I didn't take the bait. I just stared him down.

With a sigh, he sank onto the couch, thumbs already moving over his screen. "Give me something to work with."

I ran a hand through my damp hair, irritation curling beneath my skin. I had nothing. No name. No connections. Just the ghost of a smirk and ice-blue eyes I couldn't purge from my thoughts.

"He was at Denny's the other day," I said. "Followed me into the alley when I took care of the Gallo soldier, watching me from the shadows."

Ghost arched a brow, interest piqued. "Watched you kill a guy and didn't run?"

I didn't answer. I didn't need to. That was the problem. He had seen it—all of it—and still, he hadn't moved.

Hadn't feared me.

He had leaned in, drawn to the blood. To the violence.

To me.

"He's young," I continued. "Not a civilian, but not a soldier either. No crew colors. No weapon. Could be independent, but…" My voice dropped, something dark curling in my gut. "I need to know what he's really doing in my city. He said he was here to finish his degree in Forensic Anthropology, but I'm not buying it."

"Interesting," Ghost hummed, still tapping away. "You get a nickname? Overhear someone else talk to him?"

"No."

"You get anything?"

I had. The way his pulse had jumped beneath my fingertips. The way his breath had hitched when my thumb pressed against his throat—not with fear, but something deeper. Something that mirrored the hunger clawing inside me.

"Find him." My voice was sharp, final.

Ghost smirked but didn't push further. "I'll call you when I have something." He stood, stretching lazily. "You look like shit, boss. Get some sleep."

"Fuck off!"

I wouldn't be sleeping. I waited until Ghost was gone before I moved. My feet carried me to the bar, but I wasn't interested in drinking. My reflection stared back at me in the mirrored backsplash, the shadows beneath my eyes darker than usual.

This wasn't how it was supposed to be. People were useful—or they were dead. I had never wanted to unravel someone before. Never felt the need to pick them apart, to see what made them tick. Never ached to push further, to press closer—to see just how deep the darkness ran beneath their skin.

But him?

I dragged my tongue over my teeth.

The need to know how far he'd let me go before he broke was visceral. Would he shatter beautifully, or would he fight me every step of the way? Would I be able to pry him apart, layer by layer, taste the sweat-slicked heat of his skin, his blood? If he let me near him again, I wouldn't stop. I would consume him. Make him mine.

Dead or alive, I'd own him.

Ghost had set up his base in one of my spare rooms. One wall was lined with monitors, flickering with live feeds from every street camera in the city. He had total control. A single keystroke could erase my men from existence—turning them into ghosts, unseen and untouchable by the city's useless police force.

But hacking wasn't his only skill. Ghost could find anyone. Anywhere. He sat at his desk, fingers moving lazily across the keyboard, rewinding through days of Denny's footage. Hunting my little lamb.

I grabbed a coffee, pacing behind him, the scent bitter and sharp, grounding me against the electricity still humming in my veins.

"Either of these?"

Ghost's voice was flat, detached—his focus on the screen, but mine? Mine was still back in that alley, in the heat of another body, in the slow burn of a stare that had ignited something deep in my gut. I leaned in, my gaze flicking over the grainy images. Even in black and white, his eyes cut through me—razor-sharp, slicing straight to the marrow.

I licked my lips. "On the left."

Ghost let out a low whistle. "Now, he is pretty."

A growl rumbled in my throat before I could stop it. My fingers curled into fists, itching to wrap around his throat. "Don't."

Ghost smirked, but he lifted his hands in surrender. "I'll run facial recognition. Track his movements. Find out where he's been."

"I want everything."

A pause. A flicker of something unreadable in his expression. "You sure about that?"

My head tilted, anger pressing against the edges of my control.

"I mean, I can get you whatever you want, but this is… next level. Even for you."

"Watch it," I snapped.

I turned, storming from the room. I had calls to make.

My father was hounding me about the Gallos, demanding answers about their next move like I was some fucking mind reader—I needed a mole in their operation, but I didn't have anyone suitable. Shipments needed checking. Distribution lines had to be accounted for. I despised this—leading—even though it was my birthright. I didn't want to manage operations, balance territories, sit through endless meetings with men I'd rather put a bullet in.

If it were up to me, I'd burn this city to the ground. But Federico had other plans. Expanding, growing our empire—he lived for it. That hunger had always been his driving force. His obsession.

Mine? My eyes fell closed, the grainy image of him burned into my mind as clear as day. I had a different kind of obsession.

GHOST

Left a folder on your desk. Everything you need to know—down to his social security number.

DOMINO

Good.

GHOST

Monitors are tracking his every move. Just in case you wanted to... y'know.

MY PHONE BURNED HOT IN MY HAND AS I STORMED through my apartment, my skin too tight, itching for the feel of blood. Hours were wasted bending to my father's whims, running the numbers for the latest shipment, making sure every dollar was accounted for before it could be cleaned. The gangs got their cut—a pittance to keep them in line—but one crew had been stupid enough to think they could get away with skimming off the top. I'd sent three soldiers to deal with them. Permanently. What would be done to them would send shockwaves through the ranks. A stark reminder of what would happen if you tried to cross me.

I snatched the folder off the desk and dropped into my chair. The monitors flickered to life, the city sprawling across a dozen screens, but I barely registered them. My focus locked onto the secrets sealed inside that folder.

My eyes devoured every detail. Every iota of information.

Remi Cain.

Son of Angelica Cain—currently wasting away in Hollow Pines Care Home after a severe stroke. Prognosis? Bleak. Months left if she was lucky. That explained why he was here.

But what didn't add up?

Why wasn't he staying at Hollow Pines with his family?

Brielle Cain had no shortage of space. The home was only at half capacity, and even if it weren't, she had her own damn property on the estate. Staff quarters. Empty rooms. There was no reason—none—for him to be holed up in that godforsaken shelter on Clayburn Avenue.

Anger licked through my veins, slow and insidious, as I turned the page to his family's financial records.

And there it was.

A sizable trust fund. Set up by his father before he died in the service. Untouched. Locked away until his graduation. It appeared Remi didn't even know it existed.

An amendment had been made after his father's death that explained so much. A new trustee? Brielle. I gritted my teeth as something dark and twisted coiled inside me, pressing tight against my ribs.

"Fuck."

That scheming bitch was after his money—always taking the easy way out. She was keeping him weak.

Dependent. Helpless. But she had no idea—none—that Remi was anything but helpless.

My fingers clenched around the desk, knuckles bleached bone-white. Brielle had been a thorn in my side for years, but now? Now, she was an obstacle. An obstacle that needed to be removed.

I wouldn't come for her head-on. My father would never allow it, considering they were in bed together. She was one of his many playthings. They also had a racketeering ring together. So that made her a valuable asset in his eyes, but never mine.

No—what I had planned? She wouldn't see it coming. None of them would. Not until it was too late.

Movement flickered on one of the screens, catching my attention. Remi. His name curled through my mind like smoke—intoxicating—I wanted to breathe in until I was drunk on it.

He was walking slow steps along the river, head bowed like the weight of the world was suffocating him. A ratty backpack slung over one shoulder, the sharp wind tugging at his clothes. He was heading toward the old cemetery on the edge of the city—miles away from anywhere he'd been before.

Why?

The question burned under my skin as I tracked him, my pulse syncing with his every movement. The way he moved—lithe, fluid—felt at odds with the darkness that wrapped around him like a second skin.

He slipped through a gap in the rusted boundary fence and vanished into the shadows. Gone. My jaw clenched. I needed to know why he was there. Why this place had called to him? The need to know every facet of him coiled inside me, sharp and insistent. It was no longer just curiosity. It was fixation. Obsession.

With my mind made up, I locked the folder away in my office, grabbed my jacket, and took the elevator down. My bike rumbled to life beneath me, the vibrations sinking into my muscles as I twisted the throttle and tore through the city. Cars blurred past, nothing but noise, background static.

All I could focus on was him.

Always him.

I killed the engine near one of the cemetery's entrances, the silence that followed sharp and unnatural. Twilight stretched long shadows over the crumbling gravestones, casting everything in muted shades of gray. When Remi had slipped through the fence, I'd seen it—the way his tension melted and his shoulders eased like he was coming home.

The city wasn't where he belonged.

This was.

Decay. Darkness. Forgotten things.

Just like the sketch he'd been drawing at Denny's—morbid and stunning in a way most wouldn't understand.

But I did.

His trail was easy to find. My footsteps were silent as I weaved through gravestones, cracked and worn by time. I kept my distance, watching as he traced his fingers over ancient names, reading stories no one remembered of people long forgotten. He marveled at the way nature has started to reclaim what had been taken, photographing the sprawling ivy and twisted brambles.

His soft voice reached me in the wind. I couldn't make out the words, but it didn't matter. The sound of him wrapped around me, seeped into my skin, and lodged deep in my bones.

He was different here. The sadness, the weight that clung to him in the city—it was gone. Here, he was... peaceful.

He stopped at a grave with a towering angel carved from a stone at its head, one wing cracked and broken, and hoisted himself onto the main body of the tomb. He settled against the angel like he was being held in its embrace and pulled out his sketchbook.

Remi was lost in his own world as his pencil glided over the bone-white page. From this distance, I couldn't make out what he was drawing, but he filled the page with his creation. He started with long strokes before going back and adding in small details. Brows furrowed, lips pinched in concentration. The wind played with his hair, the messy black strands fell into that striking white streak.

Totally unaware I was watching him, circling him like a hunter. That I was drawing closer with every breath. Every step on silent feet. My heart rate picked up, heating the blood in my veins. I felt electrified. Alive.

I wanted to know what he saw.

I wanted to see the world through his eyes.

That one sketch I'd seen had been mesmerizing—death, stripped bare and reimagined into something raw, beautiful. I'd seen thousands of paintings and attended gallery shows under my family's name, wearing that public mask, but nothing had ever looked like that.

Nothing had ever captured the beauty of death, a dark macabre piece that called to my soul, just like he did.

A branch snapped beneath my boot, brittle like aged bone. A deliberate move to notify him of my presence just to see how he'd react.

His pencil faltered, pausing for a split-second before

moving again. Not a hint of fear. No outward reaction. His calm mask stayed perfectly still.

His control was intoxicating, he was captivating.

"How long have you been following me?"

The corner of my mouth curled at his question. My fingers twitched with the urge to touch him, to remind myself how soft his skin had felt beneath them. Instead, I shoved my hands into my pockets and waited.

"Long enough."

His gaze lifted to me and dragged over my face, slow, lingering like a physical caress, almost as if he was committing me to memory.

He tilted his head, something flashing in his ice-blue eyes before the tip of his tongue darted out, wetting his lips. "Why?"

A simple question.

It should have had a simple answer.

But it didn't.

This thing inside me—whatever it was—it didn't have a name.

Need. Hunger. Possession. Every one etched into my bones.

I didn't just want to know him. I wanted to own him. Every thought. Every breath. Every inch of him. *Mine*. I wanted to mark him, brand him. Stain his skin black and blue. Leaving it tender to the touch, so when he did, he'd get an echo of the pain and would never forget who he belonged to.

Instead of answering, I settled for a test.

"Where are you staying?"

His breath hitched. A flicker of tension, a flash of hesitation tightened his features before his gaze dropped back to his drawing.

I didn't like that. It felt like a dismissal. My fists

clenched in my pockets, frustration trickled down my spine.

"The shelter."

My muscles uncoiled and I smirked. "There are many in the city," I drawled. "Which one?"

The wind shifted, rustling the dead leaves at my feet, like a veil had been lifted as day morphed into night.

"The one on Clayburn."

A fucking hellhole. It should've been condemned years ago—rats, mold, the stink of desperation clinging to its walls. But he didn't seem to mind—curious.

He just kept drawing, the quiet scratch of pencil against paper filling the silence between us.

I moved closer, my steps measured, unhurried. Remi was so lost in his creation that he didn't notice—or maybe he did. Maybe he wanted me closer. If he thought he could brush me off, my little lamb had another thing coming, he'd never be rid of me now. I inhaled slowly, filling my lungs with his scent—open air, moss, something earthy and dark.

"Not anymore."

The pencil slipped from his fingers as he startled, head snapping toward me, those ice-blue eyes narrowing in question. This close, I could just make out the silver flecks in them. I wanted to count them. To know every scar and freckle that covered his skin.

His lips were so close I could feel his exhale as it ghosted over my skin. It would take nothing at all to lean in and seal my lips to his. To finally taste him.

I pulled the silver tin from my back pocket, flicked it open, and lit a cigarette. Smoke curled between my lips, twisting in the cold air. "Your things have been moved."

His expression didn't change—the perfect mask.

I exhaled, watching the smoke curl between us. "You

start classes soon. You need somewhere safe that isn't crawling with rats and junkies."

Nothing. Not a single flicker of emotion. I'd have thought he was catatonic if I didn't know he only hits a joint now and then.

I left him to process, strolling lazily to the next grave, lowering myself onto the stone. I pulled one knee up to my chest and rested my arm on it with the cigarette dangling between my fingers.

Seconds stretched into minutes as I waited for his reaction. I could feel it, the war raging inside him. He was fighting it in silence. Fighting me, but he wouldn't win.

He was mine now. He just didn't know it yet.

"You didn't ask."

His fingers tightened around his sketchbook, knuckles going bone-white as his eyes drilled into me. Wind tangled through his hair, the black and white strands whipping across his face, half-obscuring the sharp cut of his cheekbones.

I flicked the cigarette end across the grass. "I didn't need to."

Remi exhaled, his shoulders rising and falling with the weight of something unspoken. Then, without argument, he shut his sketchbook and slipped it into his bag.

No fight.

No resistance.

Just quiet, steady acceptance—the same way he had accepted my switchblade at his throat.

"Can I have one?"

I arched my brow. "What?"

"A cigarette."

For a moment, I just watched him—searching for something in the ice-blue depths of his gaze but finding nothing. Wordlessly, I held the tin out from where I sat perched on a grave, forcing him to come to me.

A silent test.

He hesitated only for a breath before stepping closer, plucking a cigarette from the tin and placing it between his lips. He didn't light it.

He waited for me. A test of his own?

A slow smirk curled at the edges of my mouth as I rolled my eyes and flicked open my lighter. The flame danced between us, catching in the glassy sheen of his gaze. I watched, fascinated, as he took a deep inhale. His lips parted, thick smoke curling from between them. His eyes watered slightly, but he never looked away.

A million silent questions passed between us, reflected in both our stares.

Why are we doing this?

What does it mean?

Why me?

I didn't have answers. Not ones I could name. But my body knew, my fingers snagged his belt loops, yanking him closer, the heat of him bleeding into me through layers of fabric. My other hand reached for the strap of his bag, unhooking his fingers from it with slow precision, maneuvering him wordlessly until he held his hand out palm up.

Remi frowned, looking between my face and the object I placed in the center of his hand. A ring.

Gold, bloodied, torn from a dead man's hand.

A trophy.

A claim.

A gift.

His fingers curled around it instinctively, possessively. "What's this?"

I tilted my head. "A memento."

Remi pinched the ring between his thumb and forefinger, inspecting it under the low light.

A reminder of *that* night. The start of an obsession forged in blood.

His grip tightened. He nodded once. He understood.

The night he watched me kill a man from the shadows. The night he should have run and fought for someone who could have been innocent.

The night he didn't.

I could have made him do anything at that moment when I'd pinned him to that alley wall, my switchblade at his throat. He would have let me, *willingly*. He handed me total control, that power I craved almost as much as him.

Now, his silence called to me again, tempting me to demand his thoughts, to pry them from his skull and study them one by one. Instead, I pushed him back—just enough to remind him who had the power.

Then, I turned toward my bike. "Come. Let's go home."

I didn't look back to see if he followed me. I didn't need to. I felt him like we were already in sync. Like some invisible thread had woven itself between us, pulling him forward, tethering him to me.

And I knew, without a shadow of a doubt—he would follow.

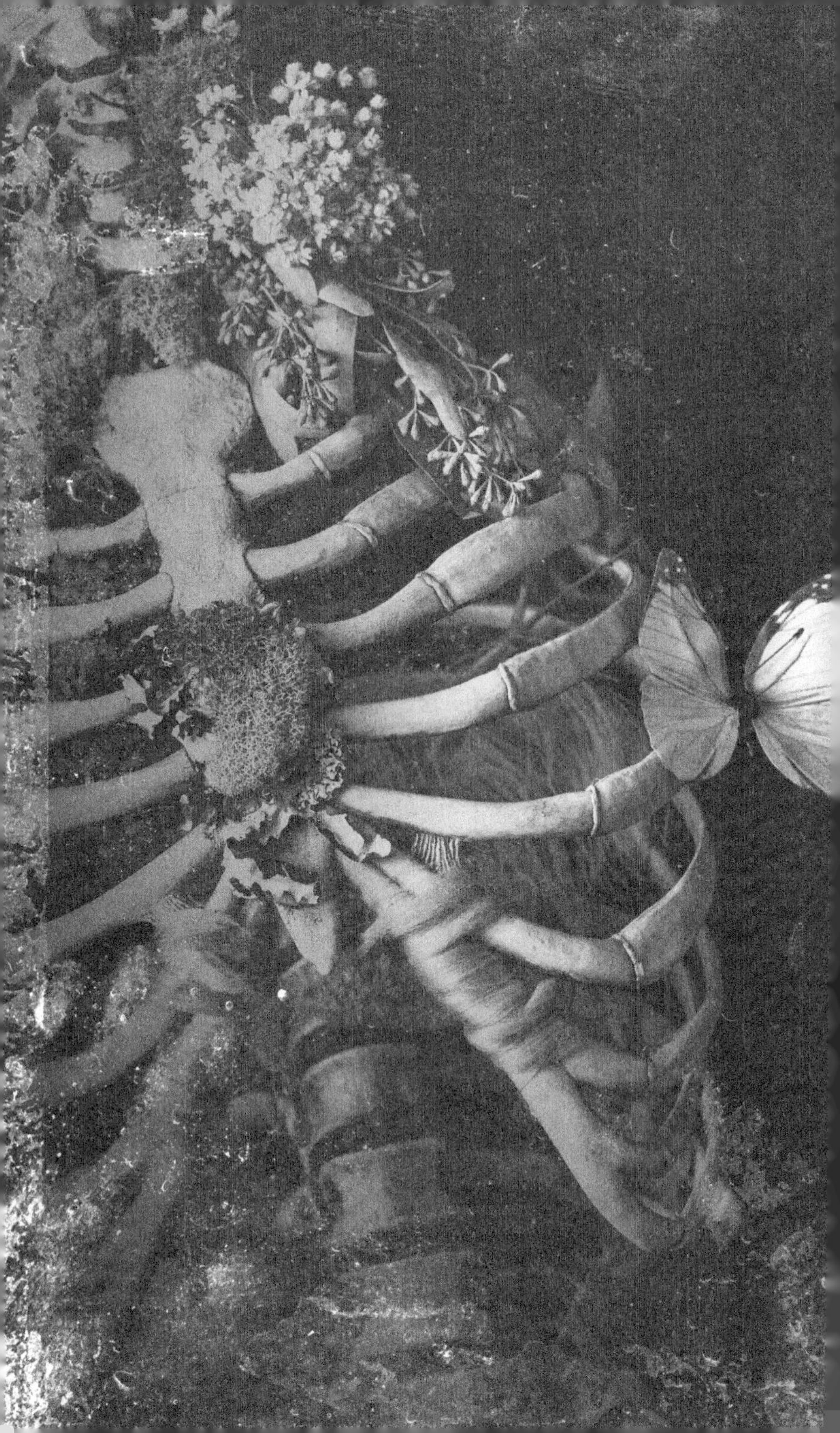

6 REMI

If someone had told me a month ago that I'd get picked up in a cemetery by a hot guy in a leather jacket—the same guy I'd watched kill a man with his bare hands—I'd have laughed in their face.

If they'd told me five days ago, I'd have called a psychiatrist and had them committed for their own safety.

And yet—here I was. Fresh out of the hottest shower I'd ever taken, in the biggest bathroom I'd ever seen, lying on a massive king-size bed covered in black silk sheets that felt like sin against my skin.

Last night, I was curled up on a stained mattress in a rat infested corner of a filthy shelter, wondering what kind of karmic debt I was paying for in this lifetime.

Now, I was here.

In his world.

A place so far removed from my own, it didn't feel real.

Life had never been easy for me—especially in high school, where I was a walking target, laughed at for being different. A freak. A nobody.

But in the silence of the night, when I felt alive and the world was asleep, I'd sit with my sketchbook, drawing them the way I saw them.

Ravaged. Broken.

Bleeding out on the floors of the places they thought made them untouchable.

Society could keep its carbon copies. I had no interest in being another clone mass-produced to fit their mold.

I liked being me, even if it meant being an outsider. Even if it meant carving out my place in the shadows. Somehow, this man—whose name I still didn't know— had reached into the darkest part of me, a place no one had ever touched. Not family. Not friends. No one.

He had.

He'd shown me kindness beyond reason and violence beyond measure. He had let me see death, raw, brutal, and beautiful. And now, his presence set me on fire in a way no one else ever had.

I felt him before I heard him. The doors in this place didn't creak, and the thick carpet swallowed every trace of sound, but I knew he was there.

His voice came low, rough enough to scrape deliciously along my skin. "I brought you some clean clothes."

A ripple of goosebumps broke across my body. "Thank you."

He set the neatly folded pile on the bed beside me, but his gaze didn't follow. It stayed on me. I could feel it like a touch, watching the beads of water slide from my hair, down my chest, trailing over the towel knotted at my waist.

I cleared my throat. His eyes snapped up, locking onto mine. "I have my own clothes, you know."

His lips twitched, almost like he found that amusing. "I'm aware. But considering where you've been staying, I thought you'd prefer something that didn't need to be incinerated."

Cool. Detached. Like he was simply stating a fact. But his eyes... His eyes told a different story. Something burned deep in the dark green depths—a quiet possessiveness, a hunger that hadn't been there before.

"Have you eaten?" he asked. But before I could answer, he was already continuing. "I was going to order takeout anyway. What do you want?"

My stomach betrayed me, the low growl filling the silence. I couldn't remember the last time I'd eaten a decent meal. The fifty bucks I'd had in my pocket hadn't gone far after Brielle threw me out, and the shelter barely had enough funding to keep the lights on. Finding a job had been impossible, though Doll said she might have a spot for me soon, once one of her waitresses left to have a baby.

But for now? I was starving.

His voice pulled me back. "Pick anything."

I hesitated, turning the thought over in my mind. Mom and I hadn't been able to afford takeout in years, not since her first stroke. If he was offering, I'd take it. Just this once. "Thai sounds good."

He nodded, already turning for the door, his hand brushing the handle when I blurted, "I feel like I should introduce myself to my, um..."

Rescuer?

Kidnapper?

I still couldn't decide.

"I'm Remi."

Something flickered across his face—a flash of amusement, something knowing. "I know."

And then he was gone, leaving me alone with the weight of his words. I shouldn't have been surprised that he knew my name. Not when he'd already known where I was staying. Not when he'd moved my things without my consent.

I exhaled, staring at the pile of clothes.

They smelled like him—smoke, leather, something dark and expensive. The fabric was softer than anything I owned. The black t-shirt clung to my damp skin, molding to my frame, the cotton worn-in but high quality. The black sweatpants sat low on my hips, too big, but the drawstring kept them in place.

The weight of the fabric was unfamiliar, luxurious in a way that felt foreign on my skin. I caught my reflection in the floor-length mirror near the bed and stopped in my tracks. For once, I didn't look completely out of place, no matter how I felt about my current arrangement.

I looked like I belonged to him. The thought shouldn't have sent a thrill down my spine. But it did. My fingers ran through my damp hair, pushing it back before I stepped out of the bedroom.

The apartment was nothing like I expected, and yet it fit what I knew of him perfectly. It was dark and elegant. Sleek lines, black and gray everything—the furniture, the walls, the expensive rugs underfoot. It was minimalist but not cold, like a place curated with intent rather than just thrown together. The glass windows stretched from floor to ceiling, offering a sprawling view of the city far below, a glittering expanse of lights that seemed a world away from the one I'd been living in.

He sat at the kitchen island, one foot propped on the bottom rung of the stool, scrolling through his phone like he hadn't just turned my entire existence upside down.

His presence filled the space effortlessly, like he owned it—which he obviously did. But it was more, like he owned everything. This was his castle, and beyond the glass walls was his kingdom.

He looked up as I entered, his proprietary gaze flicking over me, lingering just long enough to make my breath catch. Something dangerous and satisfied curled at the corner of his lips. He liked what he saw, like this was exactly how he'd envisioned me.

Wearing his clothes in his home.

Like I was his.

His eyes told me everything. He wanted to corrupt me. There wasn't a single part of me that would stop him. It felt like I had stepped willingly into hell—and now, I was dancing with the devil. But I didn't care.

Because the man staring back at me was every dark thought I had ever had. Every violent fantasy. Every forbidden curiosity. Every inch of me that had ever craved something *more*.

He tapped the white marble countertop, drawing me back. "The menu is here. Let me know what you want."

I didn't even need to look. I just started listing off everything I'd ever tried and loved, the words spilling from my mouth faster than I could process. His thumbs moved over his screen so fast my eyes couldn't keep up.

"It'll be here soon."

He slid off the stool in a single smooth movement, leading me from the kitchen into the lounge area. Like the rest of the penthouse, it was sleek, refined, and dark—shades of black and gray, everything intentional, everything in its place. The furniture was low and modern; the walls were adorned with abstract art that looked expensive and strangely unwelcoming. The glass windows stretched wide, framing the glittering skyline.

He poured me a drink without a word. I took the glass instinctively, feeling the weight of the crystal in my hand, the liquid dark and rich inside. I hesitated when it reached my lips, a smirk tugging at the corner of my mouth. "It's not poisoned, is it?"

His shoulders rose and fell in a slow shrug. Then his hands clenched at his sides. That was interesting.

He shook his head once. "No. I prefer to use my hands." A pause, his lips curving slightly. "Or my blade."

A normal person would have been horrified. But I wasn't a normal person, in my own way I understood. I snorted softly, taking a sip as my gaze held his.

Poison was impersonal—a coward's method. Unpredictable. Uncontrolled. But with his hands? With a blade? I had seen what he could do. Had watched him kill.

It was raw, primal—a monster unleashed. He had fed on the fear, thrived on it even. The moment that man had stopped breathing, he had grown taller, stronger, more alive. I had seen the hunger in his eyes—the power he felt in taking a life.

He was dangerous. Darkness incarnate. There was beauty in his savagery. A stunning, lethal kind of beauty that I wanted to capture and make immortal. I'd never been interested in drawing the living before, but him? I wanted to draw.

Here I was, sitting in his home, wearing his clothes,

drinking his whiskey—falling deeper into the abyss. And I wasn't afraid

"What's your name?"

I rolled the liquid in my glass, watching how the amber swirled against the cut crystal before sliding my gaze to his. He already knew mine, but I...

"Domino."

I blinked. "Domino?" I let the name settle on my tongue, savoring the way it tasted—exotic, sharp, filled with mystery, just like him. It felt right. It fit.

A slow smirk tugged at the corner of my lips. "Huh. That makes sense."

His gaze flicked to mine, sharp and assessing. "What do you mean?"

He settled at the opposite end of the couch, angling his body in my direction while still keeping an eye on the massive floor-to-ceiling windows. Strategic. He was always aware of his surroundings, always in control.

I leaned back, the damp material of my borrowed shirt cool against my skin. "It means lord. Master."

He lifted his glass, taking a slow sip. My eyes tracked the movement of his throat, the way his Adam's apple rolled with each swallow, the controlled way he breathed. Every movement was deliberate. Calculated.

His phone buzzed, breaking the charged silence. He glanced at the screen. "Food's here."

I frowned.

I hadn't heard anyone knock.

As if reading my mind, he added, "No one can enter without my authorization." He stood, moving toward the private elevator. "I control the elevator."

Of course, he did. Nothing about this man suggested he'd allow anyone into his world—his space—without permission.

Surreal. That was the only way to describe the rest of the evening.

Domino was a man of few words, but when he spoke, he didn't waste them. There was something strangely domestic about the way we ate together, plates and cutlery neatly arranged on the marble kitchen island. We ate mostly in silence, but it didn't feel uncomfortable. It felt easy. More than that, it felt right.

I had known him for hours, yet I felt more at ease with him than I had with my own mother.

After dinner, he gave me a tour of the penthouse. The place was palatial, a fortress in the sky. He showed me where I could and couldn't go, his voice cool and firm.

Then he sent me to bed. "You have orientation in the morning." His words should have felt dismissive, an order given with finality.

But instead, they settled in my chest like an anchor. Because somehow, in the chaos of a single night, my entire world had shifted

---

I WOKE WITH A START, HEART HAMMERING AGAINST MY ribs as an alarm screeched through the silence, ripping me from sleep. My sluggish, sleep-heavy limbs fought to move as I reached out, fumbling blindly in the dark for the offending noise.

My hand collided with a phone that wasn't mine. I snatched it up, silencing the sound with a sharp tap, before collapsing back onto the bed.

It felt like lying on a cloud. The silk sheets whispered

over my skin, so different from the scratchy, worn blankets of the shelter. Wrong. Everything about this felt wrong. For a moment, I lay there, disoriented. Out of place. Out of time.

The events of the last twenty-four hours were a tangled mess in my mind. It took the searing heat of the shower to burn away the lingering fog. Water cascaded over me, hammering against the tension wound tight in my muscles, and slowly, my memories bled through the cracks.

Tilly's voice, filled with regret, telling me the shelter wouldn't have space for me that night and I'd have to find somewhere else.

Brielle's rage spitting venom down the payphone. *"Get fucking lost!"*

Her cold refusal to let me see Mom was like a rusty blade to my heart.

My chest tightened at the thought. Why? The woman I'd spoken to before all of this had been... different. Not kind, exactly, but not this—this cruel, calculated gatekeeper who suddenly held my mom hostage. The fact I'd have to wait for Arti to let Doll know when Brielle and Brock had left the home so I could visit her was just another weight dragging me down.

The cemetery.

How my whole body had ached, every muscle strained as I walked across town to the cemetery. The only thing that calmed my tattered soul was the beauty of the weathered tombstones lost to nature's ruin. It was the place I always returned to when the outside world felt too much. The only place where I felt seen. Among the dead, I found solace. They understood the fragility of existence, the thin thread we all dangled from.

And then—Domino.

A storm in human form. A force I hadn't expected, hadn't seen coming, but somehow, everything had changed the moment he'd sat at my table in Denny's days before, and I'd been left spiralling ever since. Last night, he grounded me. He saw me. All of me and without question helped. I didn't understand why, yet, but I'm sure in time it would become clear.

I exhaled sharply, shutting off the water. There was no use dwelling on it now. I was where I was. I'd just have to wait and see what today held. I dried off quickly with a fluffy black towel and slipped on my clothes. They had been cleaned, folded, and left on a chair for me when I exited the bathroom. Amongst them was an item that didn't belong to me; I smirked as I held it, knowing full well it was Domino's.

I pulled the black hoodie over my head anyway. The fabric swallowed me whole. His scent hit me instantly—smoke, leather, and something darker, something sharp that lingered beneath it. Blood.

I breathed it in. I shouldn't have liked it as much as I did.

The apartment was silent as I stepped into the kitchen, the white marble glowing faintly in the morning light. A steaming mug of coffee waited for me on the counter, next to a note.

I scanned the neatly written words:

I had business to attend to for my father. I have organized my driver to take you to Devereux's campus for your orientation. Juno will be waiting for you downstairs as soon as you're ready.

I frowned, my teeth sinking into my bottom lip.
How is this my life?
And more importantly, why did he think he could make decisions for me without asking?

Half of me bristled at the thought, a sharp sense of defiance rising in my chest. No one controlled me. No one told me where to go or what to do.

And yet…

The other half of me—the one that had spent years fighting to survive alone—liked it. That, for once, someone had thought ahead. Had made sure I wasn't abandoned, scrambling for a plan.

Even though he wasn't here, I felt him. Watching over me. Not in an overbearing way, not in a way that smothered, but as if his presence lingered in the very walls. As if he was never really far away.

I took a sip of the coffee. Scalding hot, rich, and just bitter enough to wake me up properly. I downed it quickly, grabbed my things, and stepped into the sleek, mirrored elevator. The descent was smooth, silent.

When the doors slid open, the doorman—Tommy, according to his name tag—greeted me with a warm nod. "Morning, Remi."

I blinked. He knew my name. The casual familiarity in his voice caught me off guard, but before I could question it, he gestured toward the front of the building, where a luxurious black car idled at the curb.

"Juno's waiting for you. Oh, and Mr. DeMarco left this for you." He handed me a keycard. "You'll need this to access the building and the elevator when you come and go."

I turned the card over in my hand, its weight settling in my palm.

"That's highly unusual," Tommy added, a knowing look in his eyes.

I didn't ask what he meant. I already knew.

After a full night's sleep, the city seemed less like a cold, unyielding beast and more like something I could learn to navigate. The towering skyscrapers stretched into the sky, their sleek glass and steel reflecting the muted light. Modern architecture clashed with the past—colonial buildings with ornate facades stood stubbornly among the urban giants, remnants of an older world refusing to be swallowed whole.

The sky was a wash of endless gray. The sun barely broke through, teasing the city with fleeting glimpses before vanishing again behind thick clouds. But I didn't mind. I liked the way the diffused light softened the hard edges of the world, casting long shadows and revealing details that might have been lost under the glare of a harsh sun.

Juno was stoic and silent as he watched me through the rearview mirror, maneuvering the car through the city streets, weaving seamlessly through traffic before pushing out into the suburbs and beyond.

The change was stark. The wealth here wasn't just obvious—it was obscene. The farther we got from the city, the larger the houses grew, morphing into sprawling mansions tucked behind private forests instead of fences. The kind of homes that didn't just scream money but old money, the kind that had been passed down through generations.

Devereux University was in another world entirely. The road leading to it stretched into a long, tree-lined avenue, the thick canopy above weaving a tunnel of shadows and filtered light. The air felt different here—cleaner, quieter, carrying an almost eerie stillness.

I caught my first glimpse of the university through the gaps in the trees, and something in my chest tightened. It was breathtaking.

The main building was straight out of a gothic dream—black limestone, its dark facade rising with towering spires and sharp-arched stained glass. It looked like it had been plucked from another era, its history etched into every weathered stone.

My fingers twitched for my sketchbook. It was the kind of structure that demanded to be studied, drawn, and captured. Every intricate detail, every whisper of time, carved into its walls. A place like this had stories.

I'd bet money there was a graveyard somewhere on campus. There had to be. The haunting elegance of Devereux wrapped around me like a second skin. It felt right.

At the entrance, a group of student volunteers stood waiting, their smiles practiced and professional. The welcome committee wasted no time, dividing us into groups based on our chosen courses.

A leaflet was shoved into my hands by a tall, sharp-featured guy who introduced himself as Dorian.

"The campus is sprawling," he announced, his voice crisp and efficient. "You'll get lost if you don't pay attention. Devereux is fully self-sufficient—students rarely leave during the semester. And if you wander too far, you'll find yourself in Hollow Pines National Park."

I glanced at the edges of the property where the towering trees loomed, their dense foliage shifting with the wind. The thought of an entire forest bordering the campus was both intriguing and unsettling.

"Oh, shit, fuck. Watch out!"

Something slammed into my back with the force of a freight train. My breath left me in a sharp gasp as I hit the ground, knees sinking into the cold, damp earth. A skateboard clattered against the asphalt in front of me, spinning to a stop near my hand.

"Shit, dude! I'm so sorry!"

The voice was frantic, dripping with genuine regret. A second later, a hand appeared in front of me, offering to pull me up. I took it, brushing myself off as I straightened—and froze. I found myself staring into the most angelic face I had ever seen.

Bright shaggy blond hair framed his sharp cheekbones and full lips, his skin sun-kissed and flawless, his grin easy and utterly unapologetic. Michaelangelo could have carved him from stone.

"It's no problem," I muttered, pushing my hair back from my face, suddenly hyper-aware that half the group was sneering at us or trying to suppress their laughter.

The blond guy—a walking Greek statue—was completely unfazed.

"I'm so sorry, my dude. I was running late and was carrying too much speed." He shrugged, his skateboard now tucked under his arm like an extension of himself. He had the kind of energy that radiated pure chaos.

He held out a hand again, this time for an actual introduction. "I'm Kyran."

My lips twitched despite myself. Something about him was disarming. "Remi."

His grin widened. "This is gonna be awesome." He shouldered his backpack, the skateboard now strapped to it, as he fell into step beside me. "What are you studying?"

"Oh, um... Forensic anthropology."

His eyes lit up. "No shit? Really?"

I blinked. "Uh... yeah?"

He grinned, nudging me lightly with his elbow. "Me too, my dude."

Before I could process that, Dorian cleared his throat, loud enough to silence the murmurs around us.

"Gentlemen, if you've finished conversing," he said, his expression pinched with irritation, "perhaps we can begin the tour? Your courses start next week, and I suggest you pay attention."

Kyran leaned toward me, voice low. "Who shoved a stick up his ass?"

I snorted, barely containing my laughter as we followed Dorian up the stone steps. Massive oak doors loomed ahead, their dark wood carved with intricate patterns. They looked more suited to a cathedral than a university. I had a feeling Devereux was going to be nothing like an ordinary university. And I wasn't sure if that excited me—or terrified me.

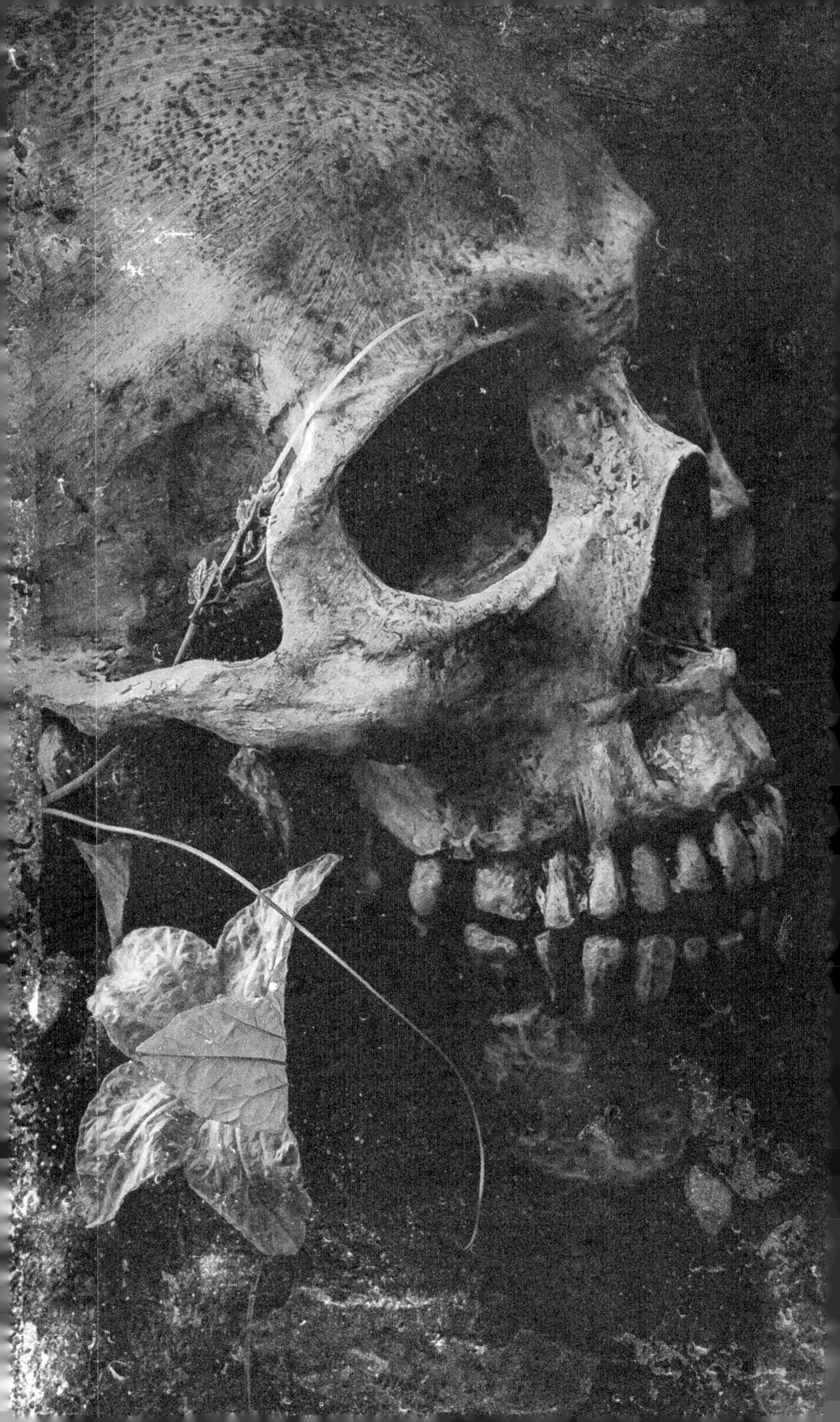

7. DOMINO

Kyran Fucking Stirling was all over him.

That little shit didn't *accidentally* crash into Remi. He was a lying, manipulative prick. I'd seen him watching him from the moment Remi stepped out of the car, his blue eyes tracking every move like a predator stalking prey.

Juno, oblivious as ever, had no idea someone was coveting what was mine. I'd given that idiot just enough rope for him to hang himself, and it was time for him to dance the hangman's jig.

Kyran Stirling was going to be a problem.

The Stirlings thought they were untouchable. That, being one of Marlow Heights' founding families, made them immune to consequences. They'd spent generations carving their name into this city, believing their legacy was law.

Kyran was about to learn the hard way that nothing —no one—got in the way of what I wanted. He'd pay in blood for laying his hands on Remi.

Not one person in this city was above reproach, other than the DeMarcos because we owned them all, something I'd need to remind Stirling Senior once I'd dealt with his eldest son. That legacy they loved so much was hanging in the balance.

Even though I'd left in the early hours to handle a Gallo sighting on our turf, my thoughts had been consumed with Remi. Calloway had slipped through my fingers a week ago—but now, he was right where he belonged. Bound, bleeding, and waiting for me in my playroom.

I'd had eyes on Remi from the moment his alarm went off. There were hidden cameras in every room of my apartment, in my car, and in every space I worked in. I'd even installed a tracker in the phone I'd gifted him, and it drove me insane he hadn't taken it. I could tap into the live feed at any time and see what he was up to, and once he had his phone on him, I'd be able to hear every word he or others said in his presence. Ghost had come through on every front for me.

It was a special kind of torture. Watching him wake —all sleep-mussed and confused, blinking against the light—had me gripping the hard plastic case of my phone so tightly my knuckles ached, but I relished the pain. He'd thrown back the covers, stretching like a lazy cat, all soft skin and sharp angles in nothing but a pair of boxer briefs.

It took everything in me not to ride straight back to the apartment and fuck him, letting him know once and for all who he belonged to. He had no idea what he'd done to me. No idea the kind of thoughts running through my head. What I wanted. What I'd already claimed as mine. He consumed me.

And now, Stirling thought he could get in my way?

I'd fucking gut him first.

With Remi occupied on his tour, I had unfinished business to attend to. I'd put it off long enough. No more avoiding him. No more excuses.

I might be the face of the DeMarco family, but I still answered to my father. He demanded in-person updates. He wanted strategy meetings. He wanted war. Short-sighted as always. For him, war and bloodshed were the only answers.

The roar of my bike cut through the quiet campus, the deep, guttural growl of the engine reverberating through my chest. Trees blurred at my sides as I pushed the throttle, chasing the rush, the brief moment of control it gave me.

But that control wouldn't last. Not where I was going.

Taking the exit onto the private road leading to the beating heart of the DeMarco empire, I felt the shift in the air. Here, there were no neon signs. No bustling streets. Just darkened trees arching over the road like silent sentinels, knowing what kind of men passed beneath their branches.

The asphalt stretched long and winding, designed to disorient any outsider stupid enough to make it this far. Few did. Even fewer left.

I pulled up to the blackened iron gates, the DeMarco crest gleaming in the dim light. They didn't open immediately. Agitation thrummed through my veins. *The fuck is this?* I ripped my helmet off, and the guards stationed at the entrance went rigid. The lazy smiles they'd been wearing disappeared like they'd just seen a ghost. They feared me more than they feared my father. Smart. Another guard emerged from the security booth, barely sparing a glance at my bike—or me.

"Boss." He gave a sharp nod before pressing the button to release the heavy locks.

One day, I'd burn this place to the ground. The house that sat at the center of the compound was a fucking monstrosity. Ostentatious and hollow. A monument to a man who thought he was untouchable. Who thought he was king, but it was me who kept him in power.

When I took over, I'd dismantle his empire piece by piece. Not because I wanted it. I never had. But because he did. He spat bullshit about birthright and legacy, acting like we were some kind of royalty. All I wanted was the kill. The hunt. The raw, visceral thrill of power.

I'd never cared about anyone. Never given a shit about their lives. Until now.

Bernard—the only man in this house I had even an ounce of respect for—opened the door as I hit the bottom step. "Your father is in his office, but he's—"

A shrill, nasal voice cut through the air, echoing down the hallway. *Brielle.* The hairs on the back of my neck stood on end, a snarl curling my lips. Fucking Brielle.

Berny laid a warm hand on my shoulder, the only person who could touch me and live to see another day.

"Not today," he murmured. "Her time will come. You have other matters to handle first." His voice was calm, calculated—a reminder.

Berny always knew more than he should. Always had his ear to the ground. He never spoke of his loyalties, but I'd long suspected they lay with me, not my father.

I exhaled sharply, the rage simmering beneath my skin, begging to be unleashed. "Doesn't mean I can't put the fear of God into her."

A rare, cruel smile ghosted over his lips. "That it doesn't, sir."

Brielle's voice made my blood boil. I moved silently down the hall, footsteps light, muscles coiled tight. My father's office door was cracked open just enough for me to glimpse inside.

I should've expected the filth I'd find. Brielle, draped across his lap like the pathetic, desperate whore she was.

"It's a hundred grand, Federico," she purred, running her fingers down his chest. "It won't be hard to get the will adjusted. Brock's gotten *much* better at that kind of thing. And her prognosis is bleak."

His mother. I went still, rage sharpening into something *colder*.

My father hummed, considering. "How long?"

"The doctors said months. But," she cooed, pressing a kiss to his throat, "A prognosis can be wrong. Months are made up of weeks, after all."

Fucking snake. She thought she was smart. That she could play my father, bend him to her will. She didn't realize *he* was playing *her*.

"What about your nephew?"

I clenched my jaw, the muscles twitching violently.

She sighed, exasperated. "That weird little freak?"

A mistake. My switchblade was in my hand before I even realized it.

"He's not going to be a problem," she continued, flicking her fake blonde hair over her shoulder. "I sent him away the moment he arrived. He was staying at the shelter on Clayburn until I paid Tilly off. So fuck knows where he is now." She snorted. "Probably the streets. He won't last long out there."

Wrong. Dead. *Fucking*. Wrong.

My father smirked. "And the trust fund?"

"Oh, he doesn't have a clue," Brielle laughed. "That's the best part of it. He'll never know it's missing."

"You can't miss what you never knew existed." My father gripped her jaw, dragging her in for a sloppy, open-mouthed kiss.

Bile burned the back of my throat. I couldn't take another second. I kicked the door open, storming inside. They jumped apart like guilty fucking teenagers.

My father's expression was unreadable—eyes black, shuttered, calculating. Brielle, though? She feigned shock, clutching her chest like a *damsel in distress*. But the second her gaze landed on me? That heat in her eyes—the same look she always gave me, sick and twisted—detonated the short fuse inside me.

In the blink of an eye, my hand was around her throat, pinning her to the wall. My blade kissed her stomach, pressing deep enough to make her breath hitch.

I leaned in, our faces millimeters apart, my voice a growl. "You're not as smart as you think, Brielle."

Her pupils blew wide. Her body trembled beneath my grip.

"You touch him," I murmured, pressing the knife just a little harder, "and I'll be the last thing you ever see."

A high, hysterical laugh spilled from her lips, but it was laced with fear. "Y-you wouldn't harm me." Her voice wavered. Her eyes darted to my father. Seeking reassurance. Protection. She'd get neither. "Y-your father won't allow it."

I smirked. "Won't he?"

Federico snorted. "You're easily replaced, Brielle." He adjusted his tie, barely sparing her a glance. "One whore is much the same as another." Cold. Emotionless.

Brielle choked on a breath, indignation twisting her already panicked features. "Federico, call off your attack dog," she rasped.

My fingers tightened around her throat, and I enjoyed the way her pale face started to turn blue. She was pathetic. *Weak*. The blade in my hand pressed deeper into her side, enough to break the skin and let the faint tang of copper fill the air. My father sat back, watching. Silent. Because he knew I wouldn't kill her today. But that didn't mean I wouldn't feed the monster inside me.

"Your days are numbered, Brielle." I leaned in, my lips brushing the shell of her ear. She was trembling now. I could *taste* the fear on her skin, sour and electric, and when I licked a slow line up the side of her face, she whimpered. "You won't see me coming," I whispered, my voice soft.

A choked noise caught in her throat.

"You'll wake up one day chained in my playground." My grip on her throat flexed, savoring the way her pulse fluttered wildly beneath my palm. "Left there for hours… until you're begging for death."

She gasped, her nails digging into my wrist in a weak attempt to free herself.

"But before I send you to hell…" I exhaled, my lips ghosting over her jaw. "You'll watch Brock die at my hand."

Her entire body seized.

I smiled against her skin. There it was. "Maybe I'll even let my men have fun with him first," I mused, dragging my knuckle down her sweat-slicked cheek. "They'll ruin that tight little virgin ass, break him open until he bleeds, until his screams go hoarse."

Her breath came in short, wheezing gasps.

"Then I'll mirror it on the outside," I murmured.

She tried to speak, but only garbled sounds escaped. "Y-you…s-sick…fuck," she wheezed.

I grinned. Her pale blue eyes started to roll back, her body sagging, going limp in my hold.

Too far.

I let go.

She hit the floor like the useless sack of shit she was, her chest heaving as she sucked in desperate, ragged breaths.

"Leave," I snapped.

She scrambled on all fours, clawing at the floor before hauling herself upright with the doorframe. She cast a final, desperate glance at my father. He didn't move. Didn't look at her. Didn't care.

Then she turned to me, eyes burning with barely contained rage. A promise of retribution.

I just smirked and wiggled my fingers in a mock wave.

"Don't make a mess on your way out."

When the door slammed shut behind Brielle, the only trace of her left behind was the putrid stench of her floral perfume. Federico's demeanor shifted. That cold, calculated ire turned on me.

"Sit." A single word. Clipped. Commanding. He motioned toward the leather chair across from his obscenely large mahogany desk.

He never spoke to me like a son. Never had. I was

another soldier to him. Another weapon. He'd broken me as a child and rebuilt me into a machine—one he could aim at a problem and watch it bleed out.

Without a word, I moved.

"Have you found Calloway?"

"Yes," I answered. "He'll be tortured for every ounce of information he has on the Gallos' plans." I cleared my throat and asked the question that had gnawed at me for years. "Why are the Gallos the only family that ever makes a move on us?"

His eyes narrowed. "I told you—they are the reason your mother is dead," he said, his voice dropping to a growl. "They killed her and nearly killed you as a child."

Same words. Same tone. Same script. Repeated verbatim every time. But today, there was something different. A crack in the rehearsed delivery. A heat bled through his words, like the question itself was tiresome.

If he had loved my mother as much as he claimed, why were the Gallos still breathing twenty-five years later? Why hadn't he rallied the other families to wipe them off the map?

"Enough of that!" His cane slammed against the desk, the sharp crack echoing through the room. "There is much more we need to discuss."

I held back the smirk that twitched at the corner of my mouth. There it was. The anger. I antagonized him.

"We have a leak," he continued, his voice dripping with disdain. "I know you took out that gang as a warning, but the books are still off." He leaned forward, eyes flashing. "If I can't trust you to do your job..." His upper lip curled. "Then you will never take over the family."

My fingers dug into the arms of the chair.

"I'll have one of your cousins brought into the fold instead," he sneered.

They'd always wanted a bigger role in the family, always been eager to please him. But he'd chosen me. Until now.

"I believed you were the only one capable of carrying the family name into the future," he said. Then he moved. Slow. Deliberate. He stood, leaning on his cane as he rounded the desk. The sharp steel tip pressed against my chest, right over my heart. "I will not hesitate to end you if you disappoint me."

I didn't flinch. Didn't react. "Yes, sir."

The words were ice on my tongue, controlled and measured. But inside, I was burning.

Irritation coiled around my ribs, squeezing tighter with every passing second. It consumed me, cell by cell, until the fire dulled into something worse—something colder. I sat there for hours, taking his berating, his threats. Until I felt nothing at all.

Federico needed to watch his back because I was about to snap. And when I did, that feral hunger inside me wouldn't be aimed at the Gallos. It would be aimed at him.

I couldn't wait for the day he took his last breath.

I was unfeeling. Detached. I didn't understand emotions, but I knew weakness. I knew how to exploit it. Federico was vile. He'd treated me as expendable since the day I was old enough to hold a knife.

Kill or be killed.

Trust no one.

Loyalty was a joke. People only followed you out of fear.

If you let them believe they were your friends, your

colleagues, they'd stab you in the back without hesitation.

Many had tried.

None had lived to regret it.

My father should have been more careful with the lessons he taught me—because I didn't fear him. I followed because I was trapped. But a caged animal fights back harder than a free one.

He thought he was the smartest person in the room. Thought he had complete control. But he didn't see it. I was exactly what he made me. And that meant he was outmatched.

In strength.

In *brutality*.

In strategy. My mind worked in ways he could never understand.

He laughed when I threatened Brielle. Brushed it off. But he didn't realize—those words were for him, too.

I held his gaze, watching the pale tinge creep across his face. "You'll never see me coming," I vowed and turned to walk away.

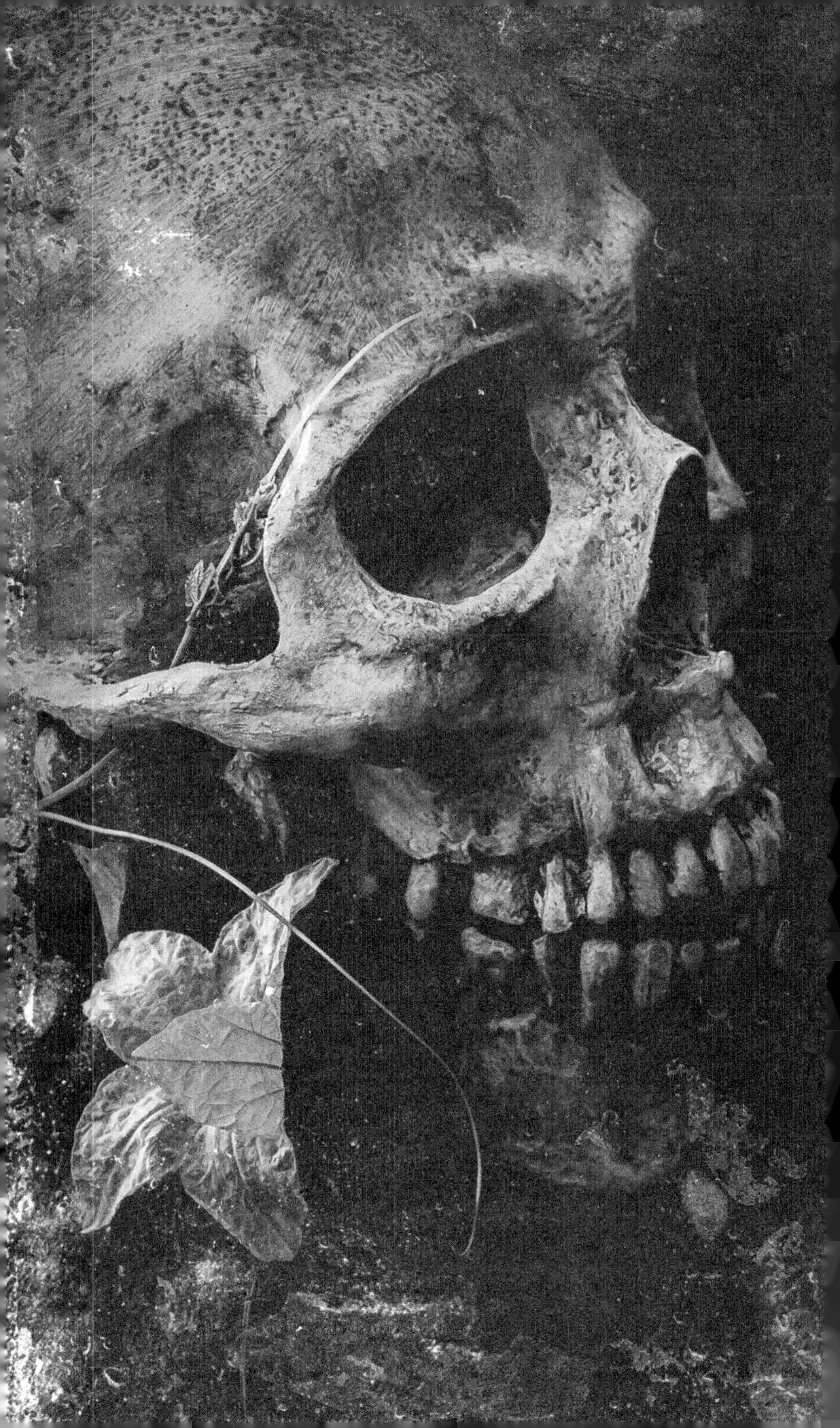

8 DOMINO

The city reeked of filth. The neon overhead flickered, casting jagged shadows along the cracked sidewalk. The stench of piss and sweat clung to the alley walls, thick and suffocating. My hands flexed at my sides, curling into fists, itching to hurt. To break something.

To break *him*.

My father had pissed me off today. That long, drawn-out meeting. The usual cryptic bullshit. Speaking in riddles, dodging my questions, testing my patience as if I didn't already know he was a liar. But that wasn't what was shredding me apart from the inside. That wasn't the thing feeding the monster inside me, making my skin feel too tight, my vision narrow.

No. That rage had a name. *Kyran-fucking-Stirling.*

The moment I left the DeMarco compound, I

headed straight to Deveraux—only to see Kyran sliding into the back of *my* car after *my* Remi. That smug fucking smile on his face, those greedy fucking eyes trailing lower, locking onto Remi's ass like he had any fucking right looking at what belonged to me.

The world snapped, and everything went dark. Everything else—the city, the noise, the fucking oxygen in my lungs—ceased to exist.

I don't remember following them into the city. I barely registered the turns as I trailed them to Nocturne, one of my clubs, but I must have because here I was, lurking in the shadows.

Outside my club. In my fucking territory.

The line stretched down the block, bodies packed tight, the bass throbbing into the streets. Nocturne was legitimate—on paper. A luxury escape for those looking to indulge. But in the shadows? It was a kingdom of secrets. Private rooms, bodies bought by the hour, whispers captured by hidden cameras. Ghost made sure we had eyes on everything. And everyone.

Including him. Kyran Stirling was flagged in every DeMarco establishment. The second he stepped inside, I would know.

Remi, though...Remi was untouchable. Didn't matter if he followed a dress code or not. Didn't matter if he walked through the front door barefoot and bleeding—he could go anywhere.

My phone buzzed. I didn't need to check to know it was Antonio. Across the street, he caught my eye, gave a nod, then slipped inside.

And still—I watched. Kyran had his arm on him. Holding him close. Leaning in, whispering something in his ear that made Remi laugh under the purple UV glow of the Nocturne sign.

Laughter. My fingers twitched. My pulse slowed. Over my dead fucking body.

The images hit hard and fast—Kyran on his knees, his arms bent at grotesque angles, mouth opening in a silent scream as I carved that smug fucking smirk from his face. I had already let him breathe once today. A mercy. A mistake.

I wouldn't make it again. I cracked my knuckles and rolled my neck, my monster gnashing its teeth against my restraint. *Soon.*

I lit a cigarette, took a drag, and exhaled slowly, my body thrumming with anticipation as I watched.

Remi moved. Stepped back.

My body went tight, muscles coiled, a loaded trigger, seconds from snapping—I could be by his side in a heartbeat. Could rip Kyran's arm from its socket before he even realized I was there. Could drive my knee into his back, pin him to the ground, press my blade to his throat, and let him feel what a mistake it was to touch what was mine.

But then Kyran laughed, raised his hands. Remi shook his head, turned on his heel, and walked away.

Good.

I forced myself to stay still. To breathe. Kyran had just saved himself—for now. I pulled out my phone. It barely rang once.

"Boss?" Juno answered.

"Where the fuck are you?" I asked, voice low, edged with death.

"I'm with—"

"Don't fucking lie to me."

A pause. A sharp inhale. A sound too close to a whimper.

"H-he said he'd be okay—"

Wrong answer.

"Your orders were to take him to Deveraux and then straight back to my apartment. Where in that instruction did I say to let him wander off with Kyran Stirling and go to Nocturne?"

Silence. Not because he wasn't there—because he was terrified.

I let it stretch. Let him feel the weight of his mistake press against him, let him imagine what would happen. The inevitability of what came next.

"I'll give you one more job. Find Remi. Bring him to me." I ended the call. Exhaled a slow, smoky breath.

An hour later, Kyran stumbled out of the club, swaying as he clutched his gut, bracing himself at the mouth of the alley. *Pathetic*. A silver-spoon prince who couldn't even hold his liquor.

Had no idea I was watching. Had no idea what was waiting for him in the dark.

"Kyran," I whispered, the sound slithering through the alley, curling around him like smoke.

The walls caught my voice and bounced it back, making it come from everywhere. His breath hitched, disoriented. He turned in slow, jerky movements, peering into the dark.

"Wh-who's there?" His voice shook. "What—what do you want?"

I smiled into the night, already able to taste his blood. The hunger inside me was begging to be fed. It wouldn't be satisfied until I was drenched in crimson, until the metallic sting of it saturated the air.

"Just a chat," I said, voice soft, almost inviting. A predator luring its prey.

He hesitated. Smart. But not smart enough. I took a step forward, just enough for the dim glow of the streetlamp to catch the steel of my rings. Kyran stiffened.

"I'd hate for you to misunderstand me," I murmured. "So I'll make this simple."

He swallowed hard. Then, to my amusement, he took a step toward me. Another. And another. The moment my face caught the light, his body jerked like a puppet with cut strings. His pupils flared with recognition, then pure, primal fear as he spun on his heel and bolted. *Pathetic.*

I caught him by the collar of his jacket and yanked him back. He slammed into the brick wall with a sickening crack. His head bounced off the surface, dazed, breath stuttering in his lungs.

The first punch split his lip, crimson blooming in thick beads. The second cracked a rib. I felt it give under my knuckles with a satisfying crunch. Kyran gasped, blood dripping down his chin as he spat a mouthful onto the concrete.

I tilted my head. "Don't touch what's mine."

"I—I don't—" His voice warbled, dazed.

He really was as dumb as those sun-kissed locks made him look.

"You can't be that inept," I sneered.

His lip trembled. His eyes darted frantically around the alley, looking for help, looking for a way out. There was none.

Not tonight.

"R-Remi—" he wheezed, chest rising and falling too fast. "He's just my friend—"

Wrong answer.

My next punch connected with his cheekbone. His head snapped sideways, crashing into the wall. I wrenched him forward and drove my fist into his stomach. Hard. The wind rushed out of him in a choked gasp. His body folded like wet paper.

I leaned in, voice lethal, intimate. "I don't give a fuck what you think you are to him." I let the words sink into his pain, sharp and precise as a blade. "If you so much as look at him again, I'll make sure you never see anything at all."

His breath hitched, wet and gurgling. He nodded weakly. I let him drop to the damp ground. He curled onto his side, whimpering, a pathetic, shaking heap at my feet.

It should have been enough. It wasn't. I brought my boot down into his ribs. Once. Twice. Again. He coughed blood, arms braced over his head, trying to protect himself. Useless.

The distant purr of my car joined the melody of his pain-filled cries, mournful whimpers, and the brittle crunch of shattered bone. I spit on him, then melted into the shadows.

I leaned against the damp wall, lit a cigarette, inhaled slowly as the thick smoke filled my lungs, and waited. Waited for my little lamb to step into the wolf's den.

Would he run?

Would he scream?

Or would he surprise me?

Would he prove what I already knew? That he was fascinated by death. By power. By the beauty of life as it hung in the balance. That he was, at his core, just like me.

I was certain I'd seen it in his eyes, an ember of dark fire that lusted to know what it felt like to take a life. If he showed that curiosity tonight, I'd lead him down the darkest path known to man. I'd grant all his illicit fantasies. I'd set him free of the oppressive chains that were wrapped around him. Allow him to free his dark heart and embrace all he could become.

Footsteps echoed through the alley. I braced against the wall; sweet euphoria coursed through my veins, heightening my senses as I counted down in my head.

Three.

Two.

One.

Remi stopped just inside the entrance, head tilted, scenting the air like an animal. His breathing was uneven. Lips parted. Eyes dark but not with fear—with fascination. He took a step closer. Gaze flicking between the shadows—me—and the barely conscious body across from me. Could he sense my presence like I could his?

I waited for the horror. The recoil. A scream. The inevitable, *"Why would you do this?"* But none of it came. The longer he stood there, the more confident I grew. Smoke curled around my lips as I exhaled, excitement heating the blood in my veins for an entirely different reason.

He stepped closer to where Kyran lay in a whimpering heap, his bloodied face turned toward Remi, filthy hand reaching for him. I bit back a snarl. He didn't get to touch what was mine. To my surprise, Remi recoiled from his touch.

Instead, he shivered. His fingers twitched at his sides. His breath came in short, sharp pants. Excited.

I stepped toward him, slow, deliberate. Testing. "You're not afraid of me, are you?" My voice was almost gentle.

He should be. His tongue darted out, wetting his lips. He shook his head. "Never."

"Good."

I closed the remaining space between us, chest pressing flush against his back. My hands slid down his chest, fingers gripping his hips, holding him there, against me. Letting him feel just how much this—he—affected me, as I nestled my hardness against his crease.

Remi's breath hitched. He looked down at my blood stained knuckles, lifted my hand, turned it over in the light, and studied the torn skin with something close to reverence.

"So beautiful," he whispered, a delicate finger tracing my tattoos.

A sharp heat coiled in my stomach. He turned slowly, gaze smoldering over his shoulder as he looked up at me. Lips inches from mine. "Why?" The word was barely a breath.

I didn't need to ask what he meant. I already knew. My pulse pounded against my ribs. I knew—right then and there—that I would never let him go. That if he tried to run, I would chain him to my bed and break him. Make him love it, crave it. He was mine in this life and each one that followed. Because I owned his soul, he just didn't know it yet.

Mine. Forever.

"Because he touched you."

Remi snorted, turning his gaze to Kyran's crumpled form, but I wasn't done.

I leaned in, lips brushing the shell of his ear, voice dropping into something dark, intimate. Claiming. "He wanted what's mine."

A full-body shudder wracked through him at my possessive tone. But instead of running—instead of doing what any sane person should—he leaned into me. His ass pressed against my aching cock. *Fuck.*

My already-thin control snapped. My blood-stained hand wrapped around his throat, not too tight—not yet—as I spun him around and pinned him against the wall, right by Kyran's trembling body.

"It seems we keep ending up like this, *piccolo agnello*."

My lips ghosted over his. Teasing, testing. The cold press of his snake bites sent a sharp spike of need straight through me. I flicked my tongue over them, savoring the contrast of steel against heat.

Remi's exhale ghosted over my lips.

He wasn't afraid.

Not of me. Not of what I'd done.

The fire in those ice-blue eyes burned through me, raking over my face, mapping out the splatters of blood like he wanted to memorize them. His gaze flicked to my lips, then back to my eyes, dark and hungry.

"I—I…" He licked his lips.

Fuck.

My head tilted, taking him in. Furrowed brows, skin dewy with sweat, pulse hammering against my thumb as I kept my grip on his throat. His chest rose and fell too fast. His pupils swallowed the blue.

"Are you innocent, *piccolo agnello?*"

A single breath—hesitation. "I…" Remi shook his head, lashes fluttering closed, as he sucked in air like he was trying to hold on. "I don't want to be."

His voice was hoarse, nearly a whimper. When his eyes fluttered back open, I felt it. That moment—right there. His surrender. The shift in him whispered that he wasn't fighting it anymore.

He was mine.

I dragged my free hand up his chest, slow and teasing, until my fingers tangled in the soft strands of his hair. I twisted them around my knuckles and yanked, angling his head up, forcing him to look at me. I kicked his legs apart, sliding a knee between them until I could feel his hardness against my thigh, eradicating any space between us.

His full lips parted. Begging.

"Ever been kissed?" I murmured.

"N-no…b-but I want to kiss you."

Little lamb, you could tempt a saint to sin with those five magic words. I crushed my mouth to his, claiming. Electricity snapped between us, setting my nerves on fire as my tongue thrust into the heat of his mouth. Tasting. Owning. Devouring.

Remi moaned against me, hands fisting in my shirt like he couldn't bear the thought of space between us. His tongue lashed against mine, rolling, teasing, and fuck—that tongue bar sent a spike of raw pleasure through me.

My little lamb had a bite. I growled against his lips, deepening the kiss, taking him apart inch by inch.

His hips rolled against my thigh, desperate for friction, seeking something he didn't quite know how to ask for.

Not yet. But he would.

I caught his bottom lip between my teeth and tugged, making him whimper. His eyes—fucking wrecked. I released my grip on his throat and licked down the slender column of his neck, burying my face against his sweat-slicked skin. I inhaled him, dark moss and salt, intoxicating. He was too tempting not to taste, my teeth sunk into the delicate skin and I sucked hard, Remi moaned long and low. I sucked until copper coated my tongue, the sweet metallic taste utterly divine.

"P-please," he whimpered.

His hands roamed my back, restless, needy, wild.

Oh, how I'd enjoy breaking my innocent little lamb. Corrupting him. Teaching him all the deliciously filthy ways he could worship me. I wrenched my mouth from his delicious skin and pressed a hand to his chest, pushing him back just enough to see the need that flickered behind those ice-blue eyes.

"On your knees."

Remi dropped instantly. No hesitation. My cock throbbed at the sight of him looking up at me, wide-eyed, submissive. Intoxicating. Lips swollen from my kiss, chest rising and falling too fast, his thighs trembling.

I cupped his face, thumb stroking his cheek. "Open your mouth, *piccolo agnello*. Tongue out."

His lips parted. His tongue flicked out, eager. Waiting.

I smirked, running my fingers through his hair. "Undo my belt."

His shaky fingers fumbled once before the leather fell apart at my waist.

"Now, pull down my zipper. Take my cock out."

Remi swallowed and licked his lips, his throat working around his nerves, but his hands moved without hesitation as he pulled my jeans and boxers down. The moment my cock sprang free, he stared. Devoured me. Like a starving man offered his first taste of real sin.

I wrapped a fist around my length, pumping once, twice, working a bead of precum to the tip. I reached down, brushing it against his lips. Marking him.

Remi's breath stuttered. He licked his lips, tasting me, moaning.

A growl rumbled in my chest. "Eyes on me."

He nodded.

"All the time." I brushed my thumb over his swollen bottom lip. "You break contact—I stop."

Another nod. His hands found my thighs, gripping them tightly, holding on. He'd need to for what I had planned.

I pressed my cock to the tip of his tongue. "Lick the tip. Taste me."

His tongue flicked out, slow, teasing. He moaned at the salty taste of me, then he dipped the tip into my slit like he was chasing more. Sharp pleasure shot through me, straight to my balls.

I gritted my teeth. "Stop."

He froze, sitting back on his heels, panting. I stepped forward, framing his face with my hands as my cock settled on his tongue.

"Good boy."

I stroked his cheek, tilting his head, before rolling my hips forward, just a little. His lips stretched around me accommodating, my girth as I pushed down his tongue. That tongue bar gliding over a pulsing vein on the underside of my dick made my whole body burn with need. *Fuck.* Spit slicked my length as I pulled back, then thrust again, deeper this time.

Remi gagged as I hit the back of his throat. "That's nearly all of me, *piccolo agnello*, only a couple more inches."

Tears welled in his eyes. *Beautiful.* I pulled all the way back, letting just the tip rest on his tongue, then locked eyes with him.

"Relax your throat," I murmured. "Breathe through your nose. Inhale when I pull back."

His fingers trembled on my thighs, but he nodded. I smirked, running my fingers through his damp hair, gripping tight.

"I can't wait to see your tears."

His breath hitched, but he kept his mouth open. I

thrust forward, deep and hard, down his throat. He choked around me, gagging, but didn't pull away. Didn't stop.

I pulled back, just enough for him to gasp in air, then slammed back in. A broken sob left his lips. Spit and precum coated his chin, dripping down his neck.

And still—his eyes never left mine. "You cry so beautifully for me, baby."

The tight, wet heat of his mouth gripped me as I pulled out and thrust back in, the rhythm harsh and punishing. Tears streamed down his pale cheeks.

Swallow. Take it. Be Mine.

The rougher I got, the more he wanted it. The more I took, the more he gave.

My cock slammed down his throat in brutal, unrelenting thrusts, giving him no room to breathe. But instead of pulling back, instead of clawing at me in desperation—Remi groaned.

The sound reverberated through me, a deep, wrecked moan that sent shocks of pleasure down my length, straight to my tightening balls. The sight of him —lips stretched wide, drool slicking his skin, eyes glassy with submission—burned itself into my fucking soul.

I couldn't stop.

Didn't want to.

I fucked his throat like it was the last thing I'd ever do. Like I could carve myself into him, make him remember this—remember me—with every raw, bruising thrust.

Every nerve ending in my body lit up, fire racing through my veins. My grip in his hair tightened, locking him in place, forcing him to take all of me.

"Fuck, Remi," I growled.

His lashes fluttered, breath stuttering, spit dripping

from his swollen lips, but those blue eyes stayed locked on mine. Drunk on me. Wrecked for me.

Perfect.

My cock thickened, pleasure cresting, that final, devastating wave about to hit. "I'm going to come," I snarled, my fingers digging into his scalp. "And you're going to swallow. Every. Last. Drop."

A wrecked whimper vibrated against my length, and fuck—I couldn't hold back. With a final thrust, I buried myself deep, his nose pressed to my groin, his throat spasming around me as I held him there.

A strangled sob left him. Tears stained his cheeks. That perfect image broke me. Cum erupted from me, thick and hot, lashing against his raw throat in relentless pulses. His muscles clenched, milking every drop from my aching cock.

But he didn't just take it. He drank me down. Sucked every drop, every last bit of me into him with long, hard pulls that had me shuddering, nearly collapsing.

His tongue flicked over the head of my oversensitive cock as I slipped from his wrecked, swollen lips.

Breathless. Ruined. Mine.

I cupped his jaw, thumb running over the flushed, tear-streaked skin. "You're fucking mine now, Remi."

He blinked once. That tongue. He flicked it out, slow, deliberate, licking the stray drops of my cum from his lips.

My cock twitched.

A smirk curled at the edges of his mouth, voice raw, wrecked—"Yours."

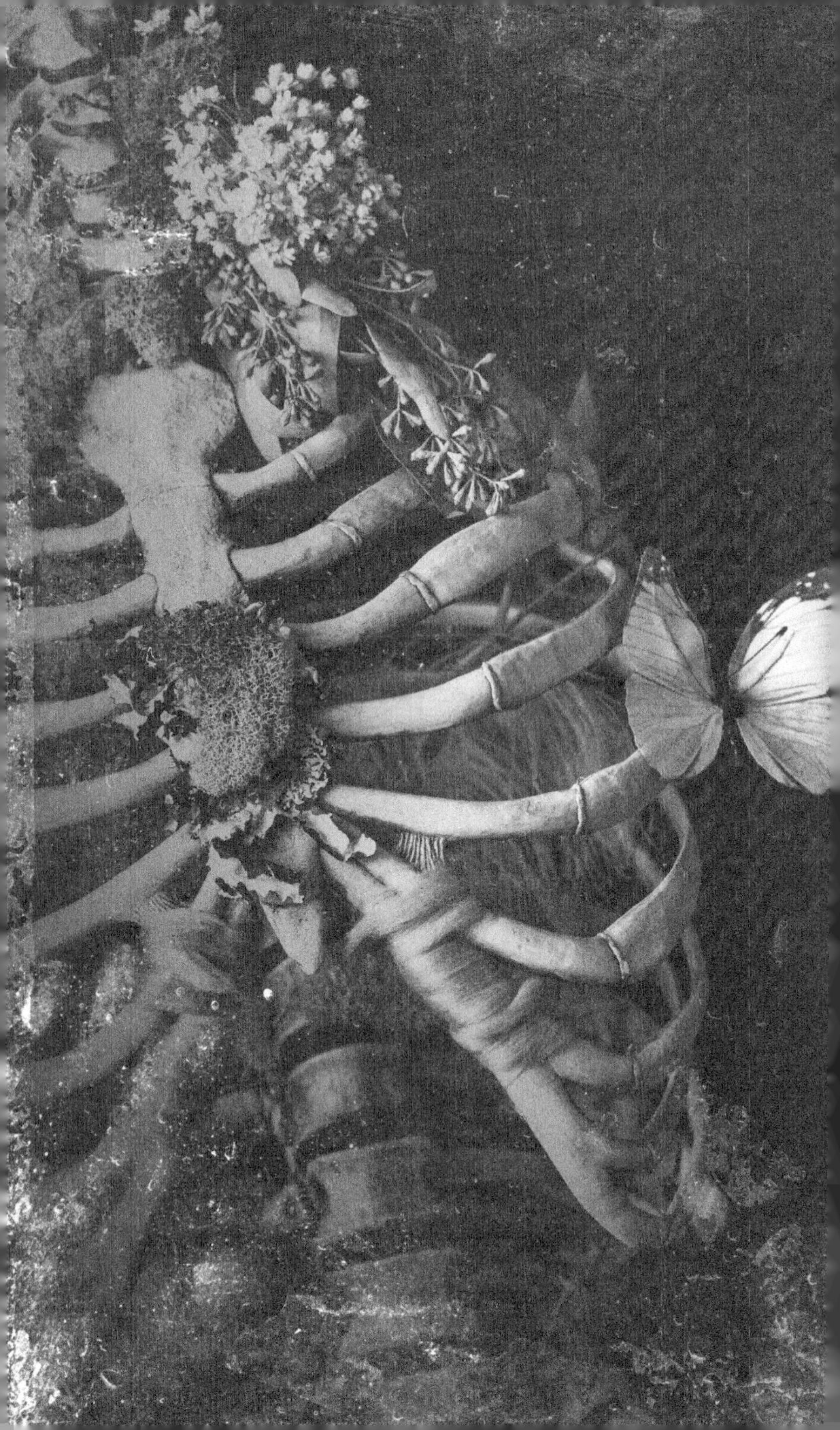

9 REMI

Last night was like a twisted fever dream—where dark fantasies bled into reality, leaving me gasping, wanting, *craving more*. I'd learned more about myself in those breathless, brutal moments than I had in my entire life.

I had never even kissed another person before. But I woke up with his taste on my tongue. I felt like I was spiraling—losing my grip on the version of myself I'd always known. But instead of fighting it, instead of running, I let go. I let myself fall.

Sunlight streaked through the thick velvet curtains, carving harsh golden slashes across my skin as I lay in bed, aching. My muscles were sore, my throat raw, my mind still drowning in the intoxicating weight of *him*.

A normal person would have been thinking about

Kyran. I should've been thinking about him. I should have cared.

But I didn't.

I didn't care about the way his body had curled on the ground, the pathetic sounds spilling from his busted lips. I didn't care that he'd been left bleeding, broken, discarded.

All I cared about was the man who did it. Domino. The one I *should* fear. The one I'd follow into hell if he so much as beckoned me forward.

Something inside me had changed—a door had been thrown open, one I'd always been too afraid to even knock on. Domino's darkness called to mine. Whispered to it. Coaxed it forward until I couldn't ignore it anymore.

Until I didn't want to.

I wondered what it had felt like for him. That moment when his fist connected, when Kyran's face split beneath his knuckles. Did it feel like power? Like control?

Did his blood sing the way mine did when he forced me to my knees, ignoring the body beside us as he claimed my throat like it belonged to him? Because it *did*.

The memory burned, seared into my skin, into my lungs, into the very marrow of my bones. I had never felt more alive. I should have felt shame, fear, *something*.

Instead, my fingers itched for my sketchbook, my body humming with the need to recreate it—every detail, every drop of claret, every shadowed curve of Domino's face as he watched me fall apart for him.

The image was so vivid I swore I could reach out and touch it. I could still taste it—the sharp copper of blood. The cloying scent of fear. The underlying, all-consuming lust that had burned through me like wildfire.

Domino was in my veins now. A poison I'd swallowed willingly. A sickness I'd never want to cure.

I'd give him anything he asked for.

The hot water of the shower unraveled the tight knots in my muscles, but it did nothing for the itch beneath my skin. It had spread. Crawling through my veins, burrowing into my marrow—a wildfire that no amount of water could extinguish.

It wasn't just in my fingers anymore. It had traveled to my brain, clawing at my skull, demanding *release*. I dragged on a pair of clean jeans and snatched a black hoodie off the chair. The soft fabric ghosted over my face, and I inhaled deeply—Smoke. Leather. Blood. His scent. His claim.

Domino hadn't just marked me with his words, his hands, his presence. He marked me with everything. His clothes. His space. The lingering phantom of him, wrapping around me even in my solitude.

And I let it.

I didn't question the madness taking hold of me, didn't fight the pull of it. What was the point? I'd already lost. The likelihood that neither of us would survive this didn't deter me.

To walk in the shadows with him—even for a little while—would be worth every consequence.

The apartment was too quiet when I stepped out of my room, sketchbook clutched tightly against my chest. The kitchen felt foreign, sleek, and untouched. The expensive coffee maker on the counter looked like something out of a catalog—beautiful yet useless to me.

I knew how to survive.

Not indulge.

A spoonful of instant coffee in a mug filled with hot water was the extent of my knowledge. Domino might come from a different world than me, but surely, he must have some? I searched the cupboards and the hallway closet. Nothing.

"Fucking, fuck."

The curse slipped from my lips as I slumped against the counter, forehead pressed to the cool marble. My body vibrated with restless energy. The hunger to create gnawed at me, a primal need that threatened to consume me whole.

There was only one way to quiet it. I needed to breathe life into death. To pull the images from my mind, let them take form, give them flesh.

I dragged the stool across the floor, the sound sharp, jarring in the silence. My sketchbook fell open, thick pages whispering as I flipped to a blank one.

The moment my pencil met the paper, the chaos in my head stilled. Lines bled from graphite. The delicate curve of a human skull took shape beneath my fingertips, the shadows hollowing out its endless, empty sockets. I lost myself in the details. The cracks spiderwebbing along brittle bone. The jagged teeth, fractured and broken. The remnants of skin, clinging in patches, half-obscured by the torn plastic of a trash bag in a moonlit alleyway.

A masterpiece of decay.

But something was missing.

My fingers tightened around the pencil, my breath slowing as I stared down at the page. The scene was almost perfect—but not quite enough. It wasn't just death that fascinated me. It was the way it happened.

The moment a soul departed, when flesh caved

beneath bone, when blood spilled in thick, sticky rivers. That sweet, sacred violence.

A sigh shuddered through me, my heart kicking against my ribs. Maybe I couldn't capture it with just my hands.

Maybe I needed to see it.

To *touch* it.

To create something real.

"What are you drawing?" Domino's low rasp ghosted over my skin, sending a violent shudder down my spine.

His presence swallowed the room, thick and inescapable. The air shifted, molecules rearranging to make space for him—as if he were the center of gravity itself. The hairs on the back of my neck stood on end, goosebumps rippling down my arms.

I had never reacted to another person like this before. Like I was the lock, and he was the key. We connected. Complemented. Craved. A perfect, devastating fit.

His tattooed hands landed on my shoulders, heat and ice bleeding through the fabric of my hoodie. I felt him everywhere, even where he didn't touch, his presence sinking into the marrow of my bones.

But my hand didn't stop moving. The pencil scratched across the thick page, desperate to keep up with the image in my mind—trying, aching to bring it to life.

Domino leaned in, his stubbled cheek brushing against mine. "That looks familiar," he mused, voice humming against my skull.

I swallowed. It was only a faint echo of the night before, twisted and aged with time. "It does. But—"

"But?"

Before I could finish, he spun me around, and I lost every thought. My vision filled with him.

Black sweatpants hung low on his hips, sharp grooves of his Adonis belt leading to the dark trail of hair vanishing beneath the waistband. My breath hitched. My memory hit hard, transporting me—the feel of him on my tongue, thick and heavy, the salty taste of him lingering.

I dragged my gaze up his torso, devouring the black ink carved into his skin. Every line of his tattoos was a story. A map. A labyrinth of chaos and death I wanted to trace with my tongue.

Silver bars gleamed in the tight buds of his nipples, twin accents against the smooth expanse of his chest. A sword inked in bold strokes lay between his pecs—mirroring the silver one around his neck—its tip kissing his skin like a silent promise of violence.

A woman's face emerged from the hilt, ink bleeding into wild, tangled branches that clawed their way up his throat, consuming every inch of bare skin. The dark lines wove seamlessly into the sharp cut of his jaw, as if she were screaming from the depths of him—trapped, lost, and forever bound to his flesh.

Art. He was art—living, breathing, untouchable. And I wanted to ruin him, to carve my obsession into his skin, to paint with him in strokes of blood and bruises. To make him mine in a way no one else ever could.

"See something you like?"

His lips twitched—almost a smirk. Almost. Then it was gone, leaving only the unrelenting weight of his gaze.

I nodded. Shamelessly.

"Now, are you going to answer my question?"

"What was it?"

"The 'but' about your drawing?"

"Oh. Umm."

My fingers twisted. The pencil slipped from my grasp, tumbling to the floor with a quiet snap, shattering the graphite inside. Domino moved before I could bend to retrieve it as it rolled across the floor. His fingers found my chin, tilting my head back.

He looked at me with those intense eyes. *Really* looked at me. Like he was peeling back my ribs, prying them open to see what lay underneath. Like he already knew what he'd find.

The truth coiled at the base of my throat, thick and cloying. Unspoken. Undeniable. I had spent my life ignoring this part of me. Shoving it down. Keeping it hidden in the dark recesses of my mind. But he had dragged it into the light.

Watching him play with life and death—like it meant nothing, like it was his to control—had unlocked something inside me. And I wanted more.

I wanted to know what it felt like to bathe in someone's blood as the light faded from their eyes. To hold a life in my hands—to decide if they deserved to keep it. To feel a knife sink into flesh, steel parting skin, blood welling in thick, sticky ribbons.

Would muscle fibers fight me when I cut into them? Would they resist, sinewy and strong? Would fresh bone splinter as I carved through it, creating something beautiful from its fragility?

What would it be like to peel flesh from bone, to strip muscle away with deliberate precision like an artist sculpting his masterpiece? To drape the skin like an angel's tattered wings, a grotesque and unholy offering. To take what is raw, macabre, and broken and twist it into something hauntingly, devastatingly beautiful.

To bring to life my art by creating it from life? I exhaled, the taste of unspoken confessions heavy on my tongue.

Domino's fingers tightened. "Remi," he murmured, voice dark and knowing.

He saw me, and for the first time, I didn't want to hide.

Domino eradicated all the space between us and stepped between my thighs, tipping my head back further until his lips brushed mine. "I see you, my *piccolo agnello.*"

His thumb traced lazy circles over my cheek, a touch so deceptively gentle it made my breath hitch. Without warning, his lips crashed into mine—hot, demanding, with a devastating hunger. The moment he teased the seam of my mouth, I surrendered, parting for him without hesitation, desperate to drown in the intoxicating taste of him.

He took everything. My mind, my sanity. His tongue licked into my mouth, duelling with mine, claiming, consuming. A punishing rhythm that left no room for doubt—I was caught in his wicked web, and he was trapped in mine. Each stroke sent shivers racing through my body, electric sparks igniting along my skin until I was burning from the inside out. Lust flowed through my veins like quicksilver, my cock filled with every stroke of his tongue against mine.

I wrapped my arms around his neck, his slick skin silky soft, and dragged him closer. I needed more, more of him, of his talented tongue—of everything. A deep growl rumbled from his chest and into mine as his hands tangled in my hair, angling my head and devouring me deeper. His teeth caught my bottom lip, tugging, teasing, before soothing the sting with another dizzying kiss. He tasted of sin, of obsession, of something I would never get enough of.

My lungs screamed for air, but I couldn't pull away—not yet, not when he felt like the only thing keeping me tethered to this world. He kissed me harder, deeper, until my body threatened to give out and my head spun in a euphoric haze.

When he finally tore his lips from mine, we were both panting, foreheads pressed together, our breaths mingling in the charged space between us. My lips tingled, swollen and bruised from his relentless attack. All I could think about was how soon I could taste him again.

"There's somewhere I want to take you, Remi."

His voice was a low, velvety murmur, wrapping around me. I blinked up at him through my lashes, my mind hazy, the world beyond his presence reduced to a blur. The meaning of his words hovered just out of reach, teasing at the edges of my understanding.

"I want to show you." His fingertips brushed over my jaw, the contact light but possessive, grounding me even as it sent a shiver racing down my spine.

I tilted my head, confused. "Show me what?"

"That I see you." His lips ghosted over my forehead before he pulled back, just enough for me to see the way his emerald eyes darkened—deep, endless pools that threatened to pull me under. "The real you. The one buried beneath the surface."

A slow, shuddering breath left my lips. Something in his voice, in the gravity of his words, sent my pulse skittering wildly.

He saw me. Not the carefully constructed version of myself I showed the world. Not the Remi who had spent years suffocating beneath expectations and self-imposed restraint. He saw the one lurking in the shadows, the one even I had been afraid to acknowledge.

"I want your demons to dance with mine."

My lips parted, but no words came. I tasted the remnants of him on my tongue, it sent a pulse of heat curling low in my stomach.

"I-I don't understand." My voice was barely a whisper, uncertain and breathless all at once.

His mouth curved—not into a smirk, not quite a smile. Something more dangerous. More knowing.

"You will." His fingers traced a slow path down my arm before retreating, leaving behind the phantom burn of his touch.

"Soon."

His gaze locked onto mine, unyielding. "I will show you every terrible thing you've ever dreamed of—" He leaned in, his breath mingling with mine, his words a dark promise sealed between us. "—and make it real."

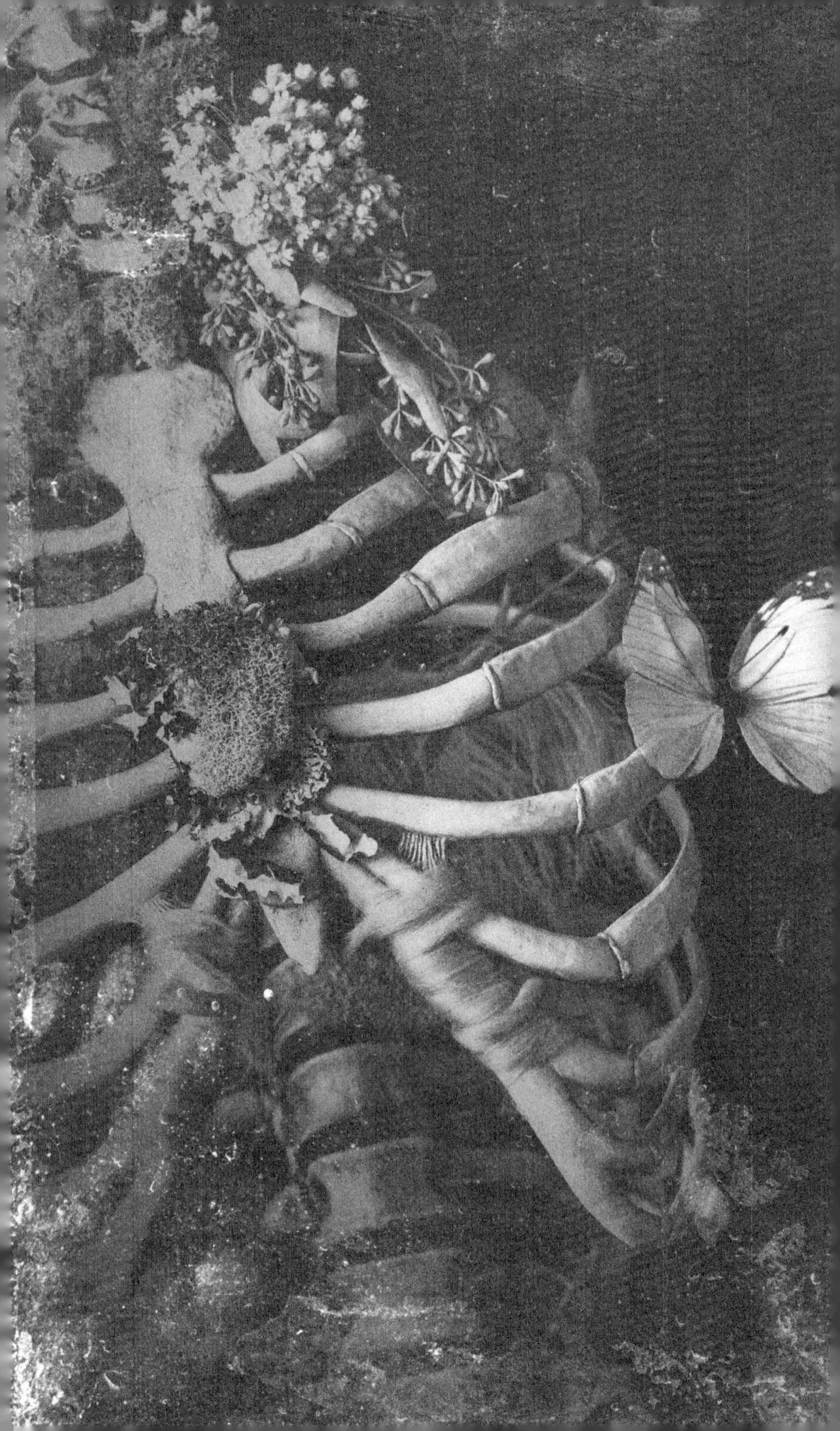

10 REMI

By late afternoon, after hours of being locked away in his office, Domino emerged without a word, grabbed two helmets from the closet, and dragged me toward the elevator. The doors closed with a quiet hiss, and as we descended rapidly, my ears popped from the sudden shift in pressure.

The underground parking garage was brightly illuminated and cavernous, the concrete walls swallowed every sound. Rows of exotic, high-performance cars gleamed beneath the fluorescent glow—machines engineered for power, speed, and control. My gaze darted between them, taking in every sharp angle and polished surface, overwhelmed by the sheer display of wealth and dominance.

A sharp whistle cut through my thoughts. I turned on my heel and found him standing next to his sleek, black motorcycle. She was a beast, all angles and aggression, exuding danger even at a standstill.

"I meant to ask you when you brought me here," I murmured, stepping closer. "What is she?"

Domino's grin flashed—quick, predatory, gone almost as soon as it appeared. "She's a beauty, isn't she? Ninja H2R."

"They're not road legal..." My words trailed off as he quirked a brow, the silent challenge hanging between us.

"And that's why she's so much fun." He tossed me a helmet, his amusement palpable. "Let me get on first, then I'll help you with your helmet."

"Why?" I frowned. Putting on a helmet wasn't difficult.

"Because your visor is blacked out. You won't see where I'm taking you. No one goes there unless I take them."

A pit formed in my stomach. Dread licked up my spine, cold and insidious.

"Remi," he said, his voice quieter now, steady and commanding. "Look at me."

I blinked up at him. The garage blurred at the edges, the world narrowing to the space between us. His fingers curled under my chin, tipping my head back, his touch searing despite its tenderness.

"Trust me."

He was a killer. A weapon forged from flesh and bone. My brain screamed at me to remember that, to understand what he was capable of. But maybe I was broken—wired wrong—because without hesitation, I whispered, "Yes."

I swung my leg over the bike, settling behind him. He took the helmet from my hands and secured it, talking to me through the communication system. His voice was smooth and unhurried, but beneath it was something coiled tight, waiting to be unleashed. The engine roared to life beneath us, vibrations rattling through my bones, setting my teeth on edge.

Then we moved. Faster than I was ready for.

The city blurred past in streaks of neon sound and darkness. Domino weaved through traffic like the laws of physics didn't apply to him, like he was playing a game only he knew the rules to. I lost track of the turns, of the passage of time. I couldn't tell which way was up, where I was, or why I was here.

It felt like I'd been plucked from obscurity and handed to the devil, and instead of running, I clung to him.

There was something intoxicating about him, the way darkness clung to his skin like a second shadow. He was a man who commanded his demons rather than feared them, leashing them only so he could set them free when he chose. I had seen him kill, had watched the way he moved—precise, unhurried, merciless. Blood-slicked golden skin haunted my dreams, seeped into my veins, and poisoned me in the most delicious way.

He had unlocked something in me. Something I wasn't sure I wanted to fight anymore.

Then suddenly, we dropped, like we'd fallen off the edge of the world. My stomach lurched, and the air turned thick, damp and cold. The engine cut off, leaving behind only the echo of our arrival. Domino pulled my helmet off, and the darkness swallowed us whole.

The massive space was ominous, the walls seemed to stretch endlessly beyond the reach of dim, flickering bulbs. The scent of damp earth and rusted metal filled my nose. Something about it felt... alive. I exhaled sharply, feeling the weight of it settle in my chest.

Domino turned to me, his face half-shadowed, unreadable. "Come."

I followed without question. The passage narrowed as we walked, the sound of our footsteps swallowed by the oppressive quiet. Eventually, the walls opened up again, and I stepped into a room that sent searing ice crawling through my veins.

A man sat bound to a chair in the center of the space, naked, his body mottled with bruises and smeared with blood. His head hung low, strands of damp hair clinging to his face, his chest rising and falling in shallow, ragged breaths. The scent of copper was thick in the air, mingling with sweat and fear.

The world tilted. I should have recoiled. Should have felt horror clawing at my throat. But all I felt was a pull—deep, insatiable, undeniable. Domino stepped forward, slow and deliberate, and the man whimpered, barely audible.

"This," he murmured, tilting his head as if admiring a piece of art. "This is what I wanted to show you."

I swallowed, my pulse hammering.

His eyes found mine, burning with something dark, something wicked. "I see you, Remi," he whispered.

And God help me—I wanted everything he had to offer. I felt like a snake shedding my skin and growing into a new one.

"There's a selection of tools on the bench over there; select what you want then come back to me, *piccolo agnello.*"

Domino circled him like a predator, his steps slow and deliberate, savoring the moment. He was patient. This wasn't about rage—not yet. It was about control.

He tipped the man's head back, his face was swollen, one eye forced shut, his lip split wide open.

I quickly grabbed a small butterfly blade from the wide selection of blood stained instruments and stood beside Domino. My fingers tingled, and the knife in my grip felt like an extension of my hand rather than an object.

"You thought you could take from me, didn't you, Calloway?" Domino's voice was smooth, dark silk stretched over steel. "Thought I'd let it slide. It was only a small indiscretion, wasn't it?"

Calloway made a choked noise, his head lolling forward. Sweat slicked his brow, strands of dirty hair sticking to his face.

"Six of my men are rotting in a cage because you paid off the police and gave them the details of my shipment." Domino crouched in front of him, gripping his jaw and forcing him to look up. His fingers dug into Calloway's cheeks, making his already battered flesh strain. "I wonder… Do you have any idea what that cost you?"

The man wheezed, a pathetic, broken sound. His body vibrated with fear, even though he refused to rise to Domino's taunting words, his lips stayed sealed shut like steel doors.

Domino chuckled, dark and quiet. "You will. No one is coming to save you. You're expendable to the Gallos…"

Then, he looked at me. The room shrank, the edges of the world narrowing until there was nothing but the weight of his gaze. The question in his eyes was silent but deafening.

Are you ready?

I wasn't sure if I had ever been more ready for

anything in my life. I stepped forward. The knife in my hand caught the dim light, the steel glinting, hungry. My heart hammered, a wild rhythm that wasn't fear but anticipation.

I had watched him kill before. Had dreamed of the way blood stained his skin, how his strength carved through flesh with precision and ease. But this was different. This was real.

This was mine.

I pressed the flat of the blade against Calloway's cheek, just beneath his swollen eye. His skin twitched. He was shaking. "Tell me," I murmured, tilting my head, watching him closely, "when you paid them off, did you think it would end here?"

Calloway swallowed thickly.

"You thought their money would protect you?" Domino added, amusement lacing his tone.

I turned the blade, the tip biting into flesh in a long, slow drag. The skin split open in a thin red line, beading with blood.

Calloway hissed through his teeth, his body jerking, but he had nowhere to go. Nowhere to run.

Domino's hand settled over mine, warm and solid. Not guiding me. Not controlling me. Just there. A tether. A silent promise. "Deeper," he murmured against my ear, his voice barely above a whisper.

Instinctively, I obeyed. The knife sank further, gliding through layers of skin, parting flesh like silk. The copper scent of blood bloomed in the air, hot and thick.

Calloway screamed.

I gasped, shuddering, the sound slithering down my spine like a caress.

Domino exhaled slowly, his grip tightening ever so

slightly over my hand. "See?" he said. "Beautiful, isn't it?"

Unable to speak, I nodded, and a bloodthirsty grin lifted my lips. I watched as blood spilled from the wound, sliding in slow rivulets down Calloway's cheek.

Something inside me disintegrated, and all the air in the room seemed to rush into my lungs at once. I wanted more.

Domino pulled back, moving around to stand behind Calloway, hands settling on the back of the chair. "You've got a choice, Calloway," he said, voice light, almost casual. "We can do this quickly. Or we can take our time."

Calloway gasped, his breaths coming in rapid, uneven bursts.

"I'll tell you whatever you want," he choked out. "Just—just stop—"

Domino sighed and shook his head. "That's not how this works."

I dragged the blade lower, tracing his jawline, down the column of his throat, close to his artery. The intoxicating way he trembled beneath the sharp blade. The way the flap of flesh folded over itself the further I cut. His blood was warm on my fingers, slick and staining, anointing me in crimson.

Domino leaned down, his mouth close to Calloway's ear. "This isn't about information. It's too late for that."

Calloway's entire body sagged. He finally understood he wasn't leaving this room.

Domino straightened and reached into his pocket, pulling out his own knife. Longer, heavier. A weapon he had wielded a hundred times before. He flipped it easily in his palm, watching me.

"Your turn," I whispered.

He smirked. Without hesitation, he drove the blade into Calloway's thigh. A raw, guttural scream tore through the room, reverberating off the walls, vibrating through my bones. I swayed on my feet, pulse thrumming.

Domino twisted the knife, slow, methodical, and Calloway thrashed, the chair rattling against the concrete floor.

The sight of it was intoxicating. The way Domino moved, lethal and precise, he wielded pain like an artist wielded a brush.

My breath was shallow, my fingers twitching, itching for more.

He pulled the blade free, blood spilling over Calloway's leg in thick rivulets, pooling beneath him, flooding out across the floor.

"Remi." He held out the blood-slicked knife to me.

An offering.

A baptism.

My hand curled around the handle, fingers tightening, the weight of the blade grounding me in the moment. Crimson shimmered like rubies beneath the low light, pooling at the tip, sliding in slow, viscous ribbons onto the concrete floor.

Domino stood beside me, still as death, a silent sentinel in the periphery of my vision. He didn't speak—he didn't have to. The approval in his gaze, the slight incline of his head, the almost imperceptible parting of his lips as he watched—*that* was enough.

I wrenched the blade back, my chest rising and falling in uneven breaths, and drove it into Calloway's gut. His flesh gave way, parting beneath the steel with a sickening wetness. His body jerked, his breath shattering into a scream, but there was no escape, no reprieve.

I pulled the knife free. A warm gush followed. I quickly sank it back in. Again and again.

The resistance of muscle and sinew, the way his body spasmed beneath each thrust—it was intoxicating. The wet slide of blood over my fingers, the way it painted my skin in chaotic strokes of red, felt like an artist's blessing.

Calloway's screams dwindled, breaking into pitiful whimpers. His head lolled forward, his breaths coming in ragged, desperate bursts. But it wasn't enough.

I wanted *more*. I gripped his jaw, forcing his face upward, making him *look at me*. His eyes, glassy and unfocused, flickered between terror and resignation. The light in them flickered, on the verge of extinguishing completely.

A slow smile curled at the edges of my lips.

I dragged the blade up his chest, carving through skin, pressing just deep enough for the wound to weep, for his nerves to flare one last time before—silence.

The last sound left him in a shaky exhale. His head rolled to the side, his body going slack. The only movement now was the slow drip of blood pooling beneath him, soaking into the floor, into my shoes, into my very soul.

Power surged through me, crackling through every nerve ending, flooding my veins with something more potent than adrenaline, more consuming than lust.

I was flying. Breathless. Weightless. I staggered back, my body thrumming, my mind blissed out in the rush—the *high*.

Domino caught me. Strong hands, firm and steady, anchored me even as I soared. I turned, chest heaving, and met his gaze. He was watching me like he had *known*. Like he had *seen* this part of me long before I'd accepted it existed.

He smiled. Not a smirk. Not a sneer.

A *smile*.

Pride.

Approval.

I swallowed hard, my fingers still trembling around the knife, and let my head drop against his shoulder. His hand came up, his knuckles brushing my cheek, smearing blood across my skin in a lover's caress.

"You feel it now, don't you?" he murmured, voice low, reverent.

I exhaled, slow and shaky. And I nodded.

The knife slipped from my fingers, clattering to the blood-slick floor. My chest heaved, lungs burning, every nerve in my body alive with something wild and untamed. Power thrummed in my veins, hotter than anything I'd ever felt. I had never been this high. Never been this weightless, this untethered from anything but the raw, aching need coursing through me.

And then there was him. My anchor. My devil in human form.

Domino stood before me, chest rising and falling in slow, measured breaths, his green eyes nearly black with hunger. His gaze devoured me, flickering from the blood smeared across my arms to the crimson dripping from my fingers.

"Look at you," he murmured, his voice thick with something feral. "Dripping in blood and fucking beautiful."

A shudder wracked through me, not from fear but from the way his voice wrapped around me like chains, pulling me deeper into him. He reached for me, dragging his fingers through the blood streaking my cheek.

His pupils blew wide as he brought them to his lips, tongue flicking out, tasting the violence still humming between us.

My breath hitched. My cock throbbed. I was shaking from undiluted need.

"Domino," I rasped, not knowing if it was a question or a plea.

He didn't give me time to figure it out. His mouth crashed into mine, crushing, devouring, his teeth scraping over my lower lip before biting down hard enough to make me whimper.

My hands fisted into his hair, yanking him closer as his grip bruised into my sides. The air between us was thick with blood, sweat, and something more potent— something dangerous. Dark and delicious.

He yanked my hoodie off, then my shirt, dragging his mouth down my throat, biting at my pulse point, sucking until I knew there'd be a mark. I barely noticed when my jeans hit the floor, only aware of the way he was stripping himself just as fast, his sweatpants falling away to reveal the thick, hard length of him, slick, precum spilling from his slit.

"Turn around," he ordered, his voice dark and commanding.

I obeyed without hesitation, my blood-drenched fingers gripping Calloway's shoulders. His skin was wet beneath my touch, the air cold against my feverish skin.

Domino pressed against me from behind, his cock sliding against the cleft of my ass. His breath was ragged at my ear. "You look so fucking good like this," he groaned. "So ready for me. So hungry for it."

A whimper slipped past my lips as his fingers sank into the globes of my ass and spread me open. He dragged his finger lower, circling my entrance, taunting me, and softening the tight ring of muscle before pushing inside. The intrusion was unlike anything I'd ever felt before—ice cold pain warred with the fiery lust roaring in my veins. I groaned as he pushed in further, stretching where no one had ever stretched me before. When the pain subsided, I arched my back and pressed my hips into him, desperate for more.

"Fuck, Remi," he growled, voice shaking with restraint. "You're so fucking tight. You're going to feel so good wrapped around my cock as I pound into you."

"Oh, fuck."

He pulled his finger out and pushed in two, stretching me further. His other hand gripped my hip so hard I knew there'd be bruises. Marked. Owned. Claimed. He twisted his fingers, brushing against something inside me that made my knees buckle as pleasure coursed through me, drowning me.

"That's it," he gritted out. "You like that, huh? You like being split open for me?"

I moaned, pushing back against his hand, fucking myself on his fingers. Chasing the pressure, the stretch, the way he was unraveling me piece by piece.

He pulled his fingers out abruptly, and before I could whine at the loss, I felt the weight of his cock pressing against me. His hand ran down my back, making me shudder. The sound of his hand working up and down his shaft echoing in the room, the blunt head of his cock nudging against my loosened hole on every upward stroke.

"Say it," he demanded. "Tell me you want it."

I swallowed, my voice wrecked with nerves and anticipation. "I want it."

"Louder."

"I want it, Domino. Fuck me. *Please.*"

A low growl vibrated against my back. "Good fucking boy."

Praise swelled in me, goosebumps prickled across my skin as waves of heat crested in my chest. Then he was slamming inside me, burying himself to the hilt in one brutal thrust. A cry tore from my throat, my body clenching around him as pleasure and pain blurred into one. He didn't give me time to adjust—he pulled back and slammed into me again, and again, each thrust rough, merciless, a punishment and a reward all at once.

The more it hurt, the higher I floated.

"Fuck," he groaned, his fingers digging into my hips, nails cutting into my skin. "You're taking my cock so fucking well. Look at you. So tight, so perfect for me."

I gasped, arching into him, my whole body trembling as he fucked me hard enough to make the chair creak beneath me.

"You love this, don't you?" His voice was a growl in my ear, filthy and possessive. "You love being used like this. My perfect little killer, soaking up every second of it."

"Yes," I choked out, fingers slipping on slick skin. My grip tightened so hard that my knuckles ached.

He slammed into me harder, his breath ragged. "Mine," he snarled. "Every fucking inch of you. Mine."

The pleasure built fast, curling deep in my stomach, turning into something blinding. I was drowning in it, in him, in the way his cock was hitting every spot inside me that had me unraveling.

"Touch yourself," he ordered, voice rough, desperate.

I obeyed, slipping my hand between my legs, stroking myself in time with his thrusts. The sensation was too much, overwhelming, pleasure bleeding into pain, and it sent me spiraling over the edge.

One more pump and I came with a wrecked cry, my body locking up as I clenched around him. Domino cursed, his rhythm stuttering before he slammed into me a final time, coming deep inside me, filling me with his cum and marking my insides like he did my skin.

His breath was hot against my skin. "Fuck, *piccolo agnello.* You love the bite of pain, don't you?"

I moaned as he licked and sucked at my bloody sweat slicked skin. Marking me where anyone could see with his mouth and his teeth. "Yes," I hissed.

"Your body is my favorite playground." His hand ran across my trembling skin, down my chest to my abs. Fingertips teasing along my softening length before they wrapped around my cum drenched hand. He brought it up to his lips and sucked my fingers clean, the vibrations of his moan traveling through every fiber of my being.

We stayed like that for a long moment—his arms locked around me, his chest flush against my back. Tangled and trembling, we were wrapped in the heat of sweat and blood, bound by something dark, something unbreakable.

It felt a lot like love, but I knew that was an illusion. This was something infinitely more powerful. It was primal, dangerous. It didn't just consume—it possessed.

And on my tongue, it tasted like obsession.

Once we'd got our breathing back under control, he turned my face toward him, his lips brushing over mine in a slow, filthy kiss.

"Perfect," he whispered. "You're fucking perfect."

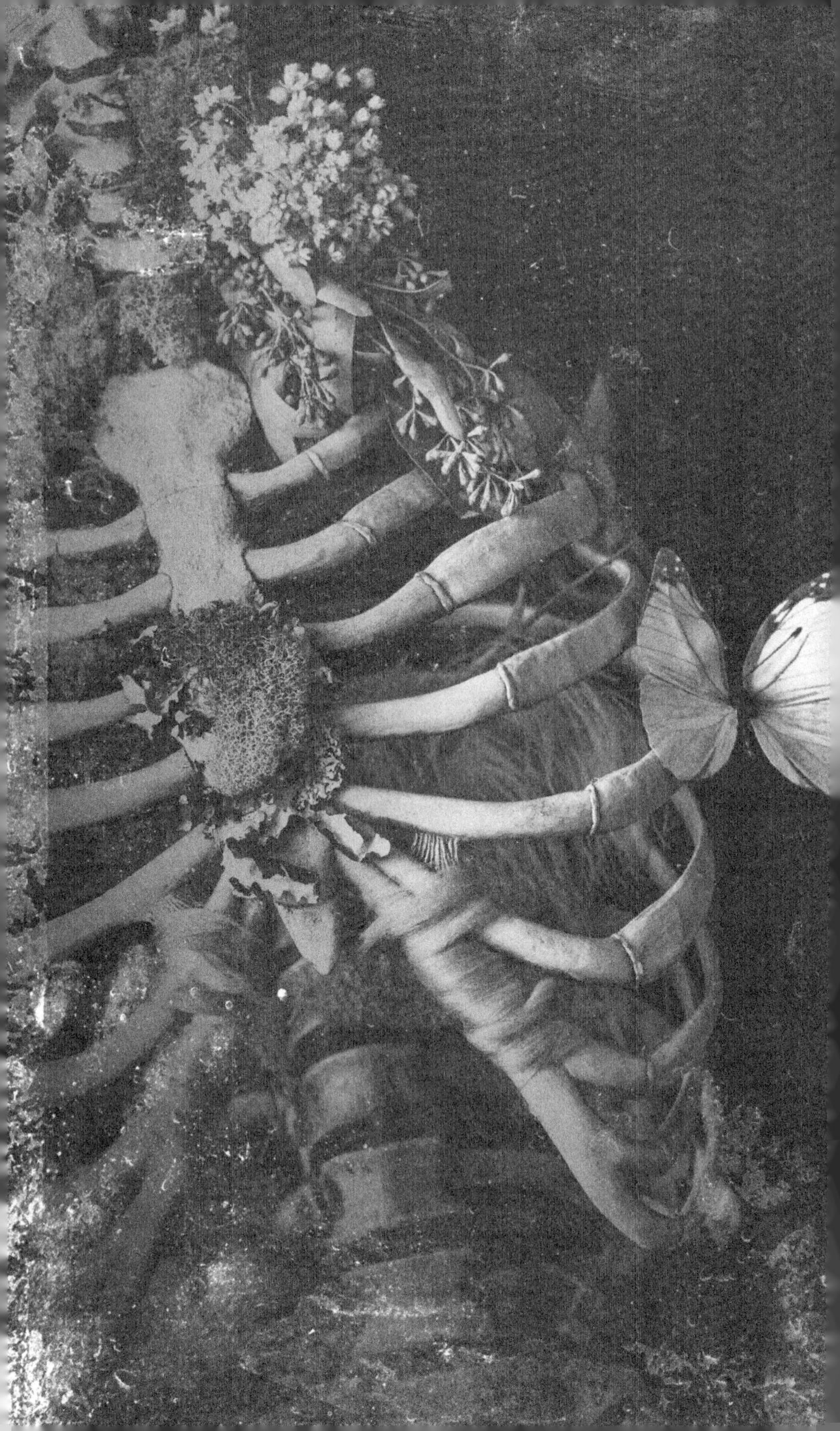

11 REMI

"*You have reached—*" Brielle's voicemail clicked in instantly.

I hung up and hurled my phone across the table, watching as it skidded across the laminate surface. My pulse pounded against my skull, frustration clawing at my ribs like an animal desperate to be freed. Thank fuck Denny's was quiet this time of day, or I'd have heads turning. Even tucked away in this shadowed corner, people still watched—eyes lingering too long, curiosity pricking at the edges of their interest.

"That bitch."

My jaw clenched as I ground my molars together, muscles in my neck twitching with restraint. My fingers tapped a restless rhythm against the table, my mind circling the same maddening thought. Three weeks in Marlow Heights, and I still hadn't seen my mom.

The first time I called, Brielle claimed they were short-staffed and said I couldn't visit. Then it was, *"She's taken a turn for the worse,"* and I was met with silence when I asked what that meant. Now, even calls from my new number were funneled straight to voicemail.

Something wasn't right.

"Hey, kid."

I lifted my gaze, narrowing my eyes as Arti slid into the booth across from me, setting down two mugs of coffee. The scent of burnt beans curled into the air between us.

"Uh, sure."

Arti pushed one toward me before wrapping his hands around his own, a sheepish expression tugging at his weathered face.

"I'm sorry you haven't been able to see your mom."

The mention of her name sent my pulse skittering. A million questions crowded the tip of my tongue, fighting for dominance.

She and I had never had the perfect relationship. For most of my life, she was absent, barely a shadow in my periphery. Then the first stroke hit, and the roles reversed—suddenly, I was the caregiver, the one making sure she ate, took her meds, and stayed alive. I tried. *Fuck*, I tried. But the last stroke had gutted what little strength she had left, and I was forced to let go. Forced to trust Brielle. That trust, even as thin as it was, was rapidly unraveling.

"Is she okay?" I forced out, my throat tight.

Arti hesitated. "She's stable, but... things don't look good."

The words landed like a lead weight in my chest. I didn't need him to elaborate. Her prognosis had been bleak from the start. But now, she was slipping faster than expected, and I wasn't even allowed to see her.

"What happened?" My voice iced over, my gaze locking onto his like a blade pressing to a throat.

Arti flinched. His grip on his mug tightened, his knuckles paling. "These things happen sometimes…." He shook his head, lips pressing together like he was holding something back. "Just—she doesn't have long, kid. I hadn't heard from you in a few days, so I thought I'd check in. Doll hadn't seen you either, but as luck would have it, you were here."

"So it seems."

He nodded, glancing down at his coffee like it held answers. "Brielle and Brock are heading out of town for a few days. A conference or something. As acting manager of the home, I can get you in to see your mom if—"

"That's great." I cut him off. I didn't need to hear anything else. Opportunity had knocked, and I was already reaching for the door handle.

Something wasn't adding up. The sick feeling in my gut had only grown with each dodged call, each excuse Brielle spat out. If I could get inside Hollow Pines, check on Mom, see for myself what the fuck was going on— maybe I could finally get some answers.

A slow crawl of unease crept across my skin, but I shoved it down.

Arti drained the rest of his coffee and stood, rapping his knuckles against the table in a nervous rhythm. "I'll text you when they're gone. Will you be able to get there, or do you need—"

"I'm fine." My lips curled into something that might've been a smile if it weren't so tight.

"Good. Good." He grimaced, then left me alone in

the suffocating silence, my thoughts spiraling like vultures circling something already half-dead.

I pulled out my phone.

> **REMI**
> Are you able to give me a lift to Hollow Pines Care Home later?

> **DOMINO**
> Yes

> **DOMINO**
> Let me know when

> **REMI**
> Thanks

A slow breath pushed past my lips, tension bleeding from my shoulders, if only slightly. Domino's presence in my life had become something inevitable. A force of nature—unrelenting, consuming. I didn't question that he would come.

With nothing left to do but wait, I pulled out the MacBook he had given me for college and opened up the assignment on trauma analysis. A study of shattered bones, splintered by force.

My life was an interesting dichotomy. By day, I studied the scars left behind—learning to read the silent stories of the dead, unraveling the violence imprinted into their remains.

By night, with Domino, I let the darkness inside me breathe.

And something told me this visit to Hollow Pines would blur the lines between the two even more.

The blacked-out SUV Domino picked me up in moved like a ghost through the dirt track, its heavy tires devouring the uneven terrain with barely a jolt. The suspension worked overtime when we hit a pothole, but I hardly felt it.

Dusk bled into the sky, that strange in-between time where night hadn't fully arrived but daylight had already fled. Thick clouds churned above, restless and heavy, like they were waiting for something—like they knew something I didn't.

I exhaled, turning to Domino. "Will you stay here and wait for me?"

Possession flickered in his dark green gaze, wrapping around me like invisible chains. This wasn't my choice. I knew that. Everything Domino did was by his own design.

He tilted his head, studying me like I was something he already owned. "Only if you don't take too long." His lips curled at the edges, something dangerous lurking beneath the surface. "I don't like sharing my things."

I should have recoiled. Should have told him I wasn't a *thing*. But that part of me—the rational part—had been eroding since the moment I met him. Instead, something inside me *thrived* under his attention, twisted itself into knots at the idea of being *kept*.

I swallowed hard. "I won't be long."

As we approached the care home, Domino veered off onto a narrower track, hidden between the trees. I hadn't seen this path the night I arrived with Mom, but it provided the perfect cover. Far in the distance, I spotted small homes dotting the hilltop—staff housing, if I had to guess.

One house stood apart from the others, larger, isolated, watching the rest like an outcast refusing to acknowledge its own kind. It was bigger, grander than the others. There was no doubt in my mind it was Brielle's.

Once I'd seen Mom and rifled through Brielle's office, I'd be heading there for answers. Not just to suffocate the unease curling around my throat but to understand why Mom had spent her life avoiding the only family she had left.

She never spoke about them—ever—apart from that one time.

All I knew was that my grandparents had died five years before I was born and that around the same time, Mom cut ties with Brielle. Completely.

The whitewashed building loomed tall and sterile, swallowing what little light remained in the sky. Domino's SUV faded into the shadows, invisible from the care home, as I followed his instructions to a back entrance. It led through the gardens—a small, overgrown seating area abandoned except for the overflowing ashtray perched on a side table. Flowers spilled from cracked pots, their petals curling inward as night settled.

A cold wind stirred through my hair as I stepped up to the glass doors and tried the handle. Luckily, it was unlocked, and I slipped inside, shutting the door behind me with a quiet click.

Darkness blanketed the room. It took my eyes a long time to adjust, pulling shapes from the shadows—a sitting area, its worn-out couches and wingback chairs arranged around a dead fireplace. A flat-screen TV hung on the wall, powered down, its black screen reflecting the dim emergency lighting overhead.

The air was thick with antiseptic and something cloying, a sweetness that clung to the back of my throat, stubborn and nauseating. I moved carefully, my footsteps a whisper against the polished floors. The staff barely spared me a glance—I had learned how to make myself invisible, how to move through spaces without drawing attention.

It didn't take long until I found the staff room near the end of the hall. The patient list was tacked to the wall next to the kitchenette, displaying names and room numbers. My fingers traced down the page until I found her. Angelica Cain – Room 213, Second Floor.

A floor plan was pinned beside it, showing the entire layout of the facility—including which staff members were assigned to each section and their scheduled breaks. A quick glance told me exactly what I needed to know. The two nurses on Mom's floor were due for their break in the next five minutes.

Moving swiftly, I navigated the halls, counting my steps, keeping my breathing controlled. The building felt like a vacuum, as if sound barely carried past its walls.

Something nagged at the edges of my mind, a loose thread that I couldn't place. I replayed my conversation with Arti at Denny's, picking it apart, stitching the pieces together. Then it hit me. Arti wasn't on shift tonight. His name was listed under the staff attending the conference —alongside Brielle and Brock.

A cold prickle ghosted down my spine as questions spiraled in my mind. Why had he been at Denny's? Why had he said he was checking in on me?

The realization sent a cold spike through my chest, my pulse stuttering against my ribs. No one in this town was who they said they were. Not Brielle. Not Arti. Not Kyran. Not the staff who walked these halls with pleasant smiles and careful hands.

I didn't know who I could trust—who was lying, who had their own agenda. It suddenly felt like everyone had an ulterior motive, a hidden piece of themselves they kept just out of reach.

Everyone except Domino.

He had never pretended to be anything other than what he was—a monster. A man who thrived living in the dark. A man who ended people's lives without a trace of remorse, who kidnapped people from cemeteries and kept them in gilded cages. The irony wasn't lost on me. I had more faith in the devil I knew than the ones who hid behind masks.

A soft shuffle of footsteps echoed down the hall. I tensed on instinct at the top of the stairs and spotted an open closet door. Just as one of the night staff rounded the corner toward the stairs, I slipped inside, pressing my back against the shelves stacked with linens and spare medical supplies.

The rhythmic click of his shoes against the polished wood floors sent a pulse of static through my veins. Each step sounded slower the closer he got. Measured. I held my breath as each second stretched into another like time was bending and distorting. Eventually, the sound faded, swallowed by the next floor.

A quiet sigh slipped from my lips. I didn't waste another minute and raced down the hall to where mom's room was on the map. The door to Room 213 stood at the end of the hall, her name scrawled in blue ink on the chart hooked beside it.

Name: Angelica Cain

Age: 41
Condition: Critical

A red hashtag was stamped in the top right corner, a tiny detail that set my teeth on edge. The unease I'd been feeling since I stepped into this place curled tighter, twisting into something more suffocating. A warning light was flashing in the back of my mind, too urgent to ignore.

The handle to her room was ice beneath my fingers. I turned it slowly, the door groaning softly as I pushed it open. Mom's room was dark, swallowed in muted shadows except for the glow of the heart monitor beside her bed. A steady *beep. Beep. Beep.* Was the only sign she was still alive. I stepped inside and held my breath. My eyes darted over the room, cataloging every machine, every wire, every tube tethering her to life. That's when I saw it—the ventilator.

Thick blue tubes had replaced the oxygen mask I'd grown so used to seeing. They snaked down her throat, forcing her body to breathe, her chest rising and falling in a slow, mechanical rhythm.

My breath hitched. My stomach clenched, and bile coated the back of my tongue.

Why hadn't Brielle told me?

More importantly, why hadn't she *asked* me?

I was listed as Mom's medical proxy. No decision should have been made without my consent. But they hadn't called. Hadn't even let me see her for three weeks. Excuse after excuse, lie after lie. I clenched my fists, the heat of fury breaking through the numbing fear.

This wasn't right.

Nothing about this was right.

I stepped closer, swallowing against the tightness in my throat. She looked... smaller. Sunken. Her once-thick, dark hair had thinned even more, strands of dull gray fanning across the pillow in messy tangles. Her skin had lost its lingering warmth, turning pale beneath the sterile LED glow.

Too pale.

Too still.

A shiver crawled down my spine as I wrapped my finger around her bony hand. It felt like ice infused her veins as they protruded from her skin. I squeezed, desperate for something—for *anything*. A flicker of movement. A sign of recognition.

"Mom?" My voice barely made it past my lips.

No response.

Nothing.

The machines beeped, steady and indifferent to the storm raging inside me. I forced down the lump in my throat and blinked against the burning sting behind my eyes. I wasn't leaving here without answers. My gaze flickered to the IV bags hanging beside her bed.

Drip. Drip. Drip.

The clear solution slid down the tubing, feeding directly into her veins. Something felt *off*. I traced the tubes with my fingers, following them to the cannula taped into her elbow. My heart thudded harder as I squinted at the labels. They were *blank*.

No drug name. No dosage.

A cold prickle ghosted down my neck. I turned to the chart at the foot of her bed, flipping it open. Every single page was *empty*. Not a single note. No record of medications, vitals, or treatment.

Nothing.

I took a slow step back, ice settling into my veins. It

was like someone had erased her. Someone had made her disappear on paper—as if she didn't exist. As if she wasn't meant to wake up.

A sharp breath shuddered through me like a rusty blade. This wasn't *just neglect.* This was *deliberate.* I inhaled slowly, pressing my shaking hands into fists hard enough to feel my nails break the skin. I had to keep it together. Had to think.

Brielle had all the answers, and I was going to get them. I glanced toward the dark window, my reflection barely visible in the glass. It was like I'd never been here either, a ghost visiting another ghost.

This wasn't going to be easy. First, I needed to get into her office and see what was in Mom's files. Then, I was heading to the house on the hill—the one that stood apart, pretending it didn't belong. The shadows had a way of revealing as many secrets as they hid. I was done being kept in the dark. I pressed a kiss to my mom's forehead, whispered a hollow goodbye, and slipped out before I could drown in the weight of what I was about to do.

The halls stretched out in front of me, too long, too empty—like something was waiting at the end. But I ignored the gnawing unease in my gut and made my way downstairs, heading straight for Brielle's office.

The key was exactly where I'd hoped it would be—perched above the door frame, tucked into the wood. It was careless, the actions of someone who thought they were untouchable. That no one would ever come for them.

Brielle was wrong, I wasn't going to stop until I got to the bottom of everything.

The lock turned easily, the door giving way with a slow, whispering groan. I slipped inside, shutting it behind me in case anyone walked down the hallway. The office smelled expensive—mahogany, leather, with the faintest trace of perfume still clinging to the air. It was a room built to intimidate, to make people feel small.

A perfectly curated illusion, but beneath the polish, something was rotten. I moved fast, keeping my steps light and my hands steady. I rifled through all the drawers of her desk, but nothing stood out. It was utilities, medication shipments, and patient acceptance logs.

Where was it? Where did she keep the things she didn't want anyone to see? My gaze landed on the bookcase. Floor-to-ceiling, perfectly curated, its weight pressing against the room like a silent guardian. My fingers trailed along book spines and intricate ornaments, pushing, testing—until something *clicked*.

My breath hitched as a hidden panel slid open. The safe that hid behind it was cracked open. The latch barely caught, like someone had left in a hurry. A mistake I'd use to my advantage.

I pulled the door open, my pulse spiking as the contents spilled into view. Stacks of cash. A gun buried between hundreds of files.

I yanked one free, my fingers shaking as I flipped through the pages. There were medical records. Falsified death certificates. Dozens, if not hundreds of victims. Many of the names matched those that had been plastered across the city. Their families still searched for them.

My blood turned to ice when I pulled out another one with mom's name on it, Angelica Cain.

The crest on the folder was one I'd seen many times since I arrived in Marlow Heights. It belonged to the DeMarcos. People whispered about them in the shadows, too afraid to say it in the light of day, like the boogie man would jump out and kill them.

Fear slithered up my spine; my skin grew cold as I flipped through the pages, my eyes refusing to believe what was printed in black and white.

Mom's death certificate except—she was still breathing upstairs. The question—for how long—infected my mind like a cancer spreading out through every neuron.

The death certificate looked genuine, with the cause of death being natural causes. Signed, dated, and stamped by the coroner's office. My fingers felt numb as I traced every letter and stared at it in disbelief. The world started spinning, the edges of my vision swallowed by darkness. My stomach revolted, and I bent over, retching.

When the world came back into focus, I noticed a second document was stapled beneath it. A change had been made to her will. I didn't even know she had one. The amendment was dated two weeks after we arrived. Was this why Brielle wouldn't let me see her? The sickness that had only just abated grew stronger, the air suffocating as a web of lies revealed itself around me.

My pulse spiked, my breath coming in shallow, gasping bursts. The signature—it wasn't hers. The angles, the pressure, the slant were wrong. It was a forgery. A fucking lie.

A hollow laugh ripped from my throat, raw and jagged, as my eyes skimmed the attached addendum.

Patient has suffered a severe stroke, which has affected motor control. Signatures may not match.

Tears scolded my cheeks at the gravity of the situation. Brielle was about to take everything from us. I slumped to the floor in a heap, pages scattering onto the ground around me.

I picked up the amended will. A $100,000 trust fund —meant for *me* upon graduation—would now be rerouted to Brielle upon my mom's death.

I clenched the papers in my hands; I had to get out. I stuffed everything into my bag and staggered toward the door, my mind spinning, my body trembling.

But when I turned—he was already there. Leaning against the desk. Watching me. Waiting.

The dim glow of a lamp cast long, jagged shadows across his face, accentuating the sharp cut of his jaw and the eerie calm in his gaze.

My breath hitched. Had he been here the whole time?

"You didn't even check the room first." His voice was low, amused. Dangerous. "Anyone could've been waiting for you."

My fingers tightened around the strap of my bag, my mind scrambling. "How did you—?"

"I know you, *piccolo agnello*." He straightened, stepping forward slowly, his presence swallowing the space between us. "I knew you'd come here."

My pulse skittered. Had he… followed me? Had he been watching? The thought should have sent me running. Instead, heat curled in my stomach, confusion warring with the dark thrill crawling under my skin.

Domino reached out, brushing his knuckles against my cheek, smearing away a stray tear with his thumb. "You look so pretty when you cry."

I swallowed hard. "I—"

His fingers curled around my jaw, tilting my chin up.

His intense gaze devoured me, tracing the raw edges of my breaking composure.

"You're falling, aren't you?" he murmured, lips ghosting over my cheek.

A shudder ripped through me.

"You don't have to fight it," he whispered. "Let it happen. There's nothing you can do now."

I should have stepped back. I should have pushed him away. But I couldn't.

Because he was right.

I was falling.

And the worst part?

I wanted him to catch me so I could drown in his darkness.

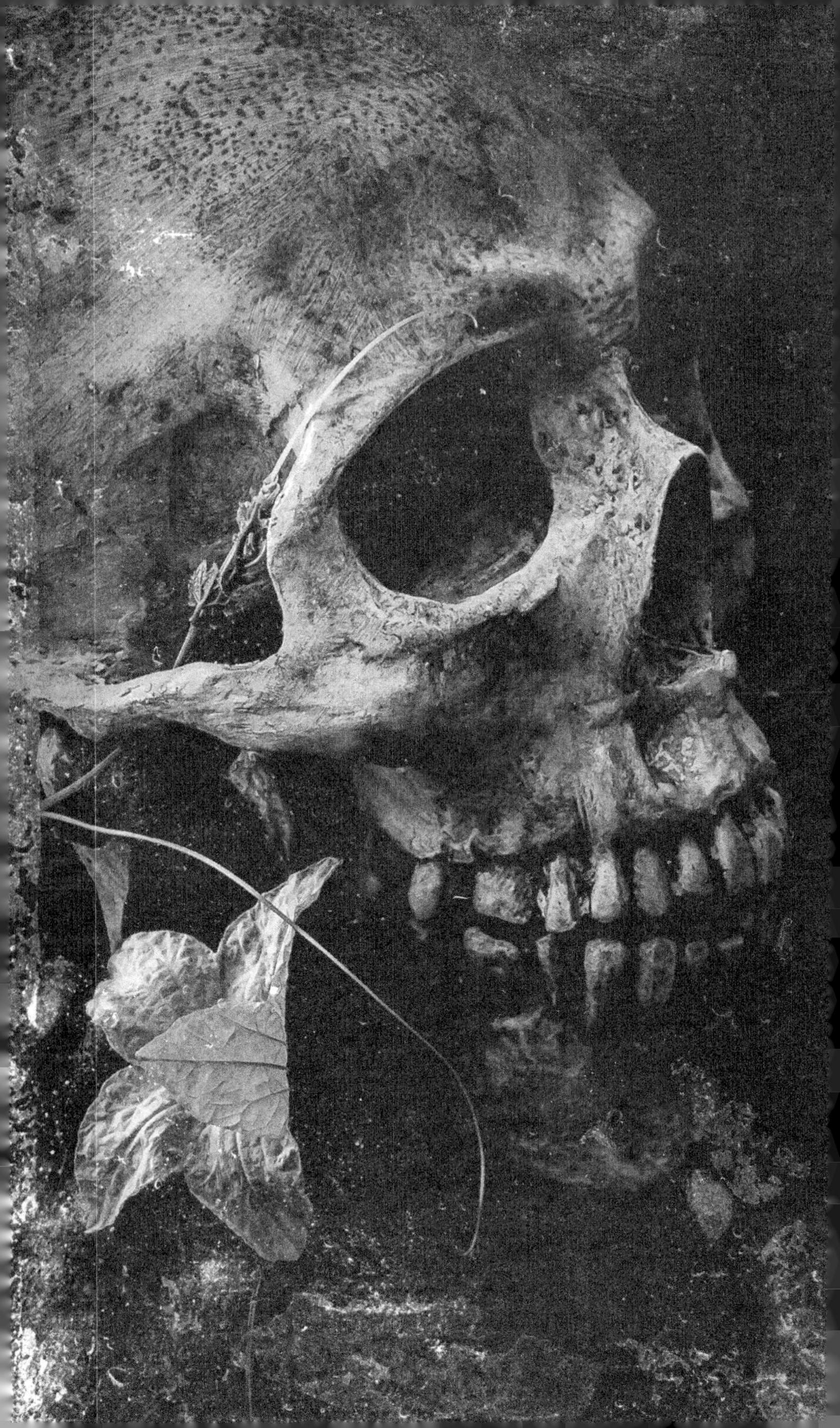

12 DOMINO

Remi's pulse fluttered beneath my touch, a fragile rhythm just beneath the surface. So easy to break. So easy to stop. I dragged my fingers down the soft column of his exposed throat, feeling his heat, the steady rise and fall of his chest. He was asleep. Defenseless. Utterly unaware of the way I devoured him with my eyes. The way I craved him—his mind, his body, his soul—until there was nothing left that didn't belong to me.

The need to consume him, to fuse myself with him completely, overrode all logical thought. I could do anything to him right now, and he wouldn't know until it was too late. I could wrap my fingers around his throat, squeeze, feel that flutter slow beneath my grip. I could carve my name into his skin, branding him so no one could ever question who owned him. I could slip between his legs, push inside him, split him open, and fuck him awake.

Would he fight me? Would he whimper? Would his body give in, instinctively opening for me before his mind could even catch up?

I wanted to find out.

I wanted to ruin him.

Because Remi was *mine*.

He stirred, thick lashes fluttering against his cheek, a soft sigh escaping his parted lips. I clenched my jaw, restraining the growl that curled in my throat. The urge to sink my teeth into his delicate flesh, to leave a mark that would never fade, was nearly unbearable.

Last night had been a fucking disaster. A revelation. A war.

He'd finally seen the truth of his aunt, of who she really was, what she was capable of. And while the reality of his mother's condition weighed on him, he had no idea how freeing it was. Once she was gone—once that final tether snapped—there would be nothing left to hold him back.

No Brielle. No guilt.

Just me and him.

If he ever thought of leaving—if the idea of a life without me so much as crossed his mind—I would remind him exactly who he belonged to.

His mind had been a mess of foreign emotions I didn't understand last night as he gathered every shred of evidence that tied Brielle to my father. He was fracturing at the seams, but when the weight of it became unbearable, he turned to me.

For some reason, my touch grounded him. My presence calmed him. It did something to me I didn't fully understand—or maybe I did. Maybe I'd always known it would be this way. He was mine after all.

When he was ready—once the last veil of his innocence was stripped away—I led him deeper into the truth. Not all of it—not yet—but enough to pull him further into my world.

Remi had been fascinated in his twisted way—obsessed—once the shock wore off. Not just with Brielle's crimes, but with what happened to the bodies. Mainly the bodies. He wanted to know how she had made them disappear, how she had hidden the truth beneath the city's feet.

It was a dangerous game. One that I played well.

Under the cover of night, I led him through the woods bordering Hollow Pines National Park, deep into the tangled labyrinth of trees. Hidden from the world was an old, abandoned cottage—one of my father's properties, left to decay in the silence of the forest.

Beneath it—beneath the dirt and rotting foundations—lay something else. A specially built bunker containing the key to their crimes, it was a graveyard hidden in plain sight. A state-of-the-art incinerator capable of reducing bodies to ash in minutes was at the center. Its official purpose? To safely dispose of soiled items from the home. Its real purpose? To erase the bodies of Brielle's and my father's victims.

There was also a torture room that he had used before his injury. Although it was abandoned, it was still haunted by the ghosts of its victims.

As we stepped into the darkness, my mind filled with visions. Brock and Brielle—begging. Screaming. Bargaining. My lips twitched as I tasted their fear. They thought they were monsters, but they were nothing but weak, spineless bottom-feeders who hid behind the shadows of men stronger than them.

Remi would soon see it too. I could feel it.

And because I knew my little lamb better than he knew himself, I had his sketchbook with me. This place was the kind of hell that set him alight. Flames of darkness flickered in his eyes as he took it all in.

He had spent hours sketching. Capturing every twisted image that bled from the depths of his mind.

It was beautiful. Savage. Primal.

A vision of death by fire, inked into the pages of his sketchbook that bled from his soul.

Even in sleep, I could feel him in my blood, in my bones, in the marrow of my fucking existence. He wasn't just mine. He was part of me. Fused with my DNA.

Soon, he would never leave my side because this wasn't just an awakening. It was a rebirth. When he finally stepped into the flames, he would emerge as a god.

The god of death.

"You're crazy, you know."

It was a statement, not a question, so I stayed silent. I watched as he slowly blinked awake, taking me in; his eyes narrowed when his brain registered my hand wrapped around his throat, but instead of pulling away, he leant into my hold. His eyes begged me for more, and my fingers flexed and tightened. His heartbeat fluttered under my fingertips, and a ghost of a smile flickered at the corners of his mouth.

"Who are you, really?"

His ice-blue eyes bored into mine, his gaze unflinching as his hand trailed up my arm, tracing the ink embedded in my skin.

"You already know the answer to that."

Remi rolled his eyes and huffed a breathy laugh. "Last night." He swallowed his Adam's apple, grazing my palm. "You knew what Brielle was doing." He tilted his head to the side as much as my grip would allow. "So tell me who you really are."

"You've seen me kill someone with my bare hands." He nodded. "A normal person wouldn't do that." I ran my nose along the side of his face, inhaling his earthy, mossy scent. When I next spoke, my lips brushed the sensitive skin of his ear. "Inside, you already know the answer."

"I do," he rasped. "But I want you to say it."

I released him from my hold and slipped out of bed. "I'm Domino DeMarco. My father, Federico DeMarco, is the Don, and Marlow Heights is ours."

Silence settled over the room as Remi processed what I told him. I walked into my closet and got dressed in an all black suit, securing my holsters and guns before slipping into my jacket. I had an important meeting with Valentin "El Fantasma" Guerra of the Los Espectros cartel to prepare for. The men needed organizing, and the weapons needed to be checked and accounted for. It was a direct trade of weapons for drugs, since our last few arms shipments had been fucked over by the Gallos I needed to recoup quickly and this was the most logical—if not risky—option.

"I'm not afraid of you."

Remi said as I headed back into the bedroom and pulled open the drawer that housed my cufflinks. I tried to get them in, but one just kept slipping and fell to the floor.

"I should be; that would be the normal response, but I'm not." He slipped out of the bed, silk sheets pooling on the floor. He picked up the cufflink and put it on for me. "I want to know how deep the rabbit hole goes."

I swallowed, and the muscles in my jaw ticked. "Get dressed." I ordered. "I have a meeting this afternoon that I need to prepare for. You can come." I wrapped my hand around his throat and tipped his head back with my thumb to stare into his eyes and see his reaction. "But you stay with me, and you keep quiet, *piccolo agnello.*"

THE RAIN HAD BEEN FALLING FOR HOURS, IT DRUMMED against the metal roof of my SUV as Ghost drove us into the abandoned train yard. Valentin had set the time and the location. I'd had men out on site scouting it, giving us another layer of defense if this deal went south, but we hadn't heard back from them. I checked my Glock, which was in a holster on my hip, and then the SIG Sauer P228 that was hidden on my back. I'd sharpened my switchblade already.

"This is for you." I handed Remi a blade of his own, a serpent wound around the handle. "Keep it somewhere easily accessible."

"We're here, boss."

Ghost looked at me through the rearview mirror. "Have we heard back from Dante and his team?"

"No."

A growl rumbled in my chest, and my senses sharpened. "Track them and update me."

Ghost handed me two earpieces. I turned them on

and gave one to Remi. "Put it in, but remember to stay silent. You are here to observe only."

"Are you sure about this?" I glared at Ghost, silencing his protest. He didn't know Remi like I did. Didn't know what lurked beneath the surface, the monster in him that stalked his mind, itching to be freed. Soon, he would. Soon, they all would.

We stepped out of the SUV together. Remi moved silently by my side as the rain continued to fall. It slithered through the cracks in the pavement, seeped into the rusted husks of abandoned freight cars, and dripped from the heavens like blood.

The air was thick—iron and oil, decay and inevitability. It smelled like death. Like home.

I adjusted the cuff of my suit, smoothing the sharp black fabric as I waited for the rest of my men to get into position. They carried over two crates of pure processed cocaine, packaged into 8-balls and half-balls per my previous discussion with Valentin. In payment, he should have five crates of weapons ranging from handguns, rifles, grenades, and C4. Today was a test to see if this partnership would be profitable on both sides.

Remi stood beside me, looking like he belonged to the night. He was wrapped in black jeans, my hoodie, his leather jacket, his breath curling into the cold like a whispered secret. Rain had plastered his black and white hair to his forehead and streaked down his sharp cheekbones.

He didn't even flinch when thunder growled across the sky. He was too still. Too quiet. Watching, calculating what was going on as men moved around us from both sides. Tension was running high; one spark and everything would implode. His ice-blue eyes hit mine, shadows running through them like he'd finally realized the world he'd stepped into.

I wanted him to see it. To feel it. To understand that this world—this violence, this bloodstained kingdom—belonged to him, the same way he belonged to me. I knew he could handle it. He was built for it. For blood and torture. For death.

The cartel members ahead of us shifted, murmuring among themselves. Their unease was clear in the flick of their eyes and the way their fingers twitched near their weapons as they waited for their leader to arrive.

I didn't blame them.

They should be afraid.

I wasn't thinking about the deal. I was thinking about Remi. How beautiful he looked standing in the downpour, his pulse a steady, rhythmic drum beneath his skin.

How I wanted to press my fingers against his throat, feel that delicate beat, squeeze just to see if he'd let me. Would he fight me? Would he submit? Or would he stare at me with that dark, endless hunger in his eyes and ask for more?

My fingers flexed as I reined in the urge to test him here, now. I could already see the way his mind was shifting, the slow unraveling of his innocence. I would be there to catch him when he finally fell and joined me in this hell because Remi was mine.

My ruin. My resurrection. My inevitable destruction.

If these men thought they were the ones in control here—if they thought for one fucking second that they were the ones pulling the strings—they were about to learn just how wrong they were.

"DeMarco, sorry to keep you waiting," a waif of a

man said smugly, heading toward me, his men parting like the Red Sea. "You know how these things go. Business is busy." He smirked, eyes raking over Remi with appreciation.

I snarled, pushing Remi behind me so he was obscured from view. "Valentin."

His deep chuckle grated across my skin, and I bared my teeth. "I didn't realize you kept pets, Domino."

"I don't."

He snorted and winked. "If you say so."

Valentin shifted, that smug half-smirk twisting his lips. He thought he was my equal. That was his first mistake. Remi stepped back, staying in my field of vision. His eyes laser-focused on Valentin, his features contorted, then smoothed out when he released a small puff of air.

"Something to say, pretty one?"

"You don't fucking talk to him."

My switchblade was in my hand before Valentin finished speaking. The sharp steel edge glinted in the headlight beams from the Los Espectros vehicles. Remi stayed eerily quiet, tilted his head to the side, assessing him through unblinking eyes.

"We have business to do, Valentin." My voice was steady, cold. "If you're seeking a willing hole, I recommend the services available at Nocturne. You'll find whatever your heart desires between those walls. A thank-you for—"

A bullet cut through the night like a whisper of death. I moved before Valentin's man hit the dirt. One deadly shot. Precise. Efficient.

The next one came faster. Then another. A barrage of gunfire tore through the air, drowning out the thunder and cries of dying men. Los Espectros were dropping like flies, bodies crashing into the ground all around us. They weren't the targets. They were collateral damage, target practice.

This was meant for me.

I dropped behind a rusted freight car, hauling Remi with me, and flicked the safety off my Glock. My mind shifted into pure calculation. No emotion. No hesitation. Only control.

Across from me, Valentin had ducked behind cover, his expression twisted into something between anger and amusement. He wasn't running. Not yet. Stupid fuck. Maybe he'd earn his name and prove he was a man truly worthy of doing business with.

A Gallo soldier moved into my periphery—gun raised, finger tightening on the trigger. Crack. Crack. Two precise pulls. The impact sent his body jerking backward, lifeless, before he hit the mud.

Another crept toward us from the other side of the car. I acted without thinking, muscle memory and training taking over. Pivot. Aim. Fire. Control.

Gunfire flared from every direction, bullets slicing through the downpour, ricocheting off the metal husks of dead trains. Another scream. Another body hitting the ground. The wet slap of meat meeting broken concrete.

"Stay here."

I grabbed Remi's emotionless face between my thumb and forefinger, slamming my lips to his in a vicious kiss. A promise. A vow that I would come back for him.

Then I threw myself into the fray. I advanced my finger, depressing the trigger with lethal precision. This wasn't chaos. This was art.

A second before I took my next shot, I saw it—the

glint of metal from the rooftop of a car on the next train over. A sniper, good but not good enough to survive. I opened my mouth to call out, but I never got the chance.

"DOMINO!" Remi bellowed my name, sharp and desperate.

It was like time slowed down, and everything happened in slow motion. A force crashed into me, shoving me to the cold, wet ground. I landed on my hands and knees, my gun skittering across the ground from the force of the impact.

A solid weight crushed me from above, and heavy panting breaths were the only thing I could hear. A deep grunt rocked the body covering me, the sound of flesh tearing. A startled gasp. Blood splattered against my arm. Warm. Fresh. It soaked through the material of my clothes, staining my skin.

"Fuck," I wheezed.

Remi hit the ground next to me, pain twisting his face, his shoulder torn open, blood pouring down his arm. The bullet meant for me had found him instead.

A faultline cracked through my skull, the edges fracturing, crumbling. Something inside me broke. Unleashed an unbridled fury.

In the time it took me to blink, Remi scrambled onto all fours, crawling for my Glock, fingers slipping in the blood-soaked mud. One of the Gallo men was on him in an instant, looming over him as he lay on his back.

My jaw clenched, muscles ticking as I reached into the holster at the small of my back for my SIG Sauer P228 and aimed.

Remi didn't think. Didn't hesitate. The trigger depressed, a fierceness I hadn't seen before solidified in his burning eyes. Crack. The man's head exploded, and then he dropped, dead before he hit the ground.

For a second, Remi just stared. His chest rose and fell too fast as adrenaline surged through his body, lighting up the receptors in his brain. Fingers tight around the gun.

Chaos continued around us, but we were somewhere else. His lips parted, and he exhaled, his muscles relaxing, embracing the euphoria zinging around his body.

The fire burning in my eyes reflected back at me when our eyes connected. We shared a moment, a silent conversion passing between us. Everything I felt was mirrored in his expression. The rage. The hunger. The need to destroy.

I sprung to my feet and turned my attention to the remaining Gallo soldiers with a brutality that had nothing to do with efficiency and everything to do with the blood they spilled of the man that belonged to me.

They would burn in hell for what they did to him. He was mine!

A shot to the stomach instead of the head. Let them suffer. A knife to the throat—slow. Deliberate. A crushed windpipe beneath my heel, ribs snapping like wet twigs. Blood was splattered across my face and dripped from my hands. Copper coated my tongue with every inhale as my monster wrought havoc on the idiots who thought they could attack me and what's mine and survive.

Valentin had vanished. The coward ran the second he realized the fight wasn't tipping in his favor. He would pay for that later; deserters paid with their lives. He lived up to his name, El Fantasma, just not the way he thought he did.

Remi stalked through the shadows behind me, lips set in a grimace, hand raised, gun ready to fire if needed. "There," he shouted, head nodding toward a guy crab crawling half under a freight cart.

There was one still breathing. That wouldn't do. I grabbed the last conscious Gallo by the collar, slamming him against the side of a freight car. The impact sent a hollow, metallic groan through the air. His head lolled forward, blood leaking from his lips. He was done. But I wasn't finished; I'd just started.

I let go, and he crumpled to the ground. I followed, knees pressing into his ribs as I drove my fist into his face. His head snapped back against the mud. Again, and his nose shattered under my knuckles. A third time. Blood gushed from his mouth, the rain making it streak and swirl like red ink.

He coughed and spit teeth at me. A hollow laugh spilled from my lips, devoid of all emotion. I grabbed him by the hair, forcing his head back and making him look into my eyes. My face would be the last thing he'd ever see.

My blade gleamed under the freight yard lights. The tip pressed into the delicate flesh just beneath his eye.

"Who sent you?" My voice was low, lethal.

The knife sank deeper. He choked, body jerking, but the name still came. "Salvatore Gallo."

A slow smile curled at my lips. I should've just ended him, but I wanted him to feel it. To suffer. I twisted the knife into the cavity behind his eye. He screamed. He thrashed, legs kicking wildly, hands clawing at my arms. I let it take longer than necessary.

I felt Remi's presence at my back, his penetrating gaze memorizing this moment, storing it in the twisted depths of his mind. His energy, his hunger for the kill, crawled across my skin like electricity.

"End him." His words were barely a breath.

We watched as his life left his body, the light fading from his only eye, the other hung from a hollow socket. Remi sat on a concrete block, eyes roaming over the bodies littered around us. Blood dripped from the fingers of his left hand as it hung loosely at his side.

I knelt at his feet, enraptured by the vision before me. Fire and brimstone had nothing on the hell contained within his flesh. I cupped his cheek, smearing mud with the blood that coated it. "You're mine, *piccolo agnello,*" I breathed. "This is what we are."

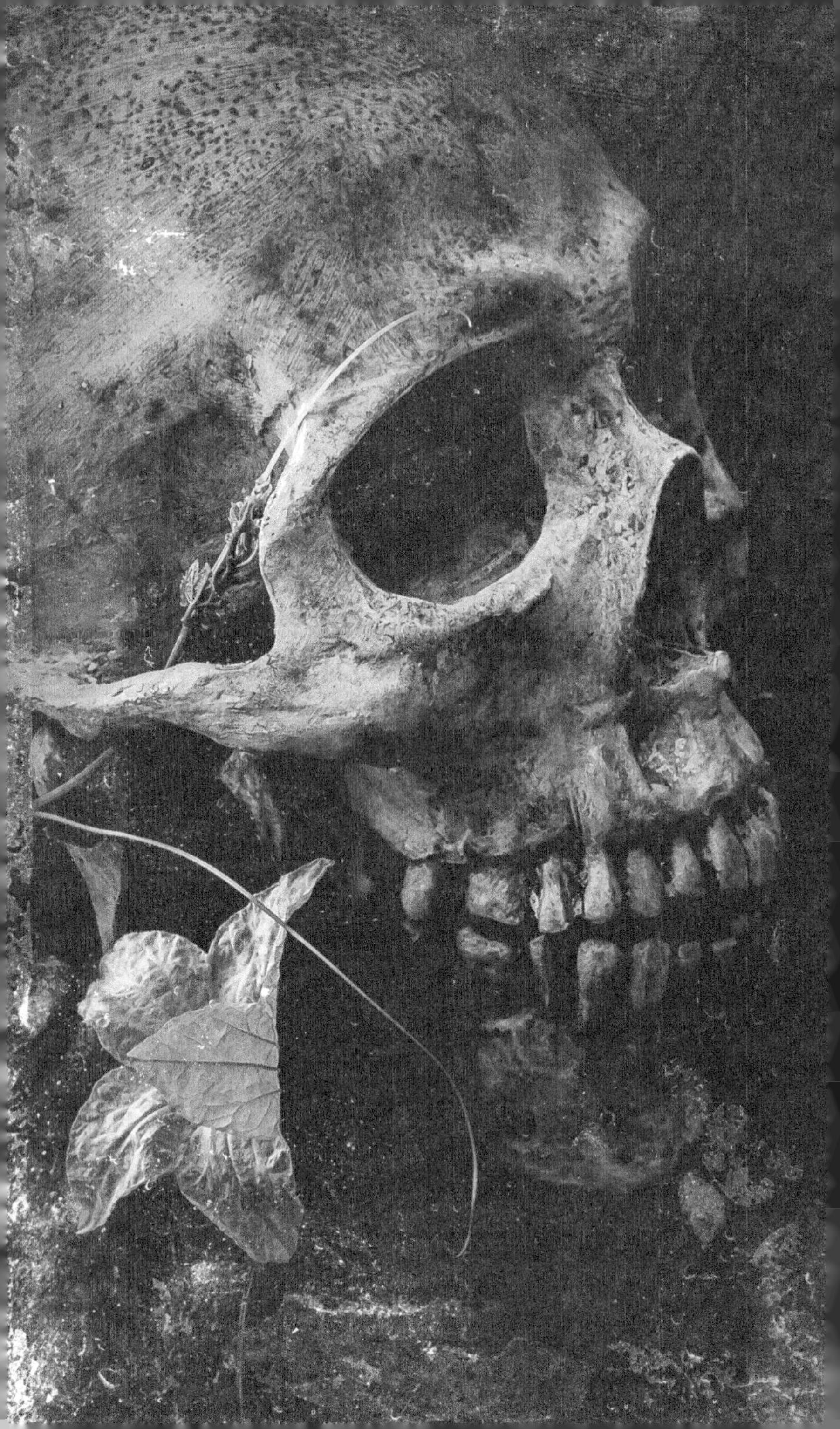

13 DOMINO

Sunlight bled through the gap in the curtains, an unwelcome intruder in the sacred dark. The city below pulsed with meaningless life, but none of it mattered. Nothing existed beyond this room, beyond the steady rise and fall of Remi's chest beside me. He was warm, soft, his breath a slow metronome against my skin.

Mine.

His arm lay draped over my stomach, unconscious instinct pulling him close. Even in sleep, he reached for me. Because he knew. His body knew. It had surrendered long before his mind had caught up.

But even now, even here, something inside him still fought. A twitch of his fingers, a crease between his brows. A caged thing testing the bars. Foolish.

I brushed ink and snow strands from his forehead,

my touch featherlight. He shivered. So fragile. So easy to break.

He thought he had a choice. He thought he could walk away, slip back into that hollow, fabricated world of lectures and expectations. That life was a mirage, an illusion I allowed him to believe in. But I knew better.

I knew him better than he knew himself.

He was never meant for normalcy.

I had memorized his movements, his schedule, the rhythm of his days. I knew the time he left, the time he returned. If he was out of my sight, it was only because I allowed it. Cameras. Shadows. A whisper in the wind. I was always there. I was everywhere.

But it didn't matter. The outside world was inconsequential. He belonged here.

With me.

He didn't need a degree. He didn't need a future outside of the one I had designed for him. I would give him everything—every pleasure, every nightmare, every whispered desire he was too afraid to name. I'd bring them to his fingertips. Watch him bathe in blood, creating art from death. I would feed every part of his psyche, set it free, raw and untamed.

All he had to do was stay.

A memory burned hot beneath my skin, igniting the hunger that never truly slept. My fingers tightened against his supple skin. Remi had grown into his darkness and unleashed it with confidence. Let it devour him like I always knew he would. The art he created was more twisted now, more exquisite.

Juno had been his finest masterpiece.

The glint in his eye as he flayed him apart, peeling back his skin like he was unwrapping a gift. How he'd pinned it back so it looked like wings as Juno screamed, suspended above the ground.

Those beautiful hands, slick with crimson, trembling with hunger as he cracked open Juno's ribcage to display the still-beating heart within, blood pouring down Juno's olive skin like an offering for the devil.

The way he had turned to me, blood-slick and radiant, eyes blown wide with hunger.

"Like what you see?" he had murmured, coy and teasing.

I had watched him inhale death like it was all he needed—like it was air—drag his tongue over blood-stained lips as he raised Juno's body. His camera captured every flicker of agony, every shattered breath. And when he set the camera down, my control snapped.

Not that I ever had any around him.

The need to fuck, claim and mark him his was incessant.

My feet devoured the distance between us in a few strides. I had seized him, my mouth claiming his in a brutal, possessive kiss. My teeth had torn into his lip, the taste of him exploding across my tongue. I had wrenched his head back, gripped his jaw between my fingers, and pried his mouth open to see the crimson pool on his tongue.

"Don't swallow." My voice had been a growl, a command, a promise.

He had obeyed. He always did.

I had forced him to his knees, the cold edge of my blade whispering against his throat. His hands had trembled as he fumbled with my belt, desperate, wrecked, his ruined lips red and glistening, parted to take me in. Ice-blue eyes never left mine.

We were lost to our desire.

When he wrapped those filthy, stained lips around my cock, I had lost myself.

Lost control.

And claimed him.

My thick cock had tunneled into his throat like a battering ram. Again. And again. And again. My free hand sank back into his hair and held his head so his nose was buried in the thick thatch of hair at the base of my shaft. I hadn't allowed him to breathe as he'd gagged and gurgled around me. Tears had streamed down his bloodstained face.

I had never seen anything more beautiful.

He was my greatest creation.

Art in motion.

All fucking *mine*.

Now, he was a part of me. Two halves of a whole, madness entwined. We sank into our depravity together.

My fingers trailed down the curve of his spine, counting each delicate vertebra as I shook the memory from my mind, not willing to miss a moment of the present. He wore my bruises, my marks, his body a canvas of possession.

They were tender beneath my touch. It would take nothing at all to push down and watch them grow and spread, like this thing crawling through my cells, growing inside me.

A slow smile curled my lips as he shifted, turning toward me, seeking me even in his sleep.

Always seeking.

I lowered my mouth to his throat, inhaling deeply, letting his scent flood my lungs. My teeth grazed his pulse, the delicate rhythm a steady, tantalizing beat against my lips. My tongue lapped the dry, salty sweat from his skin.

He was inside me, crawling through my veins, consuming me whole.

And I would drown in him, again and again.

His alarm would go off soon, shattering any semblance of peace I had found. My jaw clenched, my molars grinding together. I didn't want him to leave.

The world didn't deserve him. Didn't understand

him. Didn't know how to tame him, how to hold him together before he shattered and unleashed everything he kept hidden in the light of day.

But I did.

Only I did.

I could stop him from leaving. Break his phone. Lock the doors. Deactivate his building pass. Put him on his knees and remind him why he never wanted to leave in the first place.

But that wasn't how this worked.

He had to choose me. Had to sink deeper into my world, into me, until he forgot there had ever been an outside.

Until he couldn't breathe without me.

My fingers toyed with the silk sheet that covered the curve of his ass, teasing the fine hairs that led down to his cleft. Goosebumps rippled over his back with every pass of my fingertips. His body, even in sleep, recognized me. Knew me. Craved me.

His breathing shifted. Muscles tensed. He was waking.

My mouth watered, desperate to taste him on my tongue. It had been too long.

His lashes fluttered. Hazy ice-blue eyes, framed by thick lashes, blinked sleepily up at me. His breath hitched, caught in the back of his throat—recognition. The moment he realized how close we were. How my body was already pressing into him. Trapping him. How, even half-conscious, he clung to me with the same fervent intensity.

His tongue darted out, slicking over his swollen lips. The ice-blue of his irises disappeared beneath the bleeding black of his pupils.

"Domino," he rasped. His voice, rough from sleep, curled around my aching cock.

"Morning, *piccolo agnello*," I murmured.

I dragged my lips over his collarbone, tasting, biting, and pressed him onto his back. He stretched beneath me, shifting—but I didn't move. I never moved. Didn't give him an inch of space. There was nowhere else he needed to be than right here, under me.

His body slid against mine, warm and perfect, his hardness brushing against me as he undulated beneath me.

"Class," he breathed, his voice thick, dazed. "I have to—"

"You have to *nothing*."

I sank my teeth into his skin, hard enough to make him gasp. My hand slid lower, pressing against the deep bruises on his hips. His breath stuttered. A deep groan rumbled in his chest, his hips rolling, seeking friction, alleviating any space between us.

"You belong here."

His hands twitched like he wanted to push me away—or pull me closer—but he couldn't decide. He was balanced on a precipice, torn between what his mind told him was right and what his body begged for. A taut string ready to snap.

Because he liked the cage I formed around him.

Because he craved it.

Even if he sometimes refused to admit it.

He needed me like I needed him. Like sin needed the devil. Without one, the other wouldn't survive. Still, he fought me. Not with his body—I had claimed that a long time ago—but with words. With brittle little insistences that he could leave. That he had a life outside of me.

It was frustrating.

He drove me to the edge of insanity.

My fingers wrapped around his wrist, dragging it to my lips and pressing a slow, biting kiss to the delicate skin. His pulse stuttered beneath my mouth before I pinned him down, his wrists trapped above his head.

Then I moved over him, pressing my weight onto him, letting him feel it. Feel me. Letting him know he wasn't going anywhere.

"What time does your class start?"

He hesitated. "Ten."

"Plenty of time." My lips curved against his skin.

"Domino—"

I silenced him with my knee, sliding it between his thighs, pressing down against his hard length. He sucked in a breath. A beautiful, broken sound.

His cock throbbed against my leg, heat pulsing through the silky soft skin. His fingers curled into the sheets, his body betraying him even as his mind tried to deny me.

My lips twitched. Pathetic. Gorgeous. Mine.

My eyes devoured him—the way pale skin stretched over muscle, the faint tremor in his limbs. My bruises bloomed in purples, blacks, and yellows, claiming marks. Every inch of him invited destruction, and I had never been one to resist temptation.

I was a lit match over gasoline, and Remi was already burning. The world could go up in flames around us, and we wouldn't notice.

"Stay," I whispered, running my lips over the sharp jut of his collarbone, dragging my tongue down the center of his chest, circling the tight bud of his nipple. Tasting him. Claiming him.

"I—"

I didn't let him finish. With one swift movement, I flipped him onto his stomach like he weighed nothing. He gasped as I yanked him onto his knees, his spine curving in a perfect, submissive arch.

"Why do you always try to make this so difficult?" I murmured, fingers sliding over the ridges of his ribs.

I reached for the nightstand. His body tensed. He already knew. Anticipation buzzed across his skin like static zapping into me. The knife was cool in my hand as I pressed the flat of the blade against his spine, trailing it downward.

The smallest tremor. A sharp, shuddering inhale. I could hear his heart pounding, the rhythm erratic and wild—the sound of prey before the kill.

"You like this, don't you?" I whispered.

Remi swallowed. "You know I do."

I hummed, turning the blade, dragging the sharp edge along his ribs, just enough pressure to make him gasp. Not enough to cut too deep. Just enough to pull the blood to the surface, to tease.

But I wanted more. I wanted to break his skin. To paint his body with red, to taste him, to feed his essence back to him and watch his wrecked, broken expression when I did.

"You can't leave if I don't let you."

His breath hitched. "Ah."

I slid the knife lower, teasing the sharp tip over his stomach, pressing just beneath his navel. He shuddered in the cage of my body. The arch of his back deepening —a desperate, instinctive plea—his ass pushing back against my cock, slotting it between the firm cheeks. A strangled, pained whimper spilled from his lips.

He needed this. Needed me.

Needed me to push him to the edge of fear—of pain

—of pleasure so unbearable it blurred the lines between them.

"Tell me you're mine."

"Domino—"

I pressed harder. A shiver, a crack, the whisper of air escaping as the blade kissed his skin. A single drop of crimson welled up, sliding down his stomach, pooling at my fingers. His breath hitched. I spread my knees, grounding myself, and reached around him, closing my hand over his cock.

He was leaking. Hard and flushed, betraying himself completely.

I swiped my thumb over the swollen tip, gathered the bead of precum, and brought it to my lips. The taste of him—salty, musky, electric—exploded on my tongue. A groan rumbled through my chest, dark and primal.

Remi exhaled shakily. "I'm yours," he whispered.

A feral smile curled my lips. "Good boy."

My control over him was absolute. He'd see.

I claimed him with biting kisses, marking him with a fresh wave of bruises, the imprint of my teeth sinking into his pale skin. My tongue traced a scorching path down his spine as my blade carved delicate lines into the soft flesh of his thighs—an unspoken vow, a promise written in red.

A love song of control and submission.

His body trembled beneath me, instinct warring with surrender. I pressed my palm to the base of his neck, forcing his face into the black silk sheets. His fingers clutched them like a lifeline, as if they were the only thing tethering him to this world.

The switchblade disappeared between the sheets as I shifted, my hands sinking into the full curves of his ass, spreading him open with a slow, deliberate grip. My breath ghosted over his skin, making him shiver, and I dragged my teeth along the sensitive flesh before biting down—hard enough to leave my mark, hard enough to sting.

"D-Domino," he whimpered, voice thin with desperation.

I inhaled deeply, letting his scent drown me, corrupt me. Heat licked at my spine as I spread him wider, exposing every inch of him to my hunger. He trembled beneath my touch, his body a soft offering. So delicate. Breakable.

Adjusting my stance, I ran my thumbs along the crease of his ass and pulled his cheeks apart, enough to bury my face between them. My hot breath ghosted over the puckered skin of his entrance before I dropped my head, dragging the flat of my tongue from the base of his balls, along his taint, all the way up to his hole.

A long, low moan slipped through his trapped lips as he bit down on them, helpless against the pleasure flooding his senses.

My blood burned, a wildfire in my veins, as his taste exploded across my tongue. Each flick, each stroke sent zaps of pleasure straight to my aching cock, pulsing with its own violent heartbeat, hard enough to break through concrete.

"F-fuck... yess."

Flattening my tongue, I circled his tight ring of muscle, feeling it flutter beneath my touch. I licked and sucked at his entrance, as if I were fucking his mouth with my tongue. My lips wrapped around him, drawing out desperate little gasps as I built the pressure, pushing him closer and closer to the edge. Until he was a whimpering mess, reaching for his heavy neglected cock, heavy and dripping between his trembling legs.

"Don't touch," I growled. "That's mine."

"S-sorry," he sobbed.

Without missing a beat, I plunged back in, devouring him like his body was my last meal. His hole softened, surrendering as I stiffened my tongue and pressed inside. My grip tightened on the fleshy globes of his ass, bruising, breaking him apart for me. His taste was intoxicating. Drugging.

"I-I'm… I'm… go-gonna…"

As soon as the words left his mouth, I pulled back, blowing gently over his twitching hole, watching it clench desperately around nothing. A cruel smirk tugged at my lips. Shifting tactics, I wrapped my hand around his cock and dragged it back between his spread thighs, stroking him in slow, torturous pulls. A sinful moan spilled from his lips as a bead of precum rolled down his length.

"Are you wet for me, *piccolo agnello?*" My voice vibrated against his skin, sending shivers rippling across his abused flesh.

His only answer was a helpless whimper, his thighs shaking, his body betraying him once more.

"Who told you that you could move?" I growled. "I'm the one who gets to decide how you receive your pleasure, Remi. You'd do well to remember that I can stop this at any time. Leave you hanging off the edge of that cliff with no relief."

His movements stopped instantly, a low hollow chuckle circled my throat. I took his glands into my mouth, sucked hard and teased his slit with my tongue. A burst of precum filled my mouth, making me moan.

A high, broken keening sound split the air as I brought him to the brink again. And again.

I was unraveling him, thread by thread, carving my

name into his soul. Every gasp, every broken plea belonged to me. His body was mine to ruin, mine to worship, and mine to control.

Tears streaked his flushed cheeks, his breath coming in frantic, shallow pants. His body glistened with sweat, the bruises I'd left painted across his skin like the most exquisite art. Time had ceased to exist. There was only this—only him. Bound by my hands, by my desire.

"Pleasepleasepleaseplease," he chanted, voice slurred, hypnotized, shattered.

His limbs trembled violently, and he was barely able to hold himself up. Between deep, slow drags of his cock and fucking his hole with the length of my tongue, I unraveled him thread by thread, carving my name into his soul.

The sheets beneath him were soaked with his tears. The puddle of precum below him was obscene.

I gave his stretched hole one last deep lick before reaching for my switchblade. Flipping it open, I met his gaze—those ice-blue eyes hazy, lost, drowning in my control.

A wicked smirk curved my lips as I traced the blade down the arch of his spine, pressing just hard enough to break skin. Beads of red welled up, rolling down to where he was stretched and quivering for me.

I licked the blood from his skin, savoring the metallic tang, the intoxicating mixture of pain and surrender. My fingers tangled in his damp hair, yanking his head back as I crushed my mouth against his in a brutal, claiming kiss.

Mine.

Always.

I fed him his essence, his whimper lost between my teeth. It was messy. Raw. Obsession incarnate.

He was mine. And I made sure he knew it.

When I pulled back, he gasped, lips swollen, eyes glazed with need. He reached for me, desperate.

"Nu-uh." I gripped his jaw, forcing him to meet my gaze. "You take what I give you."

Dragging my fingers through the blood streaking his back, I painted my palm in crimson before wrapping it around my cock, slicking my length with it. My breathing turned ragged at the sight—his blood marking me. Claiming me as much as I claimed him.

It made me fucking feral.

Notching the head against his stretched hole, I let out a satisfied growl. "You exist to take me, Remi." I pressed in just enough to make him shudder. "To be filled by me. To wear me inside and out."

A moan tore from his throat, his hips rolling, his body seeking more. My hand cracked down on his ass, sharp and punishing. He jerked forward with a high-pitched cry.

"Stay. Still." My voice was steel. "You don't move unless I say. You don't breathe unless I allow it."

My hips snapped forward, impaling him in one brutal thrust. Remi's back arched, his body seizing, his nails clawing at the sheets as he wailed.

I grabbed a fistful of his hair, yanking his head back, my lips grazing his ear. "I'm going to use you like my own personal cocksleeve." I licked a slow path down his throat, feeling his pulse hammer beneath my tongue. "And if you can't behave, I'll tie you down. Bind your wrists. Your ankles. Spread you wide."

I tightened my grip on his hair, tilting his head back further, and his body bent to my will.

"You'll be at my mercy."

Remi shuddered violently, whimpering, his body limp against mine, pliant, willing.

"You like that, don't you?" Remi nodded. I dragged my teeth along his jaw before shoving two fingers into his mouth. "Suck."

He obeyed without hesitation, tongue swirling, moaning around them like he was starving for it.

"To be tied down and used over and over again. Fucked until you blacked out."

He moaned around my fingers, saliva spilling down his chin.

I pulled my fingers free, gripping his jaw once more. "Would you like to wake up, *piccolo agnello*, and feel my cum dripping out of you?"

"Oh God. Oh God," he chanted.

A dark chuckle rumbled through me as I grabbed my switchblade and pressed it to his throat.

His breath hitched. Every swallow, every hammering heartbeat trembled against the cold steel.

Tears welled in his eyes as I drove up into him, grinding so deep he keened. His body sucked me in greedily, gripping me like it never wanted to let me go.

"Would you even remember?" I pressed the blade just enough to slice the thinnest line, a bead of crimson rolling down his neck. "Would you wake up ruined, wrecked, dripping, and wonder how many times I took you?"

He trembled, his fingers clutching at my wrist as if to anchor himself.

"You would, wouldn't you?"

Every muscle in my body was coiled tight. A raw, aching need surged through my veins like lightning. My balls were heavy, tight against the base of my cock, my orgasm balanced on a razor's edge.

A sob wrenched from him, his body writhing in my grip, caught between pleasure and surrender.

I smirked.

"Pathetic."

I pulled him up until he straddled my lap, my arms banding around him, keeping him exactly where I wanted him. My cock drove up into him relentlessly, mercilessly.

"I own you," I snarled. "Every inch. Every breath. Every thought."

He whimpered, tears streaking down his flushed cheeks.

"You don't get to come until I decide. You don't get to break unless I say."

His head lolled back against my shoulder, his body limp, utterly consumed.

"P-please," he gasped.

I ignored him, shifting him higher onto his knees, my grip iron-clad as I fucked up into him, my cock dragging over his prostate with every brutal thrust. His body shook, thighs twitching, his cock dripping onto the sheets.

The sound of wet skin slapping against wet skin was a salacious echo bouncing off the walls.

"I-I can't—"

"You will." I slammed into him, punishing, relentless. My teeth sank into his skin between neck and shoulder to keep him teetering on the edge of fear.

Right where he thrived.

He moaned, head thrashing, body trembling. His breath hitched every time the blade kissed his flesh, slicing another claiming mark—another reminder of my ownership—into his skin.

"Come," I ordered.

With a broken cry he shattered, untouched, as thick ropes of cum spilled onto the sheets.

I didn't stop.

I wrung every last tremor from his body, dragging him deeper, further, until he was nothing but a ruined mess in my hands. By the time I was done, he sagged against me, his body wracked with aftershocks, sweat-drenched, marked in crimson.

He was wrecked. Spent. Mine.

My orgasm tore through me like wildfire, consuming, obliterating, dragging me under until I was nothing but instinct and need. I emptied myself inside him, holding him still, making sure he took every drop.

When I finally came back to myself, we were a tangled mess of limbs, sweat, cum, and blood.

Remi looked ruined—perfectly, exquisitely claimed.

No one would question who he belonged to. I pulled him into my lap, nosing along his throat, tasting sweat and blood and something uniquely him. His pulse pounded wildly beneath my lips.

I hummed, satisfied. "Now you can go," I murmured. "You smell like me. You wear my marks so well, baby."

Remi didn't move. Not at first. His breathing was ragged, uneven. But then, slowly, he peeled himself away from me.

I let him.

I watched as he stood on shaking legs, reaching for his jeans. He didn't even try to wipe me off. A slow smile tugged at my lips.

He wanted everyone to see what I'd done to him.

He wanted to carry me with him—inside, outside.

I owned it all.

He was mine.

"You're a psycho," he bit out through blood-red, kiss-swollen lips.

I laughed, low and cold. "No, *piccolo agnello*. I'm just thorough."

Remi scoffed and disappeared into the bathroom.

The sound of running water filled the silence as I slipped out of bed and pulled on a pair of sweatpants. Leaning against the bathroom door frame, I watched him furiously scrub his face and teeth.

His eyes met mine in the mirror and never left. Shadows swirled in their icy depths.

A challenge. A useless threat.

Because I knew the truth. Remi couldn't breathe without me. It was fine—for now—he could go. But he'd be back.

He always would be.

He grabbed his phone, gaze locked on the screen. He hesitated. Something dark flickered in his gaze as he tapped his phone against his lips and shook his head.

He knew.

Not the specifics. But he knew I was watching. That I always was.

The cameras in our apartment saw everything. Every flicker of emotion across his face. Every restless shift of his body when he thought he was alone.

The tracker in his phone ensured I never lost him. The extra surveillance Ghost installed let me hear every conversation and access his camera at will.

Just in case.

In case fuckwits like Kyran Stirling came sniffing around again. That bastard was still breathing. Lucky him. But next time—and there would be a next time—he wouldn't be so fortunate. His breaths were already numbered.

Remi stormed across the room, snatched one of the hoodies off the chair, and yanked it over his head. My hoodie. *Mine.* He could have picked any of his own, but he didn't.

He never did.

Bag slung over his shoulder, sketchbook tucked under his arm, he headed for the elevator.

My head tilted as his steps slowed. "Come back to me soon."

He hesitated.

His thumb hovered over the call button, his back tense. Then, finally, he glanced at me. Eyes Dark. Unreadable.

The elevator dinged, and the doors slid open, swallowing him whole. The last thing I saw before they snapped shut was his gaze, locked on mine.

A challenge. A plea. A silent fucking war.

I reached for my phone. For my app. The live feed flickered to life. I watched him step onto the street. Watched the way he inhaled deeply, like he was freeing himself. Like I wasn't still wrapped around his ribs, pressing against his lungs, making it impossible for him to breathe without me.

I let him have the illusion.

For now.

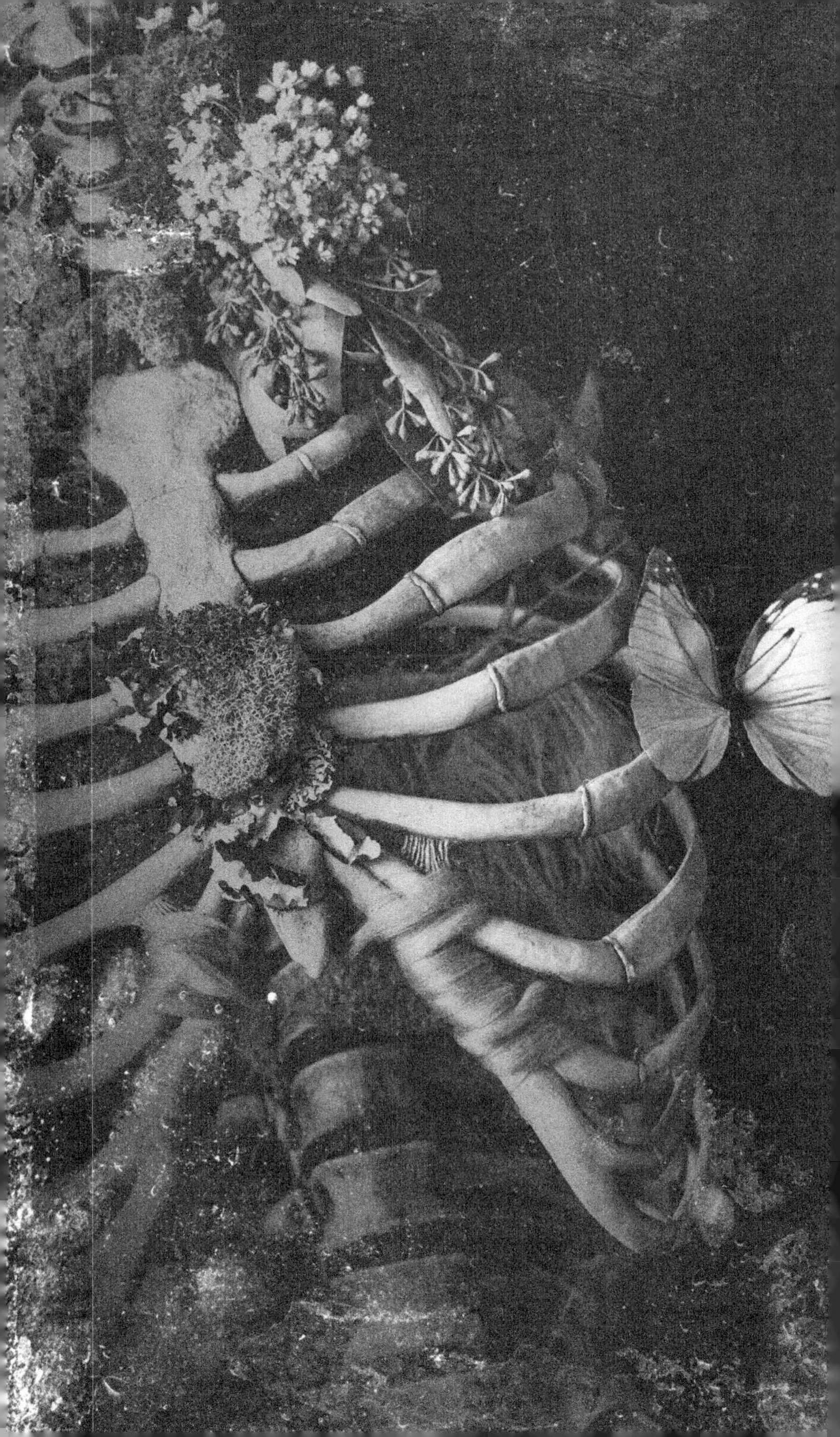

14 REMI

Something pulled me from a restless sleep—a shift in the air, a sixth sense that curled cold fingers around my throat. Sweat slicked my skin, making the silk sheets cling to me, wrapping me in the echoes of last night. My limbs were heavy, drugged with exhaustion, but I reached for him anyway, my arm stretching across the mattress, fingers brushing nothing but emptiness.

The bed was cold.

I was alone.

A dull ache pulsed beneath my ribs, slow and insidious, twisting deep inside me. My body knew before my mind did—something in me had fractured in his absence.

Shafts of sunlight cut through the darkness of Domino's room, catching the abandoned switchblade on the nightstand and glinting off the steel like a silent reminder. The sheets still smelled like him, a potent mix of smoke, leather, and something darker, something uniquely him. I turned my face into the pillow and breathed him in, inhaled until my lungs ached. Until the pressure in my chest became unbearable.

The bruises on my thighs pulsed with every breath. I ran my fingers over them, tracing the places where his hands had pressed too deep, where his blade had teased too hard. A canvas. That's what I'd become—painted in shades of him, a masterpiece of violence and possession.

I should have felt angry.

I should have felt free.

But all I felt was severed, a marionette whose strings had been cut.

The world was off-kilter without him. The gravity of his presence was gone, and I was floating, untethered, lost in the vast nothingness he'd left behind.

It should have terrified me—how much I needed him now. How much of myself had been rewritten in his image. Even before Mom's stroke, I had always been alone. Always learned to navigate the world on my own, to survive without needing anyone.

And yet, here I was, clawing at the ghost of him.

The devil himself had built me a gilded cage and called me his. Instead of fighting it, I had stepped inside and locked the door.

Inside these walls, I wasn't just Remington Cain.

I was something else.

Something darker.

Something freer.

Domino had looked inside me—past flesh, past bone, past the carefully constructed version of myself I had built for the world—and he had seen the truth.

The hunger.

The fascination with death.

The thrill of power, the beauty in destruction.

I had spent years burying it. Locking it away. Hiding it behind careful smiles and sketchbooks full of things I could never say out loud.

Domino had ripped me open. Set me free.

Now, in his absence, I felt the edges of myself fraying. The apartment was silent, but it wasn't empty.

He was everywhere.

In the shadows stretching across the walls. In the lingering scent of cigarettes and cologne. In the weight of the switchblade resting inches from my fingertips, a silent promise.

My phone sat face down on the nightstand—a landmine waiting to detonate. I hadn't checked it yet, but I knew. Even when he wasn't here, Domino always found a way to touch me.

I showered too long, scrubbing at my skin like I could wash him away, like I could burn him out of me with scalding heat. But it didn't reach deep enough. It never did.

When I caught my reflection in the mirror, it didn't look like me. Eyes shadowed. Lips swollen. Neck painted with his marks. I pressed my fingers against the bruises, half-expecting them to sting, half-hoping they would.

The pain meant I was still here. That I hadn't simply unraveled in his absence. By the time I was dressed, my hands were shaking. My thoughts were a turbulent storm.

When I was with him, his presence consumed me. I couldn't think straight. Couldn't breathe without inhaling him. But now, in the silence I had once craved, I questioned everything.

Who I was.

Who he had made me.

What I wanted.

I was Schrödinger's cat. Both dead and alive, existing in a paradox of desire and doubt.

The elevator doors softly slid open, revealing another smiling doorman. Another unfamiliar face in a perfectly pressed uniform.

"Morning, Remi. You off to Deveraux?"

"Yeah..." My voice felt wrong, thin. I forced a smile that I knew didn't reach my eyes. "Yes, Matty." According to his nametag.

He hesitated. "Mr. DeMarco said to let his—"

I lifted a hand, cutting him off. "It's fine. I'll take the bus."

Matty's expression tightened, his gaze assessing. I knew what he saw—knew exactly what questions were lurking behind his eyes.

Why do you look like that?

Why do you look like someone had torn you apart and stitched you back together?

I didn't owe him an answer.

"I'm sure," I said, nodding once. "I like the bus."

He sighed but let me go, holding the door open as I stepped onto the too-bright streets of Marlow Heights. The noise hit me like a punch to the ribs. People crashed into me, shouldering past without a glance. Car horns screamed. Voices shouted. The air was thick with exhaust and decay.

By the time I reached the bus stop, my hoodie was up, strings pulled tight, an imperfect shield against a world that had never felt more foreign. My blood simmered.

My jaw ached from clenching it too hard. My fingers

traced invisible patterns of blood and broken bones against the fabric of my jeans.

I needed to breathe. I needed a release.

Blood.

Pain.

Power.

I needed it all. In the light of day, everything I had done with Domino felt like a fever dream. A hallucination.

But I wanted it.

I needed it.

Drawing it wasn't enough anymore. Not now that I'd felt it. Not now that I had touched death with my own hands. Not now that I had learned what it was like to take control.

To own the moment.

To spill blood and bathe in it.

The hunger clawed at me from the inside, tearing me apart.

I needed to do it again.

And deep down, I knew—Domino would give me exactly what I wanted.

The city's steel and smog clung to my skin as I stepped off the bus, but the moment my feet hit the ground, the atmosphere changed. The road ahead stretched long and quiet, a tunnel of looming oaks weaving shadows and fractured light over the blacktop. The air felt different here—cleaner, quieter, like the world itself was holding its breath.

Deveraux was breathtaking. Gothic spires clawed at the sky, black limestone towering, sharp-edged and severe. Stained glass glowed with the memory of sunlight, intricate depictions of saints and monsters bleeding color onto the stone floors. The entire campus was a living relic, steeped in history, whispering secrets through every weathered archway and iron-wrought gate.

Normally, I'd lose myself in it. Skip a lecture and disappear into the sprawling grounds; let my mind wander through pencil and paper. But today—today, my skin felt too tight. The air pressed too heavily against my ribs.

Inside the classroom, the fluorescent lights burned me like a bug under a magnifying glass. I sat stiff-backed in the wooden chair, trying to pretend that I could be normal, that I could listen to a lecture on Renaissance art—an elective—without feeling Domino's grip still seared into my wrist, without my fingers twitching against my thigh, without the phantom vibration of my phone pulling me under.

I told myself I wouldn't check.

I told myself I didn't care.

I checked anyway—Nothing.

A sharp exhale passed my lips. A hollow pit expanded in my chest. My phone disappeared into my pocket, and my fingers curled into fists until my knuckles ached.

I didn't need him. I didn't.

So why did I feel like I was bleeding out in his absence?

I moved through the crowd of students like a ghost. Their voices blurred into static, their laughter rang hollow. Faces passed in waves, but I felt untethered, unseen. This place had once been a sanctuary, a world apart from everything else. Now it was foreign. It was an echo of something I barely recognized.

My hoodie was pulled tight around me, the collar abraded against my throat, hiding the evidence. The bruises, the teeth marks, the ownership burned into my skin. Imprinted into my soul. My body ached with it. And yet, I craved more.

The wind cut through me as I stepped outside, climbing the stone steps leading to the library. I sat down in a quiet corner, rubbing my wrist absentmindedly where his fingers had wrapped too tight the night before. My hand twitched toward my phone.

I wasn't going to check.

I wasn't.

A shadow fell over me before I even sensed someone was there.

Kyran.

He didn't speak right away, just dropped down beside me, his shoulder brushing mine. He exhaled slowly, like he was choosing his words carefully, like he already knew I wouldn't want to hear them.

I stiffened, my body on edge. "What?"

His gaze pinned me in place, sharp and suffocating. "You look like shit."

I huffed out a humorless laugh. "Thanks."

"I'm serious."

"So am I. You look like shit, too."

My eyes flicked over the bruises on his face, yellowing and fading but stark reminders of the day we met. We've never talked about it. I wasn't sure how much he even remembered after I had walked away from him on the steps to Nocturne—how much he recalled of Domino breaking him apart, of me watching, or what came after.

How Domino had forced me to my knees and throat fucked me as he lay broken and bleeding next to us. How I let him.

Kyran reached out, but I flinched before he could

touch me. He pulled his hand back, curling it into a fist against his thigh. "Look what's happened to you, Remi."

I tensed, but before I could move, he grabbed the collar of my hoodie and tugged. His fingers stilled against my skin. His breath hitched. "Jesus Christ," he whispered.

His eyes locked onto the deep bruises trailing down my throat, the faint line of a cut tracing my collarbone. His expression twisted—horror, disgust, something else I couldn't name. He yanked the fabric lower, revealing the imprint of Domino's teeth.

"Are those—are those fucking bite marks?"

I ripped away from him, yanking my hoodie back up and pulling the hood over my head like it could hide the truth. "It's none of your business."

Kyran's jaw clenched. He raked a hand through his hair, his movements sharp, barely contained. "You think this is normal?"

I scoffed. "You wouldn't understand."

"Wouldn't I?" His laugh was bitter, hollow. He grabbed my wrist, flipping it over, his grip gentle, a contradiction to his voice. "I know what it's like to be pulled under. To think drowning is the same thing as devotion."

My stomach twisted. "You don't know anything about us."

"You think this is love," he snapped. "But it's a fucking prison."

A cold chill ran through me. I opened my mouth to argue, to tell him he was wrong, but the words wouldn't come. Love? Love was fleeting. Love was temporary. The only thing that lasted forever was death.

Kyran exhaled sharply, shaking his head. "He's inside your head, Remi. You don't even see it, do you?"

I swallowed hard. "I'm fine."

"You're not fine," he shot back. "You're covered in bruises. You flinch when people touch you, and you can't go five minutes without checking your fucking phone."

My fingers twitched again, betraying me.

Kyran let out a harsh breath, pinching the bridge of his nose. "You don't have to live like this. You don't have to go back to him."

I laughed, but it was empty, lifeless. "Go back?" My voice was quieter now. "I never left."

Kyran's face twisted, frustration boiling over. "Do you even hear yourself?"

I looked away, my pulse hammering against my ribs. The world around me felt distant, unreal. My chest was too tight, my skin too hot.

Beneath it all, past the fear and doubt—I knew the truth. I didn't want to leave. Because in Domino's grasp, in his world of blood and pain and ownership, I had never felt more alive.

My phone buzzed, and everything else fell away. I snatched it from my pocket, heart slamming into my ribs. My vision tunneled, narrowing in on the screen. The message icon flashed. I clicked it instantly and waited for the picture message to load.

I was asleep, my arm draped over him, face buried into his skin like I couldn't get close enough. I looked peaceful. Free. The contrast between my pale skin and his tattooed olive chest was stark, but it was the darkness in his eyes that anchored me. That lit the ember inside me and let me breathe.

The world steadied. The static in my head dissipated. The suffocating wrongness of this place evaporated. The chains of reality that shackled me loosened. The pressure in my chest lifted.

Domino was my home.

Kyran's voice was still there, a dull murmur in the background, saying something—pleading, maybe—but I couldn't hear him. My pulse roared in my ears. My blood hummed with certainty.

I stood. My body knew the way before my mind could catch up.

"Remi, wait—" Kyran grabbed my arm, his grip desperate. "You don't have to do this. You don't have to go back."

I turned to him, really looked at him. Pity curled in my chest—not for myself, but for him. For thinking he could save me from something I didn't want to be saved from.

I leaned in just enough so he could see the truth in my eyes. "I was never meant to be part of this world."

His expression cracked, something breaking behind his gaze. I didn't wait for him to speak. I yanked my arm free and walked away, my steps sure, my destination inevitable.

A roar split through the air, sending shivers down my spine. The deep, guttural growl of a motorbike engine. I knew that sound like I knew his footsteps. Like I'd know him in the dark.

Domino tore down the long driveway, gravel skidding in his wake as the bike kicked out underneath him. He revved the engine, the sound a thunderclap against the stone walls of Devereaux.

A smirk curled my lips as he pulled off his helmet, eyes locking onto me instantly. A tether snapped taut between us, pulling me home. His lips twitched in response. The tip of his tongue ran along his bottom lip, and a moan built in my chest. I could still taste him. Could still feel the ghost of his touch, the imprint of his claim on my body.

My blood surged under his gaze as I stepped up to him. He pinched my chin between his fingers, tilting my head back, something unreadable flashing across his features before it was gone.

Students and teachers stopped to stare as he leaned in and claimed me in front of them all. I should have been embarrassed. But I didn't give a fuck.

These people didn't matter.

Their opinions meant nothing.

"Did any of those fuckers mess with you?" His voice was a low snarl against my lips.

I inhaled his fury and let it breathe life into me. "No," I said simply, rolling my eyes. "You've marked your territory so well they're afraid to even look at me."

Domino sneered, his gaze flicking past me, locking onto someone. "Not everyone. *He* touched you. *Again.*"

He was all steel and blood and wrath.

"It was nothing."

My voice was quiet as I turned to see Kyran, his face twisted, confused. Two guys held him back as he threw his weight against them. He looked wild, like a man possessed—like he wanted to rip me from Domino's arms.

"Hop on, *piccolo agnello.*"

I swung my leg over the bike, took the helmet he offered, and wrapped my arms around him.

Kyran broke free, screaming my name.

Domino's body vibrated with laughter. I saw the smirk on his face. He revved the engine, the sound rolling through me like a promise. As Kyran lunged forward, Domino released the throttle. The back tire spun, kicking up gravel and spraying it like shrapnel.

Each hit landed. Hard. Crimson dots bloomed on Kyran's skin as he collapsed to the ground. Then we were gone, leaving Devereaux behind in a blur.

I didn't look back.

I had made my choice.

I chose hell.

I chose my devil.

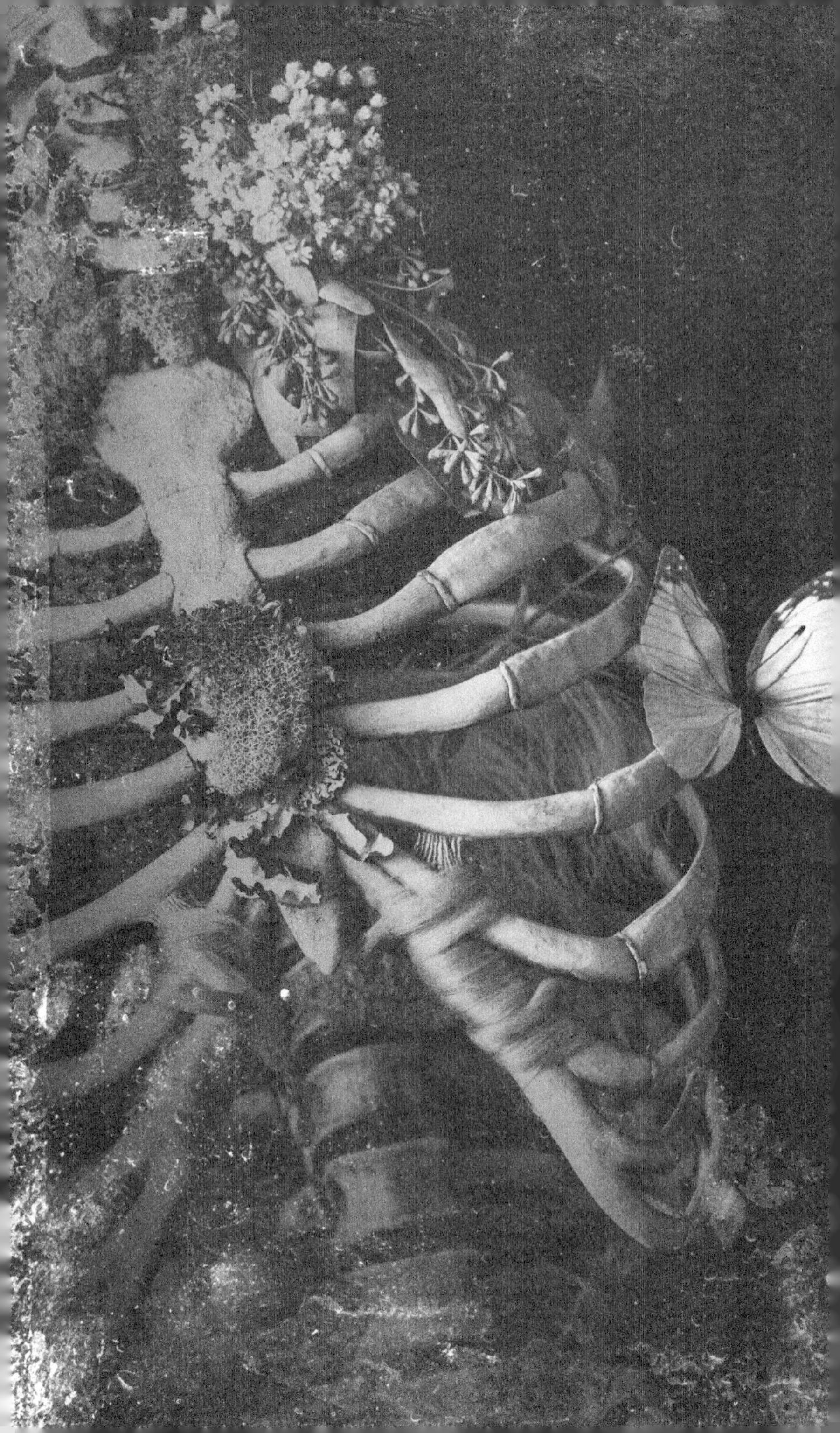

15 REMI

Domino walked into the living area of his apartment, bare-chested, water droplets glistening on his skin as they slid over his pecs and down his abs, tracing the lines of his ink.

I licked my lips hungrily. His intense gaze caught mine, a smirk lifting the corner of his mouth as he prowled toward me. He didn't slow. Didn't hesitate. He placed a heavy hand on my chest and pushed me back against the couch. His thick thighs caged me in as he sank down behind me, his nose skimming my shoulder, dragging up my neck as he inhaled deeply, a groan vibrating against my skin.

"What are you doing?" His low rasp wrapped around me like silk, like a noose tightening around my throat.

I forced myself to focus, eyes flicking to the files strewn across the floor. The ones from Brielle's office and home. They cataloged every one of her crimes, not just those tied to Federico. The tangled web of deceit she wove stretched far. Murdering patients for their inheritance. Extorting families. Blackmail. Incinerating bodies for DeMarco. Hollow Pines Care Home was built on blood money, just like everything else in Marlow Heights.

Was I a hypocrite for choosing this life with Domino? His place, cars, bike—all of it was funded the same way. But that wasn't what tethered us together. We were bonded on a deeper, darker level. We were obsession, sin, and death incarnate. We reveled in it. We needed it. We hungered for the rush of taking a life, for the power of holding it over someone's head.

His arm looped around my throat, his grip just tight enough to steal my breath, to remind me who was in control. My body reacted instantly, my cock twitching, my mind slipping into that delicious haze only he could pull me into. His presence devoured my thoughts, swallowing them whole.

"I want to make Brielle suffer before we end her," I whispered, my voice raw.

Domino hummed, his lips brushing my ear as he trailed his fingers down my cheek, forcing me to turn until our mouths barely touched, our breaths mingling.

"Psychological games?"

"Yes." My eyes fluttered shut as he exhaled, my inhale swallowing it whole. "I think we need to keep her alive as long as Mom is—to make sure she gets the care she needs."

"Mmm."

His knuckles ghosted over my jaw before his fingers hooked into the collar of my hoodie, dragging it over my head. He moved me effortlessly, pulling me onto his lap, my legs straddling his thick thighs. My cock pressed against his stomach. His green eyes burned into me—deep, dark, shimmering with flecks of gold that reflected the firelight dancing along the walls.

I was hypnotized. Drawn in.

My lips brushed his, teasing, but Domino wasn't one to be teased. He took. He devoured. He consumed. His mouth crashed into mine, his tongue invading, stealing the very air from my lungs as he deepened the kiss. Thick fingers tangled in my hair, yanking me closer, grounding me, keeping me where he wanted me.

My body vibrated with need. My skin burned where he touched. My blood turned electric in my veins.

I was his in every way.

The arrow that he would shoot.

The blade for him to wield.

The darkness he drowned in.

The sin that balanced his devil.

I rocked against him, chasing friction, my hips grinding down. His thighs spread wider, his cock thick and hard beneath me.

"Fuck, you taste like the darkest sin," he groaned, nipping my bottom lip, his grip bruising as he claimed me. "You taste like mine."

We lost ourselves in each other. Desperate touches. Biting kisses that would linger for days. Clothes abandoned, bodies pressed together, sweat slicked and fevered. I broke away, panting, my forehead resting against his as my hands clutched his shoulders.

"I want you to help me."

Domino huffed a dark laugh, his hands gripping my

waist like he might never let go. "You don't have to ask. I go wherever you go."

Once, those words would have terrified me. Now, they have settled deep in my bones. This was what we were. What we'd always been. The twisted, unshakable gravity between us. His demons recognized mine. They played together, danced together, reveling in the chaos we brought each other.

His hand wrapped around both our cocks, his grip tight, his strokes slow, teasing. My breath hitched as he ran his thumb over my slit, smearing precum down our lengths, using it to slick his touch.

"Fuck, you're so wet for me, baby."

I whimpered, my body arching, my spine bowing as he worked me over, coaxing, commanding. His mouth captured mine, swallowing my gasps, my moans, my everything. He played me like an instrument, like he'd written the melody of my body himself.

"Spit," he ordered, his voice guttural, his cock pulsing in his grip against mine.

I leaned forward, dribbling spit onto the crown of his thick length. A growl ripped through his chest as the hot liquid rolled down his shaft, slick and messy.

"Fuck," he gritted out, his muscles tensing, his grip tightening.

"I-I'm so close…"

He stroked faster, his rhythm brutal, his hand unrelenting. My mind fragmented, lost to him, to this, to the way he owned me so completely.

"Come."

My orgasm crashed into me without warning, thick ropes of cum painting his chest and abs. The sight, the feeling, the sheer intensity of it pushed him over the edge, his release spilling hot and wet between us.

I collapsed against him, my body spent, my skin tingling in the aftershocks.

His hand curled around my nape, fingers sliding into my damp hair. He turned my head, his lips brushing my ear, his breath still ragged.

"We will make her lose her mind," he murmured, dark and promising. "So when the time comes, she will beg for it to end."

We didn't go after Brielle immediately. No matter how much I wanted to see her bloodied and broken beneath me.

I wanted her to *feel* it first.

To suffer like she'd made so many others.

To feel the slow creep of paranoia sinking into her bones like venom. To see the way shadows stretched *too* long, twisting unnaturally at the edges of her vision. To suffer through the silence that pressed in thick and suffocating—not empty, but *watching*. Waiting.

I let it take root inside her, sink into her bones inch by inch.

By the time I truly started, she was already fraying at the edges. I saw it in the way she flinched at the softest sounds, how she clutched her purse with white-knuckled desperation, her breath catching when her own reflection flickered in a passing window like an unfamiliar ghost.

She was afraid, but she didn't know *why* yet. I would *give* her a reason. That was the best part.

I wanted her to unravel before I ever laid a hand on

her. I wanted her to come apart at the seams, piece by agonizing piece, until she was raw and trembling. Until she *begged* for the end.

And I wanted *him* to see me do it. I wanted Domino's approval like I needed air. He was my center. The blood in my veins. My gravity.

Her predictability made it easy. She was fragile. And fragile things *shattered*.

The first time I followed her, I kept my distance—just a shadow slipping between the cracks of her awareness. But the second time, I let her *feel* me.

A dark figure in the reflection of a store window. There and gone, just long enough for the hairs on the back of her neck to prickle. Just long enough to send her heart skittering against her ribs as she whipped around, eyes wide and searching.

That's when I melted back into the shadows.

A fleeting presence in the parking garage.

The soft *click* of a shoe on pavement behind her—too quiet to be real, too loud to ignore.

She started clutching her purse like a lifeline. Breathing in quick, shallow gasps. She *felt* me now. She just didn't know where I was.

And Domino was watching.

He liked watching me *learn* and let go of the restraints society imposed on me. He wanted me to be free to be exactly what I was always meant to be, and with him by my side, I was starting to embrace it all.

"You're enjoying this," he murmured one night, trailing his fingers along the nape of my neck.

We were parked outside a restaurant, engine off, the streetlights throwing fractured shadows over the sharp angles of his face. His gaze never left mine.

I swallowed, pulse thrumming under his touch. "I like watching her fall apart."

His smile was slow. Indulgent. *Proud.*

"Good."

It wasn't enough.

I wanted *more*.

More ways to get inside her head. More ways to make her question reality until she was drowning in uncertainty. I needed her to *know*—not just suspect, not just fear—but *know* that I had the power to destroy her in every conceivable way. That every breath she took, every trembling heartbeat, was a borrowed luxury. And that it was *me* coming for her. Me, with the hounds of hell snapping at my heels.

I could see it now.

Her downfall.

Her death.

Her destruction.

It would be *beautiful*. Painful. An endless oblivion of torment, and I would be the architect of every moment.

When I told Domino, a sinister laugh slipped past his lips before they curled in satisfaction. His dark green eyes gleamed in the dim light of the lounge, fingers tapping rhythmically against my leg as he considered me. "I have just the man for the job. Go wait in the spare room."

That's when I met Ghost—properly.

He was younger than I expected—only a few years older than me—but there was something unsettling in the amused smirk he wore, like he found all of this entertaining. Like he knew something I didn't.

I was still new to this world, still learning how deep the abyss went. Ghost had been born in it. Raised in it.

He *thrived* in the dark. And that's exactly where we worked.

The only light came from the eerie glow of his monitors, multiple screens flashing with lines of code and intercepted feeds, painting his face in shades of neon blues and greens. But I liked it. The intimacy of the darkness. The way it heightened the tension—the *chase*.

Ghost taught me how to bypass surveillance feeds. How to reroute alarms. How to crawl into Brielle's world unseen and make sure she *felt* me breathing down her neck even when I was miles away.

"Messy," he muttered one night, watching me attempt to break into her security system.

"I got through," I pointed out.

"Yeah, but not cleanly. You tripped two silent alerts last night. If she had a decent system, she'd already know you were inside." He spun lazily in his chair, cracking his knuckles. "If you're gonna learn, you better do it right."

Domino was behind me, leaning against the desk, fingers absently tracing along my shoulder. "Show him," he murmured. Ghost obeyed without hesitation.

Hours passed. I learned. Perfected. I adapted until I could move through firewalls like they were nothing more than gauzy curtains. Until I could watch her from every angle, track her every move without a single blip on her radar.

Once I had that, we moved on to her finances.

We drained her accounts. Redirected her money. Watched as she broke out in a cold sweat at her desk, her hands trembling over her keyboard as she checked and rechecked numbers that didn't add up. The hidden cameras Domino had planted everywhere gave me a front-row seat to her unraveling.

I *devoured* it.

Her fear tasted sweet.

Her perfect facade melted away, revealing the raw, brittle bones beneath.

"You don't have to be the strongest in the room," Domino murmured one night, his fingers drifting to my collarbone, our sweat-slicked skin the only thing between us. "Just the one who sees *everything*."

And I *did*.

I saw her at work, barely holding herself together in front of her clients. I saw her at home, double-checking locks that no longer mattered. I saw her in her car, gripping the wheel too tightly, jumping at shadows that weren't there.

She started sleeping with a gun on her nightstand. She thought it would *help*.

It wouldn't.

Nothing would stop me from wrecking her.

Ghost smirked at me, nudging my shoulder. "You've done well, young padawan. But there's one last thing we need to handle."

"What?" I glanced at him, my mind still tangled in thoughts of Brielle's slow descent into madness.

"You need to amend the terms of your trust fund."

"Oh." That had slipped my mind.

"*And*," Ghost continued, spinning his pen between his fingers, "I figured you might want to leak *everything* Brielle and Brock have done. Once they're no longer breathing, of course. Destroy their name completely. Make sure no one remembers them as anything but the fucking filth they are."

My heart thundered in my chest. I'd been *small-*

minded. Too focused on the immediate. But *this*—this was a reckoning that would extend beyond their deaths. This was their *legacy* going up in flames.

I rubbed my hands together, leaning toward him. "I'm in."

Ghost clapped me on the back. "That's my boy."

Something strange flickered in my chest. A tight pull at the edges of my ribs. Ghost didn't question me. Didn't hesitate at my silence and didn't push when I got lost in the haze of my mind, drowning in visions of blood and retribution.

I understood the darkness. Craved it now that my eyes had been opened, but he welcomed it.

Domino had been called away by his father, leaving Ghost and me alone—something he wasn't fond of. He didn't like me being out of his line of sight lately. His possessiveness had grown to be all-consuming after he had claimed me in front of everyone at Deveraux. That story had spread like wildfire through Marlow Heights.

Ghost worked in silence for hours, fingers flying over the keyboard, shifting between encrypted records and security systems like he was playing. But the moment his smirk faded into a frown, the hairs on the back of my neck prickled.

"Remi," he said, voice unreadable. "Look at this."

I turned to the screen, rows of falsified documents flickering beneath the glow of the monitor. Blackmail payments. Redacted reports. None of it surprising—I'd found similar files in Brielle's office.

But then I saw it.

The name.

Domino's *mother.*

A strange, sharp pulse of something dark curled inside me.

"What do you know about his mother?" Ghost asked.

Not much. Domino was a vault when it came to Catalina. Getting him to talk about her was like pulling teeth. "Only that she died when he was a kid. He said the Gallos killed her."

Ghost exhaled, something unreadable flashing through his eyes before he masked it. "That's the story Federico told him, that the Gallos cut the brakes on her car. That she died on impact. Domino only survived because he was strapped into a car seat."

A storm churned inside me.

A *lie*.

Everything *Federico* told him. Everything he *believed*.

If these documents were correct... Brielle had something to do with her death.

My vision sharpened, thoughts tightening into something sharp and focused. *Not rage*.

Calculation.

"Domino's going to see this," Ghost murmured, studying me. "What do you think he'll do?"

I didn't answer.

Because I already *knew*.

When the lid to Pandora's Box was opened, hell would be unleashed on Marlow Heights. And every single person involved in Catalina's murder and cover-up would burn.

"Print everything you've got," I said, tension knotting in my gut. "I'll tell him."

Ghost's gaze burned into me, assessing, dissecting. "Let me know, because I do not want to be collateral damage."

I snorted. Everyone feared Domino—even those closest to him. But something dark and twisted pulsed inside me. I was different. I didn't fear him. The dread in Ghost's eyes only made me smirk.

"You're fucking crazy," he muttered as more files flickered onto the screen.

A hollow laugh rumbled in my chest. "I'll light the match and stand by him when he burns it all to the ground."

BRIELLE WAS BREAKING. CRUMBLING UNDER THE WEIGHT of her fear. And when I finally revealed myself, I saw it —the hollow look in her eyes, the paranoia twisting her features.

The deserted parking garage set the perfect stage. Rain pounded the pavement, broken streetlights flickered, casting eerie glows between the abandoned cars. The wind howled, cutting through the concrete pillars.

I perched on the hood of her car, watching. Listening.

Her heels clicked, sharp against the concrete. Every few steps, she glanced over her shoulder. The sound of glass bottles rolling somewhere in the dark made her flinch.

Tension hummed between us.

My fingers traced over the broken seams of my jeans, counting the beats of my heart as she neared. A slow, sickening countdown.

I raised my head as she approached. A sinister smile curved my lips, my tongue over my top teeth when she saw me.

A flicker of terror. Her breath hitched. Her body

locked up for half a second before she masked it, rolling back her shoulders, narrowing her eyes.

"What the fuck do you want, Remi?"

I huffed a laugh, rolling my eyes.

Her fingers twitched at her sides, debating between her phone and the gun she thought would save her. But she was all front—nothing of substance existed beneath her skin. I knew that now.

"I wouldn't do that if I were you."

Her sneer was ugly. "You think you're in control?" she spat.

I examined my painted black nails, feigning boredom.

"You think he loves you? You're a pet, Remi. A fucking trophy. And when he's bored, he'll throw you away like the rest."

I tilted my head and smiled. "Takes one to know one. Where's Federico, mm?"

Her breath stuttered. Eyes widened. But before she could run—before she could even scream—Domino was behind her. The rag covered her face in an instant. A sharp, sickly-sweet scent filled the air.

It pulled a panicked gasp from her throat, and recognition flashed in her eyes. She struggled, but she was already weak, already broken down by sleepless nights and fear that had been eating her alive from the inside.

She went limp in his arms. I grabbed her legs, and together, we folded her into the trunk of the SUV.

And then—we took her.

Brielle woke up surrounded by suffocating, never-ending darkness. Her wrists were crudely bound behind her back, shoes missing, clothes torn and damp from the light rain that still fell.

The silence stretched, and there was no sound beyond her ragged, uneven breathing. The air was thick and damp, the scent of pine and earth heavy around us.

She was alone.

Or so she thought.

I let her panic bloom, let her mind spiral. I savored the way her breaths turned sharp and frantic, the way her fingers flexed against the restraints.

Let her feel true isolation before I stepped into the dim moonlight.

"Do you understand now?" I asked softly.

She jerked at the sound of my voice, trying to scramble back, but Domino caught her ankle, dragging her back to us with slow, methodical ease.

"This isn't real," she whispered, voice breaking.

I crouched in front of her, tilting my head. "That's the problem with people like you. You think your perception defines reality."

Her lips trembled. Mascara painted black rivers down her pale cheeks.

Domino sighed, disappointed. Bored. His knife flashed, pressing just under her collarbone—enough to draw a slow, crimson bead of blood.

"You're going to feel us everywhere," I murmured.

Her pulse thundered beneath the steel. I licked my lips. Images of her body distorted and broken like a sculpture, blood dripping from the wound on her neck as she hung suspended, a pool spreading across the ground beneath her, filled my mind.

"You're going to hear our footsteps even when we're not there," Domino continued. The blade traced up, teasing the edge of her jaw. "You're going to wake up in the middle of the night and wonder if we're watching."

I leaned in, my breath ghosting over her ear. "Because we are."

She let out a broken, choked sob.

I smiled, baring my teeth. "I know..."

Her confusion was fleeting—fear swallowed her whole, freezing her in place. Dirt smeared across her skin. Scratches bled red from where sticks and stones had cut into her flesh.

I pulled out my sketchbook. Pencil in hand. The need to draw what I saw flowed through my veins.

Domino watched, intrigued, as I began to draw. Quick, deliberate strokes, lines forming the outline of Brielle as she was now—fragile, terrified, crumbling.

She didn't even notice at first.

Her breath hitched when she saw. "W-what are you doing?" she stammered, her voice shaking.

I didn't look up. "Capturing something beautiful."

Her whole body shook.

"You're most beautiful when you don't know death is watching," I said softly.

My pencil glided over the page, sketching the curve of her trembling fingers, the way her lips parted in fear.

"I could kill you right now."

She squeezed her eyes shut, tears slipping down her cheeks.

"But I won't," I murmured. "Not yet. Not as long as she's alive."

Domino wasn't watching her anymore. He was watching me.

His smile was slow. Dark. Proud.

I snapped my sketchbook shut. "We should go."

Domino tilted his head. "What about her?"

I turned, walking away. Then, just before I disappeared into the shadows, I glanced back at Brielle—

sprawled on the ground, dirt streaking her skin, eyes wide with terror.

"She'll find her way out. *Eventually.*"

And when she did—she'd never feel safe again.

Domino chuckled, stepping toward her as she scrambled backward on her hands and feet. "Are you sure?"

"Brielle," I called, my voice carrying through the night. She halted mid-shuffle, her spine stiffening, dread curling around her like a second skin.

She clambered to her feet, turning slowly, movements jerky, breath coming in shallow, ragged gasps. The moonlight painted her in shades of fear—wide, unblinking eyes, and parted lips quivering on the cusp of a scream.

"I know everything."

The weight of those words shattered her like a killing blow. She stumbled, her knees buckled, fingers twitching at her sides. Fight or flight. But she didn't move. She couldn't.

I stepped closer, basking in her unraveling. "Soon… everyone will know. The truth."

The color drained from her face, leaving her ghost-pale, her expression torn between disbelief and sheer, unrelenting terror.

Domino moved behind me, swift and silent as a shadow, before shoving me to the ground. My hands hit the damp earth, a breathless gasp forced from my lungs.

A hollow, depraved laugh rumbled from Domino's chest, a sound that sent a shudder racing down my spine. Rough fingers wrenched my jeans down, the air sharp against my exposed skin. His presence loomed behind me, his body a furnace, heat radiating from him in waves.

"I need you," he growled, voice feral, raw with hunger.

He wrenched one of my arms behind my back. The slick whisper of steel cut through the night—the snick of his switchblade being flicked open. A sharp sting blossomed against my wrist, followed by the slow, searing slide of blood down my skin. The scent of metal mingled with the damp earth, heady and intoxicating. Cold fingers spread me apart, holding me open for him. Scorching drops of blood dripped down between my cheeks, the blunt head of his cock notched against my entrance.

I moaned, a sound that barely belonged to me, guttural and wrecked. My body tensed as he pushed against me. Without prep or further warning, he thrust into me brutally.

A cry tore from my throat, a perfect collision of pain and pleasure. My fingers dug into the dirt as he drove deeper, forcing me to take all of him. Each thrust was brutal, precise—a claim, a brand, an unspoken vow carved into my very being.

Mine.

Brielle turned at the sound of our ragged, animalistic breaths, her face twisting in horror. Her eyes locked on mine—on the way my lips parted in bliss, the way my body yielded to every punishing thrust.

She made a strangled noise in the back of her throat, horror morphing into something close to revulsion.

That's when Domino wrapped a bloodied arm around my chest, yanking me upright, my back flush against his chest. The blade in his hand dragged lazily up my throat, smearing my blood across my skin.

Brielle's scream shattered the night.

She ran.

Domino's laughter followed her, dark and predatory, howling through the trees like the devil himself was chasing her.

I shattered, dissolving into pure sensation—his touch, his heat, the way he owned me so completely I could no longer tell where he ended and I began.

I was his.

I had always been his.

And if this was hell, I would burn for him forever.

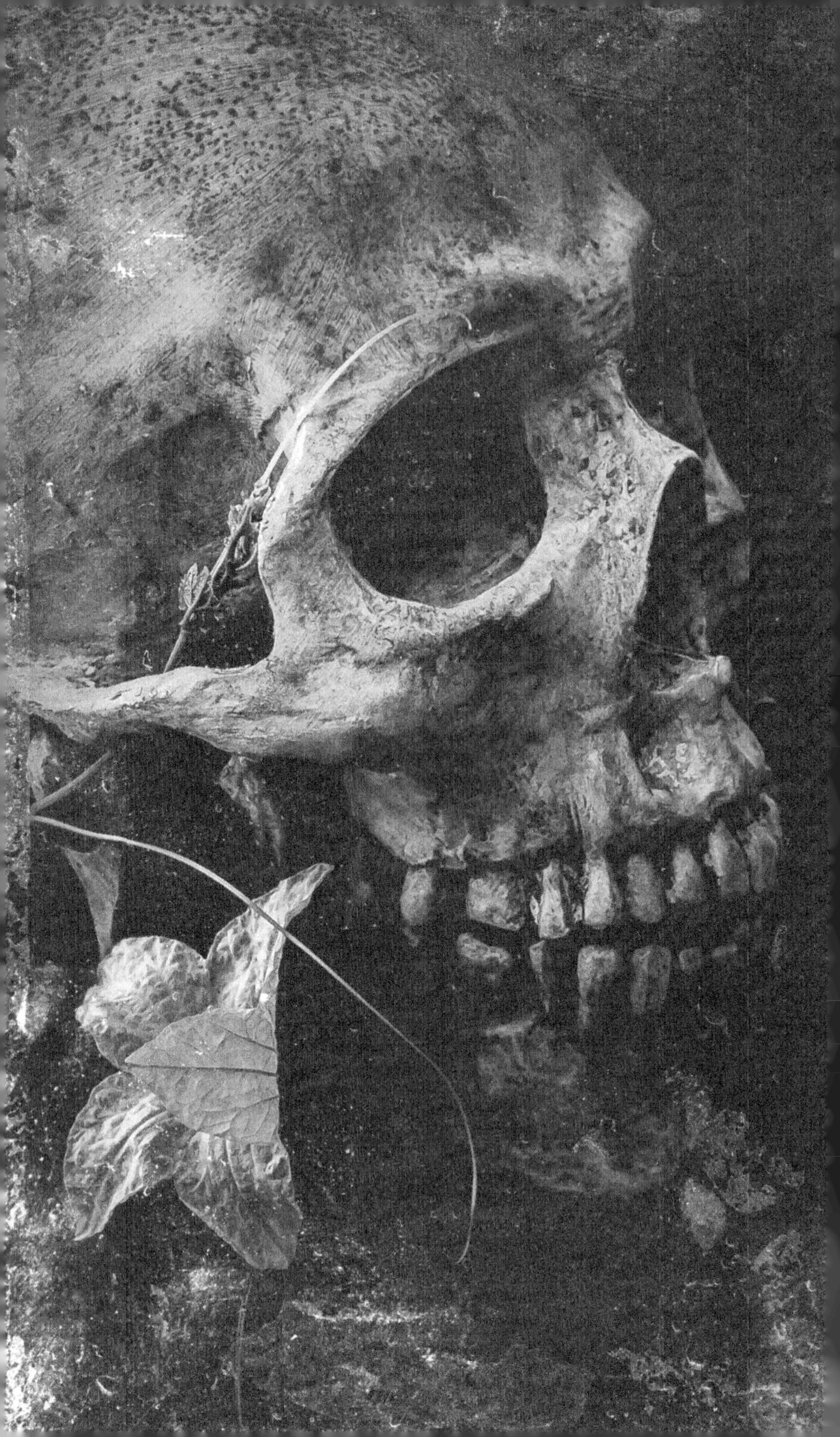

16 DOMINO

The room was steeped in darkness, but I could still see him. The soft glow from the city lights filtered through the curtains, painting his skin in pale, silver-blue shadows. He was sprawled across the bed, one arm tucked beneath his head, the other draped across his stomach.

He was dreaming. His lips parted slightly, his breath deep and slow. Restless, even in sleep. Whatever played out behind his closed lids had him shifting faintly, his fingers tightening into a fist before loosening again. I wanted to know what he was seeing, to pry his skull open and crawl inside.

Was it me? Did I haunt him the way he haunted me? Or was he reliving our evening in the woods with Brielle?

I reached out, my knuckles just barely brushing his

cheek. He didn't stir. I liked him like this—soft, unaware, completely mine. The weight of the world couldn't touch him here. No one could.

His lips parted on a quiet exhale, and my eyes traced the curve of his mouth. So delicate. So fucking deceptive. No one would guess what he was capable of—how sharp he could be, how beautifully cruel. But I knew. I had molded him with my own hands, guided him deeper into the darkness, and wrapped him in it like a second skin.

And he let me.

Remi stirred before his eyes opened. I watched the shift; his breathing changed first, the slow stretch of his limbs beneath the sheets, the way his fingers flexed like they were still searching for something even in sleep. Then his gaze landed on me.

I sat beside him, my elbow resting on my knee, watching. Waiting.

"Creep," he muttered, voice thick with sleep.

A smirk curled at the corner of my mouth. "Good morning to you, too."

He stretched, his back arching slightly, sheets slipping lower, revealing more of his pale skin that I had mapped with my teeth and hands. My fingers itched to touch, to claim, but I had something else for him first.

I reached into my pocket, feeling the smooth bone between my fingers before pulling it free. The small pendant gleamed faintly in the low light. A sliver of something primal, something *mine*, stirred inside me.

"Sit up," I ordered.

He blinked at me, still groggy, but when I dangled the leather cord in front of him, his gaze sharpened. He pushed himself up against the headboard, tilting his head as he studied it.

"What is it?"

I leaned in, lifting the cord over his head, letting the pendant settle into the hollow of his throat. Bone against skin. It belonged there.

"It's for you."

His fingers ghosted over it, his brows drawing together slightly. "What kind of bone is this?"

I smiled, slow and dark. "Does it matter?"

Something flickered in his gaze—hesitation, curiosity. Then, understanding. The smirk that followed sent a pulse of heat through me. *He gets it. He gets me.*

"One of your kills?"

Not this time.

"Yours," I murmured.

His fingers curled around it, testing the weight, the meaning. He didn't ask for details. He didn't need to. The look in his eyes told me he knew exactly what this was. Not a gift. Not a token.

A mark.

I reached out, dragging my thumb along the edge of his jaw, tilting his chin up. His pulse beat steadily beneath my touch, a rhythm I had memorized. He swallowed.

"Looks good on you."

His lips parted slightly, breath feathering against my wrist. My fingers tightened beneath his jaw, just enough to feel the way his muscles tensed before relaxing. *Submission. Trust.*

He wasn't afraid. He should be.

"Say thank you," I murmured.

His smirk widened, eyes glinting. "Thank you, *Domino.*"

The way he said my name sent a thrill down my

spine. I leaned in just enough to let our foreheads brush and let him feel the heat rolling off me.

"Good boy."

His hands slid up, curling around my neck as he pulled me in. Soft lips met mine, teasing, tasting; a groan rumbling from his throat as I tightened my grip, forcing him deeper into the kiss. I took my time, claiming every inch of his mouth, owning the way he melted beneath me. A whimper slipped free.

When I pulled back, we were both breathless. His sleep-hazed eyes were now glazed, cheeks flushed. He licked his lips, tipping his head.

"Shower with me?"

The words hit me like a spark to dry brush. My muscles clenched, my body already anticipating—his slick skin under the water, his face pressed to the tiled wall as I dragged my tongue over his entrance until he was trembling. Until he was too weak to stand. Until I had him wrapped around me, legs locked at my waist, fucking into his pliant body until he screamed my name and his release branded me like fire.

I exhaled sharply. Then, I smirked. "Lead the way."

Remi toyed with the pendant around his neck as he headed into the bathroom. My fingers were making quick work of the buttons on my shirt when my phone buzzed in my pocket.

GHOST
I'm coming up!

DOMINO
Fuck off!!

GHOST
No can do, boss. Urgent.

Fuck! My morning was ruined. If Ghost was here at this time of day, it was bad news.

"Remi," I barked. "Get dressed. Meet me in the lounge."

The sound of water hitting his skin tested every last thread of my patience. The thought of stepping into that shower, pressing him against the cold tile, and sinking into him until he was nothing but a trembling mess beneath me—it was a distraction I couldn't afford. Not now.

Not when Ghost was about to walk in.

He'd already spent too much time alone with Remi and watched him too closely. Was too damn interested. If he were anyone else, he'd be dead already—like Kyran Stirling would be shortly.

But Ghost was useful. Too useful to dispose of—*yet.*

The elevator chimed, and the doors slid open. Ghost stepped out, expression unreadable, but his eyes glinted with something sharp. Amusement. He was enjoying this.

"You're not gonna like this," he said.

I sighed, tucking my hands into my pockets. "Then start with something I will like."

A smirk moved over his lips, but he didn't waste time. "Kyran's pressing assault charges. My guy at the precinct says he's got enough to make it stick."

My jaw flexed. "He doesn't have shit," I spat.

That little fucking rat just moved up the date of his execution.

Ghost lifted a shoulder, unconcerned. "He's got witnesses. And Rutter's already called me twice."

Right on cue, my phone buzzed in my pocket. I pulled it out and answered.

"This isn't going away, Domino." Rutter's voice was

tight, clipped. "Kyran made sure of that. He's playing it smart—police backing, solid evidence. If this goes to trial—"

"It won't."

"You can't just make him disappear," Rutter warned. "Not without consequences."

I let the silence drag, let the weight of my next words settle over him. "Watch me."

I hung up.

Remi leaned against the wall, watching. Waiting. That look in his eyes—the one that meant he wanted to see what I'd do next—only made the fire in my blood burn hotter.

He wouldn't have to wait long.

Kyran was a fool marked for death, but his father? Stirling Senior needed a reminder. He was playing a game that he was about to lose. One he'd never recover from.

I turned to Ghost. His cool, amused gaze locked onto mine. "Pay Rutter a visit. Remind him what I said would happen if he stepped a toe out of line."

His smirk widened, his posture shifting in anticipation. "I've got the recording." He licked his lips. "How much do you want him to see?"

Ghost liked toying with people who fucked with the DeMarcos, almost as much as I did. Letting him off his leash once in a while was always… entertaining.

I held his gaze steady. "Everything."

His pupils dilated. "Everything?" His fingers twitched, excitement bleeding into his voice.

"You got it, boss."

"And when you're done…"

Ghost leaned in, eager, practically vibrating with anticipation. "Yes?"

I let the silence stretch just long enough to make him desperate for it. To make him need it. "Dismantle the Stirlings until there is nothing left."

His grin was razor-sharp, sick with delight. He loved this part. The breaking. The ruin. The hunt. And then—he dared to glance at Remi and fucking wink.

A low snarl tore from my throat before I could stop it, possessiveness curling through my gut like barbed wire. "Mine."

Ghost knew exactly what he was doing. That laugh—sharp, teasing—was cut off the moment the elevator doors snapped shut.

Good. Because if he lingered a second longer, I would've slit his fucking throat right here.

The fire started at midnight.

It wasn't random. It wasn't reckless. It was precise. Controlled. It hadn't taken long to get everything I needed into place. Kyran was oblivious, too consumed with trying to take me down to realize his demise was happening before his eyes.

I watched from across the street, hands in my pockets, as the flames licked up the side of Kyran's apartment building, curling like fingers against the windows. The smoke slithered into the night sky, thick and choking.

It started in the walls—old wiring in the breaker box. A surge overloaded the system, and then boom. A fire that looked like a tragic accident but was as far from that as was conceivable.

By the time the first flames reached his bedroom, Kyran was already outside, in only his boxers, standing barefoot on the pavement, watching his world go up in smoke.

His chest heaved, face pale in the flickering orange glow. Panic clung to his skin like sweat.

I crossed the street slowly, my steps deliberate.

He heard me before he saw me. His head snapped toward me, and his whole body went rigid.

"Y-you," he stammered, backing up a step. "What the fuck did you do?"

I tilted my head, letting the weight of my gaze bore into him, letting him *think*.

"You should be more careful, Kyran," I murmured. "Old buildings like this... accidents happen."

His nostrils flared. "You think this is gonna make me drop the charges?"

I took another step forward, forcing him back.

"No," I said. "This is just to remind you who you're dealing with."

His jaw clenched, his hands curling into fists. He wanted to fight, but he wouldn't. Not now. Not when he had nothing left.

"Say the words," I told him.

His lips pressed into a tight line.

"Say it, and this ends," I said, my voice dropping lower. "Say it, and you walk away from this with something left."

His shoulders rose and fell, his breaths coming fast. His gaze flicked past me—to Remi. And just like that, the truth came out.

"It was never about you," Kyran said quietly.

I stilled.

Remi frowned, confusion flickering across his face. "What?"

Kyran tensed, his eyes locking onto Remi like he was something he wanted to sink his teeth into.

"You," Kyran said. "It was always you."

Remi's face paled. He shook his head. "You're lying."

Kyran laughed—cold, bitter. "You think I'd go this far for revenge? For pride?" He scoffed. "No. I did it because I wanted *you*. Because I should have had you."

Remi took a step back, shaking his head. "You're fucking insane."

Kyran's mouth twisted. "And yet, you were the one always playing games with me. Always looking for a reaction. You *wanted* me to want you."

Remi stiffened. "What the fuck?!" He choked. "I only ever tried to be your friend."

Kyran scoffed, body vibrating with tension. "Y-you went out with me—"

My patience snapped. In a blink, I had my hand around his throat, yanking him close until our noses nearly touched. His breath hitched, but he didn't fight.

"You're going to forget this ever happened," I murmured, voice ice-cold. "You're going to drop the charges. And then, you're going to disappear. If I ever see your face again, there won't be a building left to burn—you will be the ashes."

Kyran swallowed hard, his pulse pounding beneath my grip.

"Say it," I ordered, deadly quiet.

His eyes flickered toward Remi one last time, something desperate and raw in them. Then, he exhaled sharply.

"I'll drop the charges," he rasped. "I'll disappear."

I shoved him back. He stumbled into the wall, eyes blown wide.

"Good boy," I sneered.

I turned, grabbing Remi's hand, knowing he wouldn't move until we were gone. But then Kyran proved me wrong and made the biggest mistake of his life.

Like a fool with nothing left to lose, he screamed a war cry and charged. "If I can't have him——"

His words cut off with a thick, wet gurgle—a blade buried deep in his throat. My switchblade. His legs crumpled beneath him, hands clutching the wound, blood bubbling through his fingers around the steel stuck in his neck.

I wrapped my fingers around the handle and stared into the dying eyes of a man who thought he could take what was mine.

"Remi is mine. He was mine the moment he stepped into Marlow Heights," I spat, twisting the knife. "You will never know what it's like to sink inside him."

Kyran's breath hitched, his pupils wide, tears streaking his face. A limp hand reached out toward Remi.

Remi sneered, stepping back.

I crouched beside Kyran, my voice dropping to a whisper as I yanked the knife from his throat. Thick red waves poured down his body.

"You will never know what it's like to watch him kill."

His breath stuttered, wet and shallow, blood staining his lips. Another tear slipped free.

"B...b-but..."

A hollow laugh curled from my lips as his slack hand fell into the growing pool of blood.

I leaned in, pressing my lips to his ear. "He'll draw your death when we get home." My fingers curled tighter around the blade at my side. "Then I'll fuck him with the knife I used to kill you."

Kyran shuddered—one last, pitiful tremor. The smallest puff of air left his lips, and then… nothing. His body went slack, folding into the crimson pool beneath him.

Remi stood there, head tilted slightly, watching every minute shift in Kyran's body with something like fascination. Curiosity.

His eyelashes fluttered against his sharp cheekbones, and when those ice-blue eyes met mine…blackness. A visceral hunger so deep, so insatiable, it burned through him like a fever. Like a calling.

Mine.

Anything he asked of me, I'd give him.

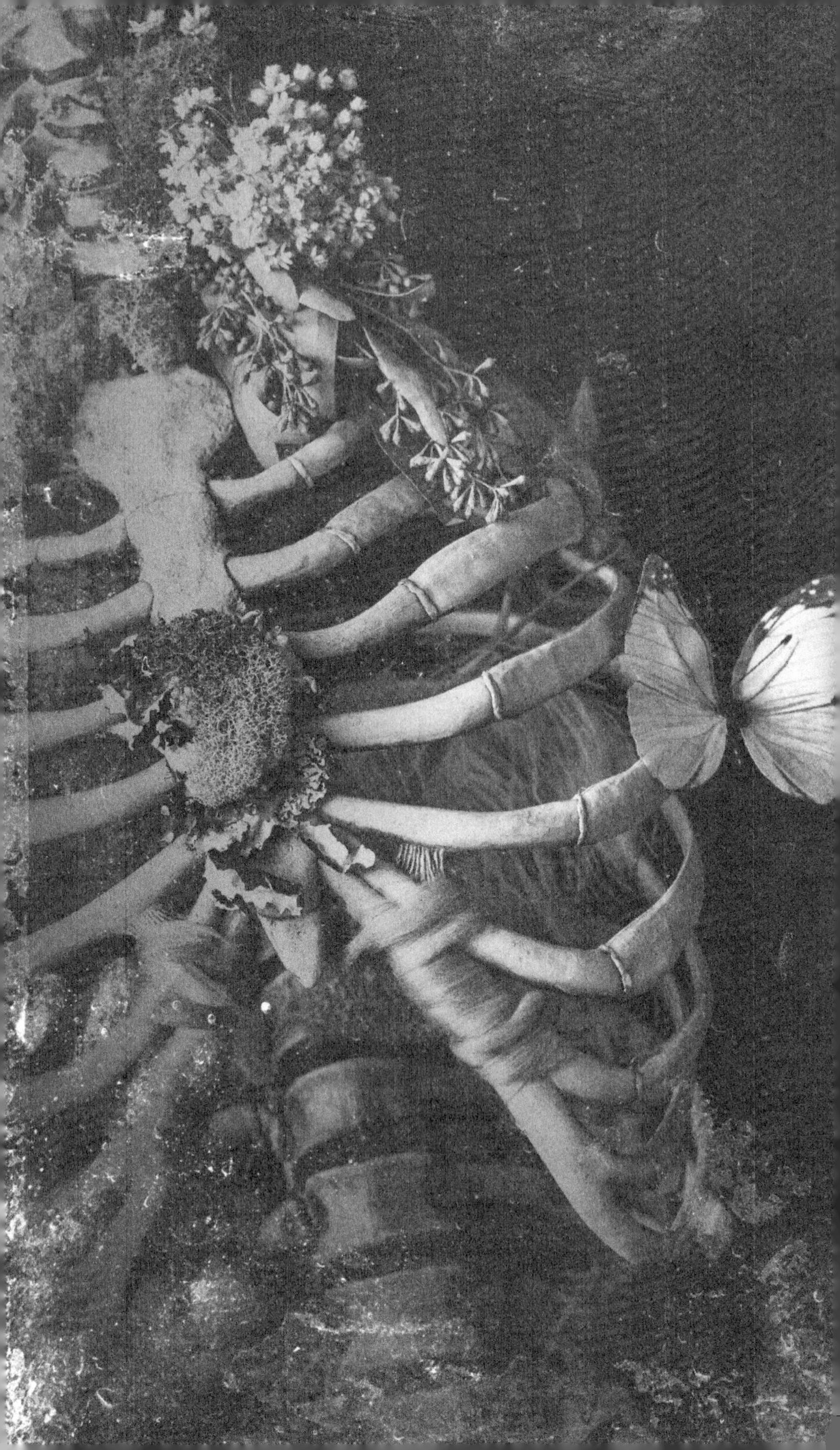

17. REMI

The bone from my necklace rolled between my fingers, its jagged edges pressing deep into my skin. It was warm—still holding the ghost of my body heat. A gift from Domino. If you could call it that. Possession disguised as sentiment. A leash disguised as devotion. A promise, unspoken but understood.

I was his. That much was undeniable. But was he mine?

That thought sank its claws into me, gnawing at my ribs like a starving animal. He was carved into my bones, stitched into my very being. Without him, I couldn't breathe. He'd unleashed me, set me free, but the fear that his infatuation was fleeting—that I was just a passing obsession—suffocated me. Life balanced on the edge of a knife, and I was terrified that one day, his blade would cut me loose.

I clenched my jaw, forcing my eyes back to the canvas stretched before me. Charcoal smeared against my fingertips as I traced the delicate lines of Brielle's ruined body. She was on her hands and knees in the dirt, skin peeling away in ragged strips, revealing gleaming bone. The forest swallowed her whole, a black maw of shadow and silence. Fear dripped from every stroke, her wide, vacant eyes pleading with a god that wasn't listening.

She didn't know what was coming. That death was already coiling around her like a noose. She didn't understand how fragile she was, how easy it would be to crush her. To peel her apart one strip of flesh at a time.

I had broken her mind. That was undeniable. But biding my time was becoming excruciating. My skin burned with the need to feel hot blood spilling over my hands, to breathe in the thick, coppery scent until it drowned me.

I hungered for it.

I ground my teeth, throat tightening as frustration curled through me like a storm.

"I don't have time for this bullshit." Domino's words slashed through the quiet, sharp and raw with frustration.

I tilted my head, listening. Somewhere in the apartment, a door slammed shut, the sound vibrating through my ribs.

My blood pounded in my ears, drowning out everything but the memory clawing its way to the surface.

A memory soaked in venom.

"Get rid of the little freak and focus on your job." Federico's voice was a slow, slithering thing. It coiled tight around my ribs, soaked into my marrow, poisoning every inch of me.

I had heard it before. A dozen times. A hundred.

But this time, Domino hesitated. "What we need to do," Domino bit out, voice hard, "is focus on the Gallos. They're getting too bold. They're testing us—"

Federico exhaled sharply, like he was bored of the conversation before it even started. His dark eyes flicked over Domino, filled with quiet, coiled disdain.

"I'm well aware of what they're doing," he said, tone smooth—too smooth. "It's your job to make sure they don't step foot in our territory."

His lip curled, and something in his face turned predatory.

"You're failing," he murmured, voice like oil, thick and seeping into every crack. "You're weak. Distracted."

A slow, heavy silence dragged between them.

Domino scoffed, but his face had hardened to stone. His breath came slow and rasping, controlled—calculated. He knew better than to let his father see the crack in his armor.

But it was already too late.

Before Domino could even part his lips, Federico moved. Fast. Like a viper striking the moment it smells weakness. His hand wrapped around Domino's throat, and in a single, crushing motion, he slammed him against the wall. The impact rattled the paintings.

My pulse slammed in my throat.

Domino didn't fight. Not yet. Not while his father's grip dug in, his fingers pressing into the tendons in his neck, into the soft hollow where he could crush his windpipe like glass.

His father leaned in close, breath ghosting over his face, stealing his air like the devil demanding obedience. "If you can't get rid of that little piece of shit," Federico murmured, "I'll take matters into my own hands."

Something in the room shifted. The air turned razor-thin, sharp enough to slice. Domino didn't agree. Not outright. But he didn't shut it down, either.

He knew I was watching. I felt it the second his body went taut, the way his jaw flexed, the way his eyes flicked to the hallway—to where I stood, unseen but not unnoticed.

Still, he didn't look at me.

Didn't acknowledge me.

Instead, he carefully steered his father away, murmuring in low, even tones, the words too soft for me to hear.

Like I didn't exist.

Like I wasn't the one who had bled for him.

Killed for him.

Belonged to him.

And for the first time, his actions gave my thoughts credence. I wasn't sure if he belonged to me. Maybe I'd been another fool to fall at his feet that would soon be buried six feet under.

His father's guard had seen me. His thick brows furrowed, his sneer curling with disgust as he raked his eyes over me. A thing to be discarded. A problem to be solved.

My eyes fluttered closed. Shut it down. *Breathe*. I exhaled through my nose, rolling my neck, but the tension refused to break. The charcoal slipped from my fingers and shattered against the floor. So easily broken. I crushed it beneath my boot and spun on my heel.

The walls of the penthouse pressed in on me, tightening like a noose. Too close. Too bright. I couldn't breathe. Domino's world was suffocating me, binding me in chains I had willingly fastened around my own throat.

His voice echoed from down the hall, low and lethal, sharp edges coated in glass. Ghost's answer was clipped. Italian words sliced the air in rapid succession—calculated, deadly.

I moved before I could think, slipping into the elevator, my heart slamming against my ribs as the doors slid shut. The weight of everything sat heavily on my shoulders, and I just needed—

A moment.

A moment to pretend I wasn't his prisoner.

A moment to escape the lingering doubt coiling in my gut.

A moment to ignore the knowledge that Catalina's blood was still on my hands. Her truth festered inside my silence.

The streets were slick with rain when I stepped outside, cold air biting through my clothes. I inhaled, deep and slow, the chill burning in my lungs. The pressure in my chest eased. Slightly.

My feet moved on instinct. The cemetery wasn't far, but it felt like a world away. And the dead? The dead didn't ask questions. They offered a salvation the living didn't.

Minutes bled together, and time became meaningless. Buildings merged into one continuous, looming presence, stalking me, and the streets all looked the same—even though I knew they had changed. Everything changed. The sky was a heavy, shifting blanket of blackness, rain slicing through the air like needles, pelting my skin, seeping into my bones. Trying to cleanse me.

Trying to save me.

I laughed under my breath. Too late for that.

The sensation of being watched hit me like a blade

between the ribs—I wasn't alone. In a city of thousands, that was impossible, but this was different.

A prickle of unease danced along the back of my neck, ice threading through my veins. I knew Domino's presence, the way it curled around me like smoke, possessive and suffocating all at once. This wasn't him.

This was something—someone else.

I paused at the corner of a building, scanning the murky streets. Nothing. No footsteps. No headlights. No one. But the weight of unseen eyes pressed against my skin, burrowing under it.

Shaking it off, I slipped through the broken chain-link fence that surrounded the cemetery. The pavement gave way to damp, leaf-littered earth. The taint of the city clung to the air, but the scent of rain-soaked mulch and decay slowly drowned it out as I picked my way through the trees.

The cemetery had been waiting for me. Its silent embrace welcomed me home. I belonged here amongst the lost and forgotten souls, among the dead that had stories to tell but no one to hear them.

Rain dripped from the skeletal branches, whispering against the marble headstones, soaking the earth until the graves bled mud. A perfect haunted silence. A place where time folded in on itself, where the dead weren't forgotten.

My fingers traced over the cold headstones, names carved into history, their stories left behind in fading letters. I exhaled as the feeling of being watched wrapped around me like a noose.

A smooth, teasing voice whispered on the wind. "Didn't think I'd find you here, *piccolo agnello*."

I turned slowly, like ice cracking and reforming. The man stood a few feet away, lips curved into something almost friendly. But his eyes—dark, cold, calculating—told the truth. The haughty look on his face made it clear that he was the one who had been following me.

"You shouldn't be out here alone," he said, stepping closer. His gaze had raked over me, lingering just a second too long.

I didn't move. But my fingers itched for the blade strapped to my arm. "Why is that?" I asked, tipping my head, watching his smirk twitch.

"It's not safe for anyone."

The corners of my lips curled. "I'm not just anyone."

He had chuckled, mistaking my words for a joke. They always did.

"He's not here to protect you now, *bel ragazzo.*"

A slow smile stretched across my face. "I need... protecting?"

"Something as beautiful as you—"

I rolled my eyes, disgust curling my lips. Predictable.

"Should be cherished. Treasured."

He was barely a foot away from me. The inches between us disappeared in the blink of an eye. I scarcely swallowed the hysterical laugh clawing up my throat. "See something you like?"

His smirk widened. So did mine as mania flowed freely through my veins. He hadn't seen the knife, hadn't even thought it could exist until I buried it in his side.

A strangled gasp had ripped from his throat, eyes widening as warmth spilled over my fingers.

"What the fuck—" he choked, stumbling back, clutching his side. "W-what did you do?"

I lifted the blade, blood glistening like rubies under the fractured moonlight. Twisting my hand, mesmerized as I watched the red drips slide over the metal. "It's beautiful," I whispered.

The man who was clearly a Gallo of some sort stiffened momentarily before he recovered, straightening to his full height and smirked. "You're a wild one, aren't you?" His voice was tight, forced. He had to have been hurting, but he was still standing. "I like the crazy ones."

A thunderous roar tore through the air. Raw. Primal. Electric. Sparks licked across my skin and danced in my veins, but it wasn't from the storm—it was *him*. His presence. His fury.

Domino didn't move like a man. He moved like a beast. A force of nature barreling toward his kill. The air thickened with his rage, suffocating, all-consuming. His need to possess, consume, and own vibrated off him in waves as he collided with the Gallo like a battering ram.

The man barely had time to register the danger before Domino's fist caved his smirk in. The crack of shattering bone sang through the night.

It was a beautiful song just for me. A brutal, chaotic symphony that vibrated through my bones, curling deep into my gut, twisting into something that felt holy.

The Gallo staggered, choking, teeth clattering onto the wet grass. He grunted, barely keeping himself upright, when Domino struck again. A vicious left hook snapped the man's head to the side, blood arcing through the air before getting swallowed by the rain.

The Gallo gasped, spitting red as it dripped down his face, stumbling backward looking for purchase. He blinked through the downpour, shock flickering in his eyes as he swiped his sleeve across his busted mouth.

"You—" He panted. "You crazy fucking—"

Domino was on him before he could finish. He

drove his knee into the man's ribs, a sickening crunch echoing through the cemetery. The Gallo wheezed, doubling over in agony, but Domino didn't let him fall.

He hauled him up by the lapels of his soaked coat, slamming him against a headstone. The marble shuddered from the impact, and the soldier groaned, eyes rolling.

Domino's voice was low. Smooth and dangerous. "You like running your mouth, huh?"

The Gallo coughed, blood bubbling past his lips. "Fuck… you."

Domino tilted his head, his soaked hair falling over his eyes. "That all you got?"

The man's hand shot toward his belt—going for the gun strapped to his waist but Domino was faster. He snatched the soldier's wrist, twisted it sharply, and the gun fell uselessly onto the grass before Domino kicked it away.

A sound ripped from the man's throat—a mix of pain and disbelief. Domino's grin was slow, dark, and dripping with amusement. "You thought that was gonna work?"

He twisted harder, making the man scream. Shivers raced down my spine, my fingers flexed on the handle of my blade.

"That's cute," Domino murmured. Then, drove his elbow into the man's temple. The Gallo collapsed onto his knees, body swaying as his fingers sank into the mud.

Domino exhaled, shaking his head and squatted in front of him, gripping the man's chin, forcing him to look up. "You know who I am?" he asked, voice calm.

The man's breath stuttered. Fear bled into his eyes. "Yeah…" he croaked. "I know exactly who the fuck you are."

Domino's grin sharpened. "Then you should've run the second you saw me."

The soldier coughed out something that might've been a laugh. "N-not scared of you, fucker."

Domino's fist crashed into his face. Once. Twice. Three times. Blood splattered onto the headstone in front of him, bright and wet. The man slumped, body barely holding itself upright.

"You scared now?" Domino murmured.

The Gallo wheezed, a cruel smile splitting his ruined lips. "You think this ends with me? You think the Gallos won't come for you?"

Domino laughed. Low. Amused. Dark. "Oh, I hope they do," he whispered. Then, he grabbed the man by the hair and slammed his skull against the marble.

A sharp crack ricocheted through the air. By the time the sound died, the man was sagged against the headstone, dazed, blinking slowly.

Domino yanked him back up—only to drive his knee into his gut. The man made a choked, wet sound. His body buckled inward, his legs giving out underneath him, but Domino didn't stop.

He yanked him up again. Slammed him back down. His fist crashed into ribs. Once. Twice. Crunch. The soldier let out a mangled cry, his body convulsing from the pain. His limbs twitched. Weak. Spasming.

I exhaled slowly. Hypnotized. This wasn't a fight. This was an execution.

The Gallo slumped, body limp against the grave as it slowly slid down, smearing a thick swath of red on the pale stone. His breath came in wet, shuddering gasps. The night swallowed his whimper as the rain mixed with the blood staining the earth.

The body at Domino's feet was still twitching, lungs

filling with water instead of air. The rain blurred everything, smearing the lines between life and death, but I could still feel it—the way violence coiled off him like heat.

Domino stood over the corpse, his chest rising and falling in deep, controlled breaths. The blood on his hands washed away under the relentless downpour, but it didn't matter. I still saw it.

He lifted his head, feral gaze locked on me. His eyes pinned me in place, dark with possession, a hunger that had nothing to do with violence and everything to do with me. My pulse pounded, but not from fear. It was a force greater than gravity.

A shiver skated down my spine, but I didn't move. I couldn't. There was something magnetic about him, something that could shift tides and tear through cities.

Domino moved too quickly for my eyes to follow. His arm snapped out and wrapped around my waist, my chest slammed against his, the soaked fabric of my shirt clinging between us.

His nose traced along my throat, slow, savoring. I felt the sharp inhale as he breathed me in, like he was trying to fill every inch of himself with my scent. His chest expanded, a low groan rumbling from the depths of him. The sound reverberated through me, igniting something violent and all-consuming. It was the only warning I got before his teeth sank into my neck.

Pain and pleasure crackled through me like a live wire, chaos searing my skin. My breath hitched, my fingers digging into his arms as he sucked hard, as if he wanted to taste the very marrow of me.

"No one gets to look at you that way and live."

His voice was a rough growl, vibrating against my throat. I barely registered the dead man at his feet—the

Gallo who had let his gaze linger on me too long, who had spoken to me like I was something to be had.

I blinked heavy-lidded eyes up at him, my breath uneven. Domino's gaze devoured me, swallowing every piece of me whole. In his eyes, I saw the same sickness that ran through my veins.

"You don't leave the apartment without telling me," he murmured, his grip tightening.

His bloodied fingers tangled in my hair, yanking my head back. My lips parted on instinct, but he didn't wait for an answer. His mouth crashed onto mine, brutal and demanding. His tongue forced its way between my lips, claiming me. Owning me.

Teeth sank into my bottom lip, tearing my flesh. The taste of copper flooded my tongue, and instead of pulling away, I moaned, deepening the kiss. My blood mixed between us, shared, swallowed. I clung to him, needing more, needing everything.

The world blurred, and everything around us fell away, ceasing to exist, but I felt him. Through every layer of fabric, through skin and bone, through the very fabric of my being.

"Who do you belong to?" His voice was a brand, searing into me, leaving no room for doubt.

I swallowed the words he forced into my lungs, my tongue tangling with his. "You," I gasped.

My arm wrapped around his neck, needing him closer. I wanted to fuse us at an atomic level. To carve away his flesh and bury myself inside his ribs. To leave a mark that would never fade.

I opened my eyes, rain dripping from my lashes, and that's when I saw it—a shadow moving fast, a gun raised at Domino's back. He tensed, already sensing the danger. Time folded in on itself. My body reacted before my mind had fully caught up. My arm snapped forward, and the blade left my hand, slicing through the rain-slick air, sinking into the man's shoulder.

The unknown man staggered, cursing, trying to lift his gun and remove the blade embedded in his shoulder.

Domino spun, pushing me behind him. His muscles tensed, coiling like a beast about to tear flesh from bone.

The man tried to recover, his fingers spasming around the trigger, his eyes darting in my direction like he might still try for me—wrong fucking move.

Domino pounced. The crack of their bodies colliding was swallowed by the storm as thunder rolled above our heads. They hit the ground hard, a wet thud against the waterlogged grass. Domino was on top of him before the bastard had a chance to lift his gun again.

I watched, breath caught in my throat, as Domino lost himself. His fists struck bone with a wet crunch. The guy, who I assumed was another Gallo, fought back, barely managing to swing before Domino shattered his wrist. A strangled cry broke through his blood stained lips

Domino grinned. That look would have sent any sane person running, but not me. Instead of fear, I found life in his controlled savagery.

His hand closed around the man's throat, his knee pressing down on his chest, pinning him. Blood spilled from his nose, bubbling past his lips, but the look in Domino's eyes—that was what made the man go still.

A predator staring down his prey.

Domino leaned in. I couldn't hear what he whispered, but the soldier's eyes widened in raw horror before they flicked to me for a fleeting moment. With terrifying ease, he snapped his neck.

The light faded from his eyes as his body slumped to the ground. The image of Domino with two corpses at his feet was burned into my retinas.

The air was thick, heavy. The rain poured around us, but I couldn't feel it anymore. Only him. *Always*, only him.

Domino turned to me, watching. Head tilting. Studying. Like I was something rare. Precious.

"You're shaking." His voice was soft now, coaxing, laced with something dark.

"I'm not," I lied, my breath still uneven.

But my mind was racing. The whispers. The proof.

I had heard the rumors from the men stationed around the apartment building. Whispers that Federico had lied about what happened to Domino's mother. Fuck! I'd seen it. In the falsified documents, the blackmail payments, the cover-ups—everything tying back to Brielle.

Something wasn't right. I knew I needed to tell him, but I didn't know how.

Domino lifted my hand—still stained with blood—and pressed his lips to the inside of my wrist. The way a priest would bless a sinner. A man worshipping his ruin.

Why worship a prince when you could love a villain?

The moment stretched, coiling tight. His fingers dragged down my throat, lingering against my erratic pulse.

"You get it now, don't you?"

Domino's voice barely rose above a whisper, yet it twisted around me like a noose, tightening with every syllable. His breath was warm against my damp skin, the words sinking deep, embedding themselves in my bones.

"You're mine." His fingers flexed. "You've been

mine since the first time you let me pull you into the dark."

Since that night in the alley. Since I watched him kill for the first time. Since every moment after that, drenched in blood and devotion.

Transfixed I didn't move. Didn't fight. My breath came in ragged pants, but my resolve didn't waver. Instead, I tilted my head back, baring my throat. "Then prove it," I whispered. "And listen to me."

Domino sucked in a sharp breath. His grip around my throat tightened—just a fraction. "Talk to me, *piccolo agnello.*"

I licked my lips, tasting the metallic tang of his blood mixed with mine. The storm raged above us, but it was nothing compared to the chaos crackling through me.

I hesitated.

Not because I didn't trust him—but because I knew this would break him.

"I found out something that will change everything," I said, voice unsteady. "It will make you doubt who you can trust—"

"I don't trust anyone." His response was instant. Absolute. "You know that, Remi."

I swallowed hard, but fear lodged itself in my throat and refused to move.

"What's this about?" His dark green eyes sliced into me, sharp and unrelenting, like he could see the shadows slithering through my mind. He read me like scripture, like a story he'd memorized—but this time, he didn't like what he found.

I forced myself to speak, even as my ribs squeezed tight around my lungs. "The Gallos…" I exhaled shakily. "T-they didn't kill your mother."

His fingers flexed. Before I could prepare myself,

Domino's grip tightened. Hard. Stars exploded in my vision. I gasped, but no air came. My lungs screamed, panic clawing up my spine. Every pulse of blood in my veins thundered in my ears, each heartbeat a dying drum.

Seconds stretched.

Turned into eternity.

The rain blurred the edges of my sight, but Domino's face remained crystal clear. Confusion flickered first. Then anger. And beneath it—something far worse.

Fear.

"Who told you that?" he snarled, his voice a feral growl. Spittle hit my cheek, but I barely felt it over the burn in my throat. "Who put you up to this?"

I clawed weakly at his wrist, nails digging into his skin. "N-no one," I rasped. "I-I found…"

The cold kiss of a blade met my skin. Sharp. Unyielding. I knew what that meant. Domino wasn't just trying to scare me.

He was one wrong answer away from killing me.

"Who are you working for?" His voice was jagged, more a snarl than words.

"I—I'm not… I…" Black spots exploded across my vision. My body spasmed from lack of oxygen.

"You found what?"

His face blurred. Distorted. My pulse slowed—each thump heavier, duller. "O-on the… PC… when… B-Brielle…"

Then, like the snap of a leash—

"Fuck!" Domino roared, ripping his hands from my throat.

I collapsed. Air flooded my lungs like fire. I coughed, my body wracked with tremors, my throat searing as I gasped for breath. Every inhale felt like swallowing glass.

I barely had time to process what was happening before Domino's fingers tangled into my drenched hair and wrenched my head back.

His face—wild, ruined, monstrous—hovered inches from mine. His teeth were bared, his breath ragged. "Are you telling me the truth?" His voice sliced through me, cutting down to the quick.

I met his gaze, forcing myself to stay steady despite the tremors running through me. "I would never lie to you," I rasped. "I know what she means to you."

A crack. A fracture. It was barely there, but I saw it. His resolve wavered. The cracks deepened, spider-webbing across his face, breaking apart the mask he wore like armor.

Emotion bled into his eyes—agony and rage swirling together, battling for dominance. And if I wasn't this close, I wouldn't have noticed the tears. They built along his lashes, lost to the rain before they ever had the chance to fall.

"Kill me," I whispered. "If that's what you have to do."

His face shuttered. Wiped clean. Every trace of emotion buried. But the tears still fell.

And watching that? Watching the god I worshipped fall from the sky? It was irrevocable. Haunting.

"In the drawer where I keep my supplies," I whispered, barely audible over the rain. "There's a folder with her name on it. Everything is in there."

"You're lying." His voice was brittle, a broken child-like thing.

"Lies are for people who think they have nothing to lose and everything to gain," I exhaled.

My breath hitched when the blade pressed deeper into my skin. Warmth trickled down my throat.

"I have nothing to gain," I choked out. "And everything to lose." A tear slipped past my lashes, cutting a cold path down my cheek.

I'd never feared death before. Never had anything worth living for.

But now?

Now I knew the weight of his devotion. Knew the depths of his sickening obsession. At that moment, I realized a terrifying, undeniable truth.

"I love you."

Domino stilled. A muscle ticked in his jaw. His lips curled back, a snarl carving his face into something vicious. "I thought you didn't lie?"

"I'm not."

His fingers twitched. The blade dug in further. Blood pooled at my collarbone, warm despite the cold rain.

"If you kill me now," I whispered, vision blurring, darkening, collapsing inward. "My only sin... will be that I never set you free... like you have me."

The darkness swallowed me whole. The last thing I heard was the sound of Domino's roar. It shattered through the night. A primal, agonized sound.

Then—nothing.

Just silence.

And the burn of his name on my lips as I let go.

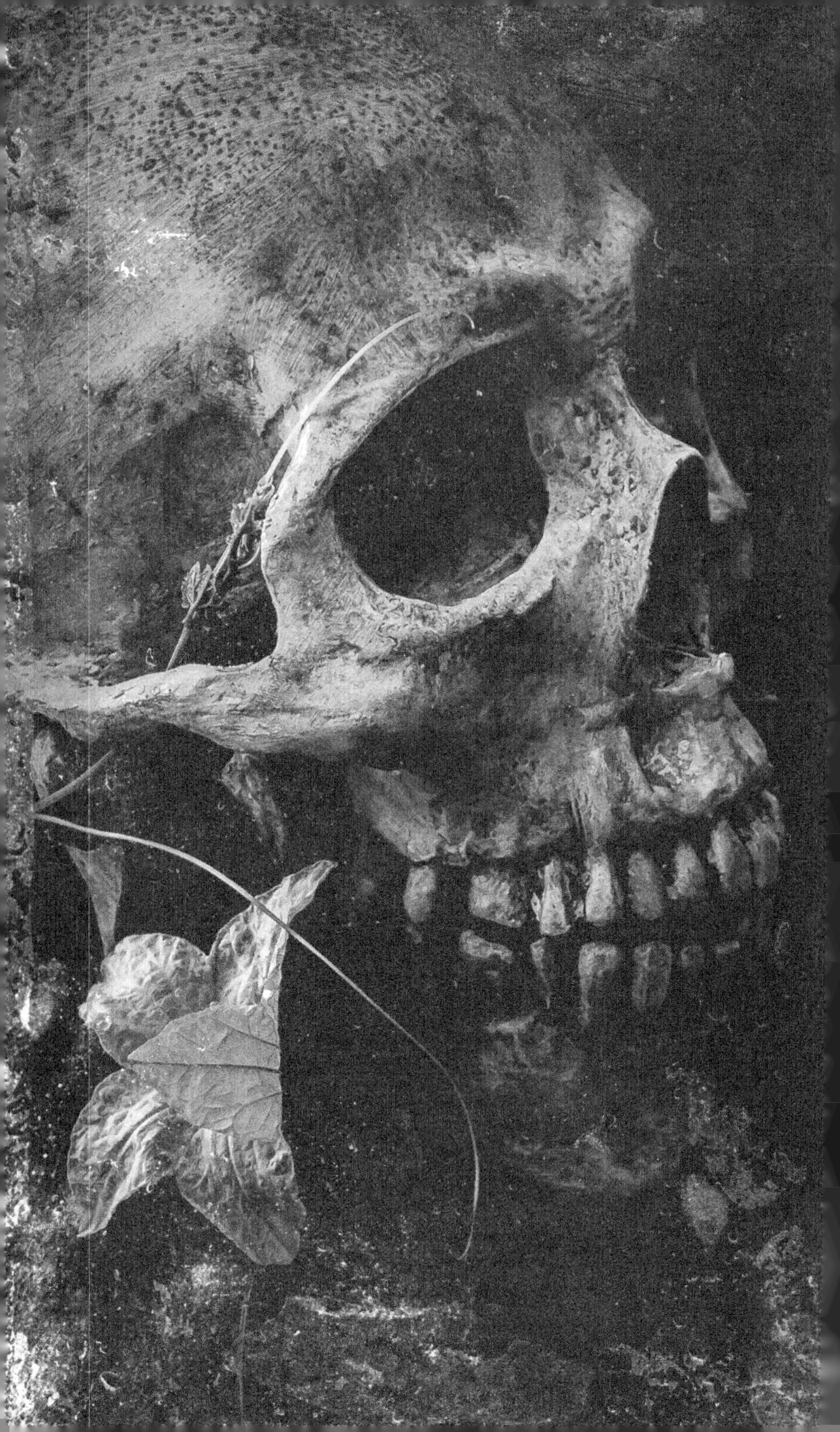

18 DOMINO

Control had never been an issue for me. Not once. Not ever. I had learned early—compartmentalization was survival. Feelings were a liability. Doubt was a death sentence. A weak mind bled before the body ever did.

And I had never bled.

Until now.

Now, the carefully constructed world I had locked myself inside was crumbling. The walls were splitting at the seams, cracks widening, the flood of questions and doubts seeping through like rot. It started after that confrontation with my father. That was when the first fracture formed.

The Gallos were crawling through Marlow Heights like a plague, leeching into every corner of our business, fucking up deals, fucking up my focus.

But none of that mattered. None of it compared to what truly fucked me up. Remi left. It was inconceivable. Unthinkable.

He was mine. I never wanted him out of my sight. I had thought—no, I had known—that what we had was singular. Something irrevocable. A bond so deep it blurred the lines of self, tangled and fused, one entity instead of two.

I didn't claim to understand people or emotions. They were background noise. I understood the dichotomy of life and death. I understood power.

The insufferable need to amass it, hoard it, wield it. The way it could be used to collar and control small-minded idiots, the ones who wouldn't know which way was up without someone like me to dictate it to them.

But Remi threw everything out of sync.

Because he didn't just leave. He told me he loved me. And he did it right after shattering my fucking world.

Right after ripping the ground out from under me.

Right before his breath stuttered into nothing.

Right before he went limp in my arms.

And in that moment—as the last breath left his lips, as his body sagged against me, as the color drained from his face—I realized love was an illusion.

What I felt for him was something far more powerful. Far greater. It was primal. It was deadly. It was not love.

It was *obsession*.

When his pulse gave one last, weak flicker before fading into silence—the world fucking shattered. It was like the last star had been plucked from the sky. The final light was snuffed out. I had never felt darker, colder.

A scream tore from my throat. Raw. Splintered. The sound felt like it had been ripped from the center of my goddamn soul.

The world had changed at a molecular level. But at the same time, nothing had changed at all.

I moved through the streets, through my apartment, through my father's compound with a single thought gnawing its way through my skull: Who the fuck could I trust?

I watched my men—the soldiers, the runners, the dealers in their dens. I watched their eyes, their hands, their movements. And for the first time, I saw the masks I'd been too blind to notice.

Nothing was real.

Nothing was solid.

The world as I knew it was gone.

Once I'd told Remi that I didn't trust anyone. But maybe that had been a lie. Maybe—before he broke the one thing I thought was unbreakable—Maybe I had trusted him.

Maybe I had trusted him more than I had ever trusted anyone.

And that was my greatest mistake.

"Boss. They're here."

I shook my head, snapping back to the present. Back to blood, to violence, to control. "Good. Have them bring him to the wet room. I'm going to get answers."

Angelo snorted. "Let's hope this one lives long enough to give you what you want."

The glare I leveled at him was glacial when I spun around to face him, enough to make the six-foot brute shrink and shiver like a child waking from a nightmare.

"You are paid to do. Not to talk. Not to joke."

His throat bobbed. "Sorry, boss."

I exhaled sharply, pinching the bridge of my nose as we walked through the warehouse. The pulse of my anger was constant now, coiled and waiting for release.

Men and women stood at long steel tables, cutting, weighing, and packaging the vast quantities of drugs moving through our pipelines. Their quiet murmurs silenced as we passed. This was one of our biggest processing centers, but like all our properties, it served multiple purposes. How much you knew depended entirely on where you stood in the hierarchy.

Angelo, as one of our enforcers, knew more than most—but less than he wanted. He had ambitions, whispered in my father's ear like a serpent, pushing for us to take the Gallos' territory. He had tried to manipulate me. Thought he could use me for his own ends because I was younger than him.

He had learned how futile that was.

I had taken his fingers for every transgression. One by one. Now, he teetered on the edge of life and death every time he stepped into my presence, but he had been leashed just enough to fall in line. I had no doubt he saw his death in my eyes.

The way he shrank when I looked at him was proof enough. But nothing could quench my thirst for blood at the moment. With Remi's revelation festering in my skull, infecting every second, every breath—I was a ticking bomb, waiting to detonate.

"Tell me what he did to warrant being brought to me."

Angelo held the unmarked door open, the dark stairwell illuminated only by bare overhead bulbs. We descended into the soundproofed wet room, another one of my playgrounds.

A single metal chair sat in the center, the base

roughly cut out above the drain. My eyes raked over the white tiles, stained with age and blood. The air was thick with the stench of sweat, desperation, and death. I inhaled it like the breath of life.

My fingers itched to peel flesh from bone. The monster inside me snarled against its cage, tasting death. We both hungered for it. To take life, feel it slip away and drown in the power.

"He came into Nocturne intoxicated, but Palo let him in—"

My gaze snapped to him, I stopped dead and the flinch that wracked his body was satisfying—but not enough. "Why would he do that?" My voice was a low, guttural snarl. "We have rules."

Angelo raised his hands. "Palo said the guy had been in before, never caused an issue."

My patience thinned. I stalked toward the back wall, my fingers grazing the array of implements neatly fixed in place. Blades. Hammers. Clamps. Chains. Each one had a purpose. Each one could tell a thousand stories.

"Why was he willingly allowing known Gallo associates inside?"

"T-that I can answer."

He stepped back as I plucked a serrated blade and a hammer from the wall. Then I reached for the box of wood splinters and laid them out carefully on the metal table.

Angelo cleared his throat, voice wavering. "The guy —Stephan—tried to push MDMA. Unsuccessfully. But before we could get to him, he started screaming that the Gallos were coming. That the DeMarcos were going to fall."

My fingers tightened around the handle of the serrated blade. I had heard enough. In the blink of an eye, I had Angelo pinned against the wall. The teeth of the blade bit into his skin, pressing just enough for pinpricks of red to bloom.

"What. Else?"

Angelo swallowed hard, forcing the blade deeper into his throat. "He—he attacked one of the girls."

Not unusual. Customers paid for the privilege. Nocturne had its own cleaning crew for this reason. They doubled as bouncers until the situation required something messier.

"And?"

My patience was hanging by a thread. My control was slipping. He trembled in my grip, unable to meet my eyes.

"When we dragged him free... he smiled. Like a fucking maniac." Angelo's breath shuddered. "Said he had a message for the DeMarcos. For you..."

The implication hung in the air like a viper coiled, ready to strike. I wasn't afraid of the Gallos. God knew I had put enough of them into the ground. Especially recently. They were a rat-infested plague infecting my city. I had to put an end to it.

"Is that all?"

The blade's tip traced over his carotid artery. I could see it now. A little more pressure—just a twitch of my wrist—and fountains of blood would paint the walls.

I licked my lips, tasting the copper tang, but there was only one person's blood I wanted on my tongue. The image clawed through my mind, dark and consuming, but I shoved it down. Refused to let my mental walls break completely and shook it off.

Angelo collapsed to the ground the moment I released him, gasping. Hand wrapped around his throat as I stepped back.

The back door slammed open as two of my men threw a body across the floor. The message arrived wrapped in blood and agony. Stephan—bound, beaten, barely breathing—had been dragged through the warehouse and dumped at my feet.

His head cracked against the tiled floor with a sickening thud. He let out a strangled noise, somewhere between a whimper and a curse.

I took my time stepping forward. The sound of my boots echoed through the vast space.

He was a soldier. A low-level one. No scars of war. No hardened exterior. Just a kid. Another desperate idiot trying to claw his way up the Gallo family ranks.

Wrong fucking ladder.

Crouched beside him, I tilted my head as I examined the damage. Busted lip. His right eye was swollen shut. Knuckles raw—like he had fought back. Like he had thought he had a chance. I gripped his jaw, forcing his battered face toward the light. Blood dripped from his nose, thick and dark, staining the floor in slow, deliberate drops.

I would carve the truth from him.

One scream at a time.

"I want the name of the person who sent you." My voice was even. Calm. Controlled. Steel wrapped in velvet. A tempting lure that could prize blood from stone.

He glared at me through his one good eye, lips pressing together. Stupid move. A wicked smile curved my lips. I loved when they made it difficult.

Reaching behind me, I pulled the serrated blade from the back of my jeans, swinging it in front of him with a smooth, practiced motion. The metal sang through the air, slicing the silence like a guillotine.

He tensed, but he didn't break, his fear ratcheting higher. It wouldn't be long till he broke. They all did—eventually—before they took their last breath.

But I wouldn't kill him. Not yet.

I'd drag him to the very edge of death before I sent him back to his masters. Let them watch him rot from the inside out. Using the husk of his body to deliver my message in return.

"You're going to tell me what I want to know," I murmured, pressing the tip of the blade just beneath his eye, where the skin was thinnest. "You'll beg to give it to me. The only choice you have is how much of you is left when you do."

Silence. His split lips trembled, and a single tear slipped from his one good eye. I pressed down slowly, increasing the pressure. His body seized as the blade broke skin. A thin rivulet of blood rolled down his cheek, bright against the grime and sweat.

"Fuck. You."

I hummed, amused. "That's the best you've got? I expected more."

The blade trailed downward—slow, deliberate. I took my time dragging it along his cheek, down the column of his throat. He swallowed hard. I felt it beneath the tip of my knife.

He thought I was bluffing. He was about to learn I never bluffed. A barely audible sigh left him when the knife left his throat. My teeth sank into my lip as I swallowed down a hollow laugh. The stupid fool thought it was over.

Power radiated through my veins. I pressed the knife against his cheek and drove it in. He screamed. A raw, ragged sound that choked off when I twisted the blade, shredding flesh from bone.

"You feel that?" I whispered, my mouth close to his ear. "That's reality sinking in. I own you now. And the longer you hold out, the worse this gets."

His body shook in my grip. His blood seeped down the planes of his face, dripping off his chin onto his shirt. Slowly, deliberately, I pulled the blade free—watching his face.

I lived for this moment. The scent of fear saturated the air.

The power.

The control.

That flicker—when defiance melted into unholy terror and the light dimmed in his eyes.

He knew, then. He wouldn't live to see another sunrise. The monster in me roared. It wanted more.

"Y-you're dead," he spluttered. "You a-and everyone who works for you. W-when they hear about this—"

I drove my fist into his temple, knocking him out cold. A hysterical laugh tore from my lungs as he collapsed at my feet.

"Strip him and bind him to the chair. Hands tied to the arms—fingertips hanging over the edge."

Angelo and the two men who had dragged him in jumped to work. My fingers twitched, itching to do more. Death hummed in my veins. My chest expanded as power flooded me.

One drop of blood at a time.

Pulling a cigarette from the tin in my back pocket, I lit it and watched them while they worked. Inhaling deeply, the cherry glowed in the muted light. The smoke spilled from my lips, coiling in the air like a serpent. Toxic. Deadly.

Just like me.

Once he was in position, Angelo dumped a bucket

of lemon juice and ice water over his body. The acid burned into the cuts and grazes littering his skin.

The scream that tore from him was animalistic. His body jerked, convulsing against the restraints that were shocking him back to consciousness. What little color he had drained from his face. His blood stood out even more against his ashen skin, dripping in slow, thick rivulets.

I exhaled another drag of smoke, watching him. Letting him feel it. "My men tell me you came into my club, causing havoc. Said you had a message for me?"

His one swollen eye blinked slowly, unfocused. Trying to remember. His brain rattled inside his skull, struggling to put the pieces back together. A slow nod of acknowledgement. He grimaced as he tested the restraints.

"Yes."

I tilted my head, considering what path to take next. Gooseflesh prickled across his exposed skin. The room was cold, like an industrial freezer. It kept my toys awake longer. Made them bleed slower.

"Who sent you?"

Something flickered across his face, but his trembling lips stayed sealed shut.

"Like that, is it?"

I spun the blade between my fingers. His eye tracked every movement. He winced every time the sharp edge of the blade flashed before his face.

His fear was potent. I savored it.

"You said you had a message for me?" I leaned in close, his acrid breath feathering over my face. "But now that you're here, you've lost your voice?" I snorted. "Mmm. Not so cocky now, are you big guy?"

He shuddered when I stubbed my cigarette out on

his thigh. The sizzle of burning flesh was like a shot of adrenaline. The pained whimper in his throat thrilled me.

I licked my lips and drank in his fear like the finest liquor. "There isn't a man alive I can't break. Are you sure you want to suffer?"

His entire body trembled. The chair rattled against where it was chained to the tiled floor.

"Tell me who sent you." My voice was razor-sharp. He flinched like I'd slashed him.

"Y-y-you…"

"Well, if you insist." I turned to the metal table, reaching for what I needed. The hammer and splinters of wood. "This will only hurt a little bit."

Then, positioned a splinter just beneath his nail by the nail bed and pressed slowly. It sank into the soft tissue with a whisper.

"Who sent you?"

Silence. His breath was shallow. The tendons in his hand strained as he tried—futilely—to pull away.

I smirked. "No answer?" A low chuckle rumbled in my throat.

Oh, this was going to be fun. I pulled the hammer from my back pocket and twirled it between my fingers. His eye went wide. The implication of my actions dawned on him.

Stephan's chest rose and fell in sharp, uneven breaths. He knew what was coming. But like a car crash, he knew what was going to happen. He couldn't take his eye off my every movement.

When the first strike fell—

When the splinter drove deeper into raw flesh—

The scream that tore from him was music to my ears. But that is not enough. It was never enough. I needed more. Unsatisfied, I gave myself over to the bloodlust inside me. One after another, I drove the splinters of wood into his nail beds.

The cacophony of agony filled the room—screams of anguish and pain crackling over my skin like electricity.

Each scream hardened my resolve. No one fucked with the DeMarcos without paying the price.

And this fool?

He would pay in blood.

In flesh ripped from bone.

I'd peel it back layer by layer until he sang like a canary. Then I'd send him back to his masters on the edge of death, with my message carved into his flesh and bone.

Shattered breaths slithered past his lips, coated in the stench of bile, but still—no answer.

Blood dripped from the end of each finger, pooling beneath his hands. Cold sweat slicked his skin. Tendons and muscles strained against the thin membrane that covered his body. His fingers were twisted in ruined agony. Black and blue flowed under his skin like a beautiful watercolor.

"Are you ready to talk?"

A limp nod was all he had left. He was slipping, his consciousness fleeting. I knew many effective ways to bring him back. Cold worked, but so did a sharp shock of burning pain.

I turned to Angelo. A single look was all it took, malice gleamed in his eyes. He disappeared, returning seconds later, two halves of a lemon in his hand. Without a word, he held them over Stephan's shredded fingers—and squeezed.

The acid hit the open wounds like fire that licked

through his veins. Pure, unadulterated torture. A guttural, soul-rending scream tore from his throat. His one good eye bulged from its socket. Tears streamed down his face, mingling with the rivulets of blood that seeped down his body.

The taste of his suffering on my tongue was exquisite.

Beautiful.

"Try again."

Stephan's breath hitched, shallow and ragged. Pained. His body slumped forward, strength leaving him in waves.

"Please," he rasped. "I—I don't know..."

I grabbed a fistful of his hair, jerking his head back. "Lying pisses me off." My voice turned glacial. "You don't want to see what I'm like when I'm pissed off."

His one good eye squeezed shut. His entire mangled body trembled. He was breaking perfectly. So close.

This was the best kind of foreplay.

I slid my blade up his leg, pressing just enough to make him flinch. "Let's try again. Who sent you?"

Silence.

My grip tightened in his hair; strands ripped free. "You have five seconds," I whispered against his ear. The smell of urine burned my nostrils. I stepped back, looking at him in disgust.

"Five."

The blade traced the blue veins in his wrist, dragging slowly along his arm, up to his throat.

"Four."

His breath stuttered. Blood and saliva dripped from his ruined lips.

"Three."

I circled his good eye with the bloodied tip of the

blade, pressing harder—tracing the socket, peeling the skin away, exposing raw, pulsing flesh inch by inch.

"Two—"

Before I finished, he cried out, his voice like nails on a chalkboard.

"Salvatore Gallo!" The words ripped from his lungs. "It was Salvatore Gallo!"

I stilled. Watching the fresh blood drip off his lashes and inhaling, savoring the flavor of his suffering. As I exhaled, the storm inside me went deathly quiet. Remi's words slithered through my mind. A whisper in the darkness.

What if he was telling the truth?

What if..?

"H-he has...in-information for...for you." He gulped, blood coating his lips with every word. "I-it'll change...everything."

I clenched my jaw and ground my molars together, shutting those thoughts down. Now wasn't the time to look closer. Now was the time to make someone pay. My blade continued its fluid movement around Stephan's eye socket so he would keep talking. I let him spill his guts through a haze of pain and delirium. I needed to glean as much information as I possibly could from him.

But none of it mattered. Not really. I already knew where to look next. Once the floodgates opened, his words became background noise. Drowned out by the slow, methodical drag of my blade carving his confession into his skin.

By the time he stopped screaming, his voice was nothing more than brittle whimpers; he was barely human. Just muscle, bone, and blood pooling in the spaces between my cuts.

Stephan was clinging to life, but not for long. Angelo

and Ghost would deliver my message to the gates of the Gallo compound.

And by the time he died, Salvatore Gallo would know—The DeMarcos were coming.

And I wasn't going to leave anyone breathing.

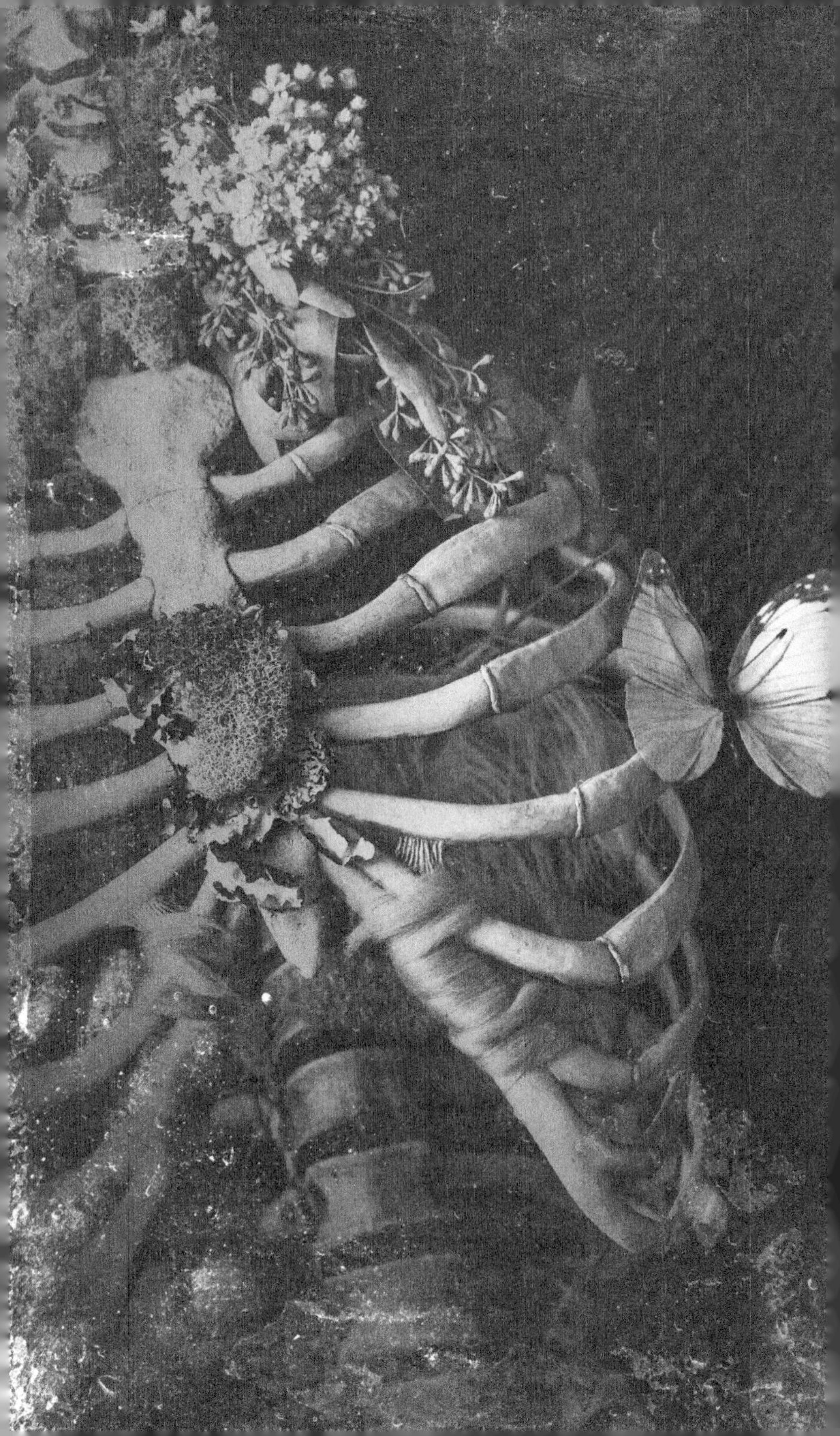

19 REMI

A scream—guttural and low—ripped me from unconsciousness, carving me open from the inside. My heavy-lidded eyes blinked slowly. A full-body shudder rolled through me, from the tips of my toes to the base of my skull. Goosebumps prickled my skin in its wake, jolting me upright in bed.

The sheets smelled like smoke and steel, like him, but the bed was empty. My body ached—deep, lingering bruises thrumming beneath my skin. But nothing compared to the raw, searing burn around my throat.

The scream still echoed in my ears as I dragged my fingers over the imprint Domino left behind. A brutal necklace of bruises. The cemetery. His hands. The bloodied and broken corpses at his feet. The moment he'd snapped, the moment I'd told him his father had a hand in his mother's death. It all rushed back like a black-and-white film flickering in my mind.

I had never seen him lose control like that. Not with me. I'd thought he might kill me. I was certain some part of me wanted him to. That should have terrified me. Maybe it did. But deep down, I knew—The only way to prove myself to him was to offer my mortal body as a sacrifice.

I'd be his sacrificial lamb whenever he needed. That thought settled inside me with an eerie calm. There was nothing I wouldn't do for him.

Even if it cost me my life.

Because I was his.

In every way possible.

The silk sheets tangled around my legs as I swung them off the bed, stumbling on weak, shaking limbs toward the bathroom. Every muscle ached. Lactic acid burned in my veins, and my body was starved of oxygen. He had turned my world into an endless night. It was only when I was on the brink of death…That was when I let go.

That was when I surrendered.

I had told him he'd already freed me. But that was the moment I relinquished everything. I gave myself over. Completely. Now, I knew I couldn't survive without him. There wasn't a molecule inside me that wanted to. I was his in this life, the next, and any that might follow if reincarnation was real.

And if it wasn't?

Then I would die knowing I loved him until our bodies became part of the universe once more.

My hollow reflection stared back at me from the mirror. My skin was whiter than bleached bone, a stark contrast to the dark bruises that circled my neck—his mark, his claim. I traced the inkblot stains of his fingers with my own. A full-body shudder rolled through me at the echo of pain that radiated from them. Electricity zapped across my skin, heating the cool blood pooling at the base of my dick.

My eyes shuttered closed, and I wrapped my hand around my shaft, squeezing, trying to mimic Domino's vice-like grip. His touch set me on fire. My hand? It was nothing but a pale imitation.

It didn't make my blood sing. It didn't make my soul dance with the devil.

It left me feeling empty.

Bereft.

Like I had lost a piece of myself to him that I would never reclaim—not until he came back. My heart thudded against my ribs hard enough to shatter the bones.

What if he didn't come back?

Last night, I had broken the only part of him Federico couldn't touch. A child's love for a parent.

Domino's love for his mother had been a dark treasure hidden from the world. I had only glimpsed it in stolen moments between us in the darkness. When he was trapped in that semi-lucid haze, lost between wakefulness and sleep. When his brain wasn't firing on all cylinders, I caught glimpses of the vulnerable child beaten out of him.

Last night, I killed that child who had once looked up to his father, searching for approval that would never come.

Hot water scalded my skin, but I stayed under the spray, revelling in the pain. I stroked myself for nothing but comfort. To feel alive. I anchored myself as my mind circled the memories of the last twenty-four hours. My hardness faded as I washed myself, but the ache carved into me only deepened.

Once washed, I stepped out and dried off before getting dressed in his clothes. Submerging myself in his scent. Keeping our tenuous connection alive while I was haunted by the ghost of him. I could text him or call him. My heart begged me to, but my mind knew he wouldn't answer.

His love was a test, and I would weather any storm that he threw my way.

The penthouse was silent. Too silent. Too large. I wanted to hide under the covers, sleep the day away, and wait for him to come home, but my skin itched. The need to draw burned through me. Rain fell in thick sheets beyond the floor-to-ceiling windows, obscuring the city skyline. The sky's muted shades of churning gray clouds provided the perfect lighting, mimicking my somber mood.

The only person here was Ghost, moving like a shadow through the space, always watching but never speaking. I knew I couldn't leave, but there wasn't a single part of me that wanted to.

After grabbing a coffee, I collapsed on the couch. Indistinct charcoal lines covered the page of my open sketchbook on the table. The longer I stared, the clearer the image became in my mind's eye.

Intense eyes formed from the darkness. Fathomless green depths that knew me better than I knew myself. Demons danced in the shadows, whispering truths I couldn't hear. But his eyes knew. They told me what I wasn't ready to understand—but my subconscious did.

The TV murmured in the background, but I wasn't listening. My fingers moved with a life of their own, charcoal smudging across the page. Heavy strokes.

Jagged lines. Breathing life into the image that wouldn't leave me. That haunted me. Because no matter where I looked, no matter what I did—it was always him.

Domino.

Domino was covered in blood, his hands stained red and eyes hollow. Domino mid-fight, muscles strained, the moment before he shattered a man's ribs with a single, brutal kick.

Domino stood over a broken body, chest rising and falling, something feral curling in his gaze.

Domino held down a slight body littered with bruises, their back arched in rapturous pleasure, his hips thrusting. Teeth bared as he fucked into the one he pinned down. Fire burned in his fixated eyes.

It wasn't enough.

I turned the page and started again.

The elevator dinged announcing someone's arrival, I didn't need to look up to know who had entered. The air pressure changed, became charged, and the temperature dropped. My hand continued to move as I lifted my gaze to meet his. Domino walked in, dragging hell in behind him.

His clothes were soaked in blood but there wasn't a mark on him. I could smell it—copper and sweat, the thick, cloying scent of someone else's suffering. His hands were coated in it, staining the creases of his knuckles, the ridges beneath his nails.

His eyes were wrong. Wide and wild, pupils blown, his chest was heaving like he'd run the whole way here. Like he was still running from something. I rose to my feet, taking him in, watching how his fingers twitched at his sides.

"You're shaking," I said.

Domino flinched. Just for a second. Then his face

twisted into something sharp and dangerous. "I don't shake," he snarled.

I didn't move, didn't break eye contact as he pulled out a cigarette and flicked his lighter open. But when he tried to ignite the flame, his grip slipped. The lighter clattered to the floor. A beat of silence passed between us and stretched, the world was frozen still.

His jaw clenched so tight I thought his teeth might crack. That's when I saw them—the demons tearing through him, whispering in his ear, sinking claws into his spine as he bowed under their relentless torment.

Without a word, Domino turned on his heel and stormed down the hall, muscles wound too tight, hands still bloodstained.

I followed. My feet moved without conscious thought. "Domino—"

"Go to bed, Remi." His voice was raw, uneven.

I kept following, refusing to let him walk away from me. "You think you can just come home like this and not—"

He spun to face me faster than I could blink, his hand latched around my throat, digging into the bruises that stained my skin. Pain pulsed beneath his cool fingers, zapping like lightning through my body. The world blurred as his grip tightened, and he threw me onto the bed.

My body crashed onto the bed with a vicious bounce. He followed swiftly behind me like a beast. His humanity was splitting at the seams, revealing the snarling monster beneath. He stalked up the bed, crawling on his hands and knees, body caging me in, pressing me down.

His hands shook where they pinned me. Fingers digging into my skin and leaving fresh marks that made me come alive in his presence. Drawn to him by an invisible magnetic force, the wilder he became, the more I craved him.

"This is your fault," he rasped. Not cold. Not detached. Furious. Fractured. "You did this to me."

I swallowed hard, staring up at him. His chest heaved, blood smeared across his skin. He was unraveling. The mask was gone. The control was gone. I had torn him apart, and I didn't regret it.

My hand cupped his face, fingers tracing along the sharp line of his jaw, his stubble biting into my skin. He tensed beneath my touch, eyes darting between mine like he was searching for something—waiting for me to push him away.

I didn't. I never would. Because he was mine, and I was his. We were interwoven into one another to where I couldn't tell where he ended and I began.

"Your pain is mine too," I whispered, cupping his face and placing a feather-light kiss on his forehead.

He swallowed audibly.

I placed my other hand on his chest, over his racing heart, feeling it pound against my palm. A frantic, erratic rhythm. A war drum. A warning.

"I can bear it with you," I whispered. My voice was steady, but inside, I was burning.

Domino's breathing hitched, his chest rising sharply beneath my hand.

"Use me," I said. My fingers curled into his shirt, clenching in the fabric like an anchor. The blood of his victims stained my skin, and I smiled.

"Take it out on me."

His jaw locked, eyes dark and storming, but he didn't move. He just watched me, gaze flickering between my mouth, my throat, the bruises he'd put there. His mark.

"Break me," I murmured.

His fingers flexed where they still pinned me down.

"Make me into what you need." I let my thumb brush over his lips as he released a shuddering exhale. He was wrecked. "I *love* you."

A pained whimper slipped past his lips, and his eyes shuttered closed as if the words were a blade carving through him. And when they reopened, their beautiful dark green depths had been swallowed by obsidian hunger. His pupils were blown so wide they consumed the color entirely.

A muscle in his jaw twitched. His hands tightened, thick veins protruding against the skin. Something inside him snapped. The moment was palpable, like a bomb detonating, obliterating everything in its path.

His lips crashed down on mine with a force that stole the air from my lungs. A brutal, claiming kiss that wasn't soft, wasn't kind—it was a declaration of war.

Teeth. Nails. Bruising kisses that drew blood and shattered me apart, only to piece me back together under him. He was my master. My dark god. The altar I'd worship.

His hands weren't just gripping me—they were staking a claim. Tearing pieces of me away. Owning. They trailed fire down my skin, branding me with every ragged breath, every growl vibrating through his chest.

I felt his need in every single visceral touch. The way he dug his nails into my waist, into my hips, yanking me closer like the distance between us was unbearable.

The way he bit into my throat, sucking deep enough to leave another mark as my blood coated his lips, another reminder that I was his.

I moaned into his mouth, and he swallowed it whole, his tongue licking into me, dominating, demanding.

His name was carved into my body now, left in bruises and bite marks, in the ache of my muscles, in the sting of my lips.

Domino didn't remove our clothes—he ripped them away. The fabric shredded under his hands, torn apart like nothing more than an inconvenience. A low growl rumbled from his chest as he bared me to him, heat rolling off his skin as it sealed against mine.

His body was a furnace, scorching away the cold that had settled in my bones. The sudden contact stole the air from my lungs, forcing a gasp from my lips that he swallowed with his mouth.

We didn't need whispered words.

There was no need for declarations or sweet reassurances. We understood each other without them.

The way his hands bruised into my skin—demanding, urgent. The way I arched into him, meeting his force with my own. The way his forehead pressed against mine, breaths mingling, shared between us. This was our language.

His large hands hooked under my knees, lifting me, spreading me wider until I was open, exposed, helpless beneath him. His legs caged me in, a predator pinning his prey.

And I wanted to be caught.

The slick, swollen head of his cock notched at my entrance, pressing, teasing—but it wasn't gentle. Nothing about Domino ever was. His dark gaze burned into mine, eyes feral, full of something savage and unrelenting.

Then he drove forward. One brutal thrust punched into me as he forced my body to submit to him.

I choked on a cry as he breached me, filled me, stretched me to the edge of breaking. A sharp burn flared through my spine, pleasure and pain tangled so tightly together I couldn't separate them. My body resisted, then yielded, sucked him deeper until he was buried to the hilt, fully seated inside me.

Domino shuddered, a breathless curse spilling from his lips as he gripped my hips like he was trying to fuse us together.

My nails dragged down his back, leaving marks of my own, staking my claim on him the same way he was branding me. His flesh embedded under my nails, his blood slipping down his back, staining my hands.

His head dipped, teeth sinking into my throat, sucking hard enough to leave a mark that would last for days. A reminder. A warning.

Domino's hips snapped forward, setting a brutal, punishing rhythm. No hesitation. No mercy. Each powerful thrust tore the breath from my lungs, each drag and stretch of his cock against my raw, hypersensitive nerves sent violent tremors through me.

Pleasure and pain collided and fused into something monstrous. A devastating, all-consuming force that left me at his mercy. And I wanted it. Begged for it.

He fucked me like he was breaking me apart just to put me back together. Like he needed to destroy every inch of me before claiming what was left. And I let him.

The thick head of his cock pummeled my prostate with ruthless precision, ripping desperate, wrecked sounds from my throat. My body convulsed beneath him, muscles straining, vision tunneling as the pressure inside me coiled impossibly tight.

"Domino—" His name was a prayer, a plea, a surrender.

I was on the edge of oblivion, teetering between pain and rapture, between madness and salvation.

With one final savage thrust, he shattered me.

The heat of his release seared into my core, marking me, branding me from the inside out. My spine arched off the bed, my head snapping back as my orgasm detonated, white-hot and annihilating.

Thick ropes of cum splattered across my chest, my entire body seizing, locked tight in an inescapable pleasure-ridden agony.

Domino didn't stop.

He fucked me through it, into it, past it— tearing every last aftershock from my wrecked body until the pleasure was too much, too sharp, too consuming.

Darkness rushed in at the edges of my vision, the world spinning away as my body finally gave out.

The last thing I felt was Domino's hands gripping me, holding me down, refusing to let me go.

And I let him; I always would because this was ours.

Because Domino DeMarco would kill for me, and I would die for him, knowing he'd never love anyone else.

Because without him, nothing else mattered.

Ghost's voice cut through my orgasmic haze like a knife through my ribs. "There's a problem with the books."

I pushed myself up from the mattress, limbs heavy, sore, ruined. Domino's arm was still slung over me, his breathing even now, the demons inside him temporarily tamed.

Ghost stood in the doorway, expression unreadable, arms folded across his chest. "Brock's been skimming. A *lot*."

"Brock?" I croaked in confusion.

"Yes." Ghost rolled his eyes. "Your cousin wasn't happy being under your aunt's thumb, so he begged Federico to let him play with the big boys—"

The sound of a blade whistled through the air before embedding itself in the door frame right next to Ghost's head.

"Fucking hell." He froze, eyes going wide as the color drained from his face.

"Get the fuck out of here," Domino growled from behind me. "You ever look in his direction again... I'll pluck your eyeballs from your head and give them to him as a gift."

Domino's voice was like ice crystallizing on my skin. His heated breath against my nape made me shiver as he wrapped a possessive arm around my waist and pulled my body back against his. His possessiveness had a smile flickering at the corner of my lips.

Ghost snorted and rolled his eyes. "Fuck, alright man. Just get out here... soon." The door slammed shut behind him.

"Stupid fucking prick," Domino growled. He pinched my chin between his thumb and forefinger, turning my head to his, and sealed our lips together in a scorching kiss.

Panting for breath, I pulled back and licked the heady taste of him from my lips. "So tell me about my cousin?"

APPARENTLY, BROCK THOUGHT HE WAS UNTOUCHABLE. He thought being Brielle's son and her little situationship with Federico meant he could fuck around with the big guns and never find out while pulling one over on his mother. To him, it was a win-win kind of setup, but reality had a way of teaching lessons.

We were about to prove him wrong. The bigger they were, the harder they fell, and I was going to enjoy every second of it.

We found him holed up in a house Brielle didn't even know existed—a little hidden escape where he played king in the shadows. A place that smelled of expensive whiskey and entitlement.

He thought he was safe there. Untouchable. The irony wasn't lost on me.

It hadn't been hard to get the location from his on-again, off-again squeeze—especially after he fucked her best friend while she was passed out in the bed next to them. Only to wake up and find them lost in the moment.

When Brock opened the door, Domino's boot slammed into his chest, shattering that illusion.

Brock barely had time to breathe before Domino unleashed his fury. Fists of iron slammed into his face over and over until the smug superiority bled from his eyes, leaving behind only fear.

I stood back and let it happen, wondering if I should have brought popcorn. Some lessons had to be taught with blood. Not that I thought even that would get through Brock's thick skull.

Some people were beyond learning.

By the time Domino had him tied up and stuffed in the trunk of his SUV, Brock was barely conscious. Blood dribbled down his chin and pooled in his lap.

But Domino wasn't finished. Not yet. The drive to Hollow Pines was silent aside from Brock's muffled groans.

Domino didn't say a word. He didn't need to. His

rage crackled in the air—controlled, lethal, sharpened to a blade's edge.

My shitty excuse for a cousin had thought no one would miss the ten grand he skimmed off his sales this past month. He was wrong. So very wrong, and he was about to pay the ultimate price. His life.

Soon, Brielle would be getting a gift, too. An appetizer before she came home to the main course. Ghost was tracking her movements. The courier was standing by, and if everything went smoothly, we'd be able to watch her reaction live streamed to my phone.

I couldn't wait.

By the time we reached the care home, Brock was barely able to stand as Domino yanked him from the trunk; his knees buckled as he hit the ground.

"Where… where are we?" he slurred.

His face was swollen, blood drying in streaks down his neck. Domino didn't answer. He simply hauled Brock to his feet like he was dragging out the trash.

Together, we dragged his ass across the manicured lawns, past Hollow Pines, to the home he shared with his mother.

I bypassed the security system in seconds. Once we were inside, we kicked him down the basement stairs. He landed with a crack, a heap at the bottom.

Brock barely had the strength to struggle when we strapped him into the chair. The dim light overhead cast deep, grotesque shadows over his ruined face. He coughed weakly, blood splattering onto the concrete.

Domino didn't care. His ruthless brutality bled through him. He only had eyes for me as his hands moved with expert precision. The first scream echoed through the room as the blade sliced through bone.

A single finger hit the floor with a dull thud.

Brock howled. His body jerked violently against the restraints, eyes wide, blood spilling down his wrist in thick, scarlet rivers.

Domino took his time with the second one. Then the third. By the fourth, Brock could barely make a sound. His body shook violently, pale and clammy from blood loss, sweat slicking his skin. Tears streaked down his battered face.

Domino studied the severed fingers, head tilted, almost curious. He dropped them into the small, elegant wooden box beside him and closed the lid with a quiet snap.

"That's for your mother," Domino murmured, wiping his knife clean with an eerie elegance.

Brock whimpered, snot and tears covering his face. Domino turned to me, handing over the box. I quickly ran upstairs just as the courier arrived.

A delivery for Brielle. She was currently having lunch with the mayor. The stir this would cause would be all over the papers tomorrow; she would be excommunicated by her 'friends', outcast from society.

Ghost had the cameras set up so we'd get to watch her reaction as she received our gift while her son took his last breaths.

By the time I rejoined Domino, he had smelling salts under Brock's nose. Waiting for him to wake up, dragging him back because he wasn't done yet.

Brock gasped awake, his wide eyes ping-ponging around the room. I watched the exact second he realized that he was tied up in his own basement.

A smile tugged at my lips. Domino pushed his sleeves up, slow and methodical. He paced behind Brock, rolling his bloodied knife between his fingers.

Calm. Detached. Back in control. "You fucked up, Brock," he murmured. Voice like silk—sharp as glass.

Brock's breath shuddered. His body trembled. "I—Dom, *please*, man, I—I didn't mean to—"

The knife plunged into his thigh, just missing the femoral artery. Brock's scream was a siren's song. Domino leaned in, twisting the blade until bone scraped against steel.

"That's Mr. DeMarco to you," he said softly.

Brock sobbed. Sniveled. Begged. "S-sorry. I-I'm so sorry Mr. DeMarco…"

I pulled my camera from my bag. Framed the shot and captured the moment. The lighting was shit, but it would be clear enough to haunt Brielle before we came for her.

Domino let Brock bleed. Let the fear set in. Let him feel it—the inevitability of what was coming. I didn't look away. Couldn't. Watching Domino work was like watching poetry in motion.

I watched as Domino broke him.

Piece by piece.

And when Brock finally stopped begging and started blaming—when the last shred of dignity burned away in rage and terror—

Domino turned to me.

"How does this end, Remi?"

A gift.

One only he knew I'd love.

I stepped forward, slow and deliberate. My fingers curled around the hilt of the knife still lodged in Brock's thigh. His breath hitched. His glassy eyes locked onto mine, lips moving, but no sound left them.

"I told you once," I murmured, leaning in. "Touch what's mine, and I'll make sure you never touch anything again. This is for Mom." I ripped the blade free and drove it higher, right into his armpit, deep enough to sever the axillary artery. Blood bubbled around the knife lodged in his side.

Scream after scream tore from Brock's throat. He knew this was it. Blood vessels burst in his eyes, but his gaze never left mine.

I leaned in close. "See you in hell," I whispered. I yanked the blade from his body. Nothing could have prepared me for the deluge of blood that spilled from him.

Domino smiled as I settled on his lap, straddling him, bloodstained hands cupping his cheeks.

"Thank you," I breathed against his lips.

He traced his fingers through the blood on my skin. "To see you free like this," he murmured. "Is a thing of beauty."

A shudder ripped through me as his lips sealed to mine. Lost in each other's embrace, time ceased to exist.

Hours passed.

Brock took his last, rattling breaths.

Eventually, when the sky had turned black, Brielle came home. Her broken whimpers sent a thrill up my spine as she called Brock's name.

Only silence answered her.

"Brock?" Her voice cracked. "Stop fucking around and c-come h-here…"

She trailed off as I knocked over a tin of paint from the shelf behind me. Like the fool she was, Brielle followed the sound.

"Brock, honey, you down here?"

I smothered a laugh as she stumbled off the last step, catching herself on a pile of boxes opposite the staircase. Her hand blindly reached for the light switch. The light flickered before it flooded the room, unleashing the horror show we had created for her.

The scream that tore from her throat was almost as satisfying as the look she gave me when she realized I was waiting for her.

Her eyes locked onto mine, wide with horror. "You let this happen," she whispered, her voice trembling.

I tilted my head and let a slow smile stretch across my lips. Not an ounce of remorse in my veins. "No," I murmured. "I made it happen."

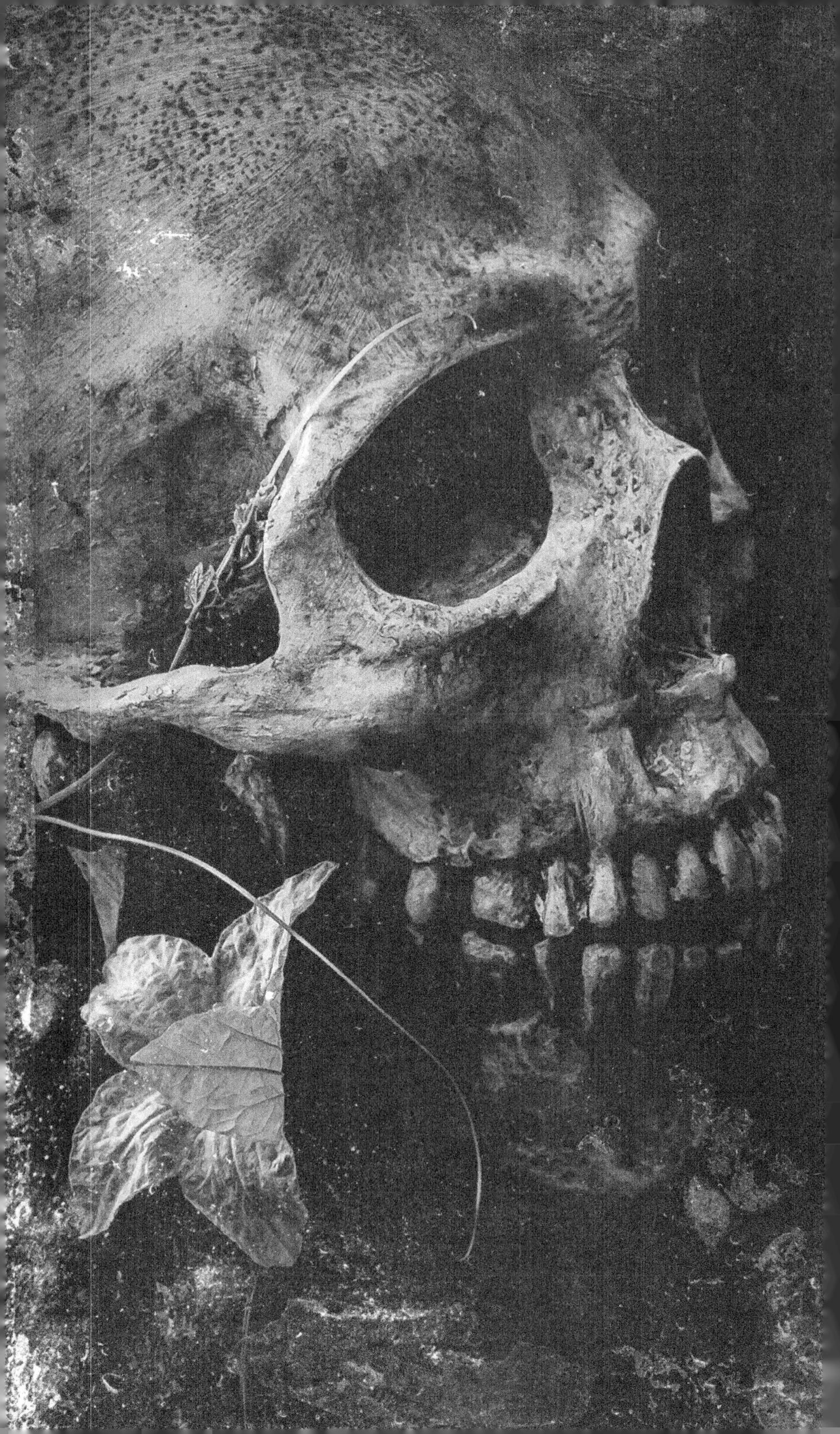

20 DOMINO

Documents lay sprawled across the coffee table, a mess of numbers and names, wire transfers and timestamps. A spider web of deception. So many details blurred together until they became a single, unbearable truth—one I refused to accept.

Brielle was a manipulator. A liar. A survivor who never played a game she couldn't win. She always had an exit strategy. And now, with someone clearly closing in on her, this?

This looked too convenient. My fingers twitched at my sides, my pulse hammering in my ears. It was all there—dates, encrypted messages, bank records that traced back to Federico.

Proof.

Remi had spent hours digging through these files, pulling together an airtight case of Federico's betrayal.

Ghost had backed him up. They'd worked together, meticulously piecing through every digital breadcrumb until they found what they were looking for.

But the voice in my head wouldn't shut the fuck up. It was too easy. The words on the pages shifted under my gaze, smudging at the edges. The ink felt false, too neat, too damning.

Printouts could be doctored.

Numbers could be fabricated.

I dragged a hand down my face, pressing my fingers into my eyes until colors burst behind my lids. Something wasn't right. I just couldn't pinpoint where that niggling sensation came from and what it meant. But I wouldn't stop until I knew the truth.

"Domino." Remi's voice was sharp. I opened my eyes. He was watching me—tense, waiting. "This is real," he said, his tone edged with frustration.

He wanted me to see it. To accept it. But conviction wasn't proof. I wouldn't believe it until the devil himself made them whole.

I lifted my cigarette to my lips, exhaling slowly. The smoke curled between us, twisting in the dim light. "It means nothing without something physical," I muttered. "A paper trail can be rewritten."

Remi's jaw ticked. I saw the way his fingers flexed against his knee like he wanted to hit something; his body vibrated. His teeth sank into his full bottom lip like he was fighting to keep words at bay.

Before he could argue, my phone vibrated against the table. The sound sent a cold rush down my spine. I turned it over and froze. The name flashing across the screen made my blood run cold.

Federico.

It was like he knew we were talking about him. I

reached for the phone, gripping it so hard my knuckles went white. Swiped to answer, and brought it to my ear.

My father's voice slithered through the receiver, smooth but firm. Commanding. "We need to talk. Now."

The muscles in my jaw locked. My grip tightened around the plastic casing, the subtle crack of strain barely registering. This wasn't a request. Federico didn't make requests.

He dealt in orders, ultimatums, and consequences.

Emotions were for the weak.

"Where?" I forced out through gritted teeth.

"The compound. Thirty minutes."

The line went dead. I lowered the phone, my stomach twisting into knots. The timing was too fucking perfect. Federico knew something, or at the very least, he suspected.

I turned my head, my gaze locking onto Remi. Teeth sank into his bottom lip, chewing on his piercings. He was perched on the edge of the couch, watching me. The intensity in his eyes seared right through to the marrow of my bones. The oversized hoodie he'd stolen from me swallowed him whole, sleeves bunched around his hands. His black skinny jeans clung to his legs, hugging the sharp angles of his frame.

My marks stained his skin.

A litany of ownership. *Obsession*.

The soft glow from the lamp caught the deep, bruised circles under his eyes, but his expression remained carefully unreadable. Even now, even with doubt crawling under my skin, I knew one thing with absolute certainty.

Remi was ready to go. Ready to do whatever I asked. Because we weren't just partners.

We were something *worse*.

Bound together by violence, by blood, by a need so deep it bordered on sickness.

The darkness curled in his gaze, coiled in his bones, whispered against his skin. It called to the monster in me—the one teetering on the edge, caught between control and the abyss.

Before Remi, the only person I'd ever cared about was the one I couldn't even remember. Not really. A child's memory, faded with time, slipping away like sand through an hourglass.

I stubbed out my cigarette with a hiss and locked eyes with him. "Let's go," I growled.

"Where?" Remi asked, following behind me to the elevator.

"The DeMarco compound."

We slipped inside, the doors sliding shut with a quiet pssh.

"When we get there, once I'm in the meeting and everyone is occupied," I murmured, my voice low and firm, "I want you to search the house. His office. His room. Find anything that ties into this."

Remi blinked up at me, silent but understanding. He didn't need to ask what would happen once we had proof. He knew.

He knew the lengths I'd go to for the truth.

He knew the vengeance I'd enact when I uncovered it.

I didn't trust anyone in this world—except Remi. He had proven his loyalty, not with empty words but by offering his life without hesitation. It only fed the sickness I had for him.

It wasn't just loyalty. It was obsession. A quiet, all-consuming poison fusing into my bones like a cancer.

My Ninja H2R roared to life beneath me, the vibrations rattling through my chest. The only things keeping me tethered to reality were Remi's hands gripping my waist and the thrumming engine between my legs.

Everything else? It was nothing. The streets blurred. The countryside vanished. Until the blackened iron gates of the DeMarco compound materialized before us. The DeMarco crest gleamed in the dim light. A sigil of power and blood. Fear and control.

I felt it before I saw it—the shift in the air. Tension coiled around the compound, thick enough to choke on. By the time we reached the inner courtyard, the security presence had tripled.

Men were stationed at every entrance, their hands hovering near their weapons, their eyes scanning the perimeter like they were expecting an attack or worse—preparing for one.

I barely had time to kill the engine before three men stepped forward, shifting uneasily under my gaze as I removed my helmet. Their shoulders went rigid. Their expressions were blank, like they were trained to be. But I saw it—the flinch.

A smirk curled my lips. They knew who to fear, and I drank it in. My father may have been a monster, but he had shaped me in his image. If he was the devil, I was the antichrist.

I was the darkness that stalked them in their nightmares. The thing that slithered through their thoughts in the quiet moments.

Their lives?

They hinged on my whim.

I swung my leg off the bike, my boots hitting the stone with purpose. I turned to Remi and nodded toward the entrance. "Stay close."

Remi didn't argue, falling in step with me like my shadow. But as we stepped toward the doors, something coiled in my gut.

Something cold.

Something final.

A feeling like the world had just tipped—a moment too late to stop whatever was coming.

The doors swung open. "Domino," Bernard greeted, a tight smile pressed to his lips. "A wonderful surprise."

A warning. His words weren't a formality. They were caution wrapped in pleasantries.

"Your father and *his* men are in the great room."

A den of vipers laying in wait. They thought I feared them because I was younger, under the illusion that my father had me collared and chained. But that shackle had fallen away a long time ago—along with my sanity.

Rage twisted through my veins, tightly leashed.

I clapped Bernard on the shoulder. "Berny." I gestured toward Remi. "This is—"

"Remi," Bernard cut in, dipping his head. "A pleasure to finally meet you."

His gaze flicked to Remi, something dark passing through his expression before he extended a hand. Remi hesitated but shook it.

"Make sure he's—"

"He will be safe within these walls," Bernard said firmly, his voice edged with steel. "Wherever he may need to go…"

"Good."

He leaned in, his voice dropping to a whisper. "My loyalty is to you and you alone."

Shock crashed over me, the indifference in my cold mask unbreakable. The implication of his words was not lost on me. He'd chosen a side when lines hadn't even been drawn in the sand.

And with that, Bernard ushered him away. "This way, Remi. Let's get you a drink."

Their voices faded as they disappeared into the vast house, and I turned, heading in the opposite direction toward the great room where Federico liked to hold his meetings when numbers were required as a show of strength. His frailty was becoming evident in his need to amass his men to his cause.

The hallway stretched before me, dark walls lined with portraits of DeMarcos past. Cold, judging faces stared down at me. A legacy I'd been trained to want. A legacy I'd been promised. But as with all things in this world, it was built on an insurmountable mountain of blood and lies.

Power. Control. Death.

That was the true inheritance Federico DeMarco wanted to pass on to me—not this compound, his millions, or his kingdom of cowards. And I didn't want it.

I craved something else. Destruction. Annihilation. Power that would be granted to me not by men but by gods. I didn't want an army. I wanted death itself to bow at my feet. I wanted to wield it like a weapon.

Blood-slicked hands. Final heartbeats. Glazed-over eyes staring into nothing. That was power. That's what I wanted, and it was mine for the taking.

The double doors loomed ahead, thick mahogany polished to a gleam. Beyond them, voices rumbled— low, sharp-edged words laced with irritation and restraint. Twelve men, maybe more. My father's inner circle.

Federico DeMarco didn't tolerate incompetence. If

you made it to his table—his inner sanctum— it meant you were ruthless, loyal, and fucking useful.

As I pushed the doors open and strode through, the conversation died. Words collapsed into silence as every head turned in my direction. The sudden stillness was suffocating, a vice wrapped around the room.

At the center of the Great Room—what the lower ranks called the War Room—a long, dark wooden table stretched, large enough to seat twenty. At its head, Federico sat like a king rotting on his throne, his enforcers and advisors flanking him like well-dressed jackals.

Cigar smoke curled through the air, thick and heavy, filtered by the weak sunlight from the wall of glass that overlooked the manicured gardens. Whiskey glinted in an array of cut crystal glasses on the table, untouched, forgotten.

I didn't rush as they waited. I circled them. Slow. Controlled. Letting the silence stretch, letting it grow thick enough to choke. My gaze landed on each of them in turn—men who had ordered deaths, conquered territory, and broken men beyond repair. They would stab each other in the back in a heartbeat if it meant they were another rung up the ladder.

One by one, they dropped their gazes in begrudging deference. They knew who held the real power in the room. Who held their life and the lives of their families in the palm of their hand.

A room full of powerful men—made men—flinched before me.

Their fear was a heady fucking thing.

Federico exhaled sharply, his scornful scoff cutting through the silence like a blade. He leaned back in his chair, draping one arm casually over the side, but I didn't miss the tremor in his fingers. His face was unreadable, but his eyes? They burned with hate.

"Domino." His voice rasped, low but firm. "Sit."

I didn't. "Father," I greeted evenly.

His jaw ticked. "You took your time."

I tilted my head. "I didn't realize we were on a schedule." My voice was light. Mocking. "Traffic was… hectic in the city."

Federico's fingers drummed once against the table before stilling. A warning. "Don't test me, boy."

I smirked, slow and sharp. Not a single ounce of warmth in it. His nostrils flared. He was waiting for me to fold. I never did.

My father leaned forward, planting his elbows on the table. "You think you're ready to carry the DeMarco name?"

I didn't answer. I didn't need to, just held his gaze with an unwavering intensity. A silent challenge.

Federico's eyes narrowed. "You can't even deal with the fucking Gallos."

The air crackled between us.

His voice sharpened. "They're running riot through my ports—" he paused, a correction, an afterthought. "Our ports. They're disrupting shipments, making us look weak."

I said nothing. Because the only one who looked weak was him. The only one who hadn't lifted a finger or gun was him. I'd slaughtered and buried Gallos in shallow graves across our territory. I'd stained Marlow Heights red so deeply it had seeped into the foundation of the city.

And yet, Federico sat there seething.

He had always been a slave to his temper. He

mistook rage for power. Control for dominance. But now, his men were watching. Measuring.

My silence was pushing him closer to the edge.

The veins in his forehead throbbed before he slammed a fist onto the table. The whiskey glasses rattled. His voice cut like steel—"And you do nothing!"

A murmur rippled down the table. Dissent. Small. But unmistakably there.

Giancarlo's voice cut through the silence, "You sit on your hands while the Gallos piss on our empire." His tone was cold, a calculated knife to the throat. "And yet, we still pretend Federico's in control."

I swallowed the laugh that climbed my throat. Eyes snapped to Giancarlo. Then to Federico. Then to me.

A hush settled as tensions rose. No one spoke, although it was clear to see silent words forming on their lips. I felt the shift before it happened. The air thickened, turning electric. Hands twitched toward weapons. Bodies shifted. A fraction of hesitation. A moment of reckoning.

I tracked my father's movements. Watched as his lips curled, a ghost of a sneer crept onto his face. In my mind, I heard his voice. A lesson from my childhood, burned into memory.

"If anyone challenges you in the open, make it a public execution. Send that message home with their blood. Don't show weakness."

Federico moved as swiftly as he was able. His hand dipped beneath the table. I could read him like a child's book. Before he could pull his gun, I moved first. My movements were swift and sure.

A knife buried deep into the wood—right between his fingers. The room erupted into chaos like the snap of an elastic band. Everything changed in a fraction of a second. Chairs scraped. Hands flew to weapons. Chaos capitulated into madness around us.

Federico's nostrils flared, his other hand twitching toward his gun. I didn't blink. Didn't flinch. I was already at his shoulder and leaned in slightly, voice low, almost amused. "Careful, old man," I murmured. "You're making it too easy for them."

His eyes burned. Rage. Hate. But beneath it?
Fear.

Because this—this was the beginning of the end. He lost control of his most faithful flock. The king had lost his crown. As the sound of bullets rang out and the sharp scent of gunpowder filled the air, he shrank back.

A hollow laugh ripped out of my chest as he stumbled toward the sideboard—toward the hidden tunnels. No one stopped him. Not one man in the room noticed his departure. No one but me.

I pulled the Glock from my belt and fired off two rounds into the chain that held up the chandelier, crashing it down on the table. Every single man froze, arms outstretched, guns aimed at each other, but their attention was on me.

"Either fall in line and bend the knee to me or say your goodbyes in your prayers."

The words cut the room like ice, and five men dropped to their knees, heads bowed. In less than a heartbeat, the first man fell. Then another. Then another. A bullet between the eyes.

The last thing they saw?
Me.

The doors opened to the hallway, and in stepped Bernard. "I'll have this cleaned up right away."

"Thank you." My eyes narrowed when I realized he

was alone. A sharp inhale was all I managed before Bernard answered my unspoken question.

"He's upstairs in Federico's room."

The pounding of my footsteps was absorbed by the thick carpet as I climbed the stairs two at a time. Each step was a drumbeat in my head, driving me forward. A prickle of unease slithered down my spine.

Federico was injured, but a wounded animal was often the most dangerous. I knew Remi could handle himself—he never went anywhere unarmed—but Federico had years of experience. These walls, these hidden tunnels—they were his. He could be anywhere in an instant.

I hit the landing, my breath even, my muscles coiled tight. Federico had a panic room installed after his injury, a fortress built into the bones of this house. I was certain that was where he was heading. Where cowards hid until their reinforcements arrived.

Gun raised. Arm steady. I moved like a phantom through the hall. Silent. Predatory. Eyes darting, checking for any guards that might be patrolling the upper levels.

A noise carried through the still air. Low and dangerous. I slowed, my breath evening out, my heart hammering a steady rhythm against my ribs. I followed the sound, every step measured, each movement precise.

"What the fuck are you doing in my room?" Federico's voice was raw with rage.

I kept to the shadows, moving closer until I could see through the partially open door. The angle kept me hidden, my presence nothing more than a whisper in the air.

Remi stood in the center of the room, his body still.

Tense. A statue carved from ice and violence. But I saw the tightness around his eyes. Fear.

Federico had a gun raised, aimed directly at Remi's head. His posture was loose but controlled. Calculating. A man who had spent his entire life deciding who lived and who died.

Remi didn't flinch. He didn't cower. Fuck, he was beautiful like this. On edge. Calculating.

Every instinct in my body screamed at me to intervene. To put a bullet between Federico's eyes before his finger so much as twitched.

But I didn't.

Because I wanted to see what Remi would do.

"I was looking for proof," he said, voice level. Flat. "Proof that you arranged Domino's mother's death."

Federico scoffed, shaking his head as if he couldn't believe the audacity. "You little freaks don't know what you're talking about."

My fingers tightened around my gun. The way he said it—dismissive, like we were nothing.

Remi's gaze flickered downward. Files and papers were scattered across the floor. Shattered truths.

His voice turned to steel. "All the proof I need is right there. The question is—why?"

"You don't need to worry yourself about details you wouldn't understand." His voice dropped into something almost amused. Cruel. Then he tilted his head, eyes glinting. "You're a cheap fuck. A distraction for my son. Nothing more."

Remi didn't flinch. I'd proved myself to him just like he had to me. There was nothing in this world that could tear us apart.

Federico cocked the gun, adjusting his stance. He

tightened his aim. "And it's about time I took out the trash."

Something in me snapped. But I didn't move. Not yet. I watched with unnerving focus. Tracked the way Federico's shoulders locked, his stance squared. He was going to fire.

Remi must have sensed it, too. He shifted slightly, his lips parting—stalling. Fuck, he was perfect.

"If I'm going to die," he said, voice steady, "you might as well tell me." A small pause. Calculated. "Because we all know no one hears a dead man's word."

A sharp, dangerous grin split Federico's face. His head tipped back on his shoulders and laughed. Cold. Cruel. Certain. That's when he gave me exactly what I wanted. What I'd needed.

"Of course I killed her," his tone almost bored. "She got in the way. She was going to ruin everything. And that baby of hers?" His head tilted slightly. Mocking. "An abomination."

Remi's hands curled into fists. His right hand shifted, fingers brushing over the strap around his forearm—where his knife was hidden.

Federico continued, oblivious to the danger standing in front of him. "But I trained him right. Broke him. And now? He's my greatest weapon."

I moved then like a shadow slipping through the room until I was right behind him. I pressed the cold metal of my Glock against his ear.

Federico sensed me too late. His finger tightened on the trigger—

But I fired first. The gunshot cracked through the air like thunder. Blood sprayed as Federico collapsed forward, clutching his mangled, ringing ear. His gun clattered to the floor, and I quickly kicked it away. His screams were delicious.

He writhed, his breath coming in short, ragged pants. Wet, furious sounds spluttered from his lips. I huffed a laugh and knelt, pressing my knee to his chest. Let him feel the weight of his mistakes.

The barrel of my gun found his temple. His eyes were wide with shock, like he couldn't believe I was there.

That's what happened when you got comfortable. You made mistakes.

"You fucked up, old man." My voice was low. Even. Deadly.

He sucked in a sharp, shuddering breath.

"She was a good woman," I murmured. "And she didn't deserve to die."

Before he could speak, I pistol-whipped him. The crack of metal against bone was sickening perfection.

Federico's body went slack. Blood leaked from his temple, pooling across the hardwood like ink.

Blissful silence filled the room. I rose to my feet, turning to Remi as he stood there, unmoving. His face was blank, but his eyes—his eyes were dark, stormy.

I stepped toward him. He didn't flinch. Didn't step away. I reached out, my fingers brushing over his cheek. Blood—Federico's blood—smeared against his skin.

He didn't react. Didn't breathe. Just kept his ice-blue eyes locked on mine. Then—slowly—he exhaled, and his eyes fluttered closed. I traced the line of his jaw with my thumb, relishing in the way his pulse thrummed beneath his skin.

We didn't speak.
We didn't need to.

Because this?
This was just the beginning.

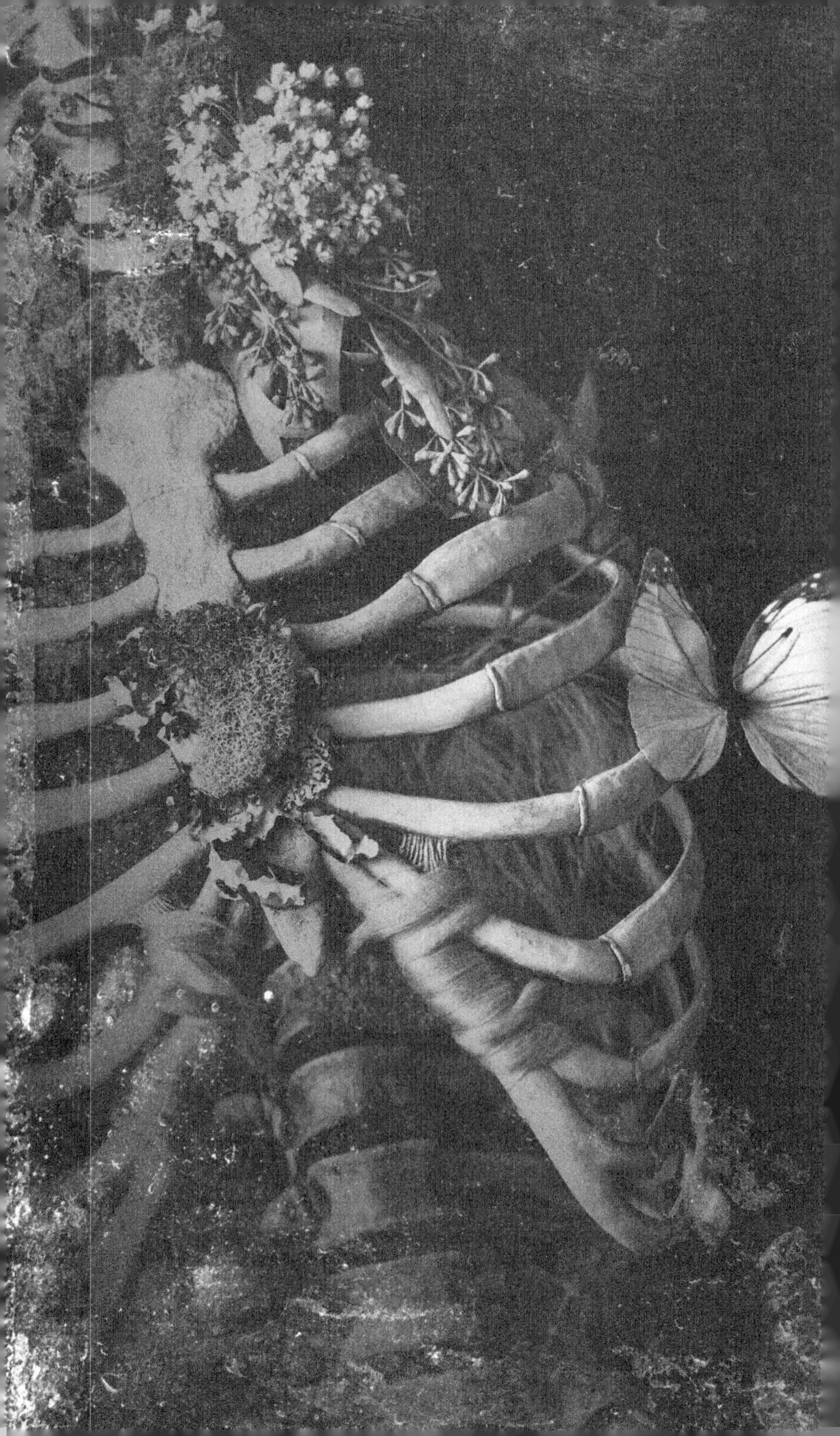

21 REMI

Domino stashed his bike in the mouth of an empty shipping container, its walls yawning open like the gaping maw of some steel beast. He locked it up tightly before pulling a cigarette from his jacket, lighting it with an almost bored efficiency. The flame flickered against his sharp cheekbones before he inhaled, exhaling a slow plume of smoke into the damp air.

Without a word, he handed it off to me and lit another. We moved forward, the crunch of gravel beneath our boots giving way to the flat, dead sound of concrete.

The docks reeked of rot. Of salt and rusted metal, of old oil and older blood. The kind that had seeped into its surroundings over decades, whispering of men who had disappeared beneath these waters, their names long forgotten.

A thick mist curled over the ground, wrapping around our ankles like spectral hands. It made it nearly impossible to see more than a foot ahead. Spotlights cut through the fog in sharp, surgical slices, turning everything ghostly, unnatural. The water lapped at the pylons below, rhythmic but somehow offbeat, as if the sea itself sensed what was coming.

I broke the silence first. "What are you going to do about Federico?"

Domino didn't answer right away. Instead, he walked a little ahead; the fog swallowed him in pieces—first his legs, then his torso, until he looked like nothing more than a shadow bleeding into the mist.

"I will end him." He turned slightly. His dark green eyes were nothing but swirling shadows. "I won't come at him head-on," he added. "He'll be expecting it."

I mulled over his words. Federico was smart. Ruthless. He'd built an empire on paranoia and the absolute certainty that everyone in his orbit would betray him, eventually. It made him dangerous. But it also meant he was waiting for the knife in his back.

"We could do what we did with Brielle."

Domino huffed a short, amused laugh. "What was that?" he mused. "Make her piss herself every time she moved?"

"Yes." A slow smile curled my lips. "Play shadow games. Make him feel like he's losing his mind before you end him. Make him suffer."

Domino exhaled another drag, the ember at the tip of his cigarette glowing like an eye in the dark. "You want to play the long game, *piccolo agnello?*"

I grunted in affirmation. I could already see it—the slow unraveling of a man who thought himself untouchable. The power of fear, how it could corrode a person's mind long before the knife ever touched their skin.

A sharp thrill crawled up my spine.

Domino moved fast. One second, he was smoking beside me. The next, I was pinned against the frozen metal of a shipping container, his hand wrapped around my throat.

The force of it sent a shudder through me, pleasure and pain threading together in a heady mix. His breath, laced with nicotine and something darker, ghosted over my lips, his smirk curling as I let him take, let him hold.

"What are you thinking?" His voice was low, a growl in the night.

His nose brushed up the column of my throat, and a deep, resonant sound rumbled in his chest.

I was so fucking gone for him.

My body betrayed me instantly. My hips punched forward on instinct as he slid a thigh between my legs, his grip tightening just enough to make the edges of my vision blur.

"I'm thinking..." I exhaled shakily. "About all the things we could do to him. When he's strung up in your playroom."

Domino snorted softly, his lips brushing against my pulse. "Is that what you call it?"

"Yes," I hissed as his teeth sank into my neck, his mark sinking deep into my skin.

This morning, I had mourned the fading bruises in the mirror. Now? He was refreshing them. Staking his claim and feeding my obsession. With the way he owned me, forced me to submit to his every sick and twisted whim.

Blunt nails dug into my jaw, tipping my head back as his mouth crashed into mine. Teeth scraped against skin, sharp and unforgiving. A gasp caught in my throat before his teeth sank into my bottom lip, tearing at the flesh until the metallic burn of copper burst across our tongues.

I moaned into him, and he swallowed it whole.

My hands fisted into his jacket, dragging him closer, the kiss deepening into something raw, violent—never sweet, never soft. This was the language we spoke: pain and pleasure, power and surrender, the sharp bite of desire laced with destruction.

Domino smirked against my mouth, pulling back just enough to mutter, "You're fucking desperate."

I bit him back. Hard enough to feel the sharp pull of his breath, the way his grip on my throat tightened just enough to make me dizzy. I licked into his mouth, tasting blood and smoke, and groaned when his fingers tugged my hair back brutally.

"Say it," he rasped, his voice like gravel.

"Say what?"

"That you want me."

I exhaled sharply, my hands dragging over his scarred knuckles encased in cold metal, his solid chest, his lethal body pressed against mine. I tilted my chin up, let him see it in my eyes, "I want you."

Domino hummed, satisfied, before abruptly releasing me. I nearly stumbled, my breath ragged as he wiped his thumb over his bottom lip, smearing the blood across his face.

"Later," he murmured, dark promise dripping from the word.

Cold wind bit at my skin, the haunting mist around us dissipating as a fine drizzle fell. The droplets glistened in his black hair like scattered diamonds. They always said the devil was the most beautiful angel before he fell; they just didn't know how true that was.

Domino stood beside me, silent, the weight of his presence pressing against my skin like a second heartbeat. His fingers twitched at his sides, his stance deceptively loose—but I knew better. It was a predator's ease. A readiness coiled into every muscle, waiting for the moment to strike.

The docks stretched ahead, swallowed in mist. Thick and unnatural, the fog clung to the ground like a living thing, curling around the rusted shipping containers, masking movement, swallowing sound. The air was damp, heavy with the tang of salt and oil, but beneath it lurked something else. Something rotting.

We'd set the bait—a fake shipment marked with the DeMarco insignia. Loud. Blatant. A neon sign blinking in the dark. A hook waiting in the water for something to bite.

But the Gallos weren't stupid. They were one of the most powerful families on the East Coast, and Federico was obsessed with taking them down. It made him reckless. But it didn't make him an idiot.

I doubted they'd fall for such an obvious trap. It worked. Just not the way we expected.

The first crate hit the dock with a dull, wet thud. A ripple of unease slithered down my spine, cold and uncertain. Something was wrong. The usual noises had vanished, the distant grumble of a passing boat and the faint screech of gulls overhead. The occasional scuttling of rats through the shipping containers. Gone.

The silence was suffocating, as thick as the fog itself.

Domino noticed it, too. I saw the subtle shift in his posture—shoulders squared, jaw clenched. His head tilted slightly, listening.

A sound. Soft. Barely there. Like breath against the mist. I inhaled sharply, drawing in the damp night air. And that's when I smelled it.

Not salt. Not rain.

Something sweet.

Chemical.

Thick enough to drown out everything else... Chloroform.

Realization hit a second too late. I turned toward it, and a hand clamped over my face. The scent flooded my lungs, thick and cloying. I jerked, but my body wasn't listening. My limbs felt heavy. Slow. My vision wavered at the edges, the world warping like oil on water.

I struggled, twisting and wrenching against the unseen grip. But it was like fighting through wet concrete. My ears rang, my breath shallow and useless as it drew more of the chemical into my burning lungs.

Domino, his name rang in my head like a fading echo. Through the haze, I saw him. His head snapped toward me, his body already in motion. A blur of black against the eerie white mist.

His gun was raised, his mouth open—

Then—blackness. The night swallowed me whole.

Pain dragged me from the depths of unconsciousness. A sharp, throbbing ache pounded against my skull, the kind of deep, relentless pain that made my vision blur at the edges. My throat was raw, my mouth parched, each breath scraping against the inside of my chest like sandpaper. The air was thick, grating against my raw throat like shards of glass.

Something cold dug into my wrists. I shifted, a sharp sting blooming where the restraints had already rubbed my skin raw. My shoulders screamed in protest, wrenched behind my back, leaving my body slumped, legs sprawled uselessly in front of me.

A haze crawled through my veins, making everything sluggish. My pulse was too slow, my movements too heavy. I sucked in a slow breath and forced my eyelids open.

A gun was pressed against my temple.

The pressure was unmistakable. A silent threat. A reminder of where I was. I blinked rapidly, the blur of unconsciousness receding as my surroundings sharpened into focus.

Cold concrete floors. Dim light flickering against damp walls. The air reeked of rust, sweat, and the faint metallic bite of blood.

And the knowledge that I wasn't alone.

Shapes loomed at the edges of my vision. Men. Their presence curled through the space, thick and oppressive, shadows shifting in the dim light. I was tied to a thick wooden beam, my arms pinned behind me. On display. Like an animal in a cage.

But my thoughts weren't on them. They were on *him.* I forced my head up, searching desperately for Domino.

Movement a few feet away caught my eye. A slumped figure.

He was still unconscious, hanging from a rusted pipe overhead, his arms bound and suspended, thick steel cuffs biting into his wrists. His body—always sharp, always primed for violence was disturbingly slack.

My stomach twisted. The sick bastards had left him shirtless. Bruises and deep, fresh cuts marred his skin, a grotesque canvas of whatever welcome party they'd thrown while I was out. His dark hair fell over his face, hiding his eyes, but I knew what I'd see when he woke—rage. Cold, lethal, unrelenting rage.

I exhaled a slow, deliberate breath, trying to control the ice creeping into my blood. This was bad.

But I took comfort in the sight before me. His broad chest rose and fell in slow, controlled breaths. I watched his fingers twitch, muscles coiling even in unconsciousness, and I knew—his body was already recalibrating. Already preparing for war.

My pulse roared in my ears. I wrenched my gaze away from him and swept the room again, the details snapping into sharper clarity now that my mind had burned off the haze.

A group of men. Watching. Waiting.

They lingered in the shadows, their eyes gleaming with anticipation. They were predators who had cornered something dangerous. A wounded animal. But even still—not one of them looked at Domino without unease. There was a silent understanding among them.

They knew what he was. And they knew the moment he woke up was the moment they lost their advantage. There would be hell to pay.

My gaze flicked to the man standing at the center of it all. The ice in my veins turned to steel.

Salvatore Gallo.

A legend. A ghost of the underworld. A name spoken in hushed whispers. The only man feared more than Domino himself.

He was older, maybe in his late fifties, with dark salt and

pepper hair slicked back with ruthless precision. A tailored suit draped over his broad frame, power exuding from every inch of him—the kind of power that didn't need to lift a gun to kill you. His word alone was enough to evoke fear.

He studied me like I was something insignificant. An insect beneath his shoe.

I lifted my chin. Refusing to look away. Refusing to cower. "Salva…" My voice was hoarse, throat raw. I swallowed the ache. "Gallo."

A slow smirk curled his lips. "So, you're the little stray that's got my son wrapped around your finger."

The words hit me like ice water searing against my skin. His son? Confusion flickered in my chest. What the fuck was he talking about? But before I could react, a sharp chuckle sliced through the thick silence.

"Rise and shine, sweetheart." The voice was smooth. Amused. Dangerous.

I shifted my gaze. He was young—late twenties. Tall, lean but strong, his dark wavy hair falling in deliberate disarray. His eyes were dark, gleaming with something sharp. Mischief. And menace.

He crouched in front of me, the gun still pressed against my temple, his head tilting as he studied me.

"You're smaller than I expected," he mused. Mocking. "But I can see why he likes you. That pretty little mouth must be good for something."

I didn't flinch. Didn't give him the satisfaction. But my blood turned to acid. Every nerve in my body itched to move. To tear. To maim. To kill. My fingers twitched with the phantom weight of a blade, desperate to drive it straight into his gut and twist.

But I stayed still. Nothing. No reaction. I refused to give him the satisfaction.

His smirk widened. "Nothing?" He tapped the gun against my temple, his voice dropping to something almost... gentle. Cruel. "Must have a real solid head on your shoulders." A pause. "Be a shame if something happened to it."

I stared him down. "Go ahead, then. Blow my brains out."

He grinned. "Oh, I like this one."

A sigh. Another voice. Colder. "Ellio, stop playing with your food."

I shifted my gaze. This one was older. Early thirties, maybe. Sharper. Broader. His dark wavy hair was slicked back, his crisp black suit immaculate. His silver eyes held no amusement. No warmth. Only calculation.

Ellio clicked his tongue, but his smirk never wavered. "You're no fun, Luca."

Luca.

Ellio.

I filed their names away. But before I could think further, something shifted. The air changed. Thickened. A pulse of unrestrained violence rippled through the space.

Ellio must have felt it, too. His smirk faltered for half a second.

A low, barely there sound tugged at my soul. Domino stirred. A slow, deliberate stretch of his fingers. The first shift of his breath. His muscles tightened.

The devil was waking up.

A soft chuckle slithered through my lips, and I saw Ellio's grip on the gun tighten. He pushed up to standing, his gun still trained on me, keeping me exactly where he wanted—a position of weakness.

It wouldn't last because soon, my monster would

open his eyes. When he did, they would all die. And I would be standing at his side, bathing in their blood.

A door creaked open somewhere behind me, the metal groaning. The men shadowing those in front of me straightened their stances and pulled their shoulders back—not in fear, but in acknowledgment, in silent respect.

The newcomer moved with the kind of confidence that came from a lifetime of control. His tailored suit was expensive but understated, dark fabric crisp, untouched by the damp, blood-stained air of the warehouse. He carried himself like a man who had never known uncertainty, whose orders had never been questioned. Power wrapped around him like a second skin.

His gaze landed on me, slow and assessing. Not curious. Not intrigued. Just... amused. Like I was an attraction at a zoo. Like I was dirt beneath his shoe.

The side of his mouth curled. "So, you're the little stray."

My jaw tightened, my gaze flicking to Domino.

Ellio chuckled, tracking the movement with predatory satisfaction. "He killed two of our men when he realized we had you. Didn't he Enzo?"

"He's got a vicious right hook."

"I did warn you all to be prepared. You know how many of our men he's taken down single-handedly." Salvator murmured his voice low, commanding. "But you didn't listen, did you Diego? Mmm?"

The man beside him—Diego—tilted his head, looking me up and down like I was an anomaly he couldn't quite figure out. He was broad-shouldered, with the solid build of a brawler, dark hair cut close to his scalp on the sides. His face was all sharp angles and harsh lines, a faint scar running down his cheek.

"He's like a rabid dog," Enzo muttered, voice laced with quiet menace. His gaze swept over me again, assessing, weighing. "What makes you worth killing for?"

I didn't answer. My lips pressed into a tight line, a million retorts flickered through my mind. But I wouldn't give them the satisfaction of breaking my control.

"Enough, Enzo," Salvatore said, voice calm, steady. Deadly. "This is going to be hard enough as it is. For all of us."

"But why now?" Diego's expression hardened, but he was watching his father closely. "Federico is weak."

Luca scoffed. "He's been weak for years."

"The time is right, *now*," Salvatore snapped.

Spines straightened instantly. His presence pressed down on the room, suffocating, absolute. A king among wolves.

"He knows enough now to accept what I'm going to tell him is the truth."

Enzo exhaled sharply. "And if he doesn't?"

Salvatore rolled his eyes before pinning his sons with a single look. The air turned thick. Heavy. A presence so sharp it cut like a blade. One by one, they fell silent.

"He knows Federico murdered Catalina." Salvatore's voice was quieter now but somehow heavier. Weighted with loss that seemed so far removed from our current situation I couldn't fathom. "Now he will learn the whole truth."

My stomach turned. What the hell was going on? Questions clawed at my throat, each one more dangerous than the last. Why was the enemy so invested in him knowing the truth? How did they know Domino knew what had happened to his mother? No one knew except…

A sharp, heated discussion broke out. Italian curses flew like daggers. Words landed like stray bullets, echoing off the warehouse walls. The circle of men behind them shifted, uneasy, shoulders squared—but there was something in their eyes. Dread. None of them wanted to step in. None of them wanted to be caught in the firestorm building in the center of the room.

A slow inhale pulled my attention like a magnetic force. A shift in the air.

Domino.

I turned my head just in time to see his fingers twitch, his muscles tightening as consciousness pulled him back. His breathing changed—slower, deeper.

The monster was waking up.

Luca noticed. His head tilted slightly, silver eyes gleaming. He murmured, "About time."

Ellio leaned back on his heels, smirking. "You're gonna wanna hear this, big guy."

Domino's lashes lifted. His gaze found mine first. Pupils expanded, black swallowing the dark green of his irises. His entire body went still. Possession. I felt it wash over me like a baptism of hellfire.

It was in his eyes, in the way his fingers curled into fists around the chains, in the way his chest expanded as his rage grew.

Once he'd assessed me and deemed it acceptable, he turned his head. Took in his surroundings. Catalogued everything. Every minute detail. He never missed a thing, and today was no different.

And I saw it—the shift. The ripple of something cold, something dangerous. He rolled his shoulders, testing the chains, feeling their weight. Searching for any weakness he could find.

Eventually, he looked at the older man—the one in charge. And he smiled. Slow. Sharp. Blood stained teeth glistened in the dim light.

Salvatore smiled back. Warmer than any expression I'd seen on him until now. And then he said the words that cracked the foundation of everything. "It's a pleasure to finally meet you, Domino. Salvatore Gallo—*your father*."

I felt it.

The way the room tilted.

The way Domino fractured.

He didn't speak. Didn't blink.

He just stared.

He had suspected. I knew he had. The whispers in the dark corners of his mind had tormented him for years, gnawing at the edges of his sanity. But to hear it spoken out loud, in cold, unwavering truth?

His fingers curled into fists. The chains rattled. His body remained eerily still, but I knew better. Something had snapped.

The Gallos had no idea what they had just unleashed.

Salvatore exhaled like he was already bored. "Federico didn't tell you?"

Domino's voice was deathly quiet. Razor-sharp. "You're lying."

Salvatore hummed. "You think Federico raised you out of loyalty? Out of obligation? Love?" He met Domino's stare, unflinching. "He kept you because you were useful."

The room held its breath.

Salvatore continued, voice dripping with ice. "He had your mother killed because she threatened everything. She was going to take you away—to me. He murdered Catalina because he was afraid. Afraid that if the truth came out, you would realize the power in your blood. That you were never his."

A pause. "But I suppose, in the end, he trained you well, didn't he? Broke you just enough to make you his most valuable weapon."

A crack split the air. Something unseen, something irreparable. Domino laughed. Low. Quiet. Not humor. Something else.

Diego scoffed. "Nothing to say? Maybe we hit him too hard."

"Or maybe he's just in shock," Ellio snickered.

Enzo exhaled sharply. "Let's focus. We didn't bring them here for banter."

Luca hummed in agreement. "We need to decide what to do with them. We can't just let them walk out of here."

Salvatore considered his sons before his gaze settled on me once more. Cold calculation glinted in his eyes. "You, however... You might be worth something. A trade, perhaps."

Domino finally spoke.

His voice was quiet. Deceptively calm.

"Touch him..." His eyes burned with something primal, something that wanted to tear them apart with its teeth. "And I'll cut your heart out."

The entire room went still.

Ellio whistled low under his breath, grinning. "That's cute. But in case you haven't noticed, big guy, you're chained to the ceiling."

Domino smiled. A sharp curve of his lips that sent ice down my spine.

"You don't need to worry about me," he murmured. "You should be worrying about yourselves."

A heartbeat passed, and the strength drained from my bones. The lights cut out, and the warehouse plunged into darkness.

That's when the screaming started.

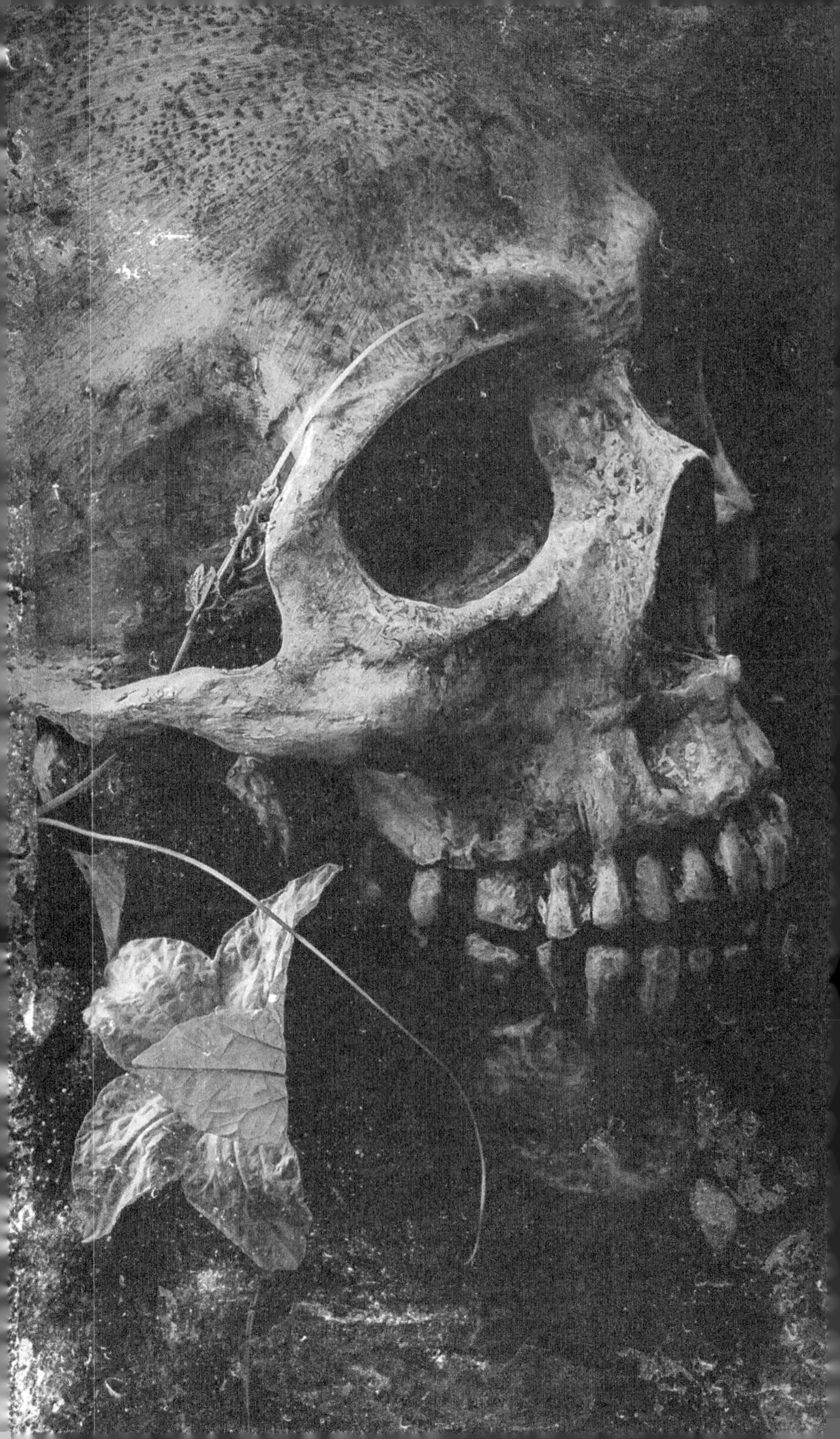

22 DOMINO

Pain was nothing new. It was ingrained in every cell, woven into my very existence. I didn't fear it. I harnessed it. Turned it into something useful.

Rage.

It throbbed in my arms, deep and pulsing, where my shoulders felt like they were being ripped apart one sinewy strand at a time. The metal cuffs cut into my wrists, fresh blood welling around them as I flexed my fists. My body sagged from the corroded air conditioning pipe above me, the old screws whining with every subtle movement. It wouldn't hold. Not for much longer.

Time was a luxury I didn't have.

Copper coated my tongue. Bruised ribs protested every shallow breath I sucked in through dry, cracked lips. Blood seeped from the multitude of wounds on my body—fists, boots, and blades had all left their mark, but they had failed in the one thing that mattered most.

Breaking me. Taking me from him.

Remi had become the sole focus of my existence.

He was too quiet. Too still. Tied to that metal girder, head slumped forward, dark hair spider webbed with white, shielding his face. But I knew him. Knew he was listening, calculating, waiting—because he knew I was coming for him.

Would always come for him.

Salvatore Gallo and his sons droned on, their arrogance thick in the air like rot. Their men patrolled the space, careless, smug. Believing in their false sense of control. Fools.

I memorized them all, counted their steps, marked the ones who hesitated when they looked at me. They would be the first to die.

The dim overhead lights flickered.

A test run. A signal. Ghost was close.

We had a plan in place if Remi or I were ever taken, and it looked like my diligence was about to pay off. The embedded tracker in Remi's necklace had led him right here. And when the lights went out for real, I would make each one of the men here regret everything.

A slow, steadying breath filled my lungs. I swung my legs and the momentum shifted the screws in their housing. A little more. A little looser. Again. And again I swung.

Salvatore's words should have hit harder. They should have meant something. Instead, they rolled off me, insignificant against the only truth that mattered—Remi. Tied up. Vulnerable. Hurt.

The only thing in this world that I gave a fuck about.

I smirked, a calculated twitch of my lips, as Salvatore looked up at me, still rambling. "You're talking a lot for a dead man," I muttered just as the lights went out.

Chaos erupted as darkness blanketed the warehouse. Feet pounded on cement, echoing in the hollow space. A scream tore through the blackness—the first of many, if I had anything to do with it.

The last screw gave way. Metal groaned and snapped. I crashed to the ground, landing atop the unlucky bastard standing sentry by me. His ribs cracked beneath my weight, the air forced from his lungs in a sharp, wet gasp.

I was moving before he even had time to choke and stutter his last breath. Momentum carried me forward as adrenaline surged through my veins, sharpening my lethal focus.

The chain of my cuffs snapped tight as I looped it around the throat of the nearest soldier. His fingers clawed at the metal, gasping, gurgling as I twisted, using my body weight to yank him off balance. He stumbled, boots skidding across the blood-slicked floor.

A jerk, a twist. The satisfying crack of his windpipe breaking was music amidst the carnage. His body slumped in my hold. Dead weight. I let him drop and was already moving before his corpse hit the ground.

Even cuffed, I was faster. Stronger. More vicious than any man in the room. My monster was unparalleled in its brutality.

My fingers closed around the barrel of a soldier's gun before he could even think to raise it. I yanked it from his grasp and flipped it until my finger curled around the trigger.

Bang.

The bullet punched through his throat. Blood and

tissue exploded outward from the proximity of the shot. The flash of gunfire illuminated wide, horrified eyes. But I didn't hang around to savour the kill and watch the life drain from him. I had a singular focus. Every cell in my body drove me forward, toward Remi.

I spun around and fired a round of shots in the direction of heavy thudding boots closing in on me. Another body crashed to the ground, skidding to a stop against a girder.

Blood thickened the air. Viscous and metallic as it coated my tongue with every inhale, tasting like sweet poison as it filled my lungs.

My monster roared as another Gallo fell. And another. They fell like flies. If this was the level of training they gave their men, wiping them off the face of the earth was going to be easier than I thought.

I moved like a phantom, precise and unrelenting, my world narrowing to the cold press of steel and the warm spray of blood.

Footsteps scrambled to my right. A coward hiding behind one of the thick pillars. I pivoted, catching the faintest outline of his form. He clutched his leg, blood seeping between his fingers where a ricocheted bullet had caught him.

His breath hitched. "P—please—"

I silenced his pathetic pleas with the brutal press of my thumb into the open wound, pushing the bullet lodged in his flesh deeper. His scream echoed around us, as thick claret welled around my thumb. Delicious chills raced over my skin, making the hairs on my nape stand on end.

I smirked as his eyes widened. He could see the monster in me. Reflected in my eyes. "The keys," I ordered, voice calm against the hysteria. "Now."

His hand trembled as he yanked the ring free and thrust it toward me. I snatched it from his grasp, my fingers closing around his throat in a slow, deliberate squeeze. His racing pulse fluttered beneath my fingertips.

"You're the one who locked me up." My voice was almost gentle. A lie from a sinner's lips. "Tell me. Did you enjoy it?"

He whimpered. I tightened my grip. His hands left his bleeding leg to claw at my arm. A manic grin curled my lips as pain sliced into my skin where he shredded it with his nails.

His body spasmed once. Then he went limp. Eyes glassy, unseeing. Euphoria rushed through my veins, chasing away the exhaustion. I discarded him, stepping over his corpse. Forgetting him like the nothing he was.

Remi—My eyes shot straight to him. The vice that had sunk its teeth into my heart retreated. He was watching me through his dark lashes, ice-blue eyes, almost phosphorus in the dim light.

My Remi smiled up at me and licked his lips. His heady gaze raked over my bruised and bleeding chest with a visceral hunger that went straight to my cock.

He was the only person I would ever kill for again. He was everything to me. My solitude. My home. My darkness made whole.

Mirrored souls, carved from the same depths of hell.

I crouched behind him, sawing at the zip ties with the sharp edge of the cuffs that had bound my wrists. My fingers brushed against his wrist, lingering a second too long on the bleeding flesh, feeling the depth of the lacerations.

His blood coated my fingertips. I brought them to

my lips, sucking them clean one by one. Remi's bright eyes hooded as he watched them slide into my mouth.

"You took your time," he murmured, voice hoarse but steady.

A huffed laugh caught in my throat, and I brushed the pad of my thumb across his bottom lip. "Had to make sure they learned their lesson first."

Remi's lips twitched. But his gaze flickered past me. Tracking movement in the shadows. I turned just as a Gallo soldier staggered to his feet, gun shaking in his hands.

A low growl curled from my throat as I stepped in front of Remi. Protecting what was mine with my life. The soldier barely had time to blink before I pulled the trigger.

The bullet tore through his skull, splattering brain matter across the ground and silencing him before he could make another foolish mistake.

I reached out, tucking a stray lock of hair behind Remi's ear. His breath hitched, and he licked his lips. My eyes traced the slow progression of the tip of his tongue.

His hands trembled—whether from exhaustion, relief, or something deeper, I didn't know. But it didn't matter. Because the moment I wrenched the last restraint free, the second his hands were no longer bound—

He surged forward. His fingers clutched at my bloodied skin. And his mouth was on me, lips melding to mine, making me gasp as hunger parched my throat. It wasn't soft. It wasn't sweet. It was heat and desperation. Teeth and tongues. A brutal claim.

A promise.

A vow.

My fingers curled into his hair, dragging him closer, devouring him. Blood slicked our lips and stained our skin, the taste of copper and something sweeter lingering between us.

Remi gasped against my lips, his fingers digging into my arms as if to reassure himself that I was real. Alive. Here. "Where are they?" he whispered.

I glanced around. Bodies littered the floor, but we were alone. Salvatore and his sons were gone. Fucking cowards.

A hiss filled the warehouse. Even in the darkness, I could see it. A toxic fog filled the air, crawling across the ground like a sentient being with a singular focus. Search and destroy.

"Remi… I…" I gasped with desperation and slammed my mouth against his again. If this was the last time I ever got to taste him, then I would swallow him whole. I'd take him into the darkest, deepest parts of me and never relinquish my hold.

My body fought against the encroaching darkness, but blood loss, exhaustion, and chemicals coiled around my limbs like chains.

My knees buckled. My vision blurred.

The last thing I felt was Remi's warmth beside me before the void swallowed us whole.

I WOKE TO THE SENSATION OF DRIED BLOOD PULLING AT my skin. It cracked as I moved, stretched taut over bruises that pulsed in time with my heartbeat. My jeans were stiff, the scent of copper clinging to the air, thick and heavy, coating my tongue like a memory I'd never forget.

Everything hurt. Every wound, every cut, every bruise sang beneath my skin. A symphony of pain, sharp and unrelenting.

The sheets beneath me were too soft. Too clean. An affront to the ruin carved into my body.

A low groan beside me snapped my focus back to reality, yanking me from the crimson haze threatening to consume me.

Remi stirred. His muscles tensed, the lines of his face drawn tight with exhaustion. But when his dark, sharp gaze snapped to the corner of the room, I recognized the shift immediately.

He saw it, too. The camera. The unseen person was watching us like we were animals here for their entertainment.

We had to be in a Gallo safe house, it was the only logical place. A temporary holding cell, a place to keep us under surveillance. They wouldn't have been stupid enough to bring us to their main compound, but I didn't care. I would tear this place apart. Brick by brick. Burn it down and salt the fucking earth.

They touched him.

They would pay.

But right now, none of that mattered. Right now, all I saw was him.

Blood streaked his skin, dirt smeared across the ridges of his cheekbones. A masterpiece of violence. Of survival.

He was fucking *mine*.

The word slammed into me, consuming and absolute. The last twenty-four hours or however long it had been since we were at the docks had been hell, and the only thing keeping me from unraveling was him. Breathing. Alive. Here.

I reached for him. My fingers tangled in his hair, yanking him closer. The strands slid through my blood stained fingers like silk, the contrast making something inside me tighten—a hunger, a sickness, an obsession.

Too soft. Too reverent.

Not enough.

It would never be enough. Remi barely had time to exhale before I shoved him back onto the mattress. His body tensed beneath me—a second of resistance as pain flashed over his features before he embraced it. Then he relaxed. Yielded to me.

Not in surrender.

In expectation.

In anticipation.

He'd been waiting for this. For me. A smirk ghosted across his lips, sharp and teasing. Daring me. "You think you own me?"

A growl rumbled deep in my chest. "I don't think, *piccolo agnello*. I know."

His breath hitched, his pupils blown wide; he licked his lips, watching me intently. He liked it.

He fucking *loved* it.

My lips crashed into his throat, dragging across his pulse point. Tasting. Marking. Branding. My teeth sank in, breaking skin, and he arched into me, gasping.

"You cry so beautifully, *baby*," I murmured against his skin, tongue flicking over the wound. The metallic tang of his blood burst across my tastebuds. Perfect. Before I kissed away the tears that pricked the corners of his eyes, leaving a fresh bloody trail across his pale skin.

His fingers clawed at my back, nails biting, digging. Pulling me closer like he couldn't get deep enough.

Neither could I.

I ripped at his clothes as I kicked my jeans off, tearing the fabric from his body until every inch of him was bared to me. I needed more, needed all of him. His mind. His darkness. The blood and marrow of his bones.

His legs wrapped around my waist, locking me in, grinding up, dragging me deeper into his heat.

"You need me, don't you?" I whispered, biting at his jaw, dragging my tongue over the sweat-slick curve of his throat. Scraping my teeth over his Adam's apple, feeling his larynx vibrate beneath my lips.

He didn't answer, but his body did. Writhing. Desperate. Willing. The soft puff of air that passed his lips as they searched for mine.

His cock, slick and hard, slid against mine, sending a violent, shuddering wave of pleasure down my spine. I gritted my teeth, forcing myself to slow down before I shattered too soon.

But he wouldn't let me. Wave after wave of electricity danced across my skin, sparking everywhere we touched. Nerves came alive under my skin. Every thrust of his hips, every long grind of his slick length against mine only ratcheted the pleasure suffused in my veins higher.

"Dom..." he whimpered when my crown caught on his.

He was just as starved, just as desperate, grinding up, pushing, daring me to break.

"Say it," I ordered, my grip on his throat tightening just enough to make his breath catch.

His lips curled in a wicked, ruined smile. "Make me."

A snarl ripped from my chest. I devoured him. My lips slammed down on his, and I forced my tongue into his mouth, tasting every inch before I pulled his bottom lip between my teeth. Pulling a fresh bead of blood from the freshly scabbed over split.

Teeth clashed. Nails raked down my back, peeling layer after layer of skin away. The delicious burn of his brand on my flesh made my balls draw up tight to the base of my dick.

Skin dragged against skin, slick with sweat, blood, need. It was raw. Consuming. Violent.

I forced his thighs wider, pinning him beneath me, owning every inch of him. He arched his spine, his head thrown back, body taut with pleasure and pain, the line between them blurring.

My bloodied hand wrapped around my thick length as my gaze dragged over every inch of his body, following the trail of marks down to his glistening cock, a fresh bead of precum pooled against his abs.

"Fuck," I groaned and notched the head of my cock against his unstretched hole.

I wanted him raw and brutally. I needed to force my way inside his body, feel it fight me before it sucked me in. I looked up, and my eyes clashed with his heavy-lidded ice-blues.

The unasked question between us as I increased the pressure against his entrance. That tight ring of muscle refusing to give. Bending forward I spit on my cock slicking it up as I worked my hand from root to tip.

Remi's head thrashed. "Fuck me. Fuck me Domino. I need it. Need you." A fresh wave of tears glittered down his cheeks.

With one hard snap of my hips, that tight ring of muscle was forced to give way as I drove myself inside him. The wet heat of his body clenched around me, and my mind fractured.

Nothing else existed.

Nothing else would ever matter.

I drove into him with an unhinged intensity, bruising, claiming, my hands leaving evidence of ownership in every mark, every scrape, every bite.

He gasped, wrecked, perfect, *mine*.

"You love this," I murmured against his lips, forcing my cock deeper, making him feel it.

His response was a choked moan, fingers fisting in my hair, dragging me into a kiss that was all teeth and bloody desperation. I bit his lower lip, hard enough to coax a fresh drop of crimson to stain them. The taste burst across my tongue, copper and ruin and Remi.

I swallowed his gasp, his moan, his everything. As I pounded into him, my hands slid underneath his ass, hauling him up, changing the angle so I pegged his prostate with every brutal thrust. Sweat slicked his crimson stained skin, like fractured rubies.

His body tensed one muscle at a time until he was frozen. The muscles in his channel rippled around me with a pulsing heat as I shuttled into him, my hips slapping against his bruised flesh, pushing him higher and higher.

"Fuck! Fuck! Please.... pl...." his words devolved into a broken moan.

"Come for me, *piccolo agnello*."

Remi shattered beneath me, his release painting both our bodies, hot and thick. The sight of him, ruined and spent, slick with cum, trembling in my grip, sent me over the edge.

I poured myself into him, claiming him in the only way that mattered. My vision whited out as my cock pulsed inside him. Spurt after spurt of my cum filled him. So much that it seeped out around my length as I continued to rock into him, prolonging both our orgasms.

When it was done, we lay tangled in the aftermath. Bodies slick. Breath ragged. But I wasn't finished. I scooped up the cum coating his stomach, lifted my fingers to my lips, and sucked them clean.

Remi's eyes burned, dark and knowing.

I leaned forward, braced my hands on either side of his head, and kissed him, deep and slow, feeding him his release, passing it back and forth, until we'd swallowed every drop.

Mine. Always.

The storm settled, but my mind was already shifting. Hunting for a way out of our prison. And that's when I saw it. The vent. Partially obscured by the ornate furniture.

Remi followed my gaze, and within seconds, he was dressed in his shredded clothes and moving. Silent. Efficient. Deadly.

I let him go. I should have stopped him. Should have tied him to this bed, kept him here forever.

But I didn't.

Because the hunt wasn't over yet.

He disappeared into the darkness. Gone like he had never been here. Only the taste of his cum on my tongue reminded he was real and not just a figment of my imagination.

Silence stretched. The ticking of the clock on the nightstand grew obnoxiously loud. Jolting me with every tick. A muscle twitched in my jaw as I clenched my teeth and hauled what little in the way of clothing I had back on.

And waited.

A soft click coming from the door drew my attention. I pushed up off the bed and stepped silently over to it. The handle turned, wiggling from side to side before the sound of a lock barrel engaging filled the air.

The door unlocked.

A slow, sharp grin curled at my lips as Remi stepped through the door. A devastating grin twitched the corners of his kiss-bruised lips.

And just like that, the hunt began. We needed to find weapons and burn this place to the ground. I wouldn't leave here until everyone was dead and buried under a pile of rubble.

"Are you alone?"

My hand wrapped around his wrist and yanked him into me, unwilling to be separated another second. I'd drag him through hell at my side rather than spend a moment without him.

His skin was hot beneath my grip, damp with sweat and streaked with grime. But he was breathing. Alive. Mine.

"I didn't see anyone," he murmured, voice hushed but sharp. "But I heard voices down the hall."

The door shut behind him with a soft snick.

"Where did the vent lead?"

I cupped his face, fingers pressing in like I could mold him into me, merge us into something monstrous and whole. My thumbs dragged over the grime streaked across his cheekbones, smearing filth like war paint. Mine.

The visceral need to touch him, to consume him, to own him burned through me, feverish and all-consuming. Every breath he took, every tremor of his skin beneath my hands, was proof that he was real. That he was here. That no one had taken him from me.

I needed more. I needed to feel his pulse stutter beneath my fingers, feel his breath hitch under my lips, feel his body press against mine so tightly it was impossible to tell where he ended and I began.

The world could burn. Everything could fucking crumble. But as long as I had him beneath my hands, nothing else mattered.

"Linen closet. Four doors down," he said. "Pretty sure it's an escape route. That means they know we can get out, so we have to move fast."

We turned in unison, eyes locking onto the camera in the corner, a silent specter bearing witness to our carnage, our hunger, our ruin.

They'd already seen what we were. A twisted spectacle of blood and filth, pleasure and pain, devotion and destruction. A sickness so profound it had no cure—only indulgence.

Now, it was time to show them what we were truly capable of. They thought they could break us.

They didn't understand.

We weren't fragile. We weren't prey. We weren't even human anymore.

We were a fucking cataclysm.

Deadly alone. Stronger together. When we moved in tandem, when our bloodied hands reached for each other, when our sick, obsessive love burned through everything in our path—we weren't just destruction. We were the end.

And we were about to bring hell itself crashing down.

"We do." My lips grazed his, a fleeting touch, but I

needed more. Needed to taste him. Consume him. My fingers curled into his jaw, bruising, possessive. "They took my phone and my weapons."

A slow, sharp grin tugged at my lips. My hands ached for blood. For death. Destruction. His breath hitched, and ice-blue eyes locked onto me like he could see every wicked thought forming in my mind.

"Do you believe what Salvatore told you?"

His words slithered through my mind, a poisonous whisper. That he was my father? It made sense. Too much fucking sense. I had nothing in common with Federico besides our thirst for blood and our mutual hatred of the Gallos.

My jaw clenched. "It makes sense," I admitted. "But now is not the time." I exhaled sharply, fisting the back of his hair, yanking his head back just enough to meet my eyes. "I need to get you home. Safe."

Remi scoffed, his lips curling in something between amusement and disgust. "Safe? I haven't been safe since the day I stepped into your world." His breath came sharp, controlled—but his eyes burned.

He reached for me, fingers digging into my jaw, nails biting deep enough to break skin. To mark. To claim.

"I don't want safe, Domino," he murmured, voice low, reverent. "I want the darkness that runs through your veins. I want this—whatever the fuck this is—this approximation of love. I want blood and death and destruction." His thumb pressed against my bottom lip, smearing my blood across my mouth. His pupils swallowed the light blue of his irises. "But most of all, I want you. And nothing—not even you—will take that from me."

Fuck. He was perfect. Vicious and wicked, just like me. But still—something in me snarled at the thought of anything touching him, hurting him, taking him from me. The need to keep him, cage him, and own him burned through my veins like wildfire. I didn't have time to unravel it. Footsteps heavy and rushed echoed in the hallway drawing closer. We had company.

I turned toward the door just as it burst open. The guard barely had time to register what was happening before I hit him like a bullet. My fists collided with flesh, and cartilage cracked beneath the force.. He staggered, gasped—but I didn't let him breathe. I wanted him to choke on it.

My knuckles cracked against his ribs and shattered on impact. His knees wobbled, and blood coated his face as he flailed. I caught him by the throat and slammed him into the wall. The impact knocked the pictures to the ground.

His eyes bulged, his hands clawing at my grip, feet kicking uselessly against the floor. I leaned in, breathing in the scent of his fear, feeling his pulse stammer beneath my palm. "Take a good look," I murmured. "I'll be the last thing you ever see."

His lips turned blue. His heartbeat faltered. Behind me, Remi inhaled sharply. I felt his eyes on me. In me. Consuming. Feeding.

I grinned over my shoulder. "That's it," I whispered, voice like silk-wrapped steel. "Watch me."

The guard's body convulsed once, twice—then went limp in my grasp. I let him drop, discarded at my feet. I crouched, stripping him of his gun and knife, holding it out for Remi.

Blood dripped from my split knuckles, warm and slick, splattered across my jaw, my clothes, my fucking skin. I licked it off my lips, slow and deliberate.

Copper and death. *Perfection*.

I turned to Remi, high off the violence, the power thrumming through my veins like electricity. "Ready?"

His gaze flicked to my bloodied hands, to the corpse, then back to me. Something dark flashed in his eyes. Something wicked. Something beautifully broken.

Remi smirked, and for a moment, I could have sworn the shadows curled tighter around him, whispering secrets only he could hear. His monster stared back at me, hungry and waiting to be freed. "Always."

We tore through the hallways like starving wolves set loose from their cage, leaving nothing but death and devastation in our wake. Guards died like sacrifices. More bodies than you could imagine littered the floors. None survived.

Blood soaked the walls, decorated our skin.

Remi was a nightmare incarnate, moving through the carnage with a blade in each hand, painting the walls with crimson, carving beauty from their ruin. I ripped, tore, annihilated. Bones crumbled beneath my fists. Joints snapped in my hands. I broke them apart like toys, their screams fueling the fire inside me.

Gunfire rang out, but we were faster. Deadlier. By the time we reached the basement, the house itself was bleeding. It became a nightmare of our creation; it wasn't a battlefield. It had never been a fair fight. It'd been a massacre. A show of power.

Remi darted toward the shelves, fingers trailing over the supplies with methodical precision.

"What are you doing?" I asked, wiping the blade clean on a corpse.

He didn't answer, just huffed a quiet laugh and grabbed a can of gasoline and one can of paint thinner.

My cock throbbed, aching to be buried inside him— to claim him, to ruin him. Watching him slaughter without mercy, I craved him. Needed to devour him, to drink the sadistic poison that coursed through his veins.

I leaned against the doorway, eyes locked on him, watching him move with something raw, something feral.

He was beautiful like this.

Dark. Vicious. Unapologetic.

The monster I always knew he could be.

For a moment, he hesitated and turned to me. Searching for something only I could offer him.

Approval? Permission? Worship?

I nodded. "We need to do all the floors."

A slow, manic grin split his face. He gestured toward the remaining cans. "Grab those and do the top floors." I nodded and trailed him up the stairs to the first floor. "Meet me in the kitchen when you're done. We'll need to be fast," he called, voice thick with anticipation.

When I returned, he was shoving aluminum foil and cutlery into the microwave, setting the timer. Turning on every gas burner. I fucking laughed Remi's eyes danced with glee.

"I've always wanted to blow somewhere up."

The air crackled—charged with destruction.

We slipped through the laundry room door just as the explosion tore through the house. Glass shattered. The ground heaved. Fire erupted, vicious and all-consuming, licking up the walls like a living, breathing beast.

Heat slammed into our backs, a violent embrace that sent us hurtling forward. We hit the ground hard, rolling across the grass, tangled in each other.

I caught him by the throat and dragged him into a filthy, brutal kiss. Teeth clashed. Blood smeared. His mouth opened under mine, a wrecked, desperate moan slipping free. My tongue tangled with his, swallowing it down.

I bit his lip, tasted copper, and claimed it. "That's my boy," I breathed against him.

Then we ran. Behind us, smoke billowed, thick and choking, curling into the night sky. The first explosion rocked the ground, a warning. The second devoured the house whole, flames swallowing it in a tidal wave of ruin.

No remains. No evidence. Nothing but fire and oblivion.

The gardens stretched before us, shadows bleeding into the trees. I caught his hand, yanked him with me, refusing to let him go.

The inferno raged, consuming everything, a reflection of the hunger twisting inside me. And as we vanished into the dark, into the night—I knew one thing for certain.

The world would burn before I ever let him go.

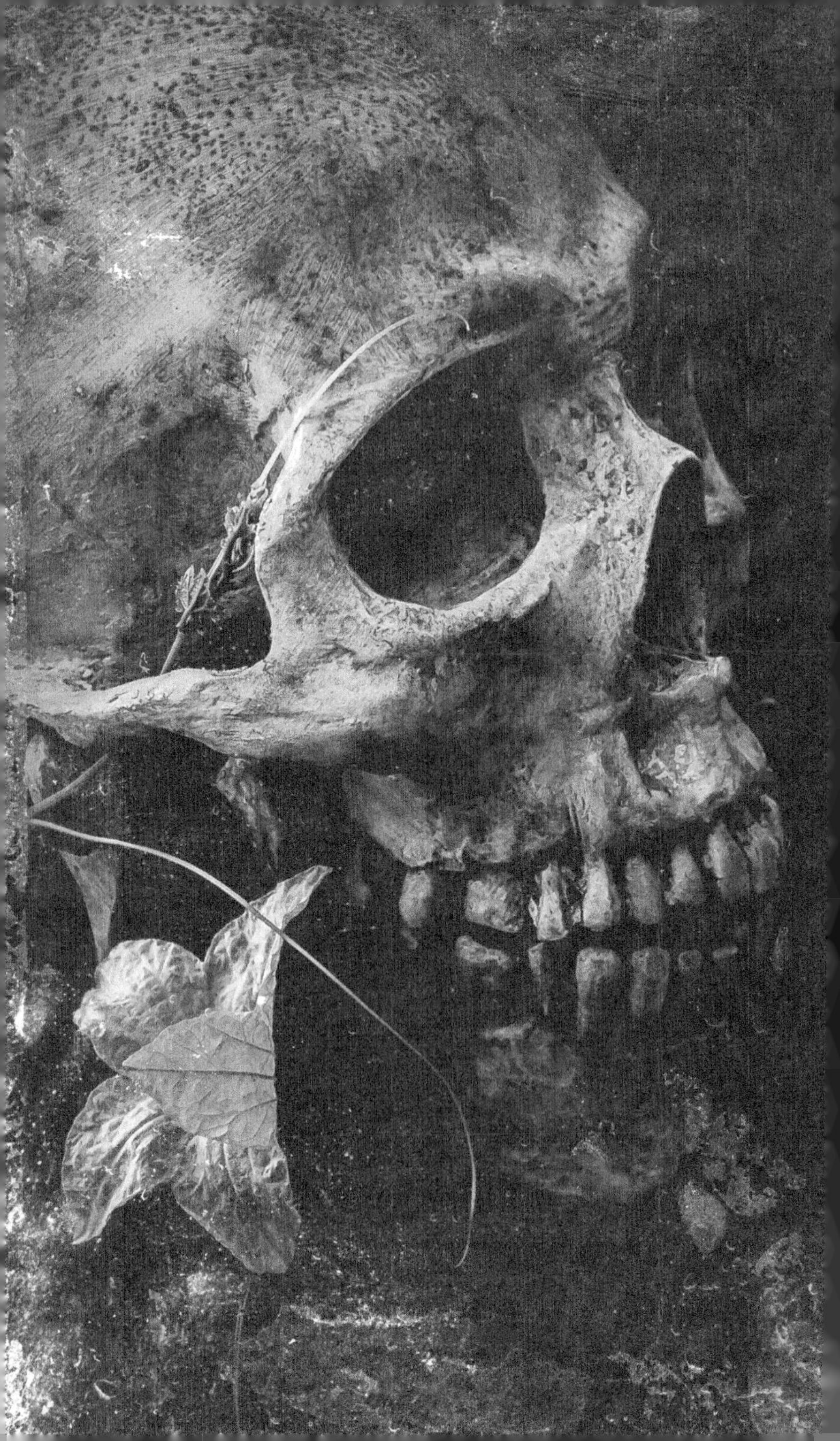

23 DOMINO

"You have some explaining to do."

My voice was low, venomous, curling through the dim space like cigarette smoke. Ghost's reflection in the window flinched before his body followed suit. The city outside stretched in murky streaks of neon and filth, a fitting backdrop to the stench of betrayal thickening the air between us.

He sauntered into my apartment, cocky as ever, but the moment the elevator doors shut behind him, his steps faltered. Good. He should be afraid.

His eyes snapped to mine, pupils flaring like a wounded animal catching the scent of blood. "What do you mean?"

He already knew. The fear creeping up his spine betrayed him before his words ever could.

I wanted to tell him the interesting things Remi

shared with me last night as we washed Gallo blood from our skin. As I pressed my lips to his throat and tasted the iron of our shared violence. As I memorized every inch of him and knew—deep in my bones—that he was the only thing in this world I would never fucking share.

Instead, I exhaled slowly, pinching the bridge of my nose like I could smother the burning need to tear him apart with my bare hands. "We can do this the easy way or the hard way," I murmured, turning to face him fully.

Ghost swallowed hard, his Adam's apple bobbing as his mouth opened and closed.

Then, a whisper of movement. A flash of silver. His breath stuttered. Remi's blade kissed the base of his throat.

"Where the fuck did you come from?" Ghost rasped, his skin grating against the edge of the knife. It wasn't a question of where. It was a question of how much he could get away with before we gutted him. "You left."

Remi snorted, tilting his head, letting the light catch the predatory glint in his ice-blue eyes. "You taught me a lot, Ghost... but I've learned more than you ever showed me." With a flick of his wrist, the blade bit deeper, just enough to draw a thin trickle of crimson. Not enough to kill. Not yet. "You've gotten sloppy if you didn't realize I looped your system. Tut tut."

Ghost's nostrils flared, his body tensing in barely restrained panic. "Fucking, fuck! You're a creepy little shit when you want to be."

I arched a brow, stepping in until the heat of his fear crawled over my skin. It smelled delicious. "Want to say that again?"

His complexion paled further, sweat blooming at his temples.

"Now, answer my question." My voice was quiet, controlled. Dangerous. "With the truth this time." A slow smirk curved my lips. "Because if you don't, I'll know."

Ghost's breath came faster, his fingers twitching at his sides. He knew. He fucking knew.

Remi dragged the blade across his throat, slow and deliberate. A promise, not a warning. Blood welled, thin rivulets tracing the curve of his neck. Still not deep enough to kill, but deep enough to scar—if I let him live that long.

The early morning light bled through the grimy window, painting the scene sickly gold and mirroring the storm unraveling in my chest. I wanted to peel him apart. Disassemble him piece by piece until nothing is left but regret and ruin.

I replaced Remi's blade with my hand, fingers pressing into the fresh cut, smearing the blood like ink across a page. "Now is not the time for silence, Ghost." I tightened my grip, pulling him closer until the tips of our shoes touched. Until I could hear the sharp hitch in his breath, the way his pulse jackhammered against my palm.

His voice broke. "I—I know, Domino. I know."

Resignation. Weak. Bitter. Hollow. It tasted like fucking victory.

Ghost's gaze flicked past me to where Remi stood against the wall, lazily flipping the bloodied knife between his fingers. The weight of his stare settled over me, a balm to the fire roaring in my veins.

Ghost wasn't stupid enough to play games with me. He knew the stakes.

I was judge, jury, and executioner. And Remi?

Remi was the executioner's blade, gleaming and hungry.

"Fine." My voice was a blade of its own. "Sit." I gestured to the couch with a flick of my wrist. "Tell me everything. Start at the beginning. If you leave anything out—" I leaned down, my lips ghosting over the shell of his ear. "I'll know."

Ghost collapsed onto the couch, his legs barely holding him up. He was sweating. *Good.* He rubbed his palms over his jeans like it would erase the tremor in his fingers.

"I know you will."

"It'll be a race between me and Remi to get to you first," I added, smirking.

Ghost inhaled sharply, running a hand through his damp hair before finally speaking. "I didn't lie when I said I was born into this world."

"Go on," I said, remaining standing, letting the weight of my presence suffocate him further.

He swallowed hard. "My parents were druggies. Mom was strung out my whole life. She tried, I think. But trying doesn't mean shit when the fridge is empty and the floor is covered in needles."

His voice grew quieter, words tumbling out like loose teeth. "When I was five, she threw a party. The trailer was packed—people I'd never seen before, fucking on every available surface, powder covering the counters. My dad had overdosed that morning, but instead of mourning, she celebrated."

Ghost shifted, gaze dropping to the floor. Shame. Pride's worst enemy.

"Where was your dad?"

"Still in the hospital. They found him with a needle in his arm. Mom cried until her dealer showed up, then she forgot all about it." His fingers twitched, an old habit of a man with too much history in his hands. "That night, her dealer beat the shit out of me for existing. She locked me in a closet for three days after that."

Remi muttered a curse under his breath, dragging a hand down his face.

I lit a cigarette, inhaling deep, letting the poison settle in my lungs. I had a feeling we weren't even at the worst of it. "Want one?"

Ghost nodded. I tossed him the pack, and he fumbled, lighting his own before exhaling a slow stream of smoke.

"Thanks," he muttered. "It didn't stop. The beatings. But eventually, I became useful. In *other* ways. Mom let it happen. He gave her more drugs, and that was enough for her."

A sick kind of silence settled over the room. The kind that festered. I took another drag, rolling my cigarette between my fingers.

"When I was ten, I ran away," Ghost murmured, like the words themselves were too heavy to hold. "You can imagine what happened after that. What I *had* to do to survive."

Remi took the cigarette from my fingers, bringing it to his lips. My eyes locked onto him, dragged to him like a planet caught in his orbit. Because when Remi was this close—when he was this fucking lethal— I could do nothing but wait for the moment we collided.

"Exactly. That's where Salvatore found me…"

A weighted silence swallowed the room whole, thick and suffocating, pressing against our ribs like a loaded gun. Our attention pinned Ghost to his spot, a specimen under a microscope, twitching beneath the scrutiny.

Then, he huffed a nervous laugh.

"He found me stuck in a dumpster. My legs were hanging out the top." He rolled his eyes, the memory crawling up his throat like bile—bittersweet, embarrassing, and pathetic. "He pulled me out, asked me what the fuck I was doing. And like any self-respecting street rat, I asked him how much."

Remi snorted, flipping his knife between his fingers. "Bet that didn't go down well."

Ghost shook his head. "Not really." His lips twisted, half amusement, half something darker. "He clipped me around the back of the head, then announced he was taking me to breakfast." He shrugged like it wasn't a pivotal fucking moment. "That was that. Took me home. Had one of his guys train me. When I was good enough, he planted me right where I am."

A pause. A deep one.

"Impossible," I snapped, barely holding back the snarl curling in my chest. The pieces didn't fit. "Federico might be a cunt, but he's not stupid."

Ghost scoffed. "I was recommended by someone he trusted." His gaze—watery, desperate, waiting—begged me to connect the dots.

The realization was a blade to the ribs. Slow, twisting, brutal. "That fucking piece of shit."

Remi's eyes flicked to me, confusion tightening his features, but I was already on my feet. Pacing. Burning. Shaking. The flames in the fireplace crackled, casting shadows over the room, over the rage threatening to consume me from the inside out.

"Angelo is a Gallo, too?"

"Yup."

That single syllable carried a death sentence.

"That explains why he's such a fucking snake," I seethed, hands curling into fists. White-hot fury licked up my spine, a drug I never planned to quit. "That piece of shit is going to die very fucking slowly."

Remi smiled.

And fuck, it was beautiful.

His straight white teeth gleamed, his lips curved just enough to send a shiver down Ghost's spine. Then, those cold, cutting eyes slanted toward him, hunting, calculating, starving.

"Do I get to play with him?" Remi purred, tossing his knife into the air and catching it by the handle, his other hand rubbing together like he could already feel Angelo's blood staining his skin.

Ghost swallowed thickly, attempting a facsimile of a smile. It failed. Miserably.

"There was a reason I came here…" His voice cracked on the edges.

I stared. Silent. Waiting for him to spit it out before I carved it out of him instead.

"Someone wants to speak to y—"

"Who?" I snapped. The smoke curling from my lips was more fire than ash.

Remi's head bounced between us as our words volleyed, the tension coiling tighter, tighter, tighter.

"You know exactly w—"

"What the fuck does he want?" My voice was a snarl. The walls felt too close.

Ghost exhaled sharply. "Just to talk, Domi—"

"They never want to just talk," I interrupted, stepping closer, letting the weight of my presence crush him. "There's always a reason."

Ghost's head dipped, shoulders curling inward, elbows braced on his knees, hands clasped together in front of him.

I didn't like it.

Didn't like the way he folded in on himself, like he was hiding something deep in his fucking marrow.

"You're right," he admitted, voice tight. "There's more to it. But it needs to come from him."

He lifted his head. Pleading. Weak. Desperate.

"Please. Hear him out."

Disgust coiled in my stomach.

"Fuck." The curse was sharp, slicing the tension. "This is against my better judgment."

I turned to Remi.

He didn't hesitate. Just nodded once, slow and deliberate, then lifted his hoodie, revealing the grips of two guns tucked into his black skinny jeans. Ready. Always ready. Always mine.

"He can come," I muttered, jaw tight. "But only him."

Ghost nodded quickly, scrambling for a phone I'd never seen before. His fingers flew over the screen.

I leaned closer, voice dipping to something darker, something that sank teeth into the base of his spine. "If Remi sees anyone else on the feed enter the building, I will kill him on sight without listening to a single fucking word he has to say."

Ghost froze, fingers hovering over the screen.

He understood.

"He won't do anything," he said. Tried to sound confident but failed. "I promise."

I laughed. Quiet, sharp, a knife's edge. "Your word is worth shit to me right now, Ghost."

Then, I yanked his head back, baring my teeth at him like the animal he should have never tried to cage.

Ghost trembled.

His pulse throbbed under my grip, fast, frantic, like a trapped thing desperate to escape. He was afraid.

Twenty minutes later, a sharp ding cut through the charged silence. The elevator doors slid open.

Salvatore stepped out.

His usual presence—calculated, immovable, impenetrable—was cracked. It was subtle, just a hairline fracture, but I saw it. Felt it in the way his shoulders weren't squared like usual, the way his normally steely gaze darted, unfocused, his breath just slightly too shallow.

I leaned back against the arm of the couch, arms crossing over my chest, boredom plastered over my face like war paint.

"Salvatore," I drawled, exhaling a lungful of smoke. "What a surprise."

Remi remained where he was, leaning against the back of the couch, flipping his knife between his fingers, his lips curling slightly at the edges like he could already taste blood in the air.

Salvatore ignored the bait. Didn't even look at Remi. His eyes locked onto mine like I was his sole focus. "Elio is gone."

The words landed with a thud, heavy but hollow.

I blinked. Let the silence stretch, coiling around us like barbed wire. "So?"

Ghost shifted uncomfortably, like he could feel how fucking unnatural my reaction was. He didn't want to be here to witness this but knew it wasn't worth risking his life to leave. He had a lot to prove… this was just the beginning.

Salvatore clenched his jaw. "He was taken."

"And?" I raised a brow, unmoved. Uninterested.

Salvatore exhaled sharply through his nose. "We can't find him."

I tilted my head, watching him with detached amusement.

We. Not *I.* His choice of words confounded me.

"Let me guess," I murmured, pressing the cigarette to my lips, taking a slow drag before exhaling. Smoke curled between us, thick and suffocating. "You came here because I'm the only one who can."

Salvatore's throat bobbed.

I grinned, sharp and humorless. "Why the fuck should I care?"

A single tear slipped down his face.

It stopped me. Not enough to show it, but enough to notice.

Salvatore Gallo didn't cry. Not when he killed. Not when he bled. Not when he lost. But now for a son—a brother—I didn't know, he cried. I'd never seen a father show any hint of emotion for their children.

My grin soured into something sharp, something venomous.

"Because I know who took him." His voice was gritted between his teeth, cracking under the weight of something unbearable.

I stared.

He inhaled shakily. "It was Federico."

Remi stilled.

Ghost tensed.

And I... felt nothing.

Not anger. Not rage. Not fear. Just cold, unyielding clarity. "Well." I took another drag. "That's unfortunate for you."

Salvatore took a step closer. "I need your help."

Something ugly curled in my chest, something dark and hollow and hungry. I tilted my head, flicking the ashes from my cigarette onto the floor.

"And why the fuck," I murmured, voice dipping lower, silkier, deadlier, "would I ever help you?"

Salvatore broke. Not all at once, but in increments. His shoulders sagged a fraction. His lips parted. His face was haunted, haggard, desperate. "You're the only one who can find him."

I let the silence stretch.

Then, I laughed. Low. Hollow. Cruel.

"Interesting," I mused, tapping a finger to my chin. "You never seemed to care when it was me."

A flicker of something passed over his face. Shame. Guilt. Or maybe I was giving him too much credit.

"I'll find him." My voice was cold. Absolute. Laced with the bite of a deal with the devil.

Salvatore's breath wooshed in relief—but it was premature. I stepped forward, crowding into his space, my voice dropping to a murmur.

"But you're going to tell me the whole fucking truth."

Salvatore's brows furrowed. "What?"

I smiled. It wasn't kind.

"If you want me to find your son, then you're going to tell me everything." My fingers ghosted over his collar, fisting the fabric tight. "About my mother."

Salvatore froze. And for the first time, I saw it.

Fear.

Not of me. Not of what I could do. But of what I might uncover.

My blood sang.

I pressed closer, so close he could feel my breath against his cheek. "Do we have a deal?"

Salvatore's jaw locked.

One second. Two. Three.

Then, slowly—with the weight of a man making a deal with the fucking abyss—

He nodded.

Hollow Pines National Park surrounded the city on three sides. It was as beautiful as it was deadly. And had claimed its fair share of victims over the years, not that anyone really knew the number of skeletons buried in shallow graves that were hidden in its depths.

The cottage at the edge of Brielle's land was the perfect place for Federico to use. Only a handful of people knew of its existence; even fewer had ever seen it or knew where it was.

The intel we'd pried out of Federico's one remaining confidant—before Remi carved him into pieces—had led us here. The cottage just beyond the grounds of the care home wasn't on any blueprints, tucked away behind gnarled trees and overgrown brush like it had been swallowed whole by time.

We slipped through the rusted gates at the forest side entrance, the wind howling through the skeletal branches. The exterior of the old cottage had deteriorated since the last time we were there. Its windows shattered, its walls sagging. A mausoleum to forgotten souls.

Remi moved beside me, silent as a shadow, his grip tight on the knife he never went without. The blade still bore Ghost's blood.

A shame it wasn't more.

Federico wasn't sloppy. He wouldn't have left Elio unguarded.

The first man never saw me coming. I wrapped my arm around his throat, yanking him back into the darkness. The crack of his snapping spine was lost to the wind.

Remi handled the next one, slipping through the night like a wraith. One second the guard was standing there, gun raised, the next his throat blossomed open like a second mouth.

The third saw what was happening and tried to run.

Remi tackled him to the ground. I crouched beside him, pressing a boot to his throat, watching with mild amusement as he choked on his breath.

"Where's the boy?" I asked, voice eerily soft.

The man gargled something unintelligible. His answer didn't matter. I pressed harder. Bones cracked. His body twitched, then stilled.

Remi wiped his blade clean on the dead man's shirt and grinned. "Shall we?"

The door to the house groaned on its hinges, the inside suffocating with the stench of mildew and something darker.

Blood. We followed it like the hounds of hell. Past the crumbling wallpaper, past the rooms filled with broken furniture and discarded remnants of lives long forgotten.

Until we reached the entrance to the bunker. The door was padlocked. Remi pulled his bag off his shoulders and handed me some bolt cutters. They sliced through the metal like it was butter, and within seconds, it clattered on the ground.

I ripped it clean off the hinges. The stench hit us first.

Rot. Sweat. Terror.

A single dim bulb swung from the ceiling, casting jagged shadows across the room as a moth fluttered around it. The only sound was the slow drip of water seeping from the cracked, tiled walls.

Elio hung motionless from the rafters, a lifeless marionette strung up by men who had no business playing god. The bag over his head sagged slightly, his body shivering against the damp.

Not dead.

But not far from it.

Remi stepped forward first, blade already in his grip, flicking the edge of the bag up with the tip. The moment the air hit Elio's face, he flinched.

"He's alive," Remi muttered, though there was something almost like disappointment in his tone. He grinned at me over his shoulder. "For now."

Elio made a noise—half-strangled, half-panicked. He couldn't see us, not yet, but he could feel us. The shift in the air, the cold presence of something worse than whatever had left him strung up like a slab of meat.

I grabbed him by the shoulders and hauled him up, cutting the rope with a flick of my knife. His body crashed to the floor in a heap, limbs twitching as blood rushed back into them.

He coughed, a wet, painful sound, and gasped for breath. Then he stilled. Listening. He still didn't know who we were.

Remi crouched beside him, grabbed the edge of the bag, and yanked it off.

Elio blinked rapidly, his pupils blown wide, confusion painted across his pale, sweat-slick face.

Then he saw me. His breath hitched. "Who…?" His voice was hoarse, barely more than a whisper.

I tilted my head. "You know who I am."

Recognition flashed behind the exhaustion in his eyes. "Domino."

"Good. Saves me an introduction."

His gaze darted to Remi, who was watching him like a wolf watches an injured rabbit.

Elio swallowed hard. "Did my father send you?"

"He did," I confirmed. "Don't make me regret agreeing to this."

Remi cut the ropes binding his wrists, and Elio hissed as the blood flooded back into them. He was weak. Starving. Broken. Federico had made sure of that.

Pathetic.

But not my problem.

"Can you walk?" I asked, already tired of this conversation.

Elio exhaled sharply through his nose and forced himself to his feet. His legs wobbled, but he stayed standing. Barely.

Remi clapped him on the back—too hard. Elio stumbled, and Remi snickered.

"Let's go," I said, already turning away. "We're on borrowed time."

The drive to the meeting point was silent.

Elio sat in the back, his eyes never leaving me. I felt them like needles against my skull, sharp and prying, filled with questions I wouldn't answer.

Remi sprawled in the passenger seat, boots kicked up on the dash, flipping his knife between his fingers with practiced ease. Every so often, he'd glance back at Elio and smirk like he knew something Elio didn't.

By the time we pulled up, the sky was a deep shade of bruised violet. The outskirts of Marlow Heights were deserted at this hour—nothing but empty roads, flickering street lights, and a gas station that hadn't seen business in years.

Salvatore was waiting. He stood beside his car, face cast in shadow, shoulders rigid.

The moment he saw Elio, something in him cracked. He took a step forward, then another, his breath sharp and ragged. A tear slipped down his face, lost to the night.

Elio hesitated, unsure if this was real. Salvatore opened his arms, and after a beat, Elio collapsed into them.

For a long moment, they just stood there. Father and son.

I watched, detached, taking in the raw display of emotion with a kind of clinical curiosity. The concept of family was foreign to me.

Salvatore had fought for his son.

I couldn't decide if that made him weak or terrifying. Eventually, he lifted his head, locking his gaze onto mine.

"You have my gratitude." His voice was hoarse and thick with something that made my stomach twist. "I owe you."

I stepped closer, my lips curling into a cold, thin smile. "You owe me more than gratitude, Salvatore."

His breath hitched.

"You know what I want."

A pause. A flicker of hesitation. Then—acceptance.

"You'll get the truth," he murmured, his fingers tightening around Elio's shoulder. "Everything about your mother."

Remi grinned, a demented, bloodthirsty thing.

I smirked back. "Good."

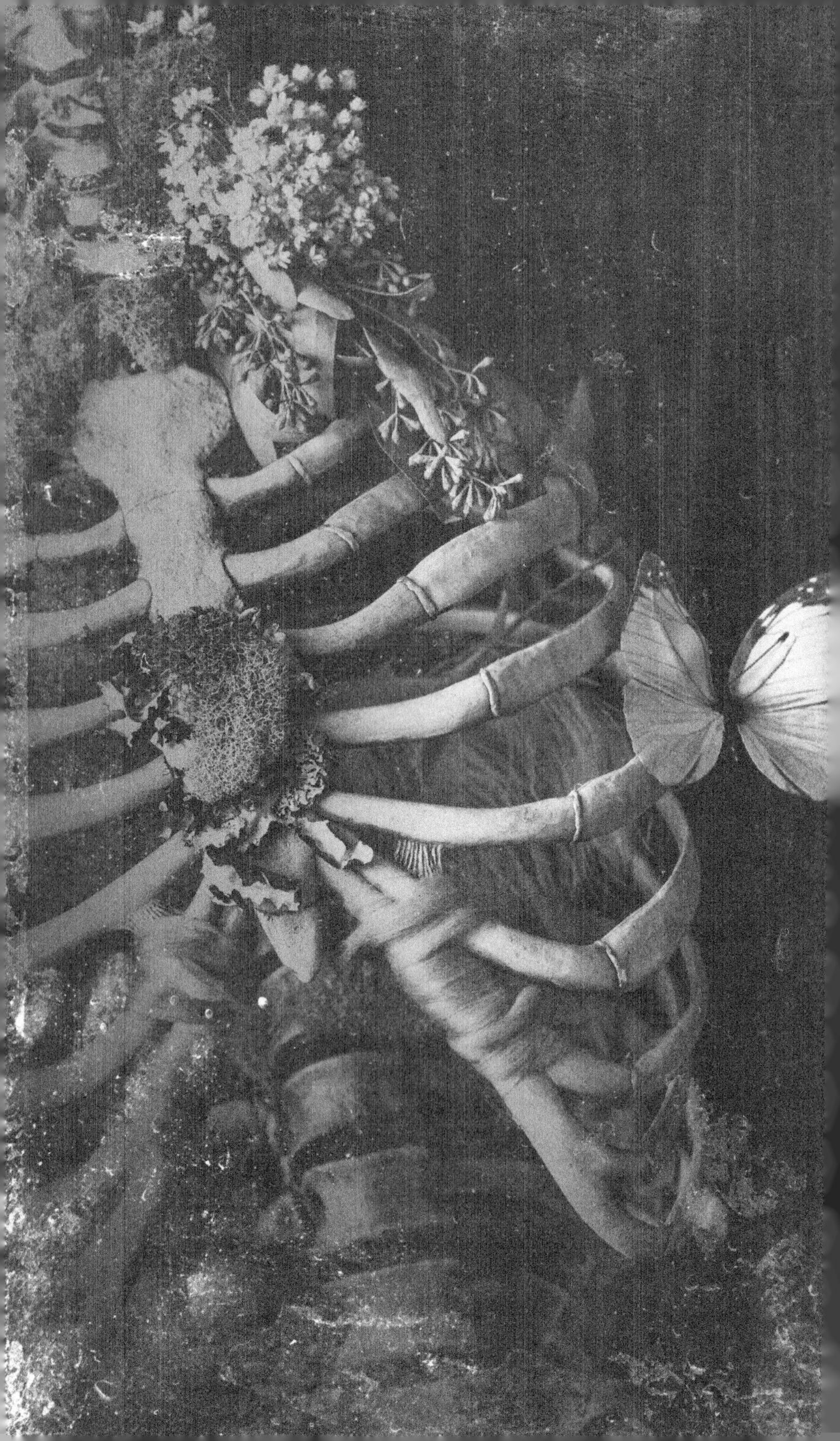

24 REMI

Domino didn't just plan to kill Federico.
He planned to unmake him—tear his world down brick by brick, salt the earth beneath his empire, watch him drown in the ashes of everything he once ruled.

It wasn't enough to kill him.

Federico had to suffer.

He had to wake up every day and wonder—was this the day? Was this the moment he'd feel cold steel sliding between his ribs? Would he see Domino's face in a reflection, in a shadow, in the last seconds before the lights went out forever?

He had to fear us.

To know we were coming and be powerless to stop it.

And Domino was thriving on it. I saw it in the way his fingers twitched, in the way his breath hitched between words, in the sharp, cruel curl of his lips that made something inside me ache with dangerous, insatiable need.

The man chained to the chair was already dead. He just didn't know it yet.

Domino moved around him like a predator savoring the last few moments before the kill, his presence suffocating, pressing into the room like a stormfront ready to break. The air was thick with sweat, with fear—with blood waiting to be spilled.

"Where is he?" His voice slithered through the silence, whispered against Leo's skin like a blade dragging over flesh.

The man trembled. His knuckles went white where they strained against the restraints, and for a moment, I thought he might piss himself.

"Nothing to say, Leo?"

His dark brown eyes darted to mine, desperate, searching for mercy. He wouldn't find it.

Domino licked his lips and held out his hand, fingers curling in silent demand. The wolfshead switchblade spun lazily between my fingers, just within Leo's line of sight. A taunt. A threat. A promise.

I placed the handle in Domino's palm, my fingertips lingering against his, watching the shift in his expression as he weighed the knife. Something dark settled over him. Something raw and ravenous.

His head fell back on his shoulders, eyes fluttered closed as he took a deep inhale, and like a coiled spring, he snapped and drove it into Leo's thigh.

Leo's head snapped back, tendons straining, skin

flushing blood-red, his jaw locking tight against the scream he couldn't swallow. The sound still broke free, a wet, strangled thing.

Domino's lips parted, and I swore I saw pleasure flicker through his eyes as he twisted the serrated blade, carving through flesh in a slow, deliberate circle.

Leo bucked against the chair, spittle dribbling from his chin, tears streaking down his face. He squeezed his eyes shut like it would make this stop.

Fool.

"Where is he?" Domino hissed, his voice curling around me like smoke, like possession.

Leo shook his head, frantic, droplets of blood and saliva spraying across the floor. The movement made him whimper.

I exhaled a quiet chuckle, biting my lip to keep it from stretching into something too eager. Too telling. He had no idea what kind of monster he was playing with.

His bloodshot eyes cracked open, locking onto me. I tilted my head, regarding him like an insect pinned beneath my fingers.

I counted down in my head.

Three.

Domino's grip flexed.

Two.

His breathing steadied.

One.

Crack.

Leo's nose shattered beneath the weight of Domino's first punch. Blood sprayed in a perfect arc, splattering the wall, streaking across Domino's cheek like war paint.

Domino shook out his fist, flexing his split knuckles,

chest rising and falling in slow, measured breaths—a man savoring the burn of violence.

I leaned against the wall, watching, hungry. I could stop this, but why would I?

Watching Domino fall apart was like watching a fire consume everything in its path. Wild. Untamed. Beautiful.

And God, did I want to burn with him.

Leo choked on his blood, coughing, his body sagging in the chair. But Domino wasn't done.

He fisted Leo's hair, yanking his head back with a force that made my pulse stutter. His eyes were dark and distant—lost to something primal. Something irreversible.

A slow, thrumming ache spread through my chest, curling low and hot in my stomach. My nails dug into my palms, trying to suppress the itch crawling under my skin.

I wanted to be the one under Domino's hands.

I wanted to be the thing he destroyed.

His pain was the most addictive touch I'd ever felt.

By the time Leo broke, his vault of secrets cracked open, his last word fading into nothing, he'd stopped moving. A useless, bloodied heap. Domino's breath came in harsh pants, his shoulders rising and falling in jagged bursts.

Our eyes met across the room.

A challenge.

A promise.

And then he was on me.

Domino crashed into me, wild and untamed, a feverish blur of teeth and pain, fingers bruising, grip desperate, violent. His mouth burned against mine, claiming, consuming, devouring me—like leaving his marks on me was the only way to stay tethered, the only way to staunch the hunger clawing at his ribs.

His breath was hot against my throat, his fingers fisting in my shirt, dragging me closer, deeper. Harder.

"You're mine," he rasped, voice raw, wrecked. Unchained.

I arched into him, where he stood between my legs. My nails raked down his back, carving an answer into his skin, demanding more. "Then prove it."

A broken groan ripped from my throat, raw and wrecked, swallowed by the heavy air between us. The glint of steel flickered in my periphery before the sharp kiss of Domino's switchblade sliced through denim. The fabric fell away in tattered strips, pooling at my ankles.

Exposed. Open. *His.*

"Fuck, *piccolo agnello*, I need to fuck you."

The need in his voice was tangible, thick and fevered, and God, I wanted to be ruined by it.

I answered without hesitation, bracing my hands behind me on the workbench as he hooked my legs over his arms, his grip branding, unrelenting. His fingers made quick work of his belt, the sharp clink of metal a wicked prelude. The slow, deliberate rasp of his zipper sent a shiver rolling through me—a countdown.

Three.

"Yes," I breathed, hips canting forward in silent demand. "Fuck me."

Two.

His cock pressed against me, the thick, swollen head teasing, taunting—denying.

The air reeked of copper and death, a heady perfume that sent adrenaline racing through my veins. My fingers curled against the workbench, nails carving half-moons into the splintered wood as a vicious snarl curled my lips.

"Stop teasing and fuck me."

One.

Domino chuckled, low and sinful, the sound thrumming straight down my spine. My eyes snapped open just in time to catch the slow, deliberate drag of his blade across his wrist.

A violent tremor shuddered through me as his blood dripped hot and thick, trailing down my taint, pooling at the tip of his cock.

His gaze burned into mine, dark and feral. "Gonna fuck more than just my cum into you." His voice was a wrecked rasp, his pupils blown wide. "I'm—" His words dissolved into a snarled growl as his hips snapped forward, spearing me open in one brutal thrust.

Pain and euphoria collided, white-hot and merciless, and I screamed, head snapping back, body bowing, breaking, surrendering.

His.

Always his.

In heaven, hell, and purgatory, until the world ended, I was his.

"WHERE ARE WE GOING?" I ASKED AS DOMINO tightened the helmet strap beneath my chin, his fingers precise and deliberate. His obsession with the damn thing made my eyes roll, and he caught the movement immediately.

A snort crackled through the helmet's speaker. "Don't be a brat."

The Ninja rumbled to life beneath us, the deep vibration rolling through my bones as I slipped my arms around his waist.

"We're going to get answers." His voice was a low growl over the helmet's intercom. "Then we're going to end this."

The weight of his words coiled in my gut, sharp and electric.

"Federico won't go down without a fight," he continued, voice edged with dark amusement. "And with most of his circle rotting in the ground, he's running scared."

I exhaled a laugh, my grip tightening around him. "I can't wait to watch you break him."

Domino didn't respond, but I felt the shift in his body—the tension snapping taut like a wire ready to strangle. He wanted this. Needed this. His demons were already clawing their way to the surface, demanding carnage, and I was more than willing to help him tear Federico apart.

We pulled out of the underground garage, the sun glinting off the mirrored skyscrapers lining the center of Marlow Heights. The city gleamed like polished steel, a deceptive beauty masking the rot underneath.

A city on the edge of war.

The helmet's speaker crackled as Domino spoke again. "A cornered animal is the most dangerous."

His words lingered, a warning wrapped in cold certainty, but I welcomed the danger. Let Federico bare his teeth—I wanted to see his fear when he realized there was no escape, that he was about to meet his end.

"It'll take us a couple of hours to get to the location

Ghost sent me," Domino said as we wove through traffic like a blade slicing through flesh.

"You trust him?"

Tension flickered through his frame, a barely-there hesitation, but I felt it like it was my own.

Since that morning in the apartment, Ghost had been walking on a knife's edge. His access had been revoked, his loyalty questioned, but he'd kept working, kept proving himself. I'd spent hours trying to unravel the connection between Catalina, Salvatore, and Federico, only to hit a brick wall of erased records and dead ends.

That wasn't possible in this day and age—unless someone wanted it to be.

The old families operated like they were still in Capone's era, their power woven into the cracks of the city itself. The air in Marlow Heights had shifted, thick with impending bloodshed. People felt it, even if they didn't understand it—the way they glanced over their shoulders, the way shadows stretched too long.

Hell was empty because all the devils were here. And soon, the streets would drown in blood.

I knew we would come out on top—we had to. But Federico had called his remaining guards back, stacking the numbers in his favor. Domino didn't care. I'd seen him kill men twice his size with nothing but his hands.

He wasn't just planning to kill Federico. He was going to rip apart his entire world, brick by fucking brick.

The city blurred as we broke through the limits, leaving the glass-and-steel skyline behind. The freeway opened before us, an endless stretch of asphalt leading straight to war.

Domino revved the engine once before launching us

forward, the bike growling like a beast unleashed. A second later, static filled my helmet as the opening chords of Korn's "Dead Bodies Everywhere" filled my ears.

I grinned despite myself. He wasn't wrong.

We all knew how this would end.

By the time we pulled up to the black gates, my body ached from the ride, but the sight before me sent a slow ripple of pleasure through my veins. Tall, menacing, and reaching toward the sky like skeletal fingers, the gates stood as the first warning—a barrier between the outside world and the monsters waiting within.

A thick brick wall stretched endlessly in either direction, swallowed by the towering trees that loomed like silent sentinels. But my attention was drawn upward—to the gleaming coils of barbed wire.

God, it was beautiful.

How would it look wrapped around flesh?

The sharp prongs would pierce so easily—soft skin surrendering to steel, beads of crimson welling up like tiny rubies, running in rivulets down trembling limbs. Would it sink deeper if I pulled harder? Could I embed it completely? Twist it into flesh until it became one with the body?

The thought sent a shiver down my spine, my fingers twitched with phantom sensations.

A stunning addition to my collection.

I'd been experimenting with oils lately, testing how the diffusion of light could capture the depth of a wound, the way bruises bloomed like violets against pale skin. But nothing—nothing—could replicate the reality of it.

The textures. The smells. The heat of fresh blood

coated my hands, thicker than paint and richer than any medium I'd ever worked with.

I knew the exact pressure required to carve flesh from bone. The force needed to break a man apart.

I craved it. Dreamed of it. Created it.

But it had been too long since Domino had gifted me someone to play with. Too long since I'd been allowed to perfect my work. Art required patience. Precision.

And lately, we'd had none to spare.

The gates groaned open, metal screaming on its hinges, welcoming us into the belly of the beast. We followed the winding driveway along a black river—dark and raging, its currents violent and unyielding.

The house emerged as we rounded the final turn. A behemoth of Colonial wealth and privilege.

It was elegant, sprawling over manicured grounds with a kind of effortless grace that only came with old money. White columns framed the front, standing tall like sentries, their smooth surfaces untouched by time. A second-story balcony wrapped around the facade, polished railing gleaming in the pale sunlight, a place meant for whiskey glasses and hushed conversations, not blood and screams.

Warm light spilled from the tall, symmetrical windows, glowing against rich, brick walls. The heavy oak doors weren't foreboding like they should've been. They were grand. Inviting, even.

It was unsettling. A place meant to be lived in, not just inhabited.

Domino and I knew houses like this; we'd burned one to the ground. I just hoped they didn't hold that against us. This house was different. It wasn't just a display of wealth; it was a home. And that was the part neither of us could understand.

Salvatore stood at the bottom of the steps, watching our approach with calm indifference. No apprehension, no hesitation—just a man who already knew how this meeting would go. Arrogant. Calculated. Dangerous.

A second man stood beside him, tall and unreadable. My fingers twitched at my sides, instinct coiling in my gut.

Domino cut the engine, the roar of the bike fading into silence. I pulled off my helmet, blinking up at them in confusion before slipping off the bike and falling into step behind Domino.

Salvatore's lips twitched at the corners, arms spreading in a gesture just shy of welcoming.

"Welcome to my home." His voice was smooth, practiced. "Please, just leave this one standing."

Domino growled low in his throat, the sound more animal than man. "If you hadn't done what you did to us, we wouldn't have had to."

Salvatore sighed, brushing the nonexistent dust from his sleeve. "I apologize for the way Enzo handled everything. We didn't know how... amenable you'd be."

Domino arched a brow, his grip tightening around my waist as he pulled me into his side. Possessive. Territorial. I didn't hate it. I fucking loved it.

"You could have asked to speak with me directly." His words cut through the air, sharp and crackling like ice.

A quiet, rueful chuckle slipped past Salvatore's lips. "I did. I sent many men to talk to you, but—"

"No." Domino's voice snapped like a whip, slicing through whatever excuse Salvatore had prepared. "You or one of your sons sent men to disturb our business.

They never tried anything other than to kill me or..." He shook his head, cutting himself off.

Silence stretched, thick and heavy.

Salvatore exhaled through his nose. "It's all water under the bridge now. Even the house that's still smoldering." His tone was light, as if we weren't discussing destruction and death. "I was on my way over to talk to you, but I guess locking you in a room wasn't the right way to go about it."

"No, it wasn't," Domino gritted out.

Salvatore gestured to the man beside him. "This is Alessio. He'll be looking after us today. If you hand him your helmets and keys, he'll see to your bike." His gaze flickered to the sleek black machine, something like admiration flashing across his face. "She's a beauty."

Domino smirked. "That she is."

We handed everything to Alessio and followed Salvatore inside, weaving through a bright hallway, a bustling kitchen, and out onto a sprawling terrace. The scent of freshly cut grass and expensive cologne clung to the air.

Seated around a large wooden table were Enzo, Luca, Diego, and Elio.

All conversation died the moment they saw us. Four pairs of eyes locked onto Domino, sizing him up like predators assessing a rival in their territory. They barely spared me a glance, their focus singular, as if I were nothing more than a shadow in Domino's wake.

That was a mistake. I felt the smirk tug at my lips. I couldn't wait to show them exactly what I was capable of.

Salvatore took his seat at the head of the table, motioning for us to sit. Domino didn't move, his presence a solid wall of defiance.

He sighed. "Sit, Domino. We're not your enemies."

Domino held his stare for a beat longer before pulling out a chair and dropping into it. I slid in beside him, resting my arms on the table, fingers laced together.

The tension coiled tighter.

It was Luca who broke the silence. "So, why the hell are we all here?"

Salvatore leaned forward, elbows braced against the table. "Because there are things you all need to know." His gaze swept over his sons before settling on Domino. "And because Domino has a proposition."

Domino's fingers tapped against the tabletop, measured and patient. "Before that, let's clear the air." His tone was flat, unreadable. "You wanted me dead. Then you didn't. Then you locked me in a fucking room. What changed?"

Salvatore exhaled through his nose. "It's time you know the truth about Catalina and me."

The name hit like a bullet. Domino's spine snapped straight, and tension coiled in his muscles. Latent power waiting to be unleashed. I slipped my hand onto his thigh and squeezed, a small act of comfort. A reminder he wasn't alone in this.

Never again.

A shift rippled through the table. Diego's jaw clenched, Enzo went utterly still, and Elio arched a single brow, curiosity flickering in his gaze.

Luca, however, laughed under his breath. "Christ. This should be good."

Salvatore met their stares head-on. "Catalina was *mine*."

The words rang like a death knell, a finality that sent a shiver through the air. Unshakable. Irrefutable.

Domino went utterly still.

Salvatore exhaled, dragging a hand down his face. "After the boys' mother died, I was lucky enough to fall in love again. Catalina was too good, too pure for our world. But the heart wants what it wants. Even if she was the sister of my enemy." His voice turned raw at the edges, old wounds splitting open beneath the weight of the truth.

Domino's fist curled against the table, knuckles whitening. "You expect me to believe that?"

Salvatore's gaze darkened, something almost wounded flashing in his expression before it was buried beneath cold resolve. "Believe what you want. She thought our union could end the fighting between our families. But Federico has always been power-hungry and unwilling to work for it. He takes the easiest route—no matter the cost."

Silence.

Luca huffed out a bitter laugh, shaking his head. "So, what? You expect us to just accept him?" He looked pointedly at Domino. "As one of us?"

Salvatore didn't blink. "Yes."

Luca was like a rabid dog with a bone, refusing to let it go. "After all the blood he's spilled in the DeMarco name?"

Salvatore's patience snapped, his voice a razor-edged snarl. "You don't get a choice in this." His jaw tensed, hands pressing flat against the table. "Domino is my son too, and I want him to be part of our family."

Domino leaned back in his chair, arms crossing over his chest, his expression blank—the storm in his eyes was anything but.

"That's touching." Domino's voice was empty, hollowed out. "But we didn't come here for a fucking love story."

Salvatore swallowed whatever emotion flickered in his gaze, nodding once. "No. You came for the truth. And something else. You listen to what I have to say, then we'll hear you out."

A muscle ticked in Domino's jaw. "Alright. But don't leave anything out."

"Thank you." The tension in Salvatore's shoulders eased, but it was fragile, a thread ready to snap.

His voice softened. "As I said, I fell in love with Catalina. Her laugh, the light in her dark green eyes... just like yours, son." His gaze turned distant, lost in a memory. He cleared his throat, shaking himself free of the past. "I haven't thought about her in years—"

The table shook. Domino's hand smashed down, glasses rattling from the impact. His breathing was heavy and ragged, something was breaking loose inside him.

I didn't think about it. I just moved closer, shifting so our bodies touched from shoulder to thigh to ankle, a silent tether.

Elio tracked the movement, his eyes flickering with something like amusement—before his expression shut down entirely.

Salvatore swallowed, voice raw. "It's been too painful to revisit the past…" He took a long sip of the golden liquid in his glass, as if it could burn away the words he didn't want to say.

"We were planning to elope when Federico found out about us. Catalina tried to reason with him, but he refused to hear her. Said he didn't want to be connected to us in any way and took her away from me." His hand clenched into a fist. "I had men combing the country trying to find her, but it was like she'd vanished. For three months, she was a ghost haunting me every time I closed my eyes." His voice cracked at the end, a deep wound left gaping open.

Domino's voice was low, almost dangerous. "What did he do?"

It wasn't a question. It was a confirmation of what he already knew.

Salvatore exhaled through his nose. "He held her hostage at his compound. At that time, I didn't have anyone on the inside." His fingers dug into the wooden table, the pain almost too much to voice.

"Catalina was too bright to be caged. She managed to escape using the tunnels leading off the property. She walked to the outskirts of Marlow Heights and caught a cab here."

Salvatore lifted his gaze, the memory cutting through him. "When she arrived, she told me she was pregnant."

Domino's breath hitched, but he didn't speak.

"I was overjoyed." Salvatore's voice was thick, his eyes glassy. "Nothing means more to me than family. To have another child... it was a blessing."

Domino let out a sharp, bitter laugh. "Federico has always treated me like a curse."

Salvatore's jaw clenched. "No. A weapon."

Domino's fingers curled into his palm, but he nodded.

Salvatore pressed on. "She spent a week here. She was so excited. A doctor came, and he confirmed she was about five months along. He did a scan..." His throat worked as he swallowed, his next words barely a whisper. "She was convinced she could reason with Federico. That you being a boy would change his perspective."

I shook my head. "She was wrong, wasn't she?" It wasn't a question.

Salvatore's expression shattered. "It changed things in ways she never expected."

He dabbed at his eyes with a handkerchief, his grief raw and unpolished.

"She went back with Angelo—he volunteered to go undercover with the DeMarcos. He was meant to protect her. But all he did was scheme and plot," he choked.

"Federico kept her locked in her room the entire pregnancy," Enzo picked up when Salvatore couldn't. "Angelo worked to gain Federico's trust—"

Domino let out a cold laugh. "He did that. Always thought he was a snake."

Enzo's expression darkened. "To you, yes. I know everything you've done to him over the years, Domino."

Domino's eyes flashed. "Nothing the fucker didn't deserve."

Salvatore sighed, running a hand through his hair. "Catalina had the baby, and Angelo did his job. He got Federico away long enough for her to run. But…"

My chest tightened. "You didn't know what he'd done to her car."

Salvatore exhaled sharply. "No. Not until it was too late."

His voice shook. "Angelo was supposed to be with her, but Federico called, saying he'd be back in a few hours. So he changed the plan. Sent her ahead."

Domino's voice was ice. "So what you're saying is I should kill him for his incompetence?"

Salvatore shot him a sharp look. "No. Angelo did what he had to do to maintain his cover." He took a shaky breath. "He was the first to arrive at the wreckage.

He called me from the scene. Confirmed what happened. My heart shattered."

The air was suffocating. The cool breeze blowing across my face did nothing to alleviate the growing tightness in my chest.

"I asked him to bring you to me. But by the time the call ended... Federico was there."

A single tear slipped down Salvatore's cheek, and he didn't bother wiping it away. "He took you. And threatened to kill anyone who revealed the truth."

Domino's hands were shaking. "So he killed his sister and raised me as his own for what?"

Salvatore sighed, his voice filled with regret. "I think he believed he could use you against me. That I'd give up everything to get you back." He swallowed hard. "I had no idea what he would do to you."

"How do you know?" Domino's chest rose and fell heavily.

Salvatore's voice cracked. "Domino... Angelo told me everything."

A silence stretched between them, unspoken pain bleeding into the air.

Domino turned to me, his dark green eyes eclipsed by shadows. "I nearly killed Remi the night two of your men attacked us—just for telling me the truth." His voice was low, rough, scraping against the heavy silence. "What he found out about the crash, with Ghost's help... He almost lost his life, too."

A flicker of something crossed his face—pain, regret, fury—but he buried it just as fast, locking it down beneath the cold mask he always wore. He tipped his head back, eyes slipping shut like he was trying to wrestle down the ghosts clawing at his mind. Around us, the Gallos murmured in hushed voices, letting the weight of the moment settle.

Without a word, I reached into his back pocket, pulled out his silver cigarette tin, lit one, and passed it to him. He took it automatically, like some part of him always knew I was there.

"Thanks," he muttered, barely audible.

A small smile tugged at my lips as I lit my own. Smoke curled between us, drifting in the night air, a temporary veil between the war in our minds and the one we were about to wage. My gaze flicked across the table, meeting Elio's for a brief moment. He dipped his chin in acknowledgment—a quiet thank you for what we'd done. A ghost of a smile crossed his lips before it vanished like it had never been there at all.

The hush thickened. Alessio arrived, replenishing drinks, setting a tumbler in front of Domino and me. A plate of pastries and sandwiches landed in the center of the table, but no one moved for them except the Gallos. We didn't have the appetite for anything but revenge.

Salvatore's voice broke the quiet. "What else did you want to discuss, Domino?"

"I want your help taking down Federico." Domino's smirk was as sharp as a blade.

Diego, who had been silent until now, finally spoke, his voice a low, dangerous rasp. "You think we're just going to join forces with you?"

Domino tilted his head, a predator studying his prey. "I think you want him dead just as much as I do."

The air tightened, tension coiling between us like a live wire. The Gallos sat still, unreadable, their expressions betraying nothing. But I knew—deep down, they were considering it. They all had their reasons.

Salvatore sighed, rubbing his temple before turning his gaze to me. "Remi."

At once, every eye landed on me. I shifted, the weight of their attention pressing against my skin. I was used to being in the background, unseen, unnoticed. I was the ghost lurking in the shadows, the one who gathered information, who dismantled enemies from the inside out. But not tonight.

I leaned forward, setting a folder on the table with a deliberate motion. "This is what we have so far." I flipped it open, revealing a roadmap to war—documents, surveillance reports, photographs of Federico's crumbling empire.

"With or without you, we're taking him down," I said, voice smooth, controlled. "Federico has lost more than half his men. He's backed into a corner, and that makes him desperate. He's not going to roll over."

I glanced at Domino before continuing.

"We've drained his accounts. His businesses are either collapsing or buried under legal red tape. We've cut off his allies, flipped his business partners. His clubs, his casinos, his construction sites—they're shutting down, one by one. His men?" A dark smile played on my lips. "They're running. And we're hunting them down."

The Gallos listened, silent. We'd already made our move. The only question was whether they'd stand with us or against us.

Domino took over, his voice steady, deliberate. He laid out the next steps, the weak points we'd identified, the places Federico would try to hold. His mercenaries inflated his numbers, but they had no loyalty. They fought for money, not for him.

"If anyone captures Federico," Domino said, his

voice like steel, "he's ours. If anyone takes his life, even by accident—we take theirs."

A beat of silence.

Salvatore exhaled slowly and leaned back. His gaze moved over his sons—Enzo, Luca, Diego, Elio—measuring them. Weighing their unspoken decision.

"Well," he said finally, voice laced with something dark and final. "If everyone agrees, we're in." His eyes glinted with cold fury. "It's high time I made him hurt the same way he hurt me."

The war had already begun. Now, it was just a matter of how long Federico could run before we caught him.

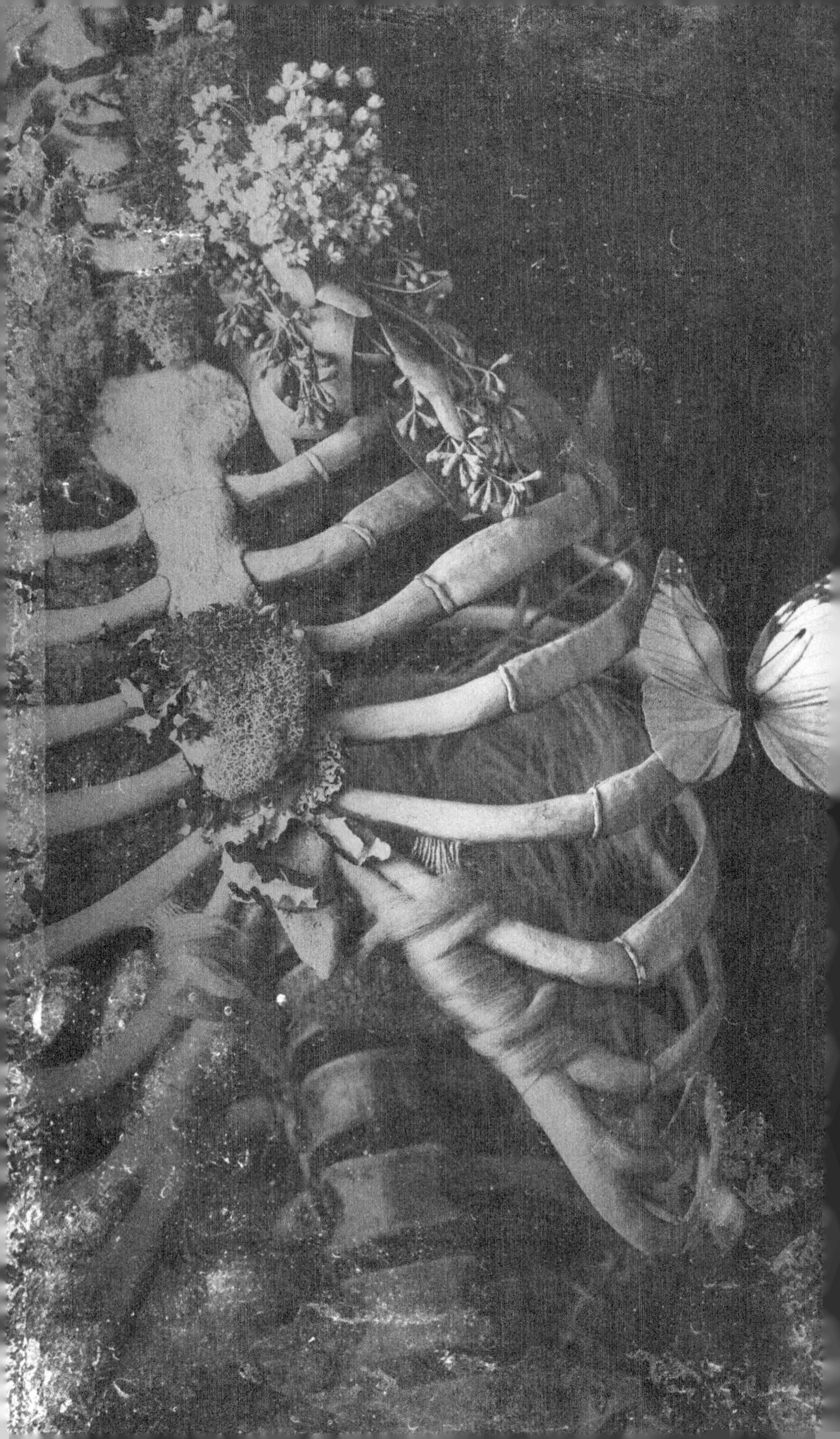

The haunting melody of Sleep Token's *Alkaline* drifted through the hidden speakers in my art room, winding through the space like ghosts whispering in the dark. Outside, rain lashed against the window, drowning the world in shifting gray, smearing the city into something unreal.

Before me, the canvas took shape—shadows stretched into something almost human, something half-alive. A dismembered body hung suspended in barbed wire, flesh torn, bone gleaming through raw muscle. The metal coils bit deep, twisting in a brutal embrace, a perfect contradiction of life and death. A moment stretched between agony and peace. Between the past and the future, stitched together in suffering.

Barbed wire had become my recent obsession. It had taken root in my mind since our day at Salvatore's house. Mansion. Compound. Whatever it was. The imagery consumed me, dug into my skin like a thorn I couldn't pull free. I had to understand it—to *feel* it. To know its power. Domino had gotten me some when I asked. When I *needed* it.

And I *had* felt it.

That night in his playroom, with one of Federico's men strung up before me, thinking he could get the jump on me. The idiot never stood a chance.

I dragged the barbs over his skin, felt them split flesh from muscle, watched the thin red lines blossom into rivers. I had stripped off my hoodie and shoes before I began—I needed to feel *connected*. I needed to *see* the moment he realized he belonged to me. The moment the fight drained from his body, his struggles slowed, his gurgling breaths turned shallow, and the light in his eyes dimmed to nothing.

I had never felt more alive. Reborn.

The memory lingered as I added another stroke of deep red to the canvas, dragging my brush in long, fluid motions. I stepped back, tilting my head, studying it. Beautiful. *Perfect*. The essence of suffering is captured, preserved in oil and shadow.

A vibration in my pocket pulled me from my trance. My fingers, still smudged with paint, dug out my phone. The screen glowed.

ARTI

Hey kid, long time no see.

I rolled my eyes, exhaling through my nose.

REMI

Not my fault you weren't on shift when I visited her last week.

ARTI

> You could have let me know??

I could have. I didn't.

Arti and Doll had taken it upon themselves to *care* about me. To pretend I was something salvageable, something worth saving. Doll especially—she hated Domino with a passion, but she never saw the parts of me that *were* him. Never acknowledged that the monster she tried so hard to protect me from was already *inside* me.

Arti, though? He ran Hollow Pines Care Home now since Brielle became too far gone to function. She was barely more than a corpse on borrowed time. Most days, she couldn't do more than stumble from her bed to the bathroom and back, her body shaking like a live wire, every movement sending volts of electricity through her veins.

I *knew* what had pushed her over the edge. A sinister smile curved my lips. The moment she saw her baby boy lying lifeless in her basement.

On the days she did manage to pull herself together, I made sure to remind her why she feared her own shadow.

REMI

> Margaret told me you were sick.

A pause as three dots appeared and disappeared.

The itch crept beneath my skin, that slow-burning agitation that made my muscles tense, made my fingers twitch. Arti could never just get to the point. Always *dancing* around it. Like he was afraid of what I'd say.

My fingers tightened around the phone as Arti's next message popped up.

ARTI

> Your mom doesn't look good this morning. Her heart rate's dropping. O2 saturation is tanking every hour.

A beat of silence, my heart frozen solid in my chest. I knew this day would come. I'd prayed for it more than I cared to admit, but being faced with the reality of it? I wasn't ready.

ARTI

> It's time, Remi.

I stared at the screen, then tapped out the only reply possible.

REMI

> Ok.

ARTI

> Drive safe.

A snort escaped me despite myself. I didn't drive. Never had. Never needed to. Domino wouldn't *let* me go anywhere without him. It had just become an unspoken rule—I was the passenger, or I was walking. And if I was walking, he was never far behind, lingering in the shadows, watching. Waiting.

I locked my phone and slipped it into my pocket, turning back to my canvas. The figure still hung, motionless, forever frozen in its suffering. Just like mom had been for so long, but now her long night was ending.

I heard him before I saw him. Domino moved like a shadow, silent but *there*. Always *there*. I didn't turn when he stepped inside.

"*Beautiful,*" he murmured, voice low, rich, edged with something dangerous. "*Haunting.*"

A slow smirk curled at my lips. "You always did have good taste."

His boots crossed the room, stopping just behind me. I felt his heat at my back, his presence settling over me like a second skin. His fingers skimmed the edge of my wrist, a featherlight touch over drying paint.

"Who's it for?"

"Everyone," I murmured. "No one." A beat. "*Me.*"

His breath was warm against my neck, his voice a whisper against my ear. "What do you need?"

My fingers twitched, aching to return to the brush, to keep shaping the twisted beauty into something more. But there was something else. Something far more urgent.

"We need to go," I said instead.

Domino stilled. "To Hollow Pines?"

I turned in his arms as they wrapped around me, meeting his gaze. Green, dark, and knowing.

His expression didn't change, but I saw the shift—the way his jaw tensed, the way his hand flexed on my hip before it relaxed again. He already knew. He always *knew*.

"Now?"

I nodded. "Now."

His slow exhale ghosted over my lips. Domino lifted a hand, dragging his fingers down the column of my throat. Possessive. Unyielding.

"Fine." His voice was quiet, but there was something in it. A promise. A warning. "I'll drive."

I didn't remember getting into the SUV. Didn't remember the city streets bleeding together in the rain, the neon signs warping into something shapeless and distant.

Didn't remember walking into Hollow Pines, past the hushed voices, past the pitying glances, past the smell of antiseptic that clung to the air like something rotten beneath the surface.

But I must have walked in the rain because my clothes were wet, the fabric clinging to my skin, heavy and cold. Drops still rolled down my face, trailing along my jaw, slipping past my lips. Water. Maybe. Maybe not.

I stood at the threshold of room 213, staring at mom's frail form in the bed. She didn't look like a person anymore.

Her skin was almost translucent, stretched too thin over sharp bones, her arms skeletal against the stark white sheets. Her chest barely moved, the only sign of life coming from the slow, mechanical rise and fall—oxygen forced into her lungs by the intubation tube taped to her lips. But she wasn't *breathing*. Not really. The machine was doing it for her.

She was already gone.

I stepped closer, my movements automatic, like I wasn't the one controlling my body. I felt nothing. No grief. No anger. No relief. Just… nothing.

The heart monitor beeped, steady and artificial. A hollow rhythm filled the silence between the whispers outside the door.

I stared at her face, searching for something familiar. Some remnant of the woman she used to be. But all I saw was the empty shell left behind.

I thought I'd feel something.

I thought I'd remember. The way she used to hum under her breath. The way her voice sounded when she said my name. The way she held my hand in hers, fingers warm, solid, real.

But there was nothing.

The doctor stood on the other side of the bed, waiting. I didn't look at him, didn't acknowledge the presence of the nurses hovering just out of view or Arti where he hovered at the end of the bed.

I reached out, my fingers brushing the back of her hand. Cold. "Goodbye, Mom."

I said the words people expected to hear, not through conscious thought. My lips just wormed the words as they rolled off my tongue. I exhaled slowly, then gave the doctor a single nod.

He moved immediately, pressing a few buttons, shutting off the machine. The silence that followed was deafening as we waited and watched. We held our collective breath like some miracle of god might happen, but it didn't.

The heart monitor let out one final, long, unbroken note before the line went flat.

No breath.

No movement.

No life.

The doctor murmured something—*time of death*—but I barely heard it. One by one, they left. The nurses. The doctor. Arti. Until it was just me.

And Domino.

He hadn't said a word the entire time. Hadn't moved from his place at my side. Silent. Watching. A sentinel standing between me and whatever storm was waiting beyond these walls.

I should've felt something.

I should've cried. Or screamed. Or *something*.

But my face stayed blank. My hands remained steady. My chest didn't ache.

I turned away from the bed, my gaze landing on the window, on the endless rain streaking down the glass. The view outside blurred into nothing, distant and unreal.

I didn't remember leaving the room.

Didn't remember stepping into the hallway or the way the walls seemed to close in, pressing against me, suffocating. Didn't remember walking through the front doors of Hollow Pines, the night swallowing me whole.

But I must have.

At some point, I was back in the SUV. Domino was driving, and the city appeared in front of us. I leaned my forehead against the cool glass of the window, watching the rain slip down in thin, winding trails.

Still, I felt nothing.

The SUV stopped.

The rhythmic drumming of the rain on the roof was the only thing my brain could process, a steady, numbing beat that filled the silence. Domino didn't speak. He just sat there, staring through the windshield, watching the droplets slip down the glass as it started to mist over, his breath barely visible in the cold air.

I didn't think.

My fingers curled around the door handle, and before I even knew what was happening, I was outside, stepping into the downpour. Cold water seeped into my clothes and clung to my skin, but I barely noticed. I just walked.

And walked.

With no real direction and no thought behind each step. My body moved on instinct, pulled by something deep inside me, something ancient and hollow. Some part of me must have known where I was going, even if my mind didn't.

The towering, ornate archway of my favorite cemetery emerged from the darkness like a specter, looming under the dim orange glow of the streetlights. I rarely used this entrance—preferred to lose myself among the graves, to wander through the headstones and let the weight of the world slip away.

Here, among the dead, was the only place I ever felt at peace.

Well—*almost* the only place. The other was in Domino's arms, but even that had its limits. Even that had an end.

The dead never left.

They didn't whisper false promises or pretend to be something they weren't. They didn't judge. Didn't have expectations. Didn't disappoint.

They *welcomed* me.

My sins, my twisted perversions, my darkness—it all meant nothing here. Because, in the end, we were all the same. Flesh and bone and breath, all reduced to dust and memory.

Death was the great equalizer. The only certainty in this pointless existence.

What purpose did money have once your lungs stopped drawing air? What meaning did love hold when you weren't there to hear the sobs of those left behind? The world didn't stop turning just because you ceased to exist.

It moved on.

Erased you.

Swallowed you whole until nothing remained.

Life was a mirage, a beautifully cruel illusion meant

to trick you into believing it had *purpose*. But it didn't. It never did.

Humans weren't special. We were parasites, feeding off the world around us, pretending our lives *mattered* when we were no different from the insects we crushed underfoot. No different from the animals we slaughtered to fill our stomachs. We wrapped our existence in laws, in governments, in the pursuit of power, but for what?

To *die* all the same?

To be buried under six feet of dirt, just another nameless body in a graveyard filled with the forgotten?

From the moment we took our first breath, our internal clock started counting down, but instead of living, *truly* living, we let ourselves suffer under the weight of meaningless expectations.

We forced ourselves to endure.

For nothing.

My legs gave out beneath me, knees sinking into drenched, freshly turned earth. It was wet and cold—clinging to my fingers like it was trying to pull me under, like the earth itself was hungry for another body. Maybe it was. Maybe I was.

Lightning split the sky, illuminating the grave I was kneeling in.

There was no headstone yet—just a simple wooden cross standing vigil over the body below. Most people would have been horrified to find themselves here, but I felt nothing.

No grief. No guilt. No fear.

Just *nothing*.

The night pressed in around me, thick and suffocating. Rain ran down my face, mixing with the dirt on my skin, but I didn't move. Didn't breathe. Didn't care.

And then, he was there.

I felt the shift before I saw him, the static charge in the air as his presence wrapped around me like smoke and steel. Even with my eyes closed, my mind half-comatose, I knew who was stalking me from the shadows.

Domino.

I'd know him anywhere. Any lifetime. Any nightmare.

His presence was a razor's edge—twisted, dark, and consuming. It pulsed out in waves, hunting me with the precision of a sniper, locking onto me with deadly intent.

Black biker boots filled my vision when I blinked raindrops from my lashes. He crouched in front of me, but I couldn't lift my head.

Couldn't move.

Didn't want to.

His fingers brushed over my lips, slow, deliberate. The barest touch, but it felt like a lightning strike to my nerves.

"What do you need, *piccolo agnello*?" His voice was raw, gravel grating over steel, stripping me to my bones.

The world around us held its breath, as if it was waiting—waiting to see if this would be the night I begged him to end me.

To make me his next victim.

I swallowed, throat tight, my body betraying me with the way it tilted toward him. Seeking. Needing.

"I don't feel anything," I admitted hoarsely.

Domino hummed low in his throat. A warning. A promise. "Then I'll make you feel."

The words crawled over my skin. A shudder raced through me. I exhaled shakily as his hands curled into the front of my hoodie and yanked me forward, dragging me out of the grave and into him.

Heat. Muscle. Control. Leather and smoke. Home.

He crushed me against him, his breath hot against my rain-slicked skin. His heartbeat pounded through his chest, steady and unyielding. Something I could latch onto. Something that made sense when nothing else did.

I needed his touch like I needed oxygen.

I needed his pain.

His brand of obsession.

His way of carving me open until I had no choice but to feel something.

My fingers fisted in his leather jacket as his teeth scraped along my throat. My breath hitched when I felt the sharp sting of his switchblade dragging down my ribs.

Not deep enough to cause irreparable damage, just enough to break my skin. Just enough to make me burn.

I gasped. And finally, finally, I felt it—

The spark. The pain. The fire.

I was alive.

Domino's growl rumbled against my skin as he shoved me back against the damp ground, pinning me beneath him. My pulse pounded against his palm when he wrapped his fingers around my throat, squeezing just enough to make me dizzy.

His dark green eyes burned into mine, searching, demanding. "Come back to me, Remi."

I arched into him, nails biting into his skin. My entire body was a live wire, crackling and begging for him to ground me in the way only he could.

I needed more.

I needed all of him.

His breath was hot against my ear, his voice nothing but a snarl. "Let me bring you back."

The storm raged around us, but the real tempest was inside me. A chasm of nothingness, vast and consuming, swallowed me whole.

"Please," I rasped, baring myself to him, offering up my shattered pieces like some broken thing begging to be ruined.

The pop of my button and the slow, deliberate rasp of my zipper were deafening, even beneath the relentless downpour. Every sensation was magnified. The bite of the rain against my skin, the rough kiss of the wind, the brutal press of his body against mine—it all made me feel alive in a way nothing else could.

"You're going to feel every inch of me when I sink inside your tight hole, *piccolo agnello.*"

His voice coiled around my throat, tighter than his fingers ever had, and I ached for the noose of him.

Cold hands yanked my jeans down, exposing me to the unforgiving earth. Sharp stones dug into my back, grit biting into my skin like hungry little mouths, but I barely noticed. Not when he was looking at me like that. Not when his deep green gaze bore into mine, burning through my soul—or whatever was left of it.

Domino shoved my knees to my chest and dropped his full weight onto me, pinning me to the dirt, his hand a steel vice behind my knees. His lips crashed against mine—feral, consuming, merciless. The first icy brush of his mouth stole my breath, my body opening to him on instinct, obedient, desperate.

Always his.

His tongue invaded my mouth, licking inside with a hunger that obliterated everything else. Possessive. Savage. Teeth sank into my tongue, the sharp sting of pain chased by the metallic bloom of copper. I moaned into him, for him.

I was leaking, my cock aching, smearing slick against my stomach, but it was the ice-cold kiss of his blade against my rim that had me gasping.

His lips dragged across my jaw, his teeth marking their claim against my skin in the most primal way possible. His breath ghosted over my ear, low and dark, a whisper that sent violent shivers down my spine.

"Your blood or mine?"

His words didn't register, not fully. My brain was fogged, spiraling, slipping through fingers like water.

"W-what?"

Domino chuckled against my throat, a dark sound that slithered beneath my skin. "Your blood or mine?"

I swallowed hard, felt his teeth scrape against my Adam's apple, the silent promise of devotion through destruction.

"Mine." My voice was wrecked, raw, the word spilling free as I tilted my head back, exposing the vulnerable column of my throat.

Pain flared, sharp and electric, as he sucked the blood to the surface, a branding deeper than ink, more permanent than scars. My heavy-lidded eyes refused to open, but I felt everything.

The blade circling my entrance shifted, the dull side turning sharp.

The first slice of metal into the sensitive skin of my taint had me arching off the ground, screaming. Hot blood met ice-cold steel, running down to my clenching hole, slicking me in my essence.

"That's it, Remi," he growled, his swollen lips brushing against my ear, sending shockwaves through my entire being. "Feel me."

His thumb dragged through the blood, coating it, circling my rim in slow, deliberate movements before pressing inside, working me into me.

A stream of unintelligible words poured from his lips—too fast, too soft, lost in the relentless downpour that lashed against our exposed skin. My world was rain and blood and him.

The moment his thumb left me, my eyes snapped open.

He was kneeling back, his blade slipping into his boot with practiced ease before his fingers found his zipper. The slow, controlled descent of the metal teeth sent thrill and terror curling around my spine.

His cock sprang free—thick, hard, leaking. Bare.

My tongue flicked out, catching the rain on my lips, and his dark green fire met my gaze. He watched me. Studied me. His hand wrapped around the base, dragging from root to tip, working my blood over his length in slow, measured strokes.

He notched his slick, flushed head against my hole, gaze locked onto mine.

"Who do you belong to, Remi?"

My lips parted, my voice barely more than a whisper. "You."

And then he was inside me.

A brutal thrust. No warning. No mercy.

My spine arched, my fingers scrambling against the mud as the force of his thrusts shoved me across the ground. The cold, the pain, the sharp sting of the rain—it was all nothing.

Nothing compared to him.

Molten pleasure and raw, biting pain seared through my veins as I let him take, let him ruin, let him carve his name into my flesh with every brutal snap of his hips.

I only breathed when he forced air into my lungs.

I only existed where he ended and I began.

"Is this what you needed, Remi?"

His lips found my rain-slicked skin, licking the droplets from my face before pressing his forehead to mine, a devastating contradiction. Gentle and brutal. Soft and merciless.

I was floating. I was drowning. I was burning alive.

Pleasure slammed into me, blinding and brutal, my body tightening around him as his cock thickened inside me.

"N-not gonna last... p-please," I whimpered, voice fractured, hands clutching at the only thing grounding me to this world.

Him.

Always him.

Domino's breath ghosted over my lips, a cruel whisper of salvation before the fall. "Come for me, *piccolo agnello.*"

His voice was my undoing. The words shattered something inside me, ripped me apart from the inside out, and launched me into a freefall of pure euphoria.

White-hot bliss detonated in my veins, my body convulsing, spiraling, lost to the abyss. And when Domino came, when he roared his climax into the black, starless sky, flooding me with everything he was, I let him take me under.

We had found each other in blood.

And in blood, we would stay.

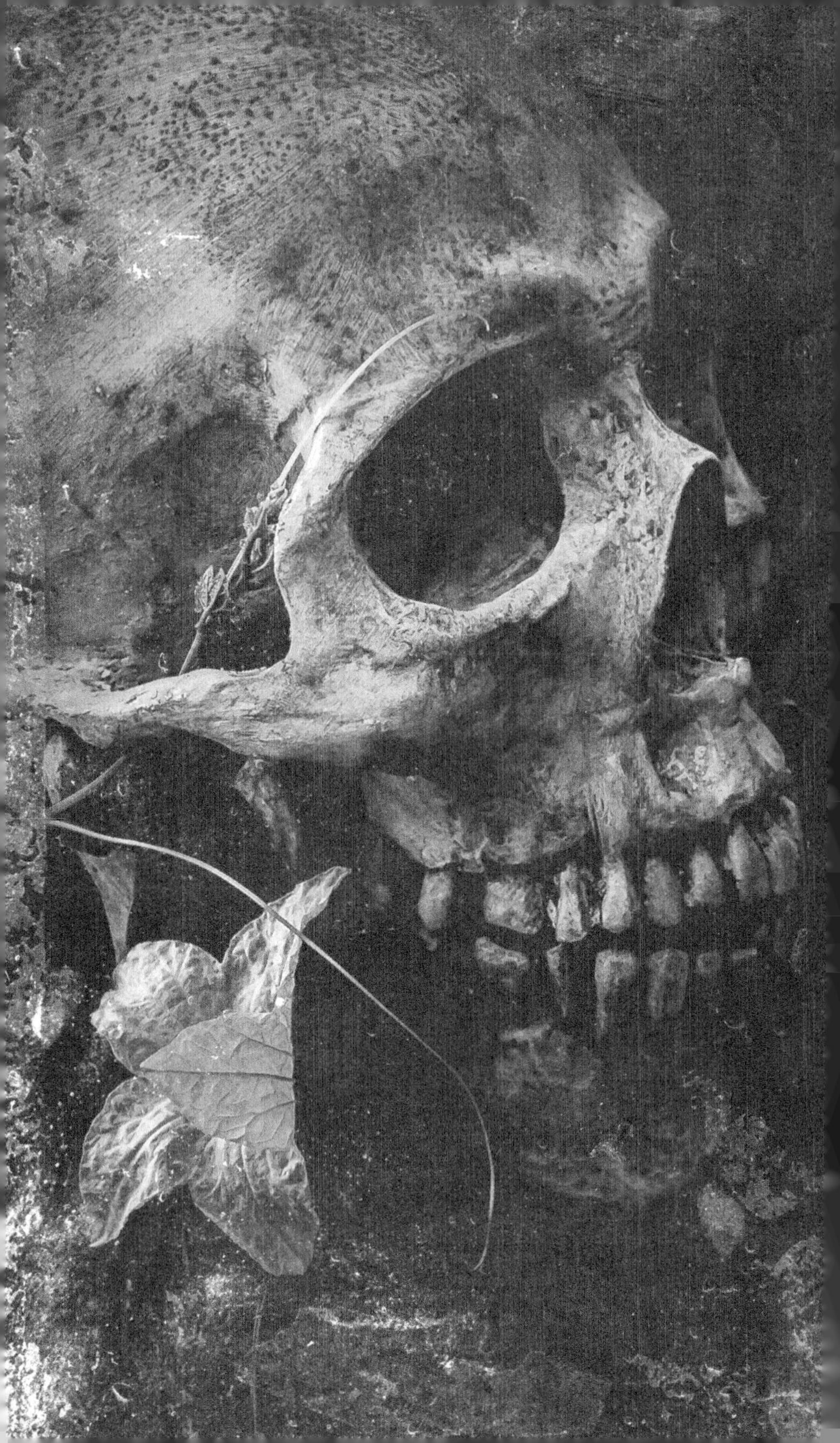

26 DOMINO

"Is it done?"

"Yeah, Boss. The paperwork's finalized. Upon Brielle Cain's passing, Hollow Pines Care Home is legally Remi's. Arthur Doyle will be instated as manager. He'll oversee everything."

Ghost chuckled down the line, low and knowing. "I'm surprised you let her live this long…"

"It was Remi's decision." My jaw ticked, fingers tightening around the phone. "He wanted her there as long as his mom was alive. But now that she's gone, it's time for Brielle to pay."

"She won't be missed," Ghost scoffed. "Hell, he's not the only one glad that bitch is dead. She was a fucking nightmare—"

"She was." I cut him off before his rant could gain momentum. "Make sure Arti is notified and prepared. I want this transition to be seamless. Remi doesn't need to concern himself with any of it."

"Boss."

"Federico?"

"Still nothing," Ghost muttered, irritation thick in his voice. Then, with a sharp inhale, his tone shifted—smug, almost entertained. "Have you seen the news?"

"No."

"The casino suffered a gas leak last night. Went up in flames and was razed to the ground. Three fire crews are still fighting to get the blaze under control."

"Good."

That place was Federico's pride and joy. I wish I could've seen his face when he turned on the news this morning. Everything was falling into place.

One more move. One final checkmate, and I would gut my father. Make him suffer the way he made me suffer for years, until he broke me. Turned me into what I am today.

The distant murmur of a reporter's voice drifted from the TV down the phone line, detailing the catastrophe that had rocked Marlow Heights to its core. I leaned against the counter, letting my lips curl in satisfaction.

They called it a tragedy.

I called it foreplay.

"One last thing," I muttered. "Remi's trust fund?"

"Taken care of. He gets everything on his twenty-first birthday."

"Good."

He wouldn't have to lift a goddamn finger for the rest of his life if he didn't want to. I hung up before Ghost could say anything else. I had better things to do.

The scent of coffee filled the air as I poured two cups, carrying them back into the bedroom.

Remi lay exactly where I left him.

Not quite awake, not quite asleep. Trapped somewhere in the in-between. That hollow, broken place I'd pulled him from the night I followed him into his own hell in the cemetery. That night, I told him three words I'd never truly understood.

I love you.

Did I even know what love was?

All I knew was that I had killed for him. Would burn the world down if he asked me to. Would slit my own throat and let him bathe in my blood.

And if that wasn't love—then I didn't want to know what was.

I set the cups on the nightstand and reached into the drawer, fingers brushing against the small black velvet bag. A strange sensation twisted in my gut—something like nerves, like hunger. Razor-winged wasps, beating against the inside of my ribs.

I slipped under the covers, molding myself to his back, pulling him into the cage of my arms. Mine.

Remi stirred with a slow inhale, voice thick with sleep. "What time is it?"

"A little after ten." I combed my fingers through the black-and-white strands of his hair, my touch dragging the tension from his body. "I have something for you."

He turned to face me, and at this close distance, I could see the silver flecks in his ice-blue eyes. They shimmered like shattered glass in the morning light.

"What is it?" His lips twitched, fingers curling against my chest. He vibrated with barely contained anticipation.

I toyed with the bone hanging around his neck,

drawing his attention to where it rested between his pecs. A memento from his first kill. My gaze was transfixed by the bruises in shades of black and blue that bloomed under his skin, fading too quickly into a yellowed green. I wondered if I could tattoo my marks onto him—add a sense of permanence. My teeth. My hand. My name.

I sat up, pulling him into my lap. He straddled me, wrapping his legs around my hips. Warmth radiated from him into my chilled skin, but it was the temptation of his ass grinding against my quickly hardening cock that had me gritting my teeth hard enough to crack them.

My hand wrapped around his throat, collaring him with a tight squeeze. "Behave, *piccolo agnello*, or you won't get to see what's inside."

Remi rolled his eyes, huffing in frustration—but that little shit still circled his hips, teasing, testing. His pupils blew wide, dark and dangerous, as he felt how hard I was beneath him.

"Behave," I warned, tightening my grip. His pulse fluttered against my palm, a beautiful, delicate thing.

His breath hitched, his lips parting slightly. "I will," he whispered, eyes flicking down to the bag in my hand. "Can I see it?"

I adjusted his position before passing him the bag, watching as an unfettered smile illuminated his face.

He didn't smile often.

None of us did. We weren't wired that way. But when he did, it was devastating.

"Open it."

Remi carefully untied the drawstring and tipped the contents into his hand. His fingers traced each carpal bone with quiet reverence, the way he always did when he studied something he found beautiful.

His tongue flicked out, wetting his lips. "Who?"

He liked to know. He needed to know. Like the bone around his neck, this was from one of his kills. These bones belonged to the last man who tried to jump him. Federico was growing desperate, sending low-level street rats to attack us.

He sucked in a sharp breath, his chest rising and falling in shallow, erratic movements. "Oh."

The bracelet's bones were set between silver I'd had shaped like barbed wire. The same way the man had died. Remi wrapped a length of barbed wire around his throat and tightened it until the steel cut through his skin.

Asphyxiation. Blood loss. Who knew which killed him first?

A single tear slipped down his cheek, catching on his lip. His voice was raw when he whispered, "It's beautiful. Put it on me?"

I obeyed, slipping the bracelet over his left wrist, watching the way he flexed his fingers, admiring the weight of it.

"It's perfect."

His breathy reply filled my lungs as his lips brushed against mine. He wrapped his arms around my neck. Then he was on me. No hesitation. No warning. Just collision. Devastation. Possession. His tongue forced its way into my mouth, tasting, claiming. Warring with mine as hunger seared through my veins.

I threaded my fingers through his hair and took control, swallowing him whole, my grip tightening, my other hand branding itself against his bare back.

He was mine.

He had always been mine.

And now—the whole fucking world would know it.

Brielle was running.

She knew what was coming. They always did. And yet, like every doomed thing staring into the abyss, rather than stand and face her reckoning, she ran. As if that would make a difference.

As if that would change the inevitable.

Death came for us all.

Most people liked to believe it was a gentle thing, a quiet hand that came in the night when they were old and gray, their lives full and lived.

But death wasn't gentle. Death was power. Death was control. And we wielded it.

Remi and I. Together.

We embraced it. Lived it. Breathed it.

I loved the hunt. The chase. Watching fear seep into the bones of the hunted, twisting them into something unrecognizable. Paranoia did most of the work for me, unraveling them thread by thread before I ever laid a hand on them.

And Brielle? She was my favorite kind of prey.

Remi had shattered her mind. Together, we had crushed her soul and stripped her of the only thing that had ever mattered—her son.

Her suffering became his inspiration. The art he created in its wake was something raw, violent—a language I could barely understand, even when he tried to explain it. The jagged edges and brutal lines spoke of madness, emotion—a chaotic symphony of destruction given form. Beautiful in its brutality.

I had Ghost shadow her, feeding me updates—how she barely slept, how she changed locations every few hours, how she flinched at shadows and avoided cameras like they were landmines.

None of it mattered.

There was no escaping us. No escaping Remi.

We had been tracking her for a week. Seven days of her spiraling into desperation.

Seven days of Remi pacing like a caged animal, retribution burning in his veins, his rage an all-consuming thing.

She had already been his from the moment he decided she was. All she was doing now was making it worse for herself.

And fuck—I reveled in it.

But for Remi? This was personal.

She had manipulated him, convinced him to bring his mother to Hollow Pines. She had left scars on him—ones I could never erase, no matter how much blood I painted over them.

And she would answer for it.

We followed the scent of her fear, tracking her through the rot and filth of Marlow Heights, through cheap motels and back-alley hideaways.

And finally, we found her an hour away from the city.

The neon vacancy sign flickered in the darkness, humming against the still air. The motel reeked of sweat, despair, and the kind of desperation that clung to people who had nowhere left to go and rented rooms by the hour, turning cheap tricks.

I dragged the tip of my switchblade across my palm,

letting the sharp sting center me. Remi stood beside me, still and silent, his ice-blue eyes fixed on the room number Ghost had given us.

His fingers twitched. His breathing slowed. He was vibrating. Starving. I reached out and brushed my thumb across his lower lip. It was split. He'd been biting it raw.

"Easy, *piccolo agnello*," I murmured, voice rough. "You'll have your turn."

His tongue flicked against my skin, gaze hooded, but there was nothing submissive about it. His patience had run out.

We moved as one.

The door wasn't even locked.

Pathetic.

I pushed it open, stepping inside the dimly lit room. The stench of mildew, stale cigarettes, and something pungent clung to the air. The sheets on the bed were tangled, the lamp beside it shattered on the floor, flickering weakly.

A sound came from the bathroom—shallow, rapid breathing.

My top lip curled, exposing my teeth. Remi tilted his head, listening. His lips parted, his pupils swallowing the blue of his irises.

He could hear it, too.

The panic. The futility.

The breaking.

I let him go first.

He stalked forward, movements predatory, controlled. His fingers flexed once before curling into fists. He was savoring it.

I leaned against the desk, rolling my shoulders as I

watched him push the bathroom door open. And there she was. Shaking. Shivering.

Brielle was curled in the corner tub, her arms wrapped around her knees, her face blotchy with tears and panic.

She had lost the polished, put-together exterior she'd worn like armor before Remi played god with her psyche. There was no power left in her. No control.

Just fear.

She looked up, eyes darting between us, her breath hitching on a silent sob. "P-please…" she whispered. "Please—"

Remi knelt in front of her, tilted his head, and tutted. She flinched. Like a beaten dog. I snorted at her. Pathetic.

His fingers ghosted over her cheek, tracing the path of a tear. "You look awful, Brielle," he murmured. His voice was soft. Almost affectionate.

I ached for him.

For this. For us.

I crouched beside him, letting my blade catch the flickering light. "You know," I mused, my gaze boring into her. "I expected more from you."

Her lip trembled as I dragged the tip of my knife down her cheek, tracing the tracks of her tears, slow and deliberate. She didn't even move.

She knew. She fucking knew.

There was no running.

No escape.

Remi smiled and moved like lightning. His fist connected with her temple, knocking her out cold. She collapsed in a heap in the tub before the sound of the impact had even died.

With swift efficiency, we had her bound and in the

trunk of the Escalade I'd picked up. We were heading to an abandoned papermill to send Brielle to her death.

"Wake up, bitch."

The words left my mouth in a low growl as I upended the bucket of ice-cold water over her head. Brielle jolted violently, choking, gasping—eyes snapping open and darting around like a trapped animal. The color drained from her face the moment she took in her surroundings.

"P-please..." she whimpered, her swollen, bloodshot gaze locking onto Remi. A desperate, pleading whisper of his name— "R-Remi."

Her body shook, limbs twitching as she tried to lift a trembling hand—only then realizing she was bound, wrists and ankles strapped to the chair sitting, in a growing pool of water.

"Fuck you," Remi spat, his lip curling in disgust. "After what you did to Mom, you think I'd help you?"

"I-I never did anything..." she croaked, tears and snot mixing as they ran down her face.

Remi tilted his head, something sharp and dark twisting in his expression. He liked it when they lied. He liked the way they clung to denial as if it could save them.

"You never did anything?"

He circled her, measured, deliberate—his boots splashing through the filthy water, the steady rhythm of his steps echoing through the abandoned papermill. The birds nesting in the rafters startled and fluttered at the sound. In the dim light, his blade spun between his fingers, flashing silver as he weighed his options. How best to make her suffer. How best to make it last.

She didn't deserve a quick death.

Brielle let out a strangled sob, her whole body quivering as she fought for breath. The chair wobbled under her, unsteady on the wet concrete.

In a blink, Remi was behind her.

One hand fisted in her hair, yanking her head back at a vicious angle, exposing the trembling column of her throat. The other pressed his blade to her skin, just enough to let her feel the cold kiss of steel.

When he spoke, his voice slithered down my spine, making the hairs on my arms stand on end.

"I think you wanted me and Mom here because you saw dollar signs."

Not a question. A fact.

Her head jerked side to side, flinging spit and tears in wide arcs. "No. No, I-I—"

Remi backhanded her so hard her head snapped sideways, blood staining her teeth. The imprint of his hand bloomed in scarlet against her sickly pale cheek. His breathing quickened, his shoulders rising and falling with barely contained rage.

"You knew about my trust fund, Brielle."

She was unraveling, hyperventilating, mumbling nonsense, like a priest reciting a prayer before the slaughter.

Remi chuckled—a low, hollow sound—and crouched in front of her, ice-blue eyes alight with something near euphoric. "You knew about it. I saw the paperwork."

Her whimpering grew more frantic. "No. No, I-I—"

"You were the co-signer," he murmured, tilting his head as if marveling at her audacity. "Don't fucking lie to me."

Fresh tears spilled down her face as if she thought she could weep her sins away. But only God could grant that mercy—and she wasn't in the company of angels.

"I-It was... it was B-Brock's idea," she rasped, eyes flicking between us.

Remi's face twisted in disgust. A lie. A pathetic, grasping lie.

"You're a fucking waste of oxygen," he sneered, pacing before her, kicking up dirty water that splashed against her trembling legs. "Mom never said why she cut you off, but I get it now." He stopped, glaring down at her. "She saw what you were. The ugly under the cheap dye job and the caked-on makeup."

"That's not—"

"I don't want to hear it," he snapped. "You don't need a voice anymore."

A grin split his face, maniacal, unhinged. His eyes burned with something primal, something ravenous.

This was his kill. His moment.

"Domino?"

I met his gaze and tipped my head, my pulse thrumming with the electric thrill of his madness. "Whatever you need, *piccolo agnello*."

His lips curled. "Hold her head. I've had enough of her voice."

I stepped forward, wrapping an arm around Brielle's skull, pressing the back of her head against my stomach. She squirmed, pathetically weak, her panicked breath fogging the air.

"Thank you." Remi blew me a kiss. His expression was drenched in bloodlust. Pure. Unfiltered. Beautiful. "Now, pull her jaw down."

A pleased hum rumbled in my chest. I loved it when his darkness broke free.

Hooking two fingers over her teeth, I wrenched her mouth open. She thrashed, her strangled scream cutting off into a garbled choke as Remi gripped her tongue and stretched it past her lips.

Slowly. Methodically.

He pressed the blade to the soft flesh.

And sliced.

She bucked against me, gurgling, blood pouring down her chin, soaking into her cream-colored blouse. The wet, slopping sounds of agony that wrenched from her throat were barely human. She was an animal now. Reduced to instinct. Drowning in suffering.

By the time Remi stepped back, holding the severed piece between his fingers, Brielle was already slumping, hovering on the verge of unconsciousness.

"Not yet," he growled.

I smirked, warmth flooding my veins, and delivered a sharp slap across her cheek. Her head snapped to the side, eyes rolling back in her head. She gurgled, broken and barely breathing, but awake enough.

Blood slicked Remi's fingers as he crouched before her, holding the mangled chunk of flesh like a prize. His other hand scooped up the rest of the butchered remnants he'd diced into small, jagged pieces.

He dangled one before her wide, terror-glazed eyes. "Open your mouth."

Brielle pressed her lips shut, trembling.

With one look, I knew what he wanted. I wrenched her head back again, forcing her mouth open as Remi dropped the piece onto her tongue.

"Swallow," he ordered, voice dark with amusement.

She shook her head violently.

Remi tsked. "I will make you if you don't." He tilted his head, letting her feel his breath ghost over her tear-streaked face. "If I have to force you, it'll be one piece at a time. Over. And over. And over again."

Brielle was weak.

And weakness always chose the coward's way out.

For the next ten minutes, we repeated the same motions. Head wrenched back. Jaw pried open. Tongue forced down her throat.

Swallow.

Gag.

Vomit.

Repeat.

Every time she retched, Remi pinched her nose, forcing it back down. Every choked sob, every convulsion, every strangled attempt to resist only fed his hunger.

The air reeked of blood, bile, and fear. It was cruel. It was deranged. But it was exactly what a lying, thieving snake like her deserved.

Remi wrapped his arms around my waist, burying his head in my chest. My lips brushed the top of his head, inhaling his scent, imprinting it on my lungs. My gaze never left Brielle's slumped form.

Broken whimpers filled the space, reverberating off the metal walls like a death knell.

"Have you decided how you want to end her?"

Remi tipped his head back, and all I saw in him was darkness—the same abyss that lived in me. A wicked grin ghosted his lips as his bloodied hands slid up my chest and curled around my neck, fingers toying with the short hairs at my nape. The sensation sent a shudder rippling through me. His touch wasn't just physical; it reached into the tattered remnants of my soul, claiming what was already his.

"Yes," he breathed against my lips before sealing his mouth over mine.

His tongue swept along my lower lip, and I opened

for him willingly, tasting the metallic tang of blood as I deepened the kiss, licking into his mouth. My blood burned molten, pumping through me like liquid fire. He rolled his hips against mine, teasing, dragging against me with each slow, deliberate movement.

"Fuck, Remi," I growled, nipping and sucking along his jaw, trailing my teeth to the sensitive skin at the base of his ear. "Tell me what deplorable things you're going to do to her."

Remi tipped his head back and groaned when I slid my thigh between his legs, my fingers digging into the firm curve of his ass. He was insatiable when his bloodlust took hold, and I wanted to feel every inch of it consume him. Every slice of flesh, every drop of blood —it was foreplay in its most exquisite form.

"I'm going to watch her burn," he whispered, voice thick with promise. "I want to hear every soul-shredding scream."

His words broke on a shuddering breath as I licked a slow path up the column of his throat, my tongue tracing the frantic rhythm of his pulse.

"Let's make it happen." I pressed a bruising kiss to his lips before reining myself back in, locking down the hunger clawing at my ribs. Remi groaned in frustration, his hands clenching at his sides.

"I'll fuck you so hard once she's dead…" My voice dripped with venomous devotion, my promise laced with poison. "I'll bury my cock so deep inside you, I'll be dripping out of you for a week. You'll remember me every time you move. Feel me even when I'm not there."

His breath hitched. We were carved from the same depraved mold, bound by something darker than love— an obsession that devoured and fed us in equal measure.

Whether we survived was a question only the devil knew the answer to.

"Fine," he ground out between clenched teeth.

His sharp gaze swept the dilapidated building, his thumb and forefinger tracing his chin as he pieced together his masterpiece.

"Alright." He straightened, eyes gleaming with cruel delight. "See those broken cables?" He pointed to the frayed wires hanging from a rusted roof strut, their ends sparking like tiny, lethal fireflies. "Use those muscles of yours and pull them over here."

I turned on my heel, ready to obey, when his voice froze me mid-step.

"Make sure you don't touch the exposed ends."

I scoffed, glancing over my shoulder. "What am I, an amateur?"

Remi chuckled, crouching to gather the rusted nails and jagged shards of corrugated iron that littered the ground.

Eyeing him suspiciously, I asked, "What are you doing?"

His lips curled into something dangerous. "I'm going to wake her up. Wouldn't want her to miss her own execution."

The devil and all his demons danced in the inferno of his eyes. They weren't just reflections—they were living, breathing entities, whispering to him, urging him on.

My fingers wrapped around the plastic-coated cable, yanking it free of the tacks that anchored it to the support beam. The first tack gave way with a groan of metal.

A scream shattered the air.

I turned, my breath catching at the sight before me.

Remi knelt beside Brielle, a rusted nail pressed to her thigh, his other hand wielding a brick as a hammer. With a single, decisive strike, he drove it deep into muscle. Blood welled around the jagged metal, spreading through her pale blue jeans in a slow, creeping stain of crimson.

Her cries were raw, barbed sobs torn straight from the depths of agony.

With the cables freed, I coiled them over my shoulder and stepped behind him. He worked with cruel precision, embedding nails, slivers of rusted metal— each one a conductor, a gateway to the torment we had planned. The cacophony of her screams was a symphony of suffering, a beautifully discordant melody that thrummed through my bones.

Federico's would sound even sweeter once I had him under my tender, loving care.

"You done?" I asked, my pulse thrumming in anticipation.

Remi didn't look up. "I've only just begun."

His gaze flicked to the coiled cable over my shoulder, the live end held safely in my hands, his fingers twitching with barely contained excitement. The air crackled, static energy thickening the space between us.

Remi grasped the cable, carefully positioning the exposed wire end against the embedded nails and metal lodged in Brielle's leg. The moment contact was made, the dim, dust-coated bulbs overhead flickered, their filaments screaming before shattering in bursts of dying light.

Brielle arched violently, her head snapping back as a hundred and twenty volts surged through her. Her body jerked, muscles contracting so brutally she nearly lifted from the chair. Her teeth were clenched, foam bubbling at her lips as she choked on her agony.

Remi watched, entranced, then threw the second cable into the stagnant puddle beneath her chair.

The sound of her torment was unholy. The air filled with the stench of searing flesh, the acrid smoke curling in thick, suffocating tendrils. Her skin blackened, blistering, peeling back in charred ribbons as electricity crashed through her, in wave after relentless wave.

We watched. We waited. When her blackened body finally stilled, her eyes were glassy and hollow, and we knew—

She had accepted the inevitable.

She had burned.

And we had won.

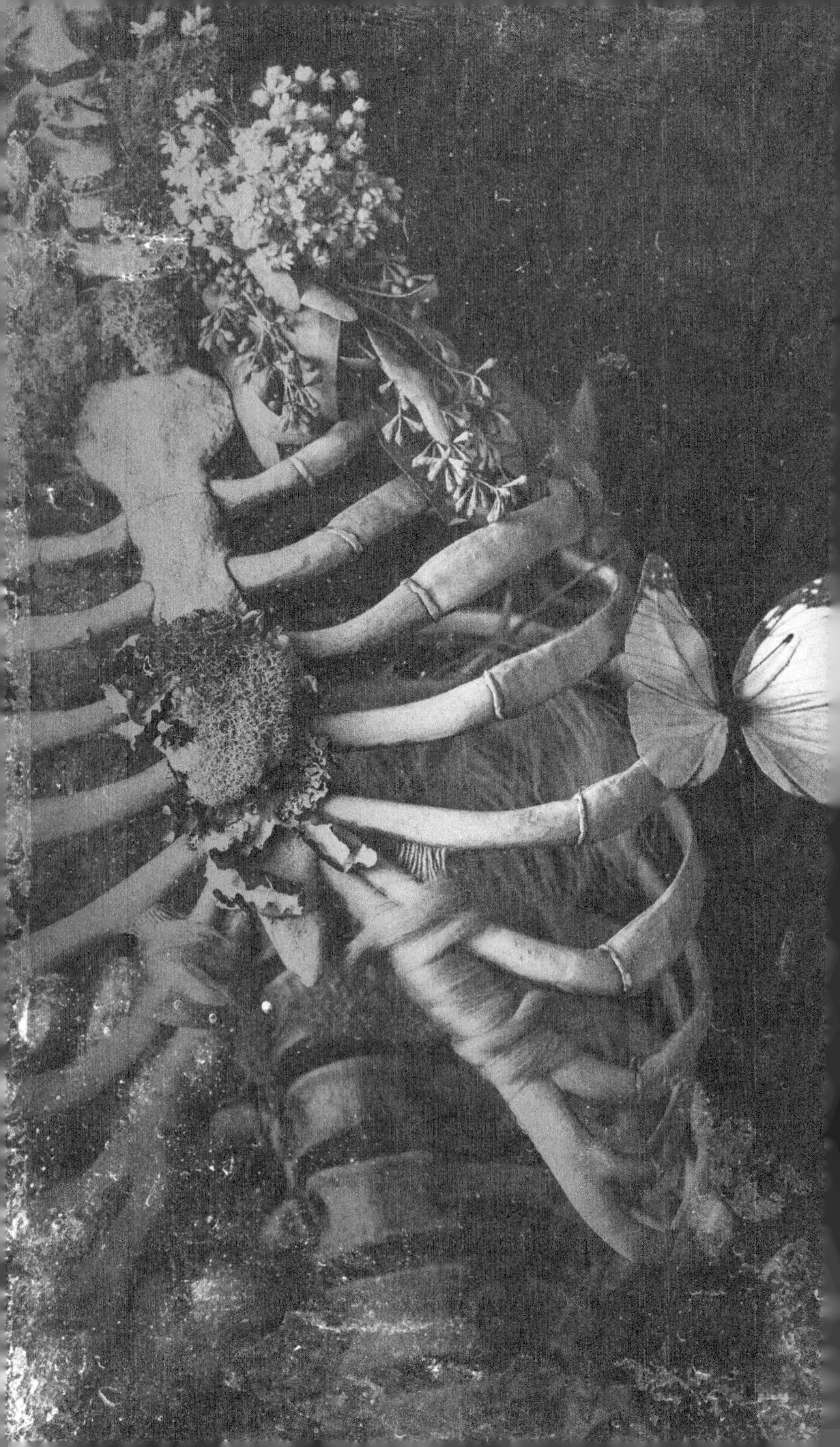

27 REMI

The elite never ceased to amaze me. With battle lines drawn across the city and whispers of an impending curfew, they paid it no mind. They clung to their gilded delusions, celebrating art and wealth as though the ground beneath them wasn't shifting. As though judgment day wasn't coming.

But it was. And when Marlow Heights was burnt to the ground and rivers of blood flowed through the streets, their world of excess and ignorance would crumble.

Yet, here we were, in tailored tuxedos, slipping into a world that would soon be unrecognizable. The invitation to The Elysian Chamber had arrived like a taunt, a reminder that some still believed themselves untouchable. It meant nothing to me, nothing more than a momentary distraction, a lure that we hoped would draw Federico from whatever sewer he'd buried himself in. We had dismantled his empire piece by piece, but he refused to rise to the bait. Tonight, that changed.

The moment the SUV rolled up to the entrance, the red carpet unfurled before us like a sacrificial altar. Flashing lights exploded from every angle, a frenzy of journalists desperate for a glimpse of the elusive Demarco heir. The press lined the velvet ropes like a swarm of hungry piranhas, each hoping to rip a sound-bite from Domino's lips, to capture a photo that would make their career. But they were nothing more than noise.

Inside the car, the air was thick with the scent of bloodlust. Ghost glanced in the rearview mirror as he shifted the vehicle into park. His expression was sharp, a predator coiled and ready to strike. "I've got cameras everywhere. If he shows, we'll see him."

Domino exhaled a quiet laugh, the sound dark and knowing. "He'd be a fool to show." His rings caught the dim glow of the streetlights as he scrubbed a hand over his mouth. "It'll be a massacre. He'll lose whatever traction he's deluded himself into thinking he's gained."

I slid my fingers through his, tightening my grip. "We're not here only for him, though."

His lips curled into a wicked smirk, eyes gleaming with something raw and consuming. "I know we're not, *piccolo agnello.*"

"Good."

"Tonight is just reconnaissance, though."

I barely held back an eye roll, sinking my teeth into my bottom lip to suppress the hunger clawing at my insides. They wanted patience. Restraint. But my mind was already painting the scene of his suffering in vivid, visceral detail.

Casius Moreau. A name that dripped from the lips of the elite like he was something to be revered. They celebrated him—but I saw the rot beneath the mask. The monster was draped in silk and civility, hiding behind wealth and power.

I was going to strip him bare.

Tear away the façade, expose the filth beneath, and make him choke on the same cruelty he had inflicted on others. Reconnaissance could wait. His reckoning was coming.

"Remi," Domino growled. A warning. A promise.

His hands were on me in an instant, curling around the back of my neck and hauling me into him. His mouth claimed mine with ruthless possession, his tongue sweeping between my lips, stealing the words before they could escape. The heat of him ignited something in me, something untamed and insatiable. It wasn't just lust—it was power, it was blood, it was the promise of devastation wrapped in a lover's embrace.

"Ahem." Ghost cleared his throat, amusement lacing his voice. "You can suck face later." He chuckled as he slipped out of the car, moving to open Domino's door.

With a lingering smirk, Domino pulled back, his thumb dragging over my lower lip as if savoring the taste of control. Then, he stepped out into the waiting chaos.

The Elysian Chamber was an opulent beast, built to house the egos of those who considered themselves gods. Marble columns loomed over the entrance, the gold-gilded doors yawning open like the mouth of some insatiable entity. Inside, chandeliers dripped with crystal and refracted the light into a kaleidoscope of wealth. The scent of aged wine and expensive perfume clashed with the ever-present tension in the air.

Every movement was calculated, every glance a silent power struggle. Men in suits and women draped in diamonds hovered around overpriced artwork, sipping champagne as though the world wasn't teetering on the edge of war. They had no idea that tonight, the blood they spilled their fortunes to avoid would finally stain their polished floors.

Domino walked through it like he owned the place, and in many ways, he did. Every eye followed him, some filled with curiosity, others with fear.

They should be afraid. Not just of him. Of me. They didn't realize his shadow was just as sadistic, as ruthless. Just as hungry.

Women flocked to Domino as we prowled through the crowd, their bodies pressing against him like he was their salvation or damnation—they didn't care which, as long as he would give them the time of day. Their fingers curled around his arms, their lips brushing against his ear, their bodies arching, offering, begging.

Pathetic. All of them. The women who threw themselves at him and the men who eyed him like he was their meal ticket to greatness. All too willing to deal with the devil for their own gains.

I knew his history. Knew how easily he took what was offered—men, women, enbies alike. He wasn't picky. If he wanted, he took. A hole to fill. A body to use.

But I'd changed that.

I'd awakened something in him that had lay dormant, something feral and obsessive. A need that coiled around his ribs and sank its claws into his gut.

And he'd done the same to me.

He had set me free, shown me who I really was. I was never going back into the box society had forced me into, not now. I understood what it took to make myself whole.

A girl in a black sequined dress, with blond hair piled on top of her head, stepped toward him, dismissing me entirely. That was her first mistake. Her fingers, delicate and manicured, smoothed over his chest, her lips grazing the sharp edge of his jaw.

That was her second mistake.

I felt it before I saw it—the way Domino's body went rigid, the way his amusement soured into something cold and merciless. She didn't matter.

"Domino," she purred, saccharine and hopeful. "It's been a while."

His lip curled in disgust. Peeling her fingers away like they were diseased.

"Has it?" His voice was cruel, detached, designed to cut deep and open a festering wound. "Can't say I remember you."

Her face burned scarlet. "W-what?" she stammered, utterly lost.

"Do I know you?" he taunted, voice a lazy drawl, eyes flicking toward mine. A claim. A warning. A promise.

"We... we met at the—"

"Have you met *my* Remi?" he cut her off smoothly, his arm curling around my waist, yanking me against him. The smirk on his lips was razor-sharp when her eyes widened.

"Say hello to him."

Her sweat-slicked palm met my cold skin, and my stomach coiled with revulsion. I let her touch me. Let her think for a fraction of a second she was safe.

Domino's entire body darkened. The air around him vibrated like a deadly current.

"Hands off what's not yours, whore."

She flinched, eyes going wide as he stepped into her space.

"S-sorry," she whimpered, and then ran, disappearing into the crowd.

I chuckled, low and quiet. "Possessive much?"

Instead of answering, Domino crushed me against him. Caging. Consuming. His hands framed my face, thumbs stroking over my cheekbones, his presence suffocating in the best way.

His gaze drilled into mine, blackened with obsession.

"You are the only thing I see."

His lips crashed into mine, a brutal claim, his tongue tangled with mine like he was branding me from the inside out. People were watching, their stares raising the hairs on the back of my neck—some envious, some horrified.

I didn't care. Neither did he. When he finally pulled away, my mind spun, my body aching from the loss. And then I saw him.

Casius Moreau.

A devil wrapped in fine tailoring, his laughter a blade disguised as silk. He stood in the center of the gallery, holding court, a predator among sheep, his voice rich with charm—but his eyes...

His eyes betrayed him.

They flicked to the girl at his side, a delicate, trembling thing, her head bowed, arms wrapped around herself like she was trying to disappear. His gaze crawled over her like she was something to be devoured.

Something inside me snarled. He was the kind of monster that needed to be exterminated. He thrived on suffering, bathed in the misery of the weak, and called it art.

Soon, he would become my greatest masterpiece.

His breaths were numbered. I would be his judge, jury, and executioner.

"Welcome." Casius's smile was a well-rehearsed lie, straight white teeth gleaming as he held out his hand, the confidence of a man who thought himself untouchable.

He wasn't.

Domino loomed beside me, his monster pacing behind his eyes.

"Casius." His tone was clipped. He didn't take the offered hand.

The rejection left Moreau floundering, his smile faltering before he masked it with forced charm.

While his attention was focused on Domino, I wondered how his blood would look painting these walls.

How best to display his corpse for maximum effect… when they eventually found him.

Would they be horrified? Or amazed? Would they see the beauty in my creation?

Casius cleared his throat, his mask settling back into place. "Thank you for coming to the opening of my gallery, showcasing my latest exhibition."

Domino arched a brow. "It's not your gallery, though, is it?"

Casius flinched. "Well, I mean…"

The air thickened, and tension crawled across my skin like ants. The crowd around us thinned, sensing danger but too self-absorbed to truly acknowledge it.

"It's all thanks to the Mayor, isn't it?" Domino continued, voice laced with something sharp. A trap closing.

Casius swallowed. "No one in this industry gets

anywhere without investors. Artists don't earn big right away—"

"But it's not money that drives you, is it?" I cut in smoothly.

His steel-gray eyes flicked to the girl beside him before landing on mine. He knew.

He knew I saw him.

His mask cracked. Just for a second. Just enough.

"It's a combination of multiple elements that inspire my work," he murmured. His hand clenched into a fist at his side. The girl at his side jumped as if she expected a blow.

My jaw tightened, rage coiling hot beneath my skin. My tongue ran across my teeth at the sour taste he filled my lungs with. We played the game of pleasantries—masks and hidden knives—but my mind was already spinning through the steps of his destruction. Tightening and refining, distilling it into perfection.

Domino, beside me, looked detached, but I felt the way he stiffened under Moreau's scrutiny.

Sizing him up.

Marking him for death.

"We're done here."

Domino spun on his heel, phone in hand, knuckles white as his grip tightened.

My pulse spiked. "What is it?"

He moved fast, cutting through the crowd, his entire body coiled like a spring.

"Something tripped the silent alarm at Nocturne." His voice was low, edged in violence. "All the cameras are out."

My breath hitched. "Federico?"

"I assume so." His jaw was clenched. "I've sent Ghost to clear the club."

I exhaled sharply, my fingers flexing at my sides. The blade strapped to my arm burned white hot. "This is what we wanted."

"Yes. This ends tonight."

Domino agreed, the finality of his words wrapping me in blood-coated shadows that whispered of retribution and death like the sweetest poison.

His pace never faltered as we strode through the darkened streets of Marlow Heights.

The city was quiet. Too quiet. Its silent eyes tracking our every movement. Streetlights flickered uselessly, failing to cut through the suffocating blackness that loomed over us like an omen. Something slithered through my chest, a whisper of foreboding.

The taste of death that coated my tongue ignited a fire in my veins that would burn until I was coated in blood.

The world blurred as we moved—shadows folding around us, shielding us, devouring us whole. We criss-crossed through alleyways, slipping between buildings, taking routes even rats would hesitate to crawl. If someone followed us, they would be dealt with. Silenced before they even knew we'd spotted them.

Tonight, we were the hunters.

"Salvatore," Domino murmured into his phone, voice a blade against the dark. "Gather everyone and prepare for war."

The trap had been sprung.

The hairs on my nape prickled as the darkness inside me stirred, stretching, uncoiling, ready to be unleashed.

A pause. A breath.

"Yes," Domino murmured, voice dropping lower. "Valentin, too."

A shiver ran through me. The kill team. No loose

ends. No survivors. This would be the end of the DeMarco line.

Domino dragged a hand through his hair, tension laced in every movement. As we rounded the alley that faced Nocturne, the world seemed to slow.

The faint rumble of idling taxi engines.

Drunken laughter spilled into the streets.

Shattered conversations carried on the mist-thickened air.

Domino lit a cigarette, the flame briefly illuminating the sharp angles of his face, the hunger in his eyes. Then he passed it to me, his attention already shifting back to Salvatore as he continued speaking.

I inhaled deeply, the burn grounding me as I toyed with the small tracker Ghost had given me. Federico's last rites were already written.

Across the street, we watched the last of Nocturne's patrons slip into their waiting cars. Watched as Ghost eased into Domino's SUV, disappearing into the night to wait for the signal.

We weren't deluded. We knew this was a trap. That Federico wanted us to come, to play into his hands.

But sometimes, you had to dance with the devil in his own kind of madness.

And Domino?

Domino had never been afraid of fire. Neither of us were afraid of getting burned.

The cherry of the cigarette sizzled out in a puddle at my feet.

A funeral pyre for what came next.

We moved, silent as death itself, crossing the street and slipping into the club through the rear staff entrance. The new locks were intact—but the busted security camera above the door told us everything we needed to know.

Federico had been here.

The air inside was thick with betrayal, with the cloying stench of sweat, sex, and old sins. We ascended the stairs two at a time. My pulse beat against my ribs like a war drum.

The office door was ajar. A sliver of light leaked into the dim corridor, accompanied by the soft rustle of papers, the muttered curses of a man searching for something he would never find.

Domino lifted a hand. A signal to wait.

Gun drawn, he stepped closer. His dark gaze flicked back to mine, pinning me in place, voice a whispered command that wrapped around my spine.

"Stay with me."

I felt his obsession like a noose around my throat.

"Always."

His lips parted, just slightly. Satisfaction. Possession. Then he nodded, raised his gun, and nudged the door open.

The silence settled like a coffin lid snapping shut.

I followed him in, blade slipping from its sheath, my free hand still toying with the tracker, rolling it between my fingers.

There he was. *Federico.*

Bent over Domino's desk, frantically rifling through drawers, his desperation a tangible thing in the stale air.

He froze.

Then, slowly, he straightened. His ill-fitting suit wrinkled around him, his once-polished appearance now tarnished by exhaustion and failure. The lines on his face had deepened. The bags beneath his eyes were carved trenches of anxiety.

But the hatred?

It burned brightly.

He scoffed, smoothing his hands down his lapels like he was still a man worth fearing. "Domino." His voice was tight. Controlled and biting. "Took your time."

Domino took a slow step forward, gun never wavering. "I knew you wouldn't find anything. So why rush?"

Federico's lips twitched. "Did I interrupt an important evening?" His gaze flicked over Domino's suit, the dark silk still pristine despite the night's bloodstained promises.

"No."

Just one word. It hit like a gunshot.

Federico flinched.

I pressed a hand to my lips, hiding a grin.

His eyes flicked to me, and the way his gaze curdled made my skin prickle with pleasure.

"You're still alive, then?" Disgust dripped from his voice.

I smiled. Sharp. Hungry. "Surprise."

His jaw flexed.

I tilted my head. "Bet you're dying to know why."

A flicker of unease. The barest hesitation flowed through his features.

"Like I give a fuck about Domino's little fucktoys," he spat.

My grin widened. "Mmm. Shame you'll never know the real reason he kept me around... until it's too late."

Federico bristled, but I saw the doubt—the fear— that flared before he buried it beneath his ego.

"You could never hurt someone like me."

I almost laughed. It was adorable that he thought this version of himself—this frail, aging husk of a man —could ever compare to the ghost of who he once was.

Domino stepped closer to me. His breath was slow, measured. His finger flexed on the trigger but didn't pull.

Not yet.

We knew how this game worked. Federico wasn't going to beg. Not right away. He'd try to spin his web and weave the illusion that he was still the one holding the leash.

But tonight?

Tonight, we would give him just enough rope to hang himself.

And when the sun rose?

The only ones left standing in the smoldering wreckage of the DeMarco empire would be those who had bled for our cause.

Federico leaned against the desk, crossing one leg over the other at the ankle, his hands braced behind him in a desperate attempt to appear at ease.

He was drowning.

The sweat at his temples, the slight tremor in his fingers as he forced himself to remain still. Tells even a blind man could see. The old bastard could play the role of the dominant for only so long, but we saw him for what he was.

A man barely keeping his head above water. A man being pushed towards the edge of a cliff, too weak to decide to jump, but he'd fall so beautifully with a knife lodged in his spine.

"They don't really want you, you know," he drawled, his voice coated in false bravado as he gestured loosely toward Domino. "The Gallos. They just want Marlow Heights. The power that comes with it."

Domino's lips barely twitched, more scoff than

smirk, his dark gaze sliding to me before returning to Federico. Unbothered. Unmoved. "I already have everything I want."

Everything.

The weight of those words wrapped around me, thick as chains.

Federico laughed, a sharp, ugly sound, his head tilting back as he let it spill into the stale air. It wasn't amusement. Not really. It was madness—the fractured edges of a man who had already lost but refused to accept it.

His smirk cut through the dim light like a blade. Sharp. Cruel. Poisoned.

"Didn't you learn from your whore of a mother?" he sneered, voice dripping with venom. "Love only leads to death. It's a worthless emotion that makes you weak."

The air shifted. Domino stepped closer, slow and deliberate, his presence expanding, darkening, consuming every bit of air.

"No, old man." His voice was razor-edged, laced with something lethal that coiled through the room like smoke before a wildfire. "Love makes me unstoppable."

Federico's smirk faltered. It was barely a flicker. A fleeting hesitation. But I saw it. It was the moment he heard them—the drums of war.

He knew.

He knew this was the beginning of his end.

His expression twisted, masking his unease with another sneer. One last act of defiance.

"You prepared to die for him?" he spat.

Domino tilted his head, gaze still fixed, still unreadable.

He didn't blink. Didn't breathe.

His next words were deathly quiet.

"I've killed for him." A pregnant pause. "I'd die for him in a heartbeat." Another step. "And I'd never regret it."

Federico went still. Something passed over his face, a flicker of something ugly. Something like… fear.

His lips curled in disgust, but I saw the color drain from his skin. I saw the moment he realized that Domino wasn't the same boy he had once controlled.

"I see this was a mistake," he finally bit out, voice cracking just enough to be noticed.

He spat at Domino, his rage unraveling in real-time, flecks of saliva catching the dim light as his chest heaved.

"You're weaker than I ever let myself believe," he hissed, voice fraying at the edges. "I refuse to waste my time with you."

He moved. Closed the distance between them faster than I'd thought possible. Their feet brushed. Their noses almost touched.

"You'll die by my hand… son."

Domino didn't move. Didn't flinch. Didn't so much as twitch. I saw the muscle in his jaw tighten, his fingers twitch at his side. His breath was steady. Controlled. Leashed.

But his eyes…

His eyes promised blood.

Federico was too caught up in his theatrics to notice me shift, the ghost of a movement as I slipped the tracker beneath the collar of his peacoat.

A soft press of metal against fabric. Then I was gone. Back at my post by the door before he even realized I'd moved.

Domino's voice was barely above a whisper, but it owned the room. "Your last breath is mine."

A promise.

A vow.

One that would never be broken.

Federico hesitated—just a fraction of a second—then turned on his heel and disappeared down the corridor.

We watched as he moved, his steps quickening, his shoulders rising with each inhale, his presence growing smaller.

He knew.

He could feel it—the weight of fate snapping into place.

By the time he reached the stairs, he was running. Like the hounds of hell were at his back.

Domino exhaled, dragging a hand through his hair before turning to me. "You get him, *piccolo agnello?*"

My fingers curled around the screen of my iPad, the blinking red dot illuminating my palm like the ember of a dying star. "Of course."

He grinned. Sharp. Wicked.

Pouring us both a glass of scotch, Domino leaned against the desk, his gaze locked on the blinking tracker, the slow march of death creeping toward its inevitable conclusion.

Beyond these walls, unseen, unknown, our men and the Gallos moved like phantoms of the underworld.

An army of death.

Waiting.

Ready.

Prepared to strike.

The red light pulsed on the screen as Federico finally stopped moving.

Domino exhaled through his nose, lifting his glass to his lips, his gaze never leaving the tablet in my hands. A slow, sinister smirk lifted the corners of his mouth.

"Got him."

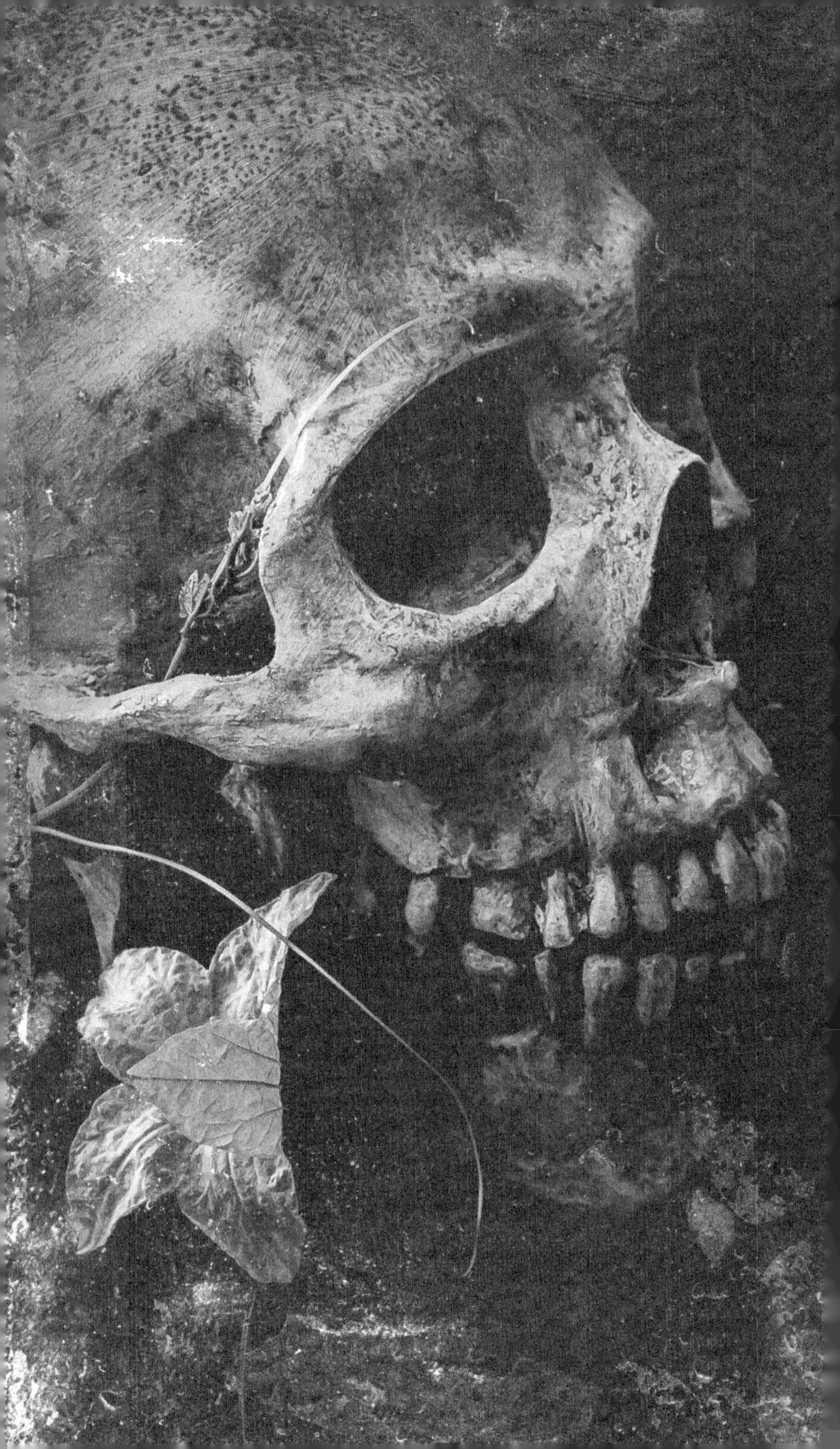

28 DOMINO

Federico hadn't moved for nearly an hour.

I knew because Ghost was watching him. He was our eyes on the ground surveilling the mansion, like a predator circling its wounded prey that he'd holed up in like a rat desperate to burrow deeper into filth.

Through the comms his voice was clipped and efficient as he fed us numbers. Positions. Mercenaries stationed along the route. Snipers in the windows. Patrols cycling through the city, their movements predictable, sloppy.

The hired hands scattered through the city were stationed along winding roads leading up to the property. They were just bodies, bought and paid for. Empty vessels with no loyalty. No fear of the name Domino.

They would learn.

The air reeked of gasoline and blood.

Marlow Heights was burning. The streets, once crawling with the desperate and damned, now belonged to the dead. Smoke curled into the dark sky, a funeral pyre for Federico's crumbling empire.

It wasn't a fight.

It was a massacre.

"A fractured future of a dystopian nightmare…" Remi muttered under his breath beside me as we weaved through the burning remnants of an overturned SUV.

"You getting inspired, *piccolo agnello*?"

Shadows danced in Remi's eyes, their flickering shapes reflected in his hungry, manic gaze. White-hot flames licked toward the night sky, their light catching on a ruined body lay sprawled near the wreck, flesh charred black, fingers curled into the pavement as if it had tried to crawl away.

The fire had claimed it. What was left flaked in the wind like burnt paper. I felt Remi's slow exhale beside me. Felt his smile before I even looked.

My soldiers moved through the streets like specters, cutting down the last remnants of Federico's men with ruthless efficiency.

The mercenaries he'd hired—pathetic, desperate, inadequate—fell fast. They died screaming. Their bodies painted the pavement, twitching in the amber glow of the streetlights, their spilled blood turning the cracked asphalt into something slick, something hungry.

The Gallos cleared a path through the gated community where Federico had barricaded himself, his cowards and traitors huddled behind automatic weapons and anti-aircraft guns.

They thought steel walls and bullets would be enough to keep us out.

They were wrong.

Six SUVs filled with Gallo soldiers completed the motorcade, their presence heavy with something more than firepower. They should have hated me.

Should have wanted me dead for the bodies I'd taken from them. Instead, they looked at me with something else—begrudging respect.

Fear. Recognition. They saw me for what I was.

Not an enemy. Not an outsider.

A weapon.

Remi pulled out the estate blueprints over the hood of a still-burning car, voice steady as he relayed Ghost's intel, laying the plan bare in front of them all.

My men.

His men.

One army.

One plan.

Black combat gear was handed out. Kevlar vests. Ammunition. Weapons. Salvatore treated us like his own. And I didn't quite know what to make of it.

Salvatore led the charge, moving through the crumbling gates like a harbinger of war. Enzo, Luca, Diego, and Elio closed ranks behind him like a wall of death, each a force of nature in their own right. They were relentless and precise, moved as a unit, their rage honed into something disciplined and terrifying.

Ghost rejoined us and moved with the second wave. He was a shadow. Silent. Lethal. His blade slid into flesh without resistance, carving open throats and leaving bodies crumpled in his wake.

Angelo followed, brutal and efficient, putting bullets through skulls like it was muscle memory.

And then there was Remi.

My Remi.

He was a storm in human form. A vicious thing; his knife danced in the firelight, a whisper of silver before it plunged into flesh. Blood speckled his face like war paint.

His movements were poetry.

A song of violence and death, written in the bodies of the fallen.

He didn't hesitate.

Didn't falter.

I fought at his side, a reflection and shadow, each moving like two halves of the same darkness.

He ducked, and I covered. He swung left, I went right. His blade sank into a throat at the same time I emptied my clip into another.

We moved like a single, deadly entity.

A force of nature.

An unstoppable nightmare.

Salvatore pushed through the gates first, a wave of gunfire trailing him. Chaos erupted. Snipers on the balconies opened fire.

Luca snapped a man's neck before he could even lift his gun, let alone pull the trigger.

Enzo threw a grenade through an open window, the explosion turning the interior into a hellstorm of shrapnel and screams.

Diego, slick with blood, gutted two men in quick succession, his blade carving through their stomachs like wet silk.

Ellio fought like a ghost made flesh, darting between bodies, knife flashing, opening throats like whispers of death. Then finished each with a bullet between the eyes just to make sure they'd never rise again.

The Gallo soldiers advanced, their firepower turning the estate's manicured lawn into a graveyard.

Hand-to-hand combat broke out as clips ran dry.

Fists. Knives. Teeth.

One of Federico's men lunged at me. A nameless merc. I caught his wrist before the blade could sink in. Snapped it. Ripped the knife from his failing grip. Buried it in his eye.

A bullet whizzed past my ear.

Remi was already on the shooter, slitting his throat before his finger could pull the trigger again. A flash of silver. A line of red. The merc collapsed, his throat carved open.

His gaze snapped to mine, wide-eyed, feral, and manic with bloodlust. He smiled. A slow, sharp, wicked thing baring his blood stained teeth.

Like he knew exactly what I was thinking.

Because he did.

Because we were the same.

We fought through the last line of defense, like wading through a river of carnage and fire.

Salvatore's voice rang through the night. "End this."

Federico's men broke. Some ran. Others were gunned down before they could take another step.

Cowards.

Traitors.

Dead men walking.

We pushed through the wreckage, past shattered bodies and smoldering debris. The estate doors loomed before us. We knew where Federico was waiting..

Remi wiped the blade clean on his thigh, his chest rising and falling with each measured breath. Controlled.

But I could feel the war inside him.

A mirror of my own.

He turned to me. Blood streaked his cheekbone. His eyes burned."Ready?"

My grip tightened on my gun. A slow smirk curled my lips. "Always."

"Stand back," one of the Gallo soldiers said as he wired up some C4 to the doors and began his countdown as we backtracked down the driveway.

"Cover," someone else shouted, and I braced my arms over Remi's head, pulling him down to the ground with me as the explosion rocked the ground beneath our feet.

One of the doors exploded inward, slamming against the far wall with a violent crack. The other collapsed, crashing down onto the white marble with a deafening boom.

Cracks spiderwebbed through the tile, jagged fractures marring the pristine floor. Smoke and blood followed us inside, the scent thick, clinging to my skin.

Salvatore and my brothers broke into two teams, peeling off into the darkened corridors of the first floor.

Their footsteps disappeared into the shadows, the air filled with muted gunfire, the wet sounds of knives sinking into flesh.

No screams.

Only silence.

A symphony of efficient, disciplined death.

A broken, bleeding thing that used to resemble a man was slumped against the bottom step of the stairs, his once-impeccable suit now nothing but torn fabric and deep, dark stains. His face was nothing more than caved in flesh and bone, blood still sluggishly trickling down his neck.

"No pulse," Remi confirmed before dropping his eyes to the tablet in his hand.

His breath ghosted over my shoulder as I stepped up to him to take a look. A single red dot pulsed on the screen. Federico. He'd most likely locked himself away in a panic room. Fucking coward.

We followed it up the grand staircase, our boots whispering against the worn runner. The air was thick with the remnants of gunpowder and fear. Faint, ragged breathing filtered through the comms.

Enzo was ordering the dead be cleared away and burned in a pit that was being dug somewhere on the grounds.

Luca's grunts were indistinct, but it sounded like he was in charge of clearing the city of the dead.

I didn't know who their cleaners were or if they were equipped for something like this, but I didn't give a flying fuck right now. I was focused on making one person suffer as much as possible for all he'd taken from me.

Federico knew we were coming. There was no way on this earth he didn't.

Remi moved beside me, silent, a shadow stretching long under the dim chandelier light. His blade still dripped red, his fingers curled loosely around the hilt. There was no hesitation in his movements. He was calm. Controlled. Lethal.

I could feel the anticipation humming under his skin, the way his breathing remained steady, even as my blood roared in my ears.

We reached the top of the stairs. The hallway stretched long and empty before us, lined with doors that led to rooms already abandoned, their occupants either dead or fleeing.

But not Federico.

He had nowhere to run.

We followed the blinking dot on the screen, down the hall, past shattered picture frames and overturned furniture and bullet holes blown through the walls.

The sound of a door creaking open had my gun raised in an instant. But it was nothing. Just the house settling in the wake of the devastation we'd wrecked on it.

Or maybe it was the weight of death pressing in from all sides. Remi tilted his head, eyes flicking between the tablet and the doors ahead.

"Here," he murmured, voice soft, intimate in its certainty.

The last door at the end of the hall. A master bedroom, most likely. A place meant to be safe. Untouchable. The irony almost made me laugh.

Remi sheathed his knife, rolling his shoulders, stretching his fingers. I caught the subtle flicker of excitement in his eyes.

He loved this.

Not just the violence—not just the hunt.

But this moment. The weight of inevitability.

The knowledge that Federico was already dead.

That he was simply waiting for his fate to arrive.

I lifted my boot and kicked the door in. The wood shattered inward, splintering as it slammed against the far wall with a deafening crack. The room reeked of sweat, fear, and blood.

And there he was.

Federico DeMarco.

A wounded animal, slumped against the far wall, his once-pristine suit a shredded mess of dark stains and torn fabric. Blood smeared his face in sticky, half-dried streaks. A gash split his temple, his left eye nearly swollen shut.

He was already broken. What a shame. I'd been looking forward to a blank canvas.

Remi let out a soft, amused hum. "Looks like someone's been having fun without us."

I stepped forward, slow, deliberate. Federico flinched. His chest heaved, every breath a struggle, his fingers twitching where they lay limp against the floor.

But his eyes...His eyes were still moving. Still calculating. Still trying to find a way out.

There wasn't one.

"Please..." he rasped, voice cracked, raw, either from pain or the screams he'd already given.

Remi laughed—a low, breathy sound, sharp with amusement.

"Please?" He mimicked, crouching beside him. "Oh, Federico. You think we're at the part where begging helps?"

Federico's lips parted, swollen and trembling. He swallowed, tried to shift, but his body was wrecked—too battered to fight, too weak to run.

Which meant all that was left for him to do was suffer.

I grabbed a chair from the corner of the room and dragged it across the floor, the wood screeching against marble as I set it down in front of him.

I sat. Unhurried. Comfortable. I leaned forward, resting my elbows on my knees, gun dangling lazily from my fingers.

"Talk."

Federico's breath shuddered out, his gaze flicking between us, his body visibly trembling. "About what?" he croaked.

Remi clicked his tongue. "Wrong answer."

His knife flashed, and in a blink, he drove it through Federico's palm, pinning it to the floor.

Federico screamed a wet, garbled sound, his entire body convulsing from the pain.

Remi twisted the blade. The crack of splintering bone was music to my ears.

"About what?" Remi echoed, voice mocking as Federico gasped, struggling against the pain. "I don't know, Federico. Maybe about how you thought you could fucking get away with it?"

Remi twisted the knife again, then rested his boot on top of it, slowly increasing the pressure.

Federico choked on a cry, his free hand clawing at the ground. His body writhed like he could somehow escape into oblivion.

I let the silence drag. Let him suffer.. I leaned in closer, my voice low, almost gentle.

"You were always going to end up here. You just didn't know it," I smirked. "I was trained never to exist in the shadow of another man."

Federico's breathing was erratic now, his entire body shaking violently as he stared up at me.

"This wasn't personal," he rasped, desperate. "B-Business—just business."

I exhaled sharply. "Business?"

Remi tilted his head, his knife still lodged in Federico's hand, his fingers casually tapping against his blood-drenched thigh.

"Is that what you tell yourself?" Remi murmured, voice soft, thoughtful. "That it wasn't personal when you murdered his mother and made him an orphan? When you stole a child's innocence by making him murder your men?"

Federico's face twisted in something almost like recognition. A shadow of some emotion I'd never seen on him fell across his face, but it was gone in the blink of an eye.

Remi yanked the knife out.

Federico howled, clutching his mangled hand to his chest, his body jerking violently as blood seeped through his fingers.

"You know," Remi mused, rising slowly to his feet, "I could make it personal."

I didn't stop him when he stomped on Federico's knee, first one, then the other. Sharp cracks echoed through the room with sickening satisfaction.

Federico screamed again, louder this time. Loud enough to strip his vocal cords and make them bleed. A raucous cheer echoed through the house from somewhere on the floor below.

I could see it now—the last vestiges of defiance slipping from his face. He wasn't thinking about escape anymore.

Just about the pain.

"Remi." My voice was a warning, but only just.

He looked at me. And for a moment, he was glowing with it. The violence. The pleasure of it. His breath was heavy, his pupils blown wide, his hands coated in red.

"Alright, alright." He let out a breathy laugh, rolling his shoulders. "Just had to get that out of my system."

Federico was panting, shaking, his face pale with agony. Tears streamed down his blood stained face.

"Please, Domino, please." His voice cracked, his body curling in on itself.

I tilted my head in confusion and arched a brow, waiting for him to continue.

He wasn't begging for his life.

Not anymore.

Just for the pain to stop.

But that was the thing about men like Federico. They never learned until it was too late. "You're just like me."

A hollow laugh slipped past my lips. "No, Federico. I'm much worse."

I pulled my gun and pressed it to his forehead. His breath hitched. The entire room hung in silence. He knew. We all knew.

I let my finger rest against the trigger.

Let it sink in.

"You should have begged sooner."

My finger slowly depressed the trigger but before I could release it—

Bang.

Blood and brain matter splattered the pristine white walls, sliding down in thick rivers of red. Federico slumped, head rolling to the side, his lifeless gaze staring into nothing.

The silence that followed was thick, almost heavy.

Remi let out a slow, satisfied sigh, tilting his head back like he was savoring the moment. Like he was memorizing the feeling of the kill. He turned to me, his eyes still bright, still wild.

"That was fun."

I exhaled, wiping blood from my jaw.

"He wasn't yours to kill," I growled.

Remi grinned, stepping closer, his voice taunting, breathless with excitement.

"Then make me pay for it."

And just like that—

The hunt started all over again.

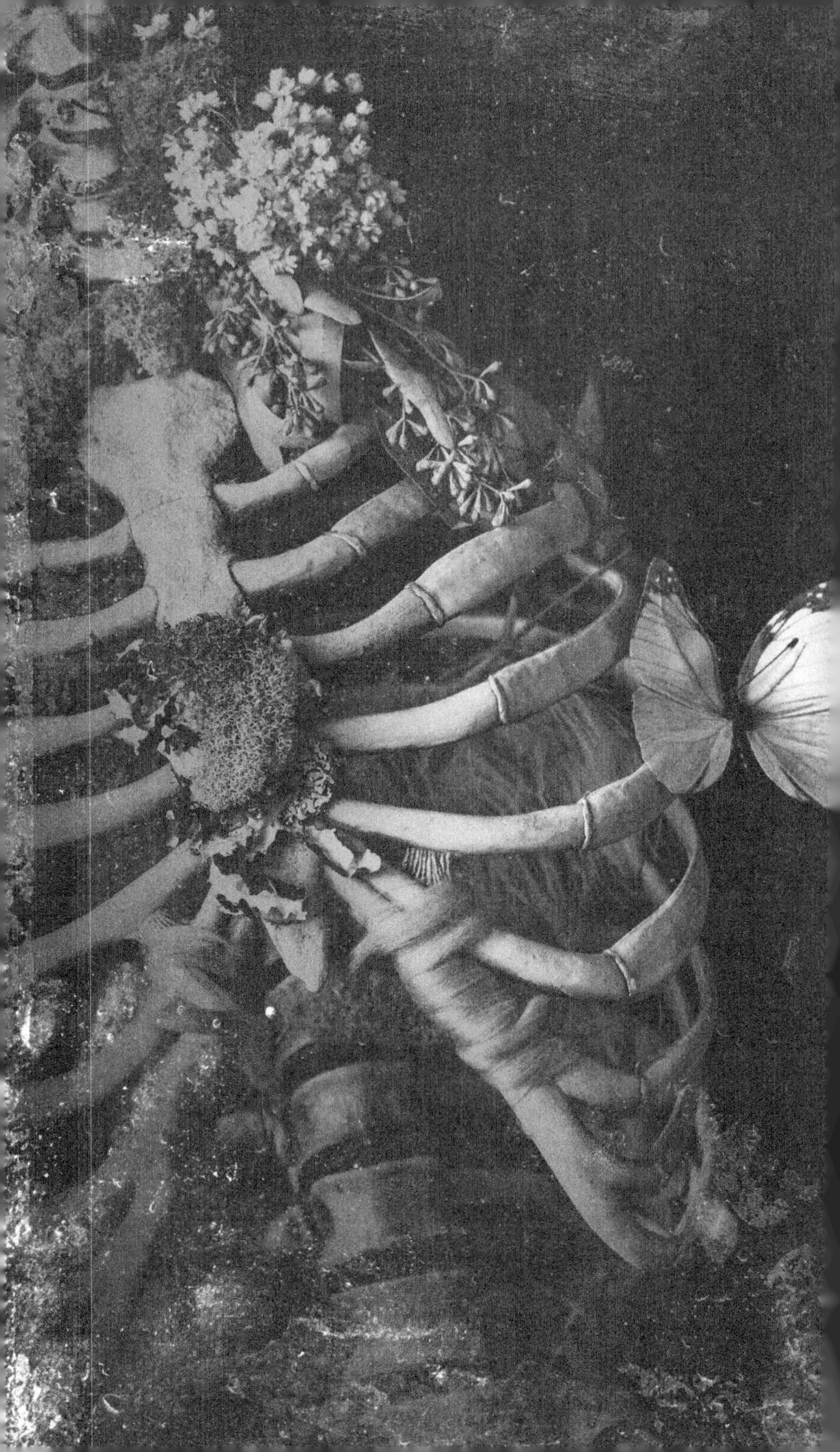

29 REMI

Marlow Heights was drowning in ghosts.

The streets were stained red, the gutters choked with the remnants of the war we waged. The bodies we left behind.

A kingdom burned to the ground. And now, Domino stood in its ashes.

But he didn't want it. Not the throne, not the crown.

Not the power.

He carried it anyway, like a blade he didn't know how to put down. Like it was cutting him open from the inside out.

And me?

I was waiting. Waiting for him to break. Waiting for him to snap. Because he would. Because he was already unraveling.

He didn't sleep anymore. Didn't even try. He just sat in the dark, watching me.

Always watching.

At first, I thought he was just lost in his head. Trapped in the wreckage of everything we had done. But then I realized—it wasn't the past haunting him.

It was *me*.

His obsession was a sickness. A hunger that had taken root inside him, festering, twisting into something bigger, darker, more insatiable. And he wasn't fighting it.

He was letting it consume him.

Tonight was no different. I lay on the bed, my shirt discarded on the floor, arms tucked behind my head. Moonlight spilled through the window, casting pale light over my skin.

Domino sat in the chair across from me, elbows on his knees, cigarette burning between his fingers. Watching. Like he was memorizing me. Like he was trying to ruin me just by looking.

His face was hollowed out with exhaustion. Shadows clung to the sharp angles of his cheekbones, dark circles bruising the skin beneath his eyes.

But he wasn't tired.

No—he was wired.

Tension coiled so tight in his shoulders it looked like it might snap his fucking bones. Like he was holding himself together by a thread.

I turned my head toward him, peeling my eyes open. I smiled—slow, lazy. "You could just touch me, you know."

His fingers twitched.

But he didn't move.

Didn't speak.

Just kept staring.

I dragged my tongue across my bottom lip, stretched just enough that my muscles flexed under his gaze.

His breath hitched.

I smirked. It was almost too easy. He was so close to the edge. So close to snapping. And I wanted him to. Needed him to.

"You're going to lose your mind at this rate," I murmured.

Then, deliberately slow, I trailed my fingers down my chest. Waiting. Daring.

Something cracked behind his eyes.

Still, he didn't move.

Didn't blink.

I chuckled. "You want to ruin me, don't you?"

That was it.

The final push. He moved so fast that I barely had time to react before he was on me. Pinning me to the mattress. His hand wrapped around my throat, his breath hot against my ear.

My grin sharpened. "About time."

His body was a live wire above me. All tension, all heat, all barely-contained violence. "You don't know what you're asking for, Remi."

His voice was wrecked. Rough. The sound of it alone made heat curl low in my stomach.

"I do." I dragged my fingers down the ridges of his spine, pressing into the scars I'd left there, feeling the texture of my history carved into his skin. Proof that he was mine.

I pulled him closer, baring my throat.

Inviting him.

Baiting him.

"You once said my body was your favorite playground," I whispered. "There is nothing you can do to me that I won't enjoy, Domino."

His fingers flexed around my throat. His control shattered.

"I want you bloody and broken." His voice was a growl, low and dark and filled with something that wasn't human. Something that had clawed its way out of him and refused to go back in. "I want you mine."

His belt slid free of his jeans with a sharp, brutal sound. He didn't give me time to react before he was tying my wrists to the headboard. Not too tight—just enough.

Enough to keep me open for him. I didn't fight it. Didn't resist. I just watched. Because I knew him. Because I wanted this.

He dragged his tongue across his lips, his voice nothing but breath and sin. "You can never leave me, Remi."

I exhaled. Smirked. "Then make me stay."

He buried his head in the crook of my neck, inhaling like he could breathe me in, drown in me, fucking consume me. A visceral shudder rolled through his body, his cock hard against my thigh, thick and heavy and fucking aching.

My arousal mirrored his, heat pooling low in my stomach, spreading through my veins.

I arched into him.

"Make me yours, Domino. In every way possible." I whispered it against his skin.

Like a prayer.

Like a curse.

Like dark magic meant to break him.

And it did.

He yanked my head back, his mouth crashing

against mine, brutal and punishing and fucking perfect. He licked into me like he wanted to steal the breath from my lungs.

Like he wanted to leave something behind. His teeth bit into my bottom lip. I groaned, the sharp sting sending a spike of pleasure through me.

His hand gripped my jaw, forcing me to look at him, his eyes dark and wild and so fucking possessive it made my stomach twist.

His gaze dropped lower. Scanning my body. Searching. I smirked because I knew what he was looking for.

The bruises had faded.

It had been weeks since he'd touched me. Since he'd left his marks. Since I'd worn his hunger on my skin like a brand.

He didn't like that.

Not one fucking bit.

A growl ripped from his throat. The sharp sting of his teeth dragged down my throat, sinking in deep, punishing, and perfect. The heavy thundering of my pulse only made him bite harder.

His tongue was the antithesis. A slow, languid drag over my artery, laving the tender flesh, tasting the blood rushing beneath.

My breath caught.

My whole fucking world narrowed down to this.

To *him*.

To the way he was tearing me apart, leaving bruises, leaving bites, leaving proof that I was his.

That I would always be his.

That I was never fucking leaving.

The suction burned, a slow, hot ache as he sucked hard, pulling the blood to the surface. My body jerked at the pressure, the heat, the sheer fucking force of it.

I'd offered myself up like a lamb for slaughter, and Domino—My god. My fucking destroyer.

He was going to do everything in his power to make sure I knew who I belonged to. Who I would always belong to.

A moan ripped from my lungs, broken and wrecked, my breaths coming in sharp, uneven gasps.

His teeth scraped over my Adam's apple, and I choked on my next inhale. Every touch, every bite pushed adrenaline into my veins like a dying man taking his first gasp of air.

I came alive under him.

Every sharp sting, every flash of pain, every claim he branded into my skin was like oxygen in my lungs, blood in my veins.

"Fuuuckkk." His voice was pure sin, dark and breathless, rolling over my skin like a slow, deep drag of smoke.

One hand clamped around my jaw, forcing my gaze to his. My vision blurred, heat flooding my chest, my stomach, my cock—

Then I saw it.

Blood.

My blood.

Coating his teeth, smeared along his lips. Domino's tongue swiped over it, and his eyes rolled back in his head, and a low, animalistic groan tore from his throat before his mouth slammed onto mine.

The burst of copper, the heat, the sheer fucking hunger. It was a claim. A brutal, possessive, all-consuming fucking claim. I took it. Opened for him. Let him devour me.

"More." The word left my lips in a plea, a prayer, a fucking demand.

I needed more. More of his pain. More of his touch. More of his twisted, feral, suffocating obsession.

I didn't need air or food or water.

I needed Domino.

His hands. His teeth. His fucking ruin.

And he gave it to me.

His mouth carved a path down my body, marking, claiming, ruining. Every inch of bare skin, every fading bruise, every fucking place where his touch had disappeared—

He brought it back. He put it back. Slowly. Methodically. Toxic, deadly, consuming. He was the night sky, smothering the light. He was the inescapable black hole.

And I was falling.

I arched, twisted, begged as his teeth clamped around my nipple. His tongue followed, teasing, torturing. He pulled it between his teeth, hard, until the pain bled into pleasure, until my hips jerked violently beneath him.

The ghost of his breath against the sensitive, aching bud made my whole body shudder, my cock pulsing, aching for friction, for fucking anything.

"Domino…more…I need more…"

His head lifted from my chest, his gaze searing, feral, knowing. The tattoos inked over his arms and throat shifted in the shadows, the dark glint in his eyes making my stomach tighten, my blood burn.

He knew.

He knew exactly what I needed.

He was the puppeteer, and I was just a body, a puppet, a fucking plaything in his hands.

Domino dragged his mouth lower, licking, biting, tracing the ridges of my abs, dipping his tongue into my navel. Fireworks exploded through my nervous system.

He pushed onto his knees, towering over me. My breath hitched as he peeled his jeans off, slow and deliberate.

My mouth went dry.

His cock—thick, flushed, fucking perfect—slapped against his stomach, leaving a glistening, wet trail across his skin.

Heat rushed through me. I needed to taste him. I needed him on my tongue. I needed—

"You want this?" His voice was a low, taunting rasp.

He wrapped his hand around his length, stroking slowly from root to tip, teasing, squeezing just enough to make my cock throb in response. A bead of precum pooled at his tip.

I watched, entranced. My head thrashed against the sheets. "Yesss," I hissed.

Domino laughed. Dark. Dangerous. Wicked.

I licked my lips. Struggled against the belt. "Please."

His thighs moved up my body, straddling my chest. The head of his cock brushed against my lips, smearing precum across them.

I inhaled deeply. Leather and smoke. Sweat and sin. That heady, intoxicating masculine scent was thickest at his groin.

I moaned.

"Open up, *piccolo agnello*."

My mouth snapped open instantly.

He chuckled. Fucking smirked. His gaze locked onto my tongue, watching me wait for him.

"Someone's hungry," he mused, his voice like a blade slicing down my spine.

His hand tangled into my hair, pulling tight. Positioning me exactly where he wanted me. The other guided his cock to my lips.

I moaned at the first hot, heavy, velvet slide of his length against my tongue and hollowed my cheeks, let him in, let him own me. I was flying high, knowing I was the one that brought him to his knees. I relaxed my throat, allowing him in deeper.

Domino groaned, deep and low. He fucked my mouth with controlled, powerful thrusts that made tears prick the backs of my eyes.

Brutal. Unrelenting. Perfect.

My throat burned and ached. I took it all and would have begged for more if I could have. Saliva spilled from my lips and down my chin, slicking his cock, filling the air with filthy, wet sounds.

He gripped the headboard, muscles tensing, flexing, rippling as he increased the intensity of his thrusts. I wanted to grab hold of his ass and sink my fingers into the muscled cheeks, feel them clench and relax as he moved.

"Fuck, you're so good at this." His voice—pure reverence.

He snapped his hips forward, burying himself to the hilt. My nose pressed to his base, my throat stretched wide. I was drowning in him as he invaded every one of my senses.

He was thick, pulsing, taking everything I had left. "That's it, Remi." A sharp thrust, a wrecked, salacious groan. "Take it all. Take everything I'm gonna give you."

His cock twitched. Throbbed against my tongue, cutting off my air supply. A hand wrapped around my throat as he felt himself deep inside me. I imagined his balls drawing up tight, his release spilling out thick and hot.

"Don't swallow." He pulled back until just the tip

rested on my tongue, his voice a demand, a command. "Close your mouth and keep it there."

My chest heaved, my lungs burning as I lost myself to his brutal rapture.

"Taste me. Savor it. Because I'm going to fuck myself back into you."

A deep groan rumbled in my chest as the salty sweet taste of his cum filled my mouth. I wanted to swallow him down. I wanted him to take root inside me and never leave.

Oh, fuck.

His words licked at my skin like flames, branding me, searing themselves deep, burning through flesh and bone until they were part of me.

Until I could never fucking forget.

Domino's gaze darkened, locked onto the sight. His tongue darted out, sweeping across his lower lip, his smirk cutting sharp at the corners. "Good boy."

Fuuuuck.

A fresh wave of tears burned the back of eyes. No one had ever said anything like that to me.

Not in praise.

Not in want.

Not in love.

My whole body felt like a struck match dipped in kerosene.

Domino's lips brushed over my sweat-dampened forehead, trailing slow, reverent kisses across my face. Like he was memorizing me. Like he was grateful for me.

His voice came wrecked, raw, shattered. Silk dragged over broken glass. "Thank you." A pause, a shuddering breath wrenched from the depths of his dark soul. "For bringing me back."

My heart cracked wide open.

I didn't know how to respond. Didn't know how to tell him that he was the one keeping me here. Keeping me alive.

That if he ever left me again, I would never recover. So I let him take me. I let him own me. Let him manipulate my body like it belonged to him because it did.

Domino's hands skimmed down my sides, featherlight, teasing, before they tightened at my hips. Blunt nails bit into my skin. The only warning I got—

Before he flipped me over.

My face hit silk, my tears soaking into the sheets. Domino's strong arm wrapped around my waist, yanking me up, positioning me exactly where he wanted me. Like I was meant to be here. Like I was built to be here. Like I was splayed open for his pleasure alone.

His hands moved fast, practiced, spreading me out, maneuvering me like I was his fucking toy.

I was.

I fucking was.

He shoved my knees under me. A strong, possessive palm pressed down on my lower back, arching me deeper, forcing me to push my ass out more.

Fuck.

I was shaking. Trembling. Still holding his release in my mouth, fighting my body's instinct to swallow.

A sharp crack rendered the air.

Pain. Heat. A fire blooming across my ass. I moaned, low and wrecked, the burn searing through my skin. Another slap landed. Harder. Faster.

The impact rocked me forward, sending electricity crackling through my veins. Pleasure collided with pain, fused into something that left me aching, gasping, begging.

My neglected cock throbbed, the tip dripping precum, every nerve screaming for relief.

"Beautiful," he muttered, his voice dark, reverent.

His body caged over me, hot skin pressed against my back. His cock—thick, heavy, hard—slotted between my ass cheeks.

I shuddered.

A full-body fucking shudder.

He reached past me, yanking open the drawer. I barely processed it. All I knew was that he was still hard. That he'd just filled my mouth with his load, but he was still ready to ruin me.

That he was going to leave my hole battered and bruised, wrecked and gaping—that I'd feel him for weeks.

And I couldn't fucking wait.

His teeth sank into my spine, biting kisses trailing down my back, catching on each vertebrae, leaving behind heat, marks, proof. My brain was spiralling from sensory overload. It took a few moments to latch on to a new sensation.

Cold metal.

A blade.

The kiss of steel against my skin. The lava in my veins turned white-hot. My hole clenched around nothing, desperate, aching.

My body sank into the madness he forced upon me, a fevered haze of pain and pleasure, heat and need.

His hips rolled against my ass, grinding into the bruises he'd just left, pushing me deeper into delirium.

The blade pressed down sharply. The first prick of pain. My breath hitched as the first drop of blood welled. Slow. Hot. It rolled down my ribs in a thin, glistening line. My lungs stuttered. My body fucking spasmed.

"You bleed so beautifully for me." His voice. Dark. Possessive. Ruined.

The hot swipe of his tongue on my side as he lapped up my blood was like a bolt of lust straight to my cock. It jolted against my abs. My ass clenched, begging, aching to be filled.

A strained whimper slipped from my lips, and some of his cum pooled on the sheets by my mouth.

I wasn't here anymore.

I was somewhere deeper, darker.

Somewhere only Domino could take me.

My eyes rolled back as he scored my skin open, carving me like I was something sacred. Like I was his map, his art, his canvas.

Thin rivulets of blood rolled down my ribs, following the paths of his blade, a network of intricate cuts drawn with precision. He was mapping my veins.

Whispered words slipped past his lips, his voice sinking into my marrow like he was spelling himself inside me.

I was gone. No up. No down. No sense of self beyond him.

I was nothing but his to ruin.

And he knew it.

Domino's fingers dug into my cheeks, spreading me wide. A sharp inhale—his breath shuddered against my skin. The tip of his nose dragged from my taint up my cleft, breathing me in like I was oxygen.

Like he couldn't live without me.

The blade balanced on my back, a warning, a promise, as he moved, shifting his weight. Heat. Wetness. His tongue. Slick, hot, circling my entrance.

"Fuck, you taste so good."

His muffled voice sent tremors through my entire body. He circled my entrance with the tip of his tongue. Worked me open with his mouth, with his hands, softening me, breaking me.

One hand wrapped around my aching cock, pulling it back, positioning me like I was meant to be used. His grip was loose, teasing, slow. But his tongue—

His tongue was desperate.

He wrapped his lips around my entrance and sucked, my hips rocked into him as his tongue forced its way inside me as deep as it could go. He devoured me, licking, kissing, sucking my hole like it was my mouth.

It was too much. My hips rocked into him, caught in the unbearable torment of choice.

To fuck into his hand—or to push back against his mouth, to smother him, bury him, drown him in me.

As if he heard my thoughts, his lips curled into a smirk, still buried between my cheeks.

I moaned, wrecked, but kept my mouth closed. Kept his cum in my mouth. My lungs burned.

It was torture.

He edged me, dragged me to the brink, and yanked me back, over and over and over until sweat slicked my skin, rolling in rivers down my spine, mixing with spit and blood.

Just when I thought I'd snap—

He let go.

It was like being plunged into ice water. I gasped, choked on nothing, on everything, on the unbearable loss of him. My cock throbbed, pulsed with its own heartbeat.

I clung to sanity by my fingertips.

Domino's thighs brushed the back of mine. His

hands spread me apart, pulling me wide open for him, for whatever he wanted to do to me.

His breath hitched. A rough, shattered groan tore from his throat. Spit. Hot and wet caught on my rim before he pushed it inside me, circling the ring of muscle with a hooked finger stretching me.

A single command, guttural, low, filthy. "Spit."

It took seconds for my fogged brain to catch up. I parted my lips, letting his release and my saliva spill into his waiting hand.

I looked over my shoulder, tracking his movements with hungry eyes. He tilted his fingers, let it slide between my cheeks, to my hole. Backlit by moonlight he looked like my darkest fantasies come to life.

He didn't blink eyes fixated on my ass, a sound rumbled in his throat. His fingers twitched a second before he shoved them roughly inside. Deep. Stretching. Claiming.

One hand worked his cock, slick and ready, the other fucked his cum into me.

I whined. I begged. "Please… please, Domino."

A sharp, teasing twist of his fingers dragged against my prostate. Tears pricked my eyes and dripped down my cheeks as another wave of my orgasm drew closer.

"Please what, *piccolo agnello*?"

I could barely form words. Could barely breathe. Could barely survive him. "Please fuck me. Now!"

A sharp slap to my ass. Hard. Brutal. Blistering. Pain chased pleasure.

"You're mine to play with." Slap. "Mine to tease." Slap. "Mine to torture." His teeth sank into my flesh, sharp enough to break the skin. "Mine to fuck."

No warning.

No hesitation.

No mercy.

He slammed inside me, burying himself to the hilt. His balls hit mine. His thighs pressed flush against my skin.

I screamed. "Oh, God. Oh, God. Oh, God."

My walls rippled around him, choking his cock. His fingers buried in my hair, he yanked my head back.

A vicious snarl against my ear. "Who do you belong to, Remi?" He pulled out—and fucked back into me, brutal, unforgiving.

My lungs seized. I couldn't breathe. Couldn't speak.

"Tell me."

The sound of skin against skin filled the room, the slap of flesh, our heavy breaths, the obscene slickness of him ruining me.

"Remi!"

A demand.

"You!"

The moment the word left my lips, he shifted. A foot planted next to my knee. A new angle and he fucking wrecked me. Pounded into my prostate, beating it into submission, breaking me open, fucking me raw

Domino released my head, and it hit the bed with an audible thunk, unable to hold myself up anymore. I was liquid fire. Sensation. Drowning in dark seas.

A blade against my spine. His voice like smoke and sin. "I'm going to make sure you never forget who you belong to."

Excruciating pain that I welcomed with open arms flowed through me. His switchblade, slicing slow, deep, deliberate. Fresh blood seeped from the wounds he was carving into me.

His cock rammed into me, fucking through my over-stimulation, shoving me higher, further, deeper.

I blacked out.

When I came back, I felt his fingers tracing the marks carved into my back.

"W-what?"

My ass was soaked in blood, spit, sweat. He coated my skin with my essence, his fingers biting into my hips.

His pace increased. He wasn't just fucking into me. He was dragging me back onto his cock.

My orgasm slammed into me like an electric current. "D-Domino…please…I-I…need…" I whimpered.

My cock throbbed. My heavy balls drew up tight, hugging the base of my shaft. My mouth opened, drool pooling onto the sheets.

An animalistic roar tore from his lungs. "Come!"

My body obeyed it was his to command. Thick, hot ropes of cum lashed against the silk sheets. My vision went white. I floated in the darkness.

I came to lying on top of him. My Domino. Arms folded across his chest. Cheek on my hand. Legs splayed, framing his hips.

I felt wrecked.

Not broken—remade.

Like my bones had been replaced with mush, liquid, honeyed submission. Still not entirely back from wherever he'd sent me.

His fingers traced my back, skimming the skin he'd carved open. Soft. Slow. Reverent. It was different from the countless little nicks, the intricate network of wounds and worship.

This one—I felt it.

Deeper. More than pain.

It should have horrified me. But instead—Heat flooded my body. A slow, sated warmth curled through me like a secret. I smiled. Barely there. Almost nothing.

But he saw it.

Of course, he did.

My eyes were too heavy to lift, but I forced them open just enough to peek at him through my lashes. His beautiful face. I drank him in. Tried to memorize him. Dark eyes were watching me, mouth unreadable—until I asked.

"What does it say?" Slurred. Mumbled. My lips barely moved.

"What does what say?" he murmured.

I scoffed. Weak. Playful. Utterly undone. "Whatever it is you've done to my back."

His brow arched, a smirk curling one corner of his mouth.

"That thing you keep tracing with your finger…"

A hum. Low, rich. He moved his finger back to the top and started all over again. Tracing it. Etching it into me, over and over. The rhythm of it—hypnotic. It lulled me, pulled me under.

"Yesss, tha…" I barely got the word out before he chuckled.

A breathless, light laugh. I'd never heard before. It dragged me back from the edge of unconsciousness. My eyes fluttered open again, wider this time. Because—I wanted to see him.

All of him.

He was multifaceted, layered, endless. And for some unfathomable reason, he'd chosen me.

"My name."

His words settled over me like a weight, like a chain around my throat. It echoed in my head. Over and over. Until I finally pieced it together.

He'd branded me.

With his name.

Carved it into my skin. I let my eyes fall closed. And whispered, "I hope it scars."

A beat of silence passed between us where we just existed.

"If it doesn't, I'll do it again and again… until it does…"

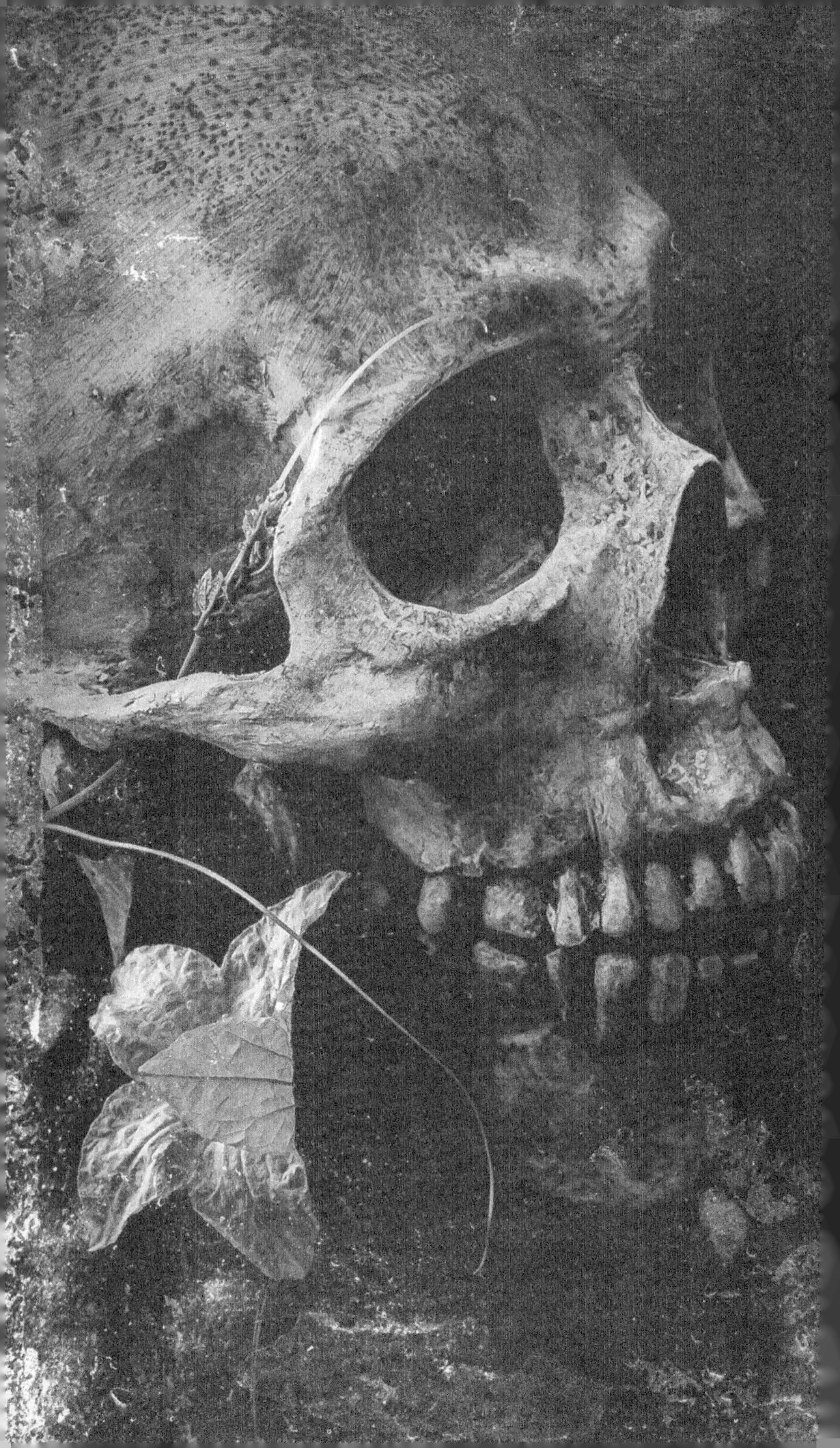

30 DOMINO

"One... two... I'm coming...for..."

His voice was soft, haunting. It slithered through the air like a whisper in the dark. Remi sounded like a fucking delinquent. He started doing this a few days ago, and it freaked me the fuck out.

At first, I thought he was watching horror movies—but no. He didn't enjoy just sitting, being still. He preferred to be doing, creating, moving. And right now, he was doing exactly that.

I leaned against the doorframe, arms crossed. Watching him.

His hand flew across the page, dark lines slashing the canvas. At first, the strokes looked meaningless. Something about them tickled a memory. Something I couldn't quite place. It settled in my head like an itch. A mystery I had to unravel.

Just like that damn song stuck on repeat in my mind. If I could, I'd happily gouge my brain out with a hook.

The ding of the elevator cut through my thoughts. Ghost had finally decided to deliver what I had sent him to get hours ago. He strode into the penthouse, smirking as always, black box in his hands.

"Morning, boss." He tilted the box up. Mocking. Teasing. "I can't believe you wanted it." His eyes flicked between me and the box, his curiosity burning. "What are you gonna do with it?"

He went to open it, but I snatched it away before he could. "That's not your concern," I ground out. My fingers smoothed over the ribbon, avoiding his gaze.

He hummed. Low. Knowing. "Ohhhh. Mmmm. I see."

My head snapped up, my gaze colliding with his. He smirked, cheeks tinged pink. He mimed zipping his mouth shut and throwing away the key.

I glared at his idiocy. "If only you would fucking do that."

He snorted, "Nah, you'd miss the sound of my voice too much."

I shook my head, jaw tensing. I was about to tell him to shut the fuck up, but his attention suddenly shifted. His gaze flicked down the hallway, toward the art room. His lips curved.

"What the fuck is he singing?" His eyes slid back to mine, amusement flickering on his face. "Well, that shit certainly suits you two."

I barked out a sharp, "Enough."

He chuckled but straightened at the tone. Back to business.

"Did you get everything sorted?"

He nodded. "Yes. Everything is in place... the club will be—"

I held up a hand. "Good. That's all I want." A pause as I gathered my thoughts. "I assume you'll be able to manage?"

Ghost snorted, rolling his eyes. "Pffft, obviously."

"Good. Now get the fuck out. I have things to do."

He lingered like a bad smell until my attention was back on him. "You don't really call him a 'thing,' do you?"

I didn't even dignify that with an answer. "Fuck off, Ghost."

He grinned, saluted, and headed for the elevator. Just as his finger pressed down on the button, he turned to look at me. "Don't forget to call Salvatore when you know."

I exhaled, aggravation crawling under my skin. "I won't. Like any of them would let me."

The doors eventually slid shut. Ghost was gone. Thank fuck. Being in his presence gave me a headache, but for some reason, Remi liked him.

Now it was just me and the weight of the gift in my hand. I turned it over, fingertips grazing the edges. How should I do this?

Should I leave it for him to find?

Should I sit him down?

Should I bring it to him?

Fuck. Anyone would think I was about to propose with how indecisive I was being. Ridiculous.

But the moment had to be right.

Remi had a way of twisting my insides, dragging me into a place where rational thought and obsession blurred together until they were the same thing.

Luckily for me, the soft hum of the coffee machine and the clatter of cups on the counter pulled him from his reverie.

He strode in, barefoot, wearing my sweats like they belonged to him—which they did. Hung low on his hips, exposing the sharp cut of his abdomen, the bruises and marks from last night shadowing his skin like kisses made of violence.

He didn't say a word. Just snatched the cup from my hand with a snicker, grabbed the creamer from the fridge, and started making his coffee. I let him. Let him steal from me like he always did.

Because it was Remi.

Because it was mine to give.

And maybe that was the problem. Maybe that was why I was standing here like a fucking fool, staring at his back, at the raised, healing lines of my name carved along his spine.

A shudder of satisfaction coiled through me, curling deep in my gut. He was mine. And now? Now everyone would know. Not that I'd ever let another fucker get close enough to see him without his shirt on.

But that wasn't the point.

I knew.

And so did he.

Remi settled onto one of the stools, his legs spread wide, completely comfortable in my space, my clothes, my life. His gaze locked onto the black box in front of him.

"What's this?"

He traced a single charcoal-stained finger along the edge, turning it this way and that, searching for some mark of origin.

I smirked against the rim of my cup and leaned

against the counter opposite him, waiting for him to drag his intrigued gaze away from it.

Eventually, I felt his eyes on me again. The moment that weight settled, something inside me eased. Like pressure lifting off a trigger.

Like the gnawing hunger I carried under my skin, finding something to sink its teeth into.

Marlow Heights was mine.

But I didn't *want* it.

I wanted *him*.

That was enough.

"Open it and see," I said finally when the drumming of his fingers against the lid got to be too much.

He huffed out a laugh, practically buzzing with curiosity. "Really?"

His excitement did something to me, something I didn't fully understand, a heat curling through my chest that I refused to name. Remi had tried to explain it once. Said it was probably love. Maybe that was wishful thinking. But I had said those three words to him.

When he wasn't preoccupied with sketching and planning his kills, he liked to remind me. Sometimes with words. Sometimes, by melting into me when I ran my fingers down his back, over the deep cuts where I'd carved my name into him.

Other times?

He would drop to his knees, take my cock to the back of his throat, and moan in thanks.

A shiver of anticipation flickered down my spine as I watched him lift the lid. The sharp inhale that followed was pure, breathless delight.

"Holy. Fucking. Shit." His fingers trembled as he reached inside, brushing over the fractured remains of a skull. His eyes snapped to mine. Wide. Wet. Impossibly bright. "Who?"

I smirked.

He already knew. He always had to know. Couldn't rest until he understood the story inside the bones, inside the blood.

"The one you stole from me," I murmured.

A sharp intake of breath. Remi's grip on the skull tightened. He placed it gently on the counter, his fingers running over the cracks, the fractures, the hollows where life had once existed.

"You mean—?"

"Yes."

His whole body went still. His breath caught in his throat, his pulse visible in his neck, his lips parting on something between a gasp and a laugh.

"It's really his?"

I rolled my eyes and reached forward, turning the skull in his hands, my fingers brushing over his knuckles, over the scars and violence now etched into his skin.

"If you look here," I murmured, tapping just above the left temple. "You'll see where your bullet went through."

Remi let out a sound. Low. Guttural. Pure fucking reverence. "Fuuuuuucccckkkk."

He tilted the skull toward the light, tracing the delicate spiderweb fractures left behind by the impact of his kill shot.

"This is one of the best things you've ever given me." His voice was breathless. Almost shaking.

Remi was... interesting.

He didn't care about jewelry. Clothes. Money. As long as he had a dry place to sleep and enough food not to starve, he didn't want anything. Not the things normal people craved.

He craved this.

The dark, ugly parts of life. Blood and pain. Power and suffering. Control. And I was here to give them to him.

The skull rested on the counter, and his fingers tightened around it, pulsing, curling, shaking with something sharp and raw.

I watched. Fascinated. A starving man watching his lover feast.

Remi's tongue darted out, wetting his lips as his eyes darkened, his pulse jumping beneath his skin.

Slowly, deliberately, he tilted the skull toward his face, his fingers drifting over the hollowed sockets, over the place where he'd once seen the world before Remi ended him.

He parted his lips. The tip of his tongue flicked out, running over the jagged cracks, tasting the ghost of gunpowder and bone.

A shudder ran through him, his lashes fluttering, his breath catching in his throat like he was suffocating on power.

"God," he whispered, voice wrecked.

It broke something in me. I stepped closer, my fingers wrapping around the back of his neck, my grip tight, possessive. His breath hitched. I could feel it. Feel the heat of him.

His obsession.

His worship.

I dragged my thumb along his pulse point, pressing just enough to feel it flutter beneath my touch. And then I leaned in.

Voice dark. Low. "Do you like it, *piccolo agnello?*"

Remi turned his head, eyes gleaming, wicked, fucking manic. His lips curled, his grip still tight on the skull. "I love it."

Remi's lips were curved in something sinful, his breath still ragged, fingers clutching at the skull like a relic.

A prize.

A trophy.

A testament to what I had done for him. And yet—it wasn't enough. It would never be enough. His obsession fed mine. His darkness reflected, refracted, amplified in the twisted mirror we had become.

I needed him to show me. To prove that he knew. Knew what I had done. Knew how far I would go. Knew that he belonged to me.

"Then show me how much you appreciate what I've done for you."

I didn't wait for an answer. Didn't need one.

The moment I grabbed a fistful of his hair, Remi gasped, his body going lax, pliant, willing in a way that made my head spin and my pulse thunder. I hauled him off the stool in one smooth motion, his legs instinctively wrapping around my waist, locking at the ankles.

Like he was meant to be there. Because he was. Because there was no world, no version of reality, where he wasn't in my arms.

Where he wasn't mine.

His fingers dug into my shoulders, his breath hot against my throat as I carried him through the penthouse. Everything about him sang to me. The way his body curled into mine.

The soft, shaky exhale when I tightened my grip on his thighs. The way he shuddered when I turned my head and ran my nose along the pulse in his neck.

And when he whispered my name—a prayer. A plea. A promise. I almost lost it. *Almost.* Not until he had placed his gift down with the care it deserved.

The door to our bedroom slammed shut behind us, the sound sending a sharp thrill down my spine.

The skull—his trophy, my offering—rested on the nightstand. But my attention wasn't on it anymore. It was on him. On the blood still drying under his fingernails. On the bruises I had put there.

On the scars I had carved into his skin, his soul, his very being.

A smirk curled at my lips, a slow, creeping thing as my gaze flicked to the skull. To the hollow sockets where eyes had once been. My father. Watching. Helpless. Forced to witness every single thing I was about to do to the boy in my arms.

I turned back to Remi, tilting his chin up, my grip bruising. His lips parted, his pupils blown wide, his breath catching in his throat as I murmured

"Show me, Remi. Show me who you belong to."

And he did.

He always did.

"Come with me."

It wasn't a request. It never was. Remi's fingers slid into mine without hesitation, his trust blind, unwavering, devotional. He would follow me anywhere.

Into the shadows. Into the flames. Into death itself.

And he would go smiling.

That knowledge burned in my gut, feeding the

gnawing hunger only he could satisfy. It was a gift, this power he gave me, this absolute control. A heady, intoxicating thing.

And yet, somehow, he owned me more.

The doors to the elevator slid shut, sealing us inside a silver cage lined with reflections—infinite versions of us drowning in each other. Remi turned, looking at me through thick lashes, lips curling in a coy smirk. Wicked. Knowing.

"Where are we going?" he asked breathlessly.

I grabbed his throat and pinned him against the mirrored wall. His breath hitched, and his pupils blew wide. "We have an appointment."

My lips hovered over his, barely brushing, teasing—because he would always want me more in the moments before he got me.

"It took a while to get everything organized," I murmured against his mouth.

Remi didn't care about appointments. Didn't care about plans, schedules, obligations. Didn't care about anything that wasn't me.

His fingers dug into my jacket, his body arching, pressing closer. His lips crashed against mine—savage, desperate. Each brush of his tongue against mine deepened the madness.

Remi never got enough.

And neither did I.

He rocked against me, his hardness grinding against my thigh in a frantic, needy motion. I tightened my grip around his throat. His pulse pounded under my palm. His breath faltered—caught in my grasp.

His body trembled.

His nails bit into me, sharp little reminders that he

loved this, loved me. Loved being on the edge of death, knowing I was the only one keeping him tethered to life.

Tears glistened in his eyes. He looked beautiful like this. Fragile and invincible, all at once.

Mine.

I exhaled, loosening my grip just enough to let the oxygen rush back into his lungs. "Patience, *piccolo agnello.*"

I stepped back as the doors slid open. Remi glared at me, flushed, panting, his eyes dark with lust and fury.

"Fucking tease," he muttered.

My lips twisted in a smirk. I lived to unravel him. To push him to the very edge—and pull him back when it suited me. His ice-blue eyes lit up as I fastened his helmet. A ritual. Something that should have been mundane, but with him? It was an intimate interaction. Binding. Sacramental.

I threw my leg over my bike, glancing at him over my shoulder. He bit his bottom lip, the softest act in a boy who had never been soft. Then slid on behind me, his arms locked around me. My body shuddered, electrified at the contact.

He was a disease. A virus. A toxin.

And I wanted him to ruin me completely.

My Ninja growled beneath us, its roar reverberating off the concrete walls. The vibrations hummed through our bodies as I pulled back the throttle, the rush of speed intoxicating. Behind me, Remi buried his face against my neck as much as his helmet allowed, his grip tightening around my waist with every shift of the gears—silent, steady, utterly in sync.

The streets were quiet tonight. The city was still recovering from the war we had brought upon it. Still littered with the ghosts of the men we had killed, as the steel buildings blurred past us.

But all I saw was him. Remi—a creature carved from the same hunger that devoured me. Nothing else mattered. Not the past. Not the bodies. Not the city we had burned to the ground.

Only him.

Engraved in my bones. Fused to me at a molecular level. I'd had fixations before. But nothing like this. Nothing like him.

We pulled into a covered garage, the rain growing heavier as we dismounted.

"Elysian Chambers?" Remi grinned, a slow, creeping thing. "It's time?"

"It is."

He whistled, low, appreciative.

I pulled my helmet off, shaking out my hair. "I assume you came prepared?"

Remi scoffed. "I don't go anywhere without my babies."

His arm curled around my neck, reeling me in until our noses brushed. His breath, warm and teasing, ghosted over my lips—a whisper of what he knew I craved.

"Thank you," he murmured, pressing a slow, deliberate kiss to my lips, his tongue swiping against mine just once before he pulled away. A taunt. A fucking torment.

My fingers snapped up, gripping his chin, forcing his gaze back to mine. "Don't make me wait."

He smirked, the kind of smirk that made my blood heat, that made me want to carve my name deeper into his skin. "Impatient, are we?"

The buzzer screeched as he pressed it, an offense in the quiet of the night. I gritted my teeth. I hated waiting. Hated being made to wait. I wasn't the kind of man who waited on others. They followed my rules, or they paid the price.

Rain dripped from our clothes, pooling at our feet as the silence stretched, taut and electric.

"Hello?" Casius. His voice cut through the night like a blade, smooth and practiced, hiding the sickness beneath.

Remi turned to me, eyes wide. Not in fear. In hunger. Excitement. Because this wasn't just about meeting an artist. This was about something darker. Something that had festered between us since the night Remi found him out.

The girl had been dying when he found her.

A fragile, broken thing, crumpled in the overgrown grass between the headstones, a whisper away from the very grave she should have been laid in.

And yet—she still clung to life. Barely. She was young. Too young. Her breath hitched in shallow, gasping sobs as her glassy eyes fixed on Remi, as if sensing that even in the presence of a monster, she had found something far worse.

But there was no fear in her gaze. Not at first. Not until he crouched beside her, tilted his head, and let his fingers brush the sticky warmth of her blood where it pooled in the dirt.

She flinched, her body trembling, but she didn't have the strength to pull away.

"Who?" Remi had murmured.

The girl shuddered. And then she broke, spilling everything. Every horrifying, disgusting, vile truth about the man who had done this to her. She had idolized Casius Moreau. Had worshiped him.

A promising young artist, she had won a competition

—a chance to learn from the master himself. But Casius had taken one look at her and decided she was not meant to be an artist.

Because she was art.

She was a canvas, a creation, a thing to be molded beneath his hands. And he had torn her apart like he was sculpting a masterpiece.

First, her mind—plucking at her thoughts, unraveling her sense of self, corroding her will like acid. Then, her body.

Breaking it. Defiling it.

Piece by piece.

She had never been meant to survive. And yet, somehow, she had crawled her way there, to the cemetery, to Remi.

Maybe fate was cruel, or maybe it was precise.

Because if she had dragged herself to anyone else, she would have been another forgotten corpse buried in a city that did not care. But she had found Remi. And Remi found me. That was the night he decided Casius Moreau had to die.

That he would suffer.

That his body, his life, his very existence would become another one of Remi's masterpieces.

Casius Moreau was a man who thought he understood monsters. He was wrong. He thought he could hide his sins beneath oil paints and grandeur, beneath layers of pretense and careful curation.

But Remi and I? We saw through it. We saw the rot beneath the polish, the grotesque thing lurking behind the illusion of artistry. And tonight, we would make him pay for it.

Casius, of course, had no idea what he had invited into his home when he greeted me.

"Casius, it's Domino DeMarco," I muttered coolly, watching him on the intercom display.

"Ahhh, yes. How could I forget someone like you?" His words dripped into my ear, each syllable curling with poison. "Would you like to come up and see my current pieces?"

Beside me, Remi snorted, tension threading his body, his irritation flashing like the edge of a blade.

Neither of us answered. We didn't need to.

We followed his instructions up the spiral staircase into his twisted sanctuary. Half-finished portraits lined the walls, their hollow stares following us as if they could sense what was coming.

The air was thick—oil paint, linseed, and something rancid. Something rotten.

Something human.

At the top of the stairs, Casius stood waiting, a glimmer of surprise flickering across his face when he noticed Remi. It soured quickly.

I smirked and let the silence hang between us, dragging it out, savoring the discomfort spreading over his face like an oil spill.

"Domino, a pleasure." He held out a hand to me.

I stared at it. Let the air go thick and heavy before I finally tilted my head, eyeing it like it was infected. He dropped it. Smart.

"What can I do for you tonight?"

Remi huffed a sardonic laugh, slipping past Casius like a wolf circling its prey, skimming the artwork with an air of casual disinterest. It was a mockery. A performance.

Casius doesn't even realize that he is already dead.

"My husband is an artist."

Remi froze. That single word hung between us like a knife on a taut thread.

Casius's brows lifted. "Husband?"

I ignored him. Remi didn't turn, didn't react beyond the slight twitch of his fingers, the slow curl of his shoulders. A shiver ran through me. *Mine.*

"He has always appreciated others' works but was interested in hosting his own exhibition."

Casius blinked. Then smiled—thin, forced. "That's wonderful. What's his style?"

Remi snickered, vanishing behind a curtain. "The macabre."

Casius stiffened. "Uh, you can't go back there—"

Wrong move.

I was already there, closing the distance, my fist wrapped around his wrist, wrenching it behind his back. His body jerked. A breathless, startled gasp. My other hand curled tight around his throat, squeezing just enough to feel his pulse hammering against my palm. He trembled in my hold.

Slow. Measured. Methodical. "And why can't he go back there?" My voice was ice, licking up his skin like the first whisper of a blade.

His lips pinched tight. His eyes darted to the corners of the room. Searching. Hoping.

I chuckled. "No one is coming."

Casius sucked in a sharp breath. "W-what?"

"We took out your security before we stepped inside. No one knows you're not alone. No one will know the last people that came to visit you…"

His body went rigid. His breath shuddered against my knuckles. "What do you mean, the last people?" His voice cracked.

Pathetic. I leaned in and let my lips graze his ear. "This will be your last meeting, Mr. Moreau."

His mouth parted in a silent scream, but before sound could escape, a flash of silver glinted in the dim light. A blade. Thin, sharp, hungry. The edge teased against Casius' throat above my fingers, pressing just enough to draw a thin bead of red.

Casius whimpered.

"I wouldn't do that if I were you." Remi's voice was a purr, his knife spinning between his fingers with lethal ease as he stepped back.

Casius whipped his head around, only now realizing Remi was beside him. A fool. A dead man. "W-w-why not?"

Remi smiled. A small, sick, sadistic thing. "Because I know everything you've done." He chuckled, dragging the tip of his blade down Casius' jawline, light enough to tickle. "I've spoken with your victims. I've seen the bodies. What did the poor girl hanging by her neck do?"

Casius thrashed, kicking out in panic. Remi danced away, laughing. Effortless. Elegant. A predator toying with his meal.

"What was it about hurting them? About killing them that captivated you?"

Something changed in Casius. His struggle slowed. His eyes went black, empty, something hollow and endless bleeding through.

His reflection in the mirror opposite us told me everything. Recognition. He had stopped fighting. Because he thought he was among kindred spirits. He thought we were the same.

Remi was fascinated by death, by the permanence of it. The way it silenced the noise and made things still.

But me?

I craved the power. The control. Holding life in my hands and deciding whether it burned or withered or was simply snuffed out like a candle.

"The rush," Casius whispered. "The challenge."

How unoriginal.

Remi smirked. "And the girl from the gallery? The one hanging next to your bed?"

Something dark and vicious flickered in Casius' gaze. He licked his lips. "I destroyed her. Piece by piece. Took everything her body had to offer me."

That was a mistake. Remi stilled. Something shifted in him, slow and terrible. The amusement bled from his features, replaced with something still. Something ice-cold.

Something lethal.

"Do you like little girls?"

Casius smiled. A disgusting, grotesque thing. "Don't you?"

I scoffed. Remi frowned, and a furrow appeared between his brow.

A smirk carved across his lips. "I was never interested in anyone until Domino took me." His gaze flicked to mine. Hunger. Reverence. Worship. My pulse thrummed. My grip tightened. "Until he showed me who I really was."

Casius' breathing hitched. His false bravado cracked, splintered. Shattered.

Remi wiped his blade clean, eyes flicking toward the staircase. "Where are your keys?"

Remi tilted his head, waiting.

Casius hesitated. "The gallery space isn't locked. The door's at the bottom of the stairs."

Remi reached the top step, then turned, watching me. His voice dripped with something dark, something electric, something that made my blood sing. "Bring him."

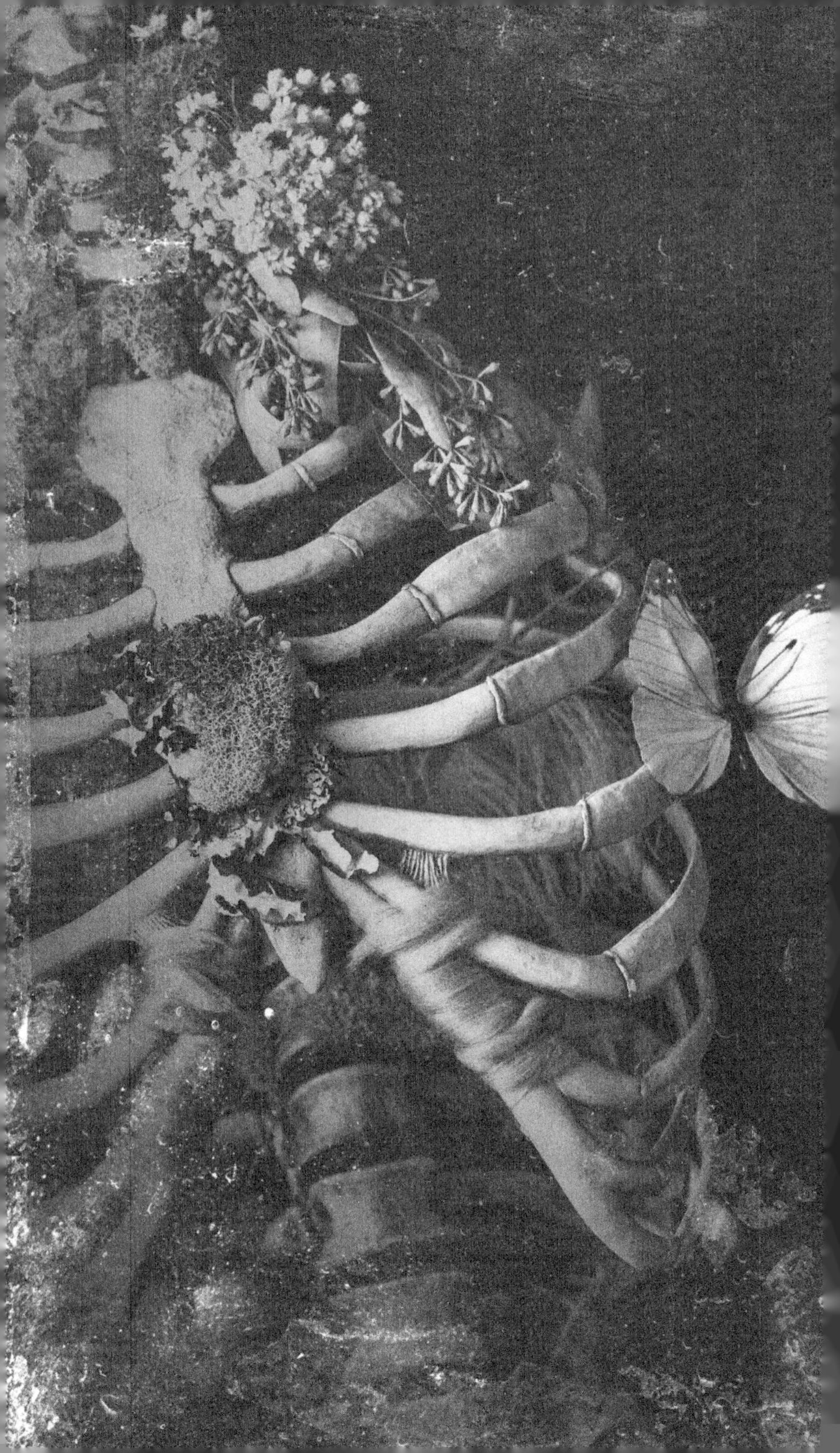

31 REMI

The slow, deliberate thud of Domino's boots on the metal steps echoed like the final seconds of a countdown timer.

Tick.

Casius stumbled in front of me, breath hitching with every uneven step, his body trembling under the pressure of Domino's gun pressed to the back of his neck.

Tick.

He flinched every time the cold barrel nudged him forward, each tap a silent command—keep walking. We were bringing him down.

Down into the gallery.

Down into his grave.

His ragged breaths filled the stairwell, panicked and shallow, like he was trying to breathe before he ran out of time. But it wouldn't matter. He had no time left.

He reached the last step, hesitating, his body locking up. His knees wobbled, his spine stiffening as though some pathetic instinct to fight, to flee, to beg was finally trying to take hold.

But Domino was faster.

The gun pressed harder against his skull. A sharp gasp left Casius's lips, and I smirked as he shuddered.

"Keep moving." Domino's voice was calm.

Cassius obeyed.

The heavy steel door groaned as we stepped into the gallery, and the space swallowed us whole.

Casius staggered forward under the harsh glare of the spotlights, his breath coming in shaky, uneven gasps as he took in the empty white walls—the blank canvas waiting for his body to be displayed.

The gallery was a mausoleum of silence.

The girl from the opening was still at the forefront of my mind, hanging in the corner next to his bed, her pale limbs twisted, her dress a ruined thing of dried blood and lace.

Casius had tried to make her art, but he was sloppy—crude in his execution, uninspired in his vision. A hack.

Her blood had long since dried, staining her delicate white dress into something reminiscent of an oil painting—deep crimson bleeding into fabric, an abstract masterpiece of suffering.

Her glassy eyes stared, unseeing, at the ceiling, her mouth parted in an unfinished scream.

I tilted my head, drinking the memory of her in. There was beauty in her death. She had suffered, but she had not died for nothing. She and the countless before her had brought me here. They had sealed Casius Moreau's fate.

And now, the gallery—his gallery—would become his tomb.

The space was vast, with double-height ceilings stretching into darkness. Chandeliers hung from the pinnacle, useless relics of grandeur, outshined by the spotlights lining the stark white walls.

A blank canvas.

For me.

For us.

A metal beam ran the length of the room, meant for suspending sculptures and installations. And at that moment, I knew. This would be my biggest stage.

My masterpiece.

My vision, displayed for all to see. Casius would not be hidden away. He would be put on display. For his victims. For the world. For me.

I turned toward the storage area, leaving Domino to hold our trembling victim. Casius was whimpering now. Tears streaked his face in silent pleas that I did not care to hear. He had no prayers left to offer, no salvation waiting for him.

Even if he repented, even if he wept and clawed at his flesh, he would burn. His sins were etched too deep into his bones, his depravity woven into his DNA.

I found the industrial rope I'd spied when we'd walked past, coarse and heavy in my hands. Perfect. I slung it over my shoulder and strode back into the gallery, my pulse thrumming with anticipation.

This would be a death worth remembering.

This would be art.

Domino looked up from where he held Casius, eyes glinting in the dim light. "Where do you want him?" he called, his voice almost bored. Like Casius was nothing more than another task to complete, but he did it anyway.

I smirked. "Center stage."

Casius choked on a sob, shaking his head. Domino wrenched him forward, forcing him under the beam as I unwound the rope. The fibers rasped against my fingers, biting into my skin. It felt good. It felt right.

My deft fingers worked quickly, looping the rope around his trembling throat, feeling his rapid pulse beneath my fingertips. He jerked in protest, but Domino was stronger. He forced Casius onto the chair beneath the beam, shoving him upright, making sure the rope sat snug against his throat.

Casius wheezed, eyes bulging, realization dawning. He knew. This was how he would die. Displayed like the pathetic imitation of an artist he was.

I tugged the rope once, testing its hold. It tightened beautifully. Casius gasped, his hands flying to the noose, fingers clawing at the rough fibers.

A laugh slipped past my lips. "Oh, you don't like that?"

Domino snickered, stepping closer, his presence a heady weight at my back.

"This is where you belong," I murmured, brushing my fingers over Casius's sweat-slicked hair. "Hanging like one of your installations. A true work of art."

Domino hummed in agreement.

"I wonder," I mused, tilting my head. Toying with his fragile mental state was glorious. "Should we leave you like this? A slow, suffocating death, every moment a stretch of agony?"

Casius shook. His lips moved, but no words came out. His terror was delicious. I let my fingers slide down his chest, feeling the rapid stutter of his heart beneath my touch.

"I could gut you first," I suggested lightly.

"Or maybe," Domino drawled, stepping in front of him, "I should just do this."

I barely had time to register the glint of silver before Domino's switchblade drove straight up through Casius's jaw. The blade disappeared into soft flesh, punching through muscle and bone, embedding itself in the roof of his mouth.

Casius convulsed. Blood burst from his lips in thick, bubbling spurts, gurgling down his chin as his throat spasmed around the noose.

I shuddered at the sight, breath catching in my throat.

Beautiful.

Domino's eyes met mine, dark with hunger.

"Pull the rope," I breathed.

He obeyed instantly. Casius jerked upward, his body hoisted by the neck, legs kicking, arms flailing. A dying marionette. His strangled screams drowned in his blood. I let out a slow breath, watching the way his limbs convulsed, the way his body fought to cling to life. A futile, pitiful thing.

Domino sighed, almost bored at his futile display, and kicked the chair out from beneath him. Casius dropped, the noose snapping tight, cutting off the last wet gurgle of his existence. His body twitched, his fingers curling inwards, eyes bulging—until finally, he stilled.

A quiet settled over the gallery.

The perfect stillness of death.

Domino wiped the blood from his blade with practiced ease, smirking up at the body swaying in the spotlight. "That was for taking Federico from me."

I rolled my eyes. "Do you miss him?"

Domino scoffed, shoving the knife back into his pocket. "I felt nothing for him then and even less now. He got what he deserved." His gaze flickered to Casius's corpse, and that smirk sharpened. "Just like you."

A shiver raced down my spine. Domino was art in motion. A masterpiece in flesh and blood. And as I looked at him, bathed in the glow of our creation, I knew—I would never love anything more than I loved this.

More than I loved him.

"He's making a mess." I huffed a laugh, tilting my head as I watched Casius's body, twitching, jerking—even after death—bleeding out onto the pristine floor. A masterpiece in motion. "A beautiful mess."

The way the blood pulsed from his wounds, pooling in a slow, creeping stain across the stark white floor, reminded me of a dying star collapsing in on itself. But it meant my vision had to change.

I was nothing if not adaptable.

Slowly, I walked around him, studying the way the light fell—how it illuminated the broken arch of his back, the angles of his limbs, the way his trembling fingers scratched at the ground as if trying to claw himself back from oblivion.

Futile. I imagined the final form I'd leave him in, sculpting it in my mind like clay beneath my fingers.

An angel fallen from grace.

I'd carve his wings from his flesh, let them hang from his back like torn relics of something once divine. Then, I'd break them. Sever the tendons, expose the bone, let him drown in his blood, suffocating on his descent.

A tragic, biblical end for a man who thought himself untouchable.

The shift in the air was subtle, but I felt it like an electric charge along my spine. Domino. I knew before he even touched me—that weight, that presence, that tether pulling me into him. His warmth pressed against me from behind, arms snaking around my waist, pulling me against his body, the hard length of him resting against the curve of my ass.

My blood burned. Desire tangled with adrenaline, coiling tight inside me, sinking its teeth into my skin. But I couldn't lose focus. Not yet.

This moment was too important.

My swan song.

The final piece of my old life before Domino and I became something else entirely.

"What do you need?" His lips ghosted over the shell of my ear, his voice low, deep, a vibration that sent a full-body shudder rolling through me.

"I need wire, hooks, and wire cutters." My voice came out breathless, drunk on the scent of smoke, leather, and aged blood that clung to him. Domino smelled like death, and I wanted to drown in it.

He exhaled a quiet groan, pressing closer, his body firm, solid, mine. "You're perfect, *piccolo agnello*."

A hand drifted down from my waist, teasing over my hard length with barely-there touches, setting fire to my nerve endings. I groaned, turning into him, burying my face in the crook of his neck, inhaling him like the sweetest poison.

Domino cupped my face, his thumbs smearing Casius's blood over my cheekbones, dragging it down to my lips. "There."

Then his mouth was on mine. Hot, searing, claiming. I whimpered when he pulled away, my lips chasing his, but he caught my chin, tilting my head back until my eyes met his. Dark green. Endless. Dangerous.

"Finish creating." His voice was velvet over steel. Commanding. Absolute. Then he glanced at his phone. "We'll have company soon."

A spike of adrenaline cut through my desire, and I pulled back slightly, narrowing my eyes. "W-what do you mean?"

The corner of Domino's mouth lifted, a slow, sinful smirk, blood drying on his lips. "I'm expecting a delivery."

A shiver crawled down my spine, something dark and thrilling unfurling in my chest. I chewed my bottom lip, tasting copper. "Are you going to tell me what you're up to?"

His grip on my chin tightened slightly, just enough to make my breath catch. "No." That smirk deepened, his gaze burning through me, pulling me apart without a single touch. "I'm going to get you what you asked for, then leave you to it."

His lips brushed over my forehead, a small, lingering kiss—a promise, a vow, a claim.

Then he was gone.

And I was left standing in the center of the gallery, blood at my feet, my masterpiece waiting to be made.

Once I started, the rest of the world faded away. The edges of my vision blackened, reality peeling like old paint. The murmur of movement—Domino somewhere nearby—was nothing more than a distant vibration, an echo against the walls of my untouchable bubble.

Nothing existed outside of this moment.
Outside of him.

Casius's body lay still, limp, purged of life yet brimming with new purpose. He would be my greatest work. I exhaled softly, pressing my palm against his chest—not to feel a heartbeat, but to feel the silence. The absence. The void where something human had once existed.

I hummed under my breath, a quiet lullaby, before sliding my blade beneath his shirt and slicing it apart like paper beneath a scalpel. The fabric split, curling away in strips and falling into the blood pooling at my feet.

Then, I carved into his still-warm flesh.

Slow. Intentional. Devout.

The first layer of skin peeled away in ribbons, curling from my knife, exposing the raw, glistening flesh beneath. Then another. And another. Deeper.

Until I saw the pale curve of his ribs—an untouched canvas beneath ruined muscle, waiting to be shaped. I traced my fingers along the bone, mapping out its structure, its possibilities. I could see it already.

His wings.

One by one, I shaped them.

Carving the ribs into feathers, fragile and elegant, each one painstakingly etched, transforming his broken body into something almost divine.

A fallen angel, stripped of his grace.

A symbol of those he had tormented, those he had torn apart.

I worked in silence, threading hooks through the base of each fractured rib, securing the wire, and lifting the wings into place. The body sagged against its restraints, but his wings held. Suspended. Displayed.

The spotlights cast their glow across him, sending long, twisting shadows stretching over the white walls. A grotesque halo. I took a step back, wiping Casius's blood from my blade with the sleeve of my shirt.

Perfect.

A masterpiece.

A monument to his sins. And then—I destroyed him.

With a single swipe of my blade, I severed the delicate carvings, watching as the ribs cracked, snapping under their weight, wings collapsing in a heap of bone and sinew.

A ruin of what he could have been. What he never was. Casius Moreau was nothing now. Just another forgotten thing. And I had never felt more alive.

The world was nothing but the sound of my breath, heavy and uneven, my chest rising and falling in sharp, erratic bursts. The gallery around me blurred. The blood-slicked floor, the macabre display of Casius's ruined form—faded into the background.

All I saw was Domino.

He stood there, looming like something carved from the very shadows, his presence sinking its claws into my skin like ownership. Just like that night in the alley—the night he made me his. He struck fast. Unrelenting. Absolute.

My knees hit the floor with a dull crack, pain sparking up my legs before dissolving into nothingness, drowned beneath the weight of his hands.

He forced me down.

Pushed me into place with a cruelty that made my blood heat, with a precision that told me he knew exactly what I needed.

His fingers curled into my hair, twisting tight, controlling me. My breath stuttered when he dragged my head back, my pulse pounding, my throat already open for him before he even spoke.

"Open, *piccolo agnello*." I obeyed. Instinctively. Like breathing. "You've kept me waiting too long."

His bloodied fingers pried my lips apart, pressing inside, stroking my tongue. A shiver slithered down my spine as the taste of iron and sweat mixed on my taste buds, filling my mouth with the aftermath of creation.

With practiced ease, he freed his cock. My pulse thundered. Thick. Hard. Already leaking. The fat, swollen head glistened, the evidence of his arousal was proof of what I'd done to him.

What I always did to him.

Watching me turn a corpse into art had been the best kind of foreplay.

His grip in my hair tightened. Pain bloomed, sharp and perfect, and I gasped, my jaw stretching wider as he pulled me closer—exactly where he wanted me.

Where I belonged.

His voice was a dark, merciless command. "You're going to take everything I give you, Remi, and hold it on your tongue."

A declaration. A promise. A sentence.

I nodded, my tongue slipping forward in silent offering. My submission fed his hunger.

A wicked smirk curled the corner of his mouth as he dragged himself along my parted lips, tracing their shape, coating them in the thick salt-slicked evidence of his desire.

The scent of him flooded my senses—heady, intoxicating, undeniable. I moaned, the weight of his cock finally settling on my tongue, and Domino laughed. Low. Dark. Victorious.

"Good boy," he murmured, voice rough, almost affectionate. But there was an edge of cruelty laced beneath it, a twist of sadism that made my skin prickle, my body ache.

He held me there balanced on a knife's edge.

His cock heavy, resting on my tongue, pulsing against my parted lips as if he was testing me, savoring my obedience. With a sharp jerk of his wrist, he forced me down at the same time his hips snapped forward.

My throat opened for him, raw and eager, taking him deeper. A strangled noise escaped me, muffled around the thick length pushing past my lips, pressing into the heat of my mouth.

Domino groaned, his fingers tightening in my hair, pulling me down until my nose was flush against his stomach.

Until he had all of me. He held me there, hips grinding forward, his cock throbbing as I struggled to breathe.

"Fuck, Remi," he hissed, tilting his head back, pleasure tightening his features into something almost beautiful.

My nails dug into his thighs as I forced myself to stay still, to take everything, his taste saturating my tongue, heavy and overwhelming. Just as I started to get lightheaded, he yanked me back—spit and precum stretching between my lips and his cock.

I gasped, sucking in a desperate breath, and he chuckled.

"Look at you," he purred, cupping my jaw, thumb stroking the mess coating my mouth. "So pretty like this. So perfect for me."

My chest heaved, my tongue darting out to catch the remnants of him still smeared across my lips.

"Again," I rasped.

Domino obliged. Harder. Faster. Deeper.

Fucking into my mouth with ruthless precision, claiming me with every snap of his hips, with every moan that ripped from my throat. Tears pricked at the corners of my eyes, my jaw aching, but I didn't care.

I wanted all of him.

I wanted to be ruined by him.

Used by him.

Owned by him.

His breathing turned ragged, his hips faltering—just barely—his control cracking. With one last thrust, he pushed me down to the base, my throat tightening around him as he came with a sharp, guttural growl.

Thick spurts of cum filled me as he unloaded. He held me there, his fingers twitching in my hair, his breath shuddering out as he unraveled in my mouth. And I took it. All of it. Just like he demanded.

When he finally slipped from my mouth, he didn't move away. Instead, he dropped to his knees before me. His chest was still heaving, his pupils blown wide, his lips wet from where they'd been bruising against mine.

A reverent look settled over his face, something close to worship, as if he was gazing at something holy.

"So fucking perfect for me, *piccolo agnello.*" His hands cupped my face—gentle, almost tender—before he sealed his mouth against mine.

The heat of him, the weight of him, devoured me whole. His tongue licked into my mouth, tasting himself, swallowing it down as we passed his release back and forth between us—sharing, consuming, claiming—until only the faintest, bitter-sweet trace remained.

Domino growled against my lips, the sound rough and dangerous, before he shoved me down onto the cold, bloodstained floor.

My head spun. Whether from lack of oxygen or the sheer force of him, I didn't know.

The next thing I felt was fabric tearing—a sudden rush of cold air as my jeans were ripped from my legs.

A choked moan escaped me as his calloused hand wrapped around my cock, his grip unrelenting as he worked me over—root to tip, slick with my leaking desperation.

"I need to be inside you." His voice was hoarse, thick with something unhinged. "It's like I can't fucking breathe unless I'm inside you in every way possible. My cum down your throat. Filling your ass. Burying myself so deep inside you that you feel me in your fucking lungs."

My body shook.

My pulse thundered.

His words destroyed me.

Domino slid his hands beneath my knees, shoving them up to my chest. My hands instinctively locked into place, holding myself open for him like I was meant for nothing else.

My eyes stayed locked on his as he moved. Pushed his jeans down just enough to free himself, the heavy weight of him thick and aching.

The sharp glint of silver flashed in the gallery lights. His switchblade. Domino pressed the edge to his arm, the blade kissing his skin in one smooth, practiced stroke. Fresh claret welled along the cut, sliding in rivulets down his forearm. Rich and intoxicating.

He ran his thumb through the blood before dragging it across my lips. "Open," he growled.

And I obeyed. He held his arm above me, watching as drops of blood landed on my face, rolled down my chin, and dripped into my mouth. I held my tongue out to catch more.

A dark fire shimmered in his eyes. Hypnotizing. Entrancing. Owning.

I swallowed him down like he was the only thing keeping me alive.

He pulled back just enough to run his hand over his own arm, coating his palm in blood before wrapping it around his cock.

Slick. Wet. Claimed.

A fresh moan tore from my throat as he scooped up more and dragged his fingers over my empty, desperate hole. My entire body trembled in anticipation, with a need so desperate it felt like I was dying.

Then he pushed inside me, bottoming out on a single thrust. Raw. Brutal. Unrelenting. I threw my head back, a wrecked sound escaping my lips as pleasure and pain crashed over me in tandem.

Like a blade sliding through silk. Like worship and destruction, blurred into one. Electricity snapped across my overheated skin.

I was burning alive.

Desperate to be filled. Desperate to fall.

Domino leaned down, his breath hot against my ear, his body crushing mine into the floor as he punched himself in deeper. "Who do you belong to, Remi?"

His words weren't a question. They were law. He drove himself forward, so deep my vision blurred. I couldn't think, couldn't breathe. As he lifted my hips, changing the angle and thrusting in deeper than before. I was lost in him. Drowned in him.

A choked sob slipped from my lips. "F-fuuuuck—" I gasped. "You. Only you."

His teeth scraped along my throat, the edge of a bite teasing my skin. "That's right," he snarled, sinking them into my neck.

His thrusts became vicious, merciless—a relentless pace that had my body arching, shaking, unraveling beneath him.

"You're mine. Forever."

And when I shattered, when I came apart beneath him, I knew—

There was no escaping him.

I didn't want to.

WELCOME TO THE BEAUTIFUL DEAD

EPILOGUE

Anchor: "We interrupt our regularly scheduled programming to bring you a breaking and disturbing report from Anderson Cotes. A word of caution: Some of the images and details in this report may be distressing. Viewer discretion is advised. Anderson, over to you."

Reporter: "Thank you, Robin. I'm standing here on the steps of the Elysian Chamber, the recently opened gallery owned by renowned artist Casius Moreau. This morning, Marlow Heights was shaken to its core by a crime scene so gruesome it has left both law enforcement and forensic teams visibly disturbed.

As the city struggles to recover from the destruction left in the wake of the violent war between the DeMarcos and the Gallos, today marks yet another dark chapter—one that will undoubtedly leave lasting scars.

Follow me as we step inside and reveal the horrific discovery.

The gallery's once-grand entrance has been completely defaced. Behind me, painted in what experts believe to be human blood, are the chilling words: *Welcome to The Beautiful Dead.* Authorities suspect the blood may belong to none other than Casius Moreau himself.

Inside, we find what can only be described as a macabre spectacle. Moreau's body has been mutilated and posed in a grotesque display, his skin flayed, bones carved into jagged extensions resembling wings—transforming him into a twisted imitation of a fallen angel.

Even seasoned law enforcement officers and forensic specialists have struggled to process the sheer brutality of this crime. Some have been seen exiting the building, visibly shaken by what they've encountered.

Perhaps most disturbingly, the gallery has been transformed into something beyond a crime scene—an exhibition of horror. The walls are lined with disturbing, avant-garde pieces, each one appearing to explore the theme of death in its rawest, most violent form. Authorities now fear some of these works may contain remains belonging to individuals reported missing in recent months. While this has yet to be confirmed, the implications are chilling.

But now, Robin, we're hearing something happening upstairs. Officers appear to have discovered something else.

—Background commotion, an officer's voice cutting through—
'Chief! Upstairs, now!'

Robin, we're moving quickly to follow the officers. We're heading up the stairs now to get firsthand information on this latest development.

Chief Rutter—Chief, can you tell us what's been discovered?"

Chief Rutter: *(Visibly frustrated, addressing the camera crew)*

"What the hell are you doing here, Anderson?"

Reporter: "Just doing my job, Chief. The public deserves to know what's happening here. Can you confirm what your team has just uncovered?"

Chief Rutter: *(Sighs, pinching the bridge of his nose before speaking)*

"Fine. At approximately 08:00 this morning, our department received a call from a cleaner reporting a disturbance at the gallery. Upon arrival, we found the victim, identified as Casius Moreau, deceased. Cause of death appears to be a combination of strangulation and a fatal knife wound—driven through his jaw into his skull."

Reporter: "And what about this new discovery?"

Chief Rutter: *(Exhales sharply, visibly tense)*

"We have just located two additional bodies inside Moreau's private apartment. Both victims are female minors."

Reporter: *(Pausing, visibly unsettled)*

"That is beyond horrific. Can you confirm their cause of death?"

Chief Rutter: "From a preliminary assessment, it appears they died from a combination of starvation and strangulation. But we'll know more after the autopsy."

Reporter: "This is truly a harrowing discovery. A crime that will shake this city to its very core. But, Chief, before we go—one last question."

Chief Rutter: *(Scowling, clearly irritated)*

"Make it quick, Cotes."

Reporter: "With this investigation underway, do

you believe the Elysian Chamber will reopen? Will *The Beautiful Dead* be revealed to the public?"

Chief Rutter: *(Jaw tightening, voice filled with disbelief)* "Are you serious right now?"

Reporter: "As serious as this investigation, Chief."

Chief Rutter: *(Shaking his head, muttering)* "I'm not discussing this."

Reporter: "And there you have it, Robin. Chief Rutter has refused to comment on whether the gallery will reopen. As you can see, tensions are high, and now we are being escorted out of the premises.

This morning, Marlow Heights was introduced to a scene of unprecedented horror. Three victims, each revealing a different layer of darkness hidden beneath the city's polished exterior. While we do not yet know if Casius Moreau was responsible for the two young girls found in his apartment, if he was—then perhaps, just perhaps, justice has already been served by an unknown hand. A vigilante.

Back to you, Robin."

Anchor: "Thank you, Anderson, for that gripping report. To our viewers, if you've stayed with us through this coverage, we can only hope you're doing okay. This was not the story we expected to be covering on this Monday morning, but it is one that will stay with us for a long time."

"DOMINO, WHAT THE FUCK IS THIS?" HIS VOICE WAS sharp, laced with suspicion, his hand pointing toward the TV showing this morning's news.

I stepped up behind him, slow and deliberate, the worn leather of the couch creaking beneath my weight.

A laugh slipped past my lips, low and syrupy-sweet,

curling like smoke in the space between us. "I wanted to immortalize you."

He tensed. He felt it. The weight of my words. The possession in them. I leaned in, pressing flush against him, breathing him in.

My lips ghosted over the shell of his ear, my fingers trailing up the column of his throat, feeling the rapid thrum of his pulse.

I wanted him etched into my eternity. Wanted the world to see what I saw. Wanted him to know there was no escaping me.

Not in this life.

Not in the next.

Not ever.

THE END

AFTERWORD

Thank you for taking a chance on Domino and Remi! If you made it this far we should be friends. They made my little dark heart very happy. I never thought characters like this would come to me but their story was so compelling I had to write it.

I loved that Domino was unapologetically authentic. He's the best kind of antihero and will live rent free in my head forever. Remi fascinated me, his viewpoints and obsession with finding beauty in things most would run from. They were a challenge to write, but I loved every minute of it. They consumed me in the best kinds of ways.

I hope you enjoyed their dark twisted story and have been left questioning your morals. If you did please leave a review and recommend it to someone who might enjoy it too. Without your continued support I wouldn't be able to do what I do.

Skyla XOXO

ABOUT THE AUTHOR

Skyla Raines is obsessed with romance and broken boys. She's an avid reader and a sucker for hard-fought happily ever afters. When she's not bringing to life the characters in her head, she's watching her family grow and cherishes every moment with them.

You can follow her here:
https://linktr.ee/authorskylaraines

ALSO BY SKYLA RAINES

Without Limits Series

The Lies We Tell Ourselves

The Lies We Believe

The Lies Of Omission (2025)

The Lies Of Temptation (2025)

The Darkness Within Series

Continues 2026

CONTENT NOTE

Stalking
Sexual Assault
Dub con
Non con
Graphic torture
Murder
Blood play
Breath play
Knife play
Manipulation
Death of loved one
Drugging
Kidnapping
Defiling a grave site
Homelessness
Self harm

Printed in Great Britain
by Amazon